He flashed a smile, one that was too handsome for his own good. His body was too broad, too strong, and it threatened to intimidate. "I'm sorry about the ticket. I should have looked into it last night. I always park there, so my son thinks the spot is mine."

Impatient now, Lauren failed to see what difference that made. "There wasn't a vehicle in it when I got there, nor a sign saying it was a privileged space."

"My motorcycle was in the shop."

"And this is supposed to concern me, Mr.——?"

"DiMartino." He extended his hand, but she didn't take it. She had no intention of getting cozy. "Nick DiMartino," he finished, lowering his arm without a flicker on his face to show his thoughts.

"Well, Mr. DiMartino," she began, her tone tight and controlled, "I'd like to know why I got this parking ticket, and since you claim to have rights on that spot, you'll have to enlighten me. Because I'm not going to pay seventeen dollars and fifty cents for something when I didn't break the law."

"I agree. Tear it up."

His quick reply threw her, but she recovered. "Wouldn't you just like that? I don't pay and then I end up with a warrant out on me."

"I never said that." He put his hands up, backed away and turned toward the town clerk who had been following the entire exchange with her mouth half open. "Maxine, what knucklehead put this parking ticket on the Falcon?"

Pink Moon

STEF ANN HOLM

MIRA®

ISBN 0-7783-2086-3

PINK MOON

Copyright © 2004 by Stef Ann Holm.

www.MIRABooks.com

Printed in U.S.A.

For Gloria Dale Skinner and
a friendship that has spanned over a decade.
I'm truly blessed to have you in my life.

Prologue

La faccia della luna è come un sentinel—tutto vede.
The moon's face is like a sentinel—it sees everything.

She came to Bella Luna under a waxing moon, her little son's hand grasped tightly in hers. The hour approached five o'clock, the time when rubber-booted fishermen drank coffee and prepared their boats in the early morning.

A low-lying mist cloaked the town in a thin wash of gray watercolor. Shop fronts were quiet and darkness filled the windows.

She stood at the corner, indecision softening her posture, the suitcase handle in her grasp held firmly.

Vacated canneries rose behind her on a long length of pier that still remained standing because of luck and the ingenuity of the Italian immigrants who had built it a hundred years ago. A soft blue patina gave color to the timbers.

Spread before the woman, the coastal town emerged

in a dawn attempting to break through the foggy curtain. Steam curled from the water-heater vents on the roof of the Wharf Diner. A signboard in front of Wong's Pizzeria creaked on rusty hooks.

The streets were narrow, barely accommodating two cars at a time. Flower boxes at the curbs held a plethora of color: vibrant red geraniums, blue lupines and golden orange California poppies.

Slick and wet, the street captured the woman's and her son's reflections. She wore an ivory cardigan sweater and a knee-length skirt with a pair of canvas tennis shoes minus socks. Her bare legs were nicely shaped, the calves trim and the ankles slender. Dark hair the shade of strong tea was brushed into a generous ponytail, revealing an oval face with perfectly arched eyebrows and red lips.

The boy was different, somewhat unusual. He probably hadn't ever played T-ball, dug for clams on the beach or belched in a library. His small face appeared even smaller under the black-framed eyeglasses that were reminiscent of Clark Kent's. A well-worn cape was tied around his narrow shoulders—a superhero's flowing red garment that had the power to make the impossible happen.

She said something to her son, then they stepped off the curb and headed toward the Tidewater Motel.

Otis Duncan had just entered his tiny grocery store on Seal Avenue when she passed by, but his presence went unnoticed.

Having lived in Bella Luna, California, all his sixty-eight years, he had watched people come and go. Some left for bigger cities and better jobs, while others settled in, only to realize the small town was too isolated, so they often moved on to places like Santa Cruz.

Those with family trees dating back to the 1700s, along with the generations of fishermen's families, were the truly content ones. These folks couldn't imagine a day without observing the sunset blaze a path across the sea, or marveling in the beauty of the wind-gnarled cypress growing on the rocky cliffs. For them, Bella Luna was their heart and their home.

Otis Duncan—"Dunk" as his friends called him, and everyone considered him their friend—knew his final resting place would be in the old cliff cemetery where, in spirit, he'd still feel the salt winds on his face.

Dunk turned on the lights and gazed out the grocery window, momentarily seeing his brown face and woolly hair in the glass. With the fragrant smells of ripe cantaloupe and the fresh strawberries from Oxnard filling the store, he pondered the newcomers' fate as his gaze strayed to the lightening sky.

Like a phantom globe, the nearly full moon was shrouded by a mantle of creamy pink. This unpredictable phenomenon seemed to take place only on a small stretch of northern California coast. Not much was known about it other than its appearance was dictated by the tides. The Italian fishermen who'd founded the town had been so enamored of its romantic beauty that they had named the port Beautiful Moon—Bella Luna.

Under such a breathtaking sentinel, a history of superstitions arose. During the last pink moon, Anthony DiMartino's boat motor died on the day when the rockfish were cloistered in the kelp beds and he missed an entire day of good fishing. Sam Wong had received good news that day—he was going to become a grandpa. On the same occasion, Verna Mae Gonzales, owner of the Wharf Diner, had a mainline pipe bust and her best waitress ran off without notice.

A pink moon meant something unexpected was going to happen. People's lives would be affected, and the tides, while strong and steady, would crawl more slowly onto the shore as if cautious about the outcome.

Dunk couldn't help thinking that this woman and her funny-looking little boy might change Bella Luna in some way. Why exactly, he couldn't quite pinpoint.

But what he did know was that just as surely as sunshine followed rain, either a great happiness or a tragic misfortune was going to befall someone in Bella Luna.

One

It's that bitch of a moon.

Nick DiMartino knocked back a bottle of Corona, a lime wedge shoved through the neck. While he listened to his younger brother talk about his upcoming wedding, the beer quenched his thirst after a nine-hour workday.

Three generations of DiMartino men sat together at one of the Wharf Diner's deep blue vinyl booths.

Sixty-two-year-old Anthony DiMartino kept his thick black hair cut short. Shallow age lines mapped a face that had been shaped by marine air from a lifetime of casting nets into the sea and hauling in fish by the ton. Sicilian ancestry gave him his strong work ethic and Catholic values—two traits he'd instilled in his sons.

John DiMartino, the eldest, had just turned forty-one and had been married for six years. Danny, at thirty-seven, was barely a year younger than Nick, the middle child. Three sons for a man whose olive-brown eyes reflected his good soul and caring heart.

Taking another sip of beer Nick glanced at his own young son, and his chest tightened with a love so fierce it could almost take his breath away. As he often did, he tried to visualize what his son would look like when he was older. Right now he was fearless. Maybe he'd become the quarterback on the football team or student-body president in high school. Whatever his son did, he would enjoy the challenge of being the best at it.

Nicholas Anthony DiMartino Jr. had been nicknamed Nicky-J—the *J* for Junior. A shaggy head of dark hair was covered by a backward San Francisco Giants baseball cap, while an indecipherable stain spotted his shirt-front. He was all boy; all afterburner and no rudder. A very unpredictable six-year-old who always warmed Nick's heart to the core.

Nicky-J took two steak fries off his plate and made guns out of them. Slivers of fried potatoes in each hand, he aimed at the ketchup bottle in front of his uncle John.

"Pshew! Pshew!" he said, then reloaded after eating both of his weapons.

If Nicky-J could climb on it, he'd jump off it. He got pleasure from throwing rocks off the pier and playing with burning firewood when the family had a big bonfire roaring on the beach. Nicky-J was drawn to everything dangerous—skateboards and BMX bikes and anything that could career out of control. It wasn't unusual for him to come through the back door with blood on his elbows and knees. His calamities had made him well acquainted with the local emergency-room doctors and nurses.

"Dad, are we almost done?" he asked, talking through the food he chewed.

"Mouth closed, dude. We don't want to see it once it's off the plate." Nick shoved a napkin at him—which he deftly turned into a mock parachute for the ketchup cap.

"Heather asked me to help her address the invitations tonight," Danny said, drawing Nick's attention. "My handwriting sucks. I told her to use labels off the computer and she said there's no way she's doing that. It isn't personal enough. What's the difference?"

John shrugged. His richly tanned complexion came from working alongside their dad every day. "Women want a wedding done their own way. Don't argue about it. Print if you have to."

"What do you think, Dad?" Danny asked, easing back into the booth with his arm draped across the tufted vinyl.

"Your mother and I eloped." Anthony examined a healing cut in the tough skin of his palm. "There weren't any invitations." His chin shot up. "But by Christ, don't get any ideas. Heather's parents are shelling out money on this thing."

"Not a chance of us slipping out for a quick ceremony. I want to see her walking down the aisle on her dad's arm and in a wedding dress."

John teased, "You just want to take off her wedding dress."

"How come you'd wanna do that, Uncle Danny?" Nicky-J finished off his plain cheeseburger in one bite and tossed a crescent of leftover bun onto his plate. "She can't do it herself? Just like she can't bait her own fishing hook?"

Danny lifted Nicky-J's ball cap, ruffled his hair, then settled the hat back on front ways. "Something like that, bud. Girls need help with certain things."

"Yeah..." His face scrunched in thought. "Like learning how to make fart noises under their armpits."

"Grandma still hasn't gotten a good armpit honk right," said a smiling Anthony, causing a peal of laughter to erupt from Nicky-J.

Watching the two of them interplay evoked feelings in Nick he had tried hard to suppress all week. Out of mind, out of reality—or so he'd been telling himself.

Nick's gaze fell on his son and held fast. The pounding of his pulse hammered through his veins. Tension held him in its grip.

The aroma of clam chowder and strong coffee fused with the hot oils of hamburger patties and onions cooking on the kitchen grill, but Nick's thoughts drifted away from the smells of the Wharf Diner. His mind fast-forwarded to what his future might be like if he couldn't stop his ex-wife from interfering in his and Nicky-J's life.

If Debbie had her way, Nicky-J would be living in metropolitan Los Angeles with her and Steve, her new husband of two years. Not a chance in hell was that going to happen if Nick had anything to say about it.

Anger simmered close to the surface as Nick remembered the day he'd been served with the legal papers. They'd come out of left field—he'd had no warning, no preparation. Debbie was suing him for school-term custody of Nicky-J—she wanted him ten months out of the year with weekends and holidays negotiable—and Nick could have their son for the summers unless they made other arrangements.

With the papers still hot in his hands, he'd called his ex and asked her what the hell she thought she was doing. She broke down crying, saying she regretted not being there for Nicky-J when he was a baby. She wanted another chance. He'd argued that life didn't give chances to fix past mistakes like the one she'd made. She insisted she'd fight him in court, and the papers were proof she was serious that she felt she had just as much right to their boy as he did.

An interim custody hearing was scheduled in two weeks.

The date was coming up faster than Nick was prepared for—if he ever would be. His attorney, Bruce Harmon, was working overtime to make sure they had everything they needed to challenge Debbie and Steve.

Nick couldn't see how this could possibly go to trial since she left Bella Luna when Nicky-J was less than a year old. Bruce told him judges often ruled a boy needed his mother as well as his father, but this was a case of abandonment—sort of.

A possible strike against Nick was that he'd never legally filed as the primary custodial parent because he and Debbie worked out their own visitation schedule after their divorce. His lawyer had advised him to get the details in writing, but Nick had felt that had been unnecessary since his divorce had been simple, no fault, and Debbie had opted out of alimony.

So how could she be proved to be unfit if Nick hadn't pursued a legal recourse from the beginning?

But there'd been no point in hammering out a binding custody agreement. They had a mutual understanding that Debbie could see Nicky-J whenever she wanted. She was the one who chose to make her visits infrequent. A couple of times, Nick flew with Nicky-J to L.A. for his stay at Debbie's condo. Nick camped out at a nearby motel for the weekend. There was no way he was leaving his son without being a phone call away.

Nicky-J loved his mom and talked about her, had many photos of her in his bedroom and called her on the phone—but his son was well adjusted where he was. Where he was going to stay.

Debbie didn't have a clue about what it took to be a responsible parent. Nick had been content to live with things the way they were for the past five-plus years. But now she was changing everything and it had him on the verge of blowing a fuse.

While Nicky-J had a relationship with his mother, he had no idea his parents were about to battle for him in a court of law. And that's the way Nick intended to keep it. Because this situation wasn't going to get out of control. Nick wouldn't let things go that far, not while he had a breath in his body.

Gazing out the window, Nick collected his thoughts, trying to keep from revealing the heavy emotions he felt inside. White breakwater hit the ridge of rocks as the tide turned. Seagulls swooped down on the pier to roost on the rope-bound pilings.

"Dad, are we almost done yet?"

Nick swallowed the thickness in his throat, drank the last of his Corona and said, "Don't you want dessert?"

"Yep." Nicky-J's little hands attempted to manipulate his fork and knife into a teepee. The silverware clattered onto the table.

Nick's dad leaned toward his grandson. "Grandpa will buy you a slice of chocolate cake."

Looking into Nick's face, the boy grinned with a smile missing some teeth. "I want candy."

"Your teeth will rot out," Danny said, his boyish face handsome, a carbon copy of their father's. He bumped his knuckles over Nicky-J's chin. "It's already happening now, bud."

"This tooth got knocked out. 'Member when I rode my bike into the gutter and my handlebars smacked me in the *mawuff*." Nicky-J had his permanent two top and bottom teeth, but was missing a few others, the rest still baby teeth. This caused his speech to be slurry and marbled sometimes.

"But it would've gotten a cavity if you hadn't knocked it out of your mouth," Danny said.

"I brush. Dad makes me."

Nick snorted. "The knucklehead shoots toothpaste around the sink edge and smoothes it in. He says he's caulking the cracks." He flipped open his wallet and fingered the bills.

"You really do that, bud?" Danny asked.

"I wanna be a carpenter just like my dad." Nicky-J dug deep into his jeans pocket, yanked out his red Hot Wheels convertible Ferrari Spider, then stuffed it back for safekeeping. This check was done several times a day to make sure the prized possession was still there.

"Put your money away," Anthony said, flashing a clip of folded bills. "I've got it."

"You bought last time, Dad," John protested while reaching for his wallet. He paused after viewing the inside and coming up short. "Nick, front me a ten-spot."

"Nobody's fronting anything. I've got it." Anthony slipped two bills beneath the check. "Nick, where's your motorcycle? It's not in your parking spot."

"The clutch blew out," Nick replied, remembering

with displeasure what had happened that morning when he tried to start his bike. The custom-built soft-tail ran great, was practically new, and for no good reason had died.

"I called Danny for a ride this morning." Nick nudged the saltshaker in line with the pepper. "We dropped the bike off at Moon Cycle on the way in. Otto said there's no reason that clutch should have failed."

Anthony rubbed his dark-stubbled jaw and said, "It's that bitch of a moon. I'm waiting for my turn. You know something's going to happen. You just don't know what it'll be—good or bad."

John rose to his feet and stretched his muscles. Spindrift and windburn chapped his rugged face, his jaw bristled with a day's growth of beard. "I've got to get home to the wife."

"Say hi to Felicia for us," Danny said to John. "You need a ride, Nick?"

"No. Otto called and said I can pick up the bike," Nick replied, taking Nicky-J by the back of the head and giving him a noogie. "It's running great now. Otto and Nubs couldn't find a problem."

"It's that bitch of a moon," Anthony repeated, cracking his callused knuckles. "Good Christ, I hope to God my truck starts. I have to drive up to Carmel tomorrow."

"Nick, you want to have breakfast tomorrow?" Danny asked.

"Can't. I have to file a permit at city hall when they open."

The DiMartinos exited the Wharf Diner together, talking and joking around as they approached Anthony's '59 Chevy Apache pickup that had seen better days. On its rear bumper, a faded sticker read: *If this truck was a horse—I'd have to shoot it.*

Danny's face broke into a broad smile. "Hey, Dad, when are you going to get rid of this shitty truck?"

"Why not castrate me?" Anthony replied with his stock answer, affectionately running his hand down the battered white side. "I've had this baby since before you were born."

"And it shows," Danny said with a chuckle.

As they went their separate ways, Nicky-J's slurred question sliced through what was left of the May day. "What's *cashtrath* mean?"

"You remember that time we went to my uncle Hal's ranch and you saw him use a knife on one of the calves?" Nick said.

His son winced. "You think Grandpa really wants Uncle Danny to cut off his nuts?"

"Naw. He's just funning with him."

An afternoon sun had begun to lay a fiery streak across the sea, the whole coast aflame with its radiant orange light. The long beach was empty. Only the seabirds were there to watch the encroaching evening. As they made their way down Main Street, Nicky-J stopped short.

"Dad!" He yanked on his father's shirt. "Somebody's parked in our spot. Should we spit on the windshield?"

"Nobody's spitting on anything."

"But 'member you told me about that time you spit on a guy?"

"Not on purpose. I was sneaking my uncle's chewing tobacco and spit it out—I didn't mean to nail my cousin who was standing in the way."

A white Ford Falcon, an early sixties model in good condition considering its age, was parked in the slot that Nick used when he came to town. The space was at the pier-front, and not really a space at all. Nick had sort of turned it into one and the city ended up painting a line on either side the last time they were striping the main road.

Everyone knew he had a claim to that spot for his personal use. He liked its convenience to the Wharf Diner, and to the Outrigger Pub where he went if he was in the mood for a drink and conversation. It went without saying that the locals left it vacant for him; something he hadn't asked for, but made use of anyway.

"Oh... Well, can we spit anyway?"

"Nobody's spitting on anything." Nick took a closer look, then commented to Nicky-J, "Whoever it is got a parking ticket."

Lauren Jessup had lived most of her thirty-five years on the water, whether it was the Willamette River winding through Portland, the Puget Sound, or the northern stretch of the Pacific Ocean. Having spent so much time in ports of call, no matter where she went, she always smelled a river or the sea in her mind.

She was sensitive to the water's power, felt a kindred spirit to its ebb and flow and to the way a moving current never seemed to have a beginning or an end.

Her life was like that.

Aside from that year in her last foster home, she couldn't remember when she'd held on to something with a past or promise of a future. She just moved with the flow, went where they placed her and tried to attach herself along the banks. But the placements never worked out for long. As a child, somebody always came and got her, pulled her back into the current where she had to swim with the other fish or sink trying to get out of their way. She'd be caught again, placed with a new couple and would hope for the best.

But the best hadn't come until she was in her senior year of high school. Thank God—and she meant that with all her heart—for the Saunderses. If it weren't for them, she'd have no basis on which to build her life. Even to this day, breaking her old patterns was still difficult.

She moved through towns, much like a pebble washes up on a shore. Sometimes she stayed a while, sometimes she let the tide pull her back before she could get her feet wet.

This lifestyle had been much easier before Billy, her son, her pride and joy, had been born. He was the angel in her life, the piece of her that was good and special.

He had turned six several months ago when they were in Ukiah. She gave him a party—just the two of them. She bought a two-layer chocolate cake and wrote *Happy Birthday Billy* in blue. The evening was spent in a weekly-rate motel room, filled with newspaper streamers and as many balloons as she could afford. She'd saved a little extra over the past year, knowing exactly what she'd get him for his sixth birthday.

Billy liked looking at the night sky, he was fascinated by the moon and its orbits, the rings around Saturn, and the red face of Mars—all seen from picture books. After he blew out his candles she gave him a certificate and told him she'd registered a star in his name. He'd hugged her and held on, thanking her, and then they'd gone outside to try to figure out which one was his. Without a telescope, they had to pretend they knew which one. He wanted to make a wish, and she knew without his asking, what that wish was.

Lauren, with Billy holding her hand, walked purposefully through Bella Luna, glancing in window fronts and reflecting on their lives.

Looking back now, what seemed like a special birthday gift was nothing more than a bleak substitute for what she knew Billy really wanted. A house, a yard, a puppy.

A father.

Billy rarely complained; he was so good, her heart squeezed just thinking about him.

She couldn't keep packing up and leaving—not for herself or, more importantly, for her son.

Waitressing—quite badly—at that last coffee shop, she'd been busing a table when she'd picked up a postcard that had been left behind. The picture on the front was of Bella Luna, a place so serene and picturesque, its image brought a smile to her lips. If there was a heaven on earth, Bella Luna had to be the closest thing to it.

Lauren knew right away that she had to come and see it for herself. But she had no expectations, she never did.

Everything she and Billy owned fit in their car, a relic but reliable. She packed up their clothes and the photo albums that documented her son's life—something she'd never had—along with their possessions she called heart-treasures. They were things that wouldn't matter to anyone else, but they meant the world to the two of them.

When they arrived in Bella Luna she hadn't counted on everything being bolder, brighter in color, than they had appeared on that discarded postcard. The ocean was a seafoam green she'd never seen before. And the sky, it was like blueberries and cream, so vibrant it seemed unreal. Like a bowl of colored candies available for her pleasure… She wanted to sample all that there was.

The smells were familiar and inviting. The lingering fishy odor from the Fruitti di Mare Cannery, a comfort, as odd as that sounded. And the fragrance of spring flowers. They filled every street, exploding with blooms like rays of promise, of hope.

There were several places in town she could ask for a job. Her specialty was cooking. She had a gift, a talent that maybe she'd gotten from her birth mother. Somewhere, something in her blood gave her the ability of conjuring tastes and flavors when she looked at food. It might be an undressed hen and wild sage with button mushrooms, a navel orange and star anise, or a combination of spices she could physically smell inside her mind and break down into what she needed to re-create it for real.

She'd never had any professional training. Like the pianist who can play by ear, she could cook from her soul. The trouble was, there weren't many jobs for women who weren't professional chefs. Lauren's experience came by way of diners and cafés, and once a truck stop in Puyallup when she'd had to fill in for the greasy cook who'd had his head busted open in a beer-bottle fight. That was before Billy.

Billy, who right now gazed up at her through black-framed glasses that made his hazel eyes appear larger than they were. He got his hair color from his father, a lighter sandy shade than her own dark brown. His facial structure wasn't quite decided yet, a blend of both hers and Trevor's, and she hoped whoever's features he ended up favoring, Billy would have a face that was strong and confident.

Strength and reliance—two traits she would need right now if she was to get anywhere in the next few moments.

Barely twenty-four hours in town, she woke up to discover she had a parking ticket to sort out.

"How come the police didn't want us parking our car there, Mom?" Billy's red cape fluttered in the morning ocean breeze, the new hem knocking at the backs of his knees.

"I don't know." She pushed the glass door to city hall open, Billy alongside. "There wasn't a No Parking sign."

He shifted his gaze to his mother. "What are you going to do?"

Lauren had to rein in an impulse to throw her arms around him and kiss his cheek.

"Get us out of it," she said, holding fast to the $17.50 citation.

The building interior was hospital sterile with speckled linoleum floor tiles and Venetian blinds covering the windows. There was a single long counter that handled every problem from registering a car to applying for a marriage license.

A man was ahead of her, tall and broad shouldered. He wore jeans, the kind that were bleach-washed and a softly faded blue. They molded to his butt and hugged his hips, not too tight, but in a way that drew her attention. His nearly black hair rested on the collar of a cambric shirt, the tail tucked in yet casual. He put his hands on the counter, leaning forward and resting his weight in a pose that was both relaxed and friendly. He had wide hands, large and strong. The skin was tanned, the nails clipped short. A watch encircled his wrist, a cell phone clipped on his belt. He had a boy with him, who from the back, appeared to be around Billy's age.

Lauren and Billy were barely in line a short moment when the boy turned and stared at Billy through the most intriguing eyes. They were a marine blue that faded to a lighter, more dominant shade closer to the tiny black spheres of his irises. He was a rumpled little boy, but cleanly dressed. He wore high-top, lace-up work boots; a carbon copy of his father's—or who she assumed was his father.

"It's not Halloween," the boy said, his face a dusting of sun freckles. "How come you're wearing that?"

Billy didn't slouch under the question, he never did. The costume was a present from Mrs. Saunders for Halloween two years ago. A godsend, Lauren thought, after what had happened the day after the package arrived. The red cape had taken on a special meaning, a vital necessity that her son's life depended on.

"It protects me and my mom," Billy said.

The man turned toward them, his posture tall and sure as he rose from reclining against the counter. He drew himself up to his full height, something she guessed was six foot three—or thereabouts. His hair caught her attention first, the way that he combed it back from his forehead, somewhat like the movie actor Andy Garcia. The line of his nose gave his face a proud look, his mouth and jaw finishing the image. He probably had the nicest set of lips she'd ever seen, and her heart jumped a little as she gazed at them. His eyes, as far as she could tell, were the same combination of colors as his son's—he wore sunglasses with lenses that didn't give her a clear view.

Slowly, he slipped them off the bridge of his nose, tucking the temple into his shirt pocket.

"Whaddaya mean?" the boy questioned, his eyes narrowing as if he'd just been told the moon was made from cheese. "You think you're a superhero?"

"No. I have magic."

"Anyone can do magic if you know the tricks. My uncle Danny can make a quarter disappear. You got any Hot Wheels?"

"No."

"You got any BMX stuff?"

"No. I have an airplane." Billy pulled one of his miniature airplanes from his pocket. They were old—she'd bought them at a secondhand store—die-cast and sturdy, the green paint still on most of the parts. The plane had metal blades for the propellers that were activated by the flick of a finger.

"I got some airplanes, too," the boy commented, studying the offering without reaching for it. "Where's your dad?"

"I don't have one."

The boy gazed up at Lauren for the first time, almost an accusation, or perhaps she was sensitive and imagined it as he asked, "Why not?"

"Nicky-J," the man spoke, his voice baritone rich. The hairs on Lauren's nape tingled, an involuntary reaction she couldn't explain. "You don't ask questions like that."

"Why not?"

"Because it's impolite."

"But, Dad—"

"Dude, it's not cool."

Nicky-J must have understood the message that way, because he stuffed his hands in his pockets and looked down at the tips of his boots. "Are we almost done?"

"Yeah, it'll be just a minute," the father replied, but he did so while leveling his eyes on Lauren.

She was right. His eyes were as distinctively blue as his son's, a color that was so unusual it was almost hard to gaze away.

"Sorry about that," he said. "He's always asking questions. If he'd only ask that many in school."

Lauren smiled, what else could she do. She didn't instantly warm to strangers. It was hard for her to make connections. It took longer than these brief minutes to form an opinion, to feel as if she could let down one of her many guards.

"Here's your copy of the permit, Nick," the clerk said after returning to the counter. She was midfifties, slender, wearing horn-rimmed glasses and her hair up in a sixties-style twist.

"Thanks, Maxine. Appreciate it." He took the document and rolled it into a tube, his fingers encircling the paper as if it were one more piece of paper to keep sorted in his life. "I can't knock anything down or put anything up without this place wanting to know about it first."

"We just like to see your handsome face in here, Nick," she flirted, her pink lipstick the shade of frosted watermelon.

"You won't see it for a while if I can help it." He took his son by the back of the head, ruffling the boy's hair, then nudging him forward just as the clerk asked Lauren what she could help her with.

"I'd like to discuss this parking ticket I got." She laid the citation on the counter. "A mistake has been made."

The clerk's expression went from jovial to business-like in half a second. "No, this is a parking ticket, and if it was on your car, you've parked incorrectly."

"But that's what I'm questioning—I didn't park incorrectly. I used the space by the pier, the one in front. There wasn't a single sign posted telling me I couldn't."

"You own a white Ford Falcon?" A man's voice was so close to her ear she practically jumped, her arm instinctively coming around Billy's slight shoulders.

Nick—the name the clerk had called him—had re-appeared. He must have been listening in, and his question put her on the defensive for reasons she didn't care to examine at the moment.

"Yes, I do. Is there a crime in that?"

"No," he replied, the one syllable spoken in monotone.

"You took our parking spot." Nicky-J's statement caused Lauren's mouth to fall open.

She grew baffled, beside herself. "I didn't see anyone's name on it."

"There's not," Nick interjected. "Nicky-J, go sit on that bench."

The hallway was bracketed on both sides by benches, the kind that appeared more suited to a church than to a city building.

Nicky-J scuffed and shuffled, plopping onto the bench and dragging out a car from his pocket. He slid the wheels across the seat and made crashing noises when the car zipped over the side and thunked onto the floor.

Dragging her attention back to Nick, who stood a head taller than her, Lauren waited for him to elaborate.

He flashed a smile, one that was too handsome for his own good. His body was too broad, too strong, and it threatened to intimidate. "I'm sorry about the ticket, I should have looked into it last night. I always park there, so my son thinks the spot is mine."

Impatient now, she failed to see what difference that made. "There wasn't a vehicle in it when I got there, nor a sign saying it was a privileged space."

"My motorcycle was in the shop."

"And this is supposed to concern me, Mr.—?"

"DiMartino." He extended his hand, she didn't take it because she had no intention of getting cozy. "Nick DiMartino," he finished, lowering his arm without a flicker on his face to show his thoughts.

Since the clerk had made herself unavailable by taking a phone call, Lauren was left to question Nick.

"Well, Mr. DiMartino," she began, her tone tight and controlled. "I'd like to know why I got this parking ticket, and since you claim to have rights on that spot, you'll have to enlighten me. Because I'm not going to pay seventeen dollars and fifty cents for something when I didn't break the law."

"I agree. Tear it up."

His quick reply momentarily threw her, her wits scattering before falling neatly back into place.

"Wouldn't you just like that? I don't pay it and then I end up with a warrant out on me. I'm not stupid."

"I never said that." He put his hands up, backed away and turned toward the clerk who'd been following the entire exchange with her mouth half-open.

Nick muttered beneath his breath, a long exhaled oath she didn't fail to notice was packed full of frustration. "Maxine, what knucklehead put this parking ticket on the Falcon?"

"Now, Nick, don't you go taking anything out on me." She studied the ticket, then nodded. "Officer Carlyle."

"You tell Doug I appreciate the favor he thinks he was doing for me, but it was a big mistake and he's got to cancel the citation."

"I can have dispatch call him on the radio," Maxine said. "I heard the boys were over at the Wharf having breakfast."

"Get him on and I'll talk to him."

Lauren watched as the call was made and Nick talked to a person on the line. Their verbal exchange sounded legitimate. When he hung up, he took the ticket and tore it in half.

"You're off the hook, ah—what's your name?"

She hesitated, licked her lips and wondered if he'd really taken care of things. Omitting her last name, she admitted to, "Lauren."

"Okay, Lauren, you're in the clear. Good to go, have a nice day and all that."

He wasn't glad about a damn thing, she mused. His eyes were covered up by the sunglasses once more, giving her no opportunity to read anything further in his expression except for what was on his lips. At present, a line of displeasure and a half smile.

Smiling? Over what? Maybe this was going to be one of those small towns that didn't give an outsider a chance. Clearly this man pulled a lot of weight in the community, something that made her both curious and on guard.

To Maxine, Lauren asked, "Why does he have so much clout in this town?"

Stated simply, Maxine replied, "He's Nick DiMartino."

Nick had the decency to appear modest, embarrassed by the comment.

"Nick's family supports all town causes," Maxine added, "so we support the DiMartinos."

The two pieces of the ticket on the counter seemed to be proof he had some pull, so perhaps she owed him. He had, after all, gone out of his way to help her. At least he had some morals, if not kind decency.

"Thank you for your time," she said.

"Not a problem." He walked toward his son, who leaped off the bench's back. He'd climbed up there and now made the three-foot descent with a smack of his boots and a grunt.

"Are we done, Dad?"

"Yeah, we're outta here."

"Do we have to buy Miss Applegate some good-smelling paper for the last day of school?" Nicky-J's chin jerked down in a mope as he walked alongside his dad toward the door. "Can't I just give her a mouse, because hers died? She's still got the empty cage on her desk and I miss having Cheddar crawl up my arm and tickle me."

"You give a lady a present that *she'll* like, not what you like. Miss Applegate will appreciate scented stationery."

"Miss Applegate's not a lady, she's my teacher."

Nick opened the door, looked down his shoulder at Lauren then left.

"Mom?" Billy's voice sounded distant as her attention was pulled toward Nick's retreating form.

"Mom," Billy said once more. "That boy goes to school, how come I can't?"

"Um." She blinked out of her trance and focused on her son. "You will when it's time for the first grade."

"That's going to be this year—you said."

"Yes, you're right." She'd taught him the alphabet, shapes and colors, numbers, and how to write his name. Although he'd never been tested, she felt he was intellectually advanced for a boy his age. But Billy needed to socialize, be around other six-year-olds, make friends and build lasting relationships. Time was up. He needed to go to school like the other children.

She wanted him to be all the things she never was—secure, happy, confident and open.

Billy grabbed the faded edges of the cape, wrapped his arms in red, then murmured as if making a wish, "Mom, I want to go to first grade here."

"We'll see" was all she could offer. "I don't have a job yet and it might not work out."

He took her hand. Squinting through his glasses, he tightened his fingers. "You better look for one. I'll go with you."

They walked hand in hand into the morning sky, her son the thread that kept Lauren's patchwork life pieced together.

Two

The moon arose in a bad mood.

The grocery-store front was capped by red-and-white-striped awnings, the window glass brightly painted with today's specials. Fruit baskets, tilted for the customer's inspection, were filled to the brim. Oranges, lemons, mangoes, green apples, grapefruits.

It was inevitable that Lauren would end up here, taking in the visual delights of produce. She began to imagine how tart the zest of lemons would be or how sweet the juice of the mangoes. Bringing to mind how they would taste against her tongue made up for her less than smooth beginning to the morning at city hall.

The rest of Lauren's day had been spent visiting the several restaurants in town, talking with managers and seeking positions in the kitchen. Luck wasn't on her side. Nobody needed a cook, not even a waitress—something she preferred not to do but would if she had to. The last place she'd gone, the Wharf Diner, hadn't given her an answer at all. Verna Mae Gonzales, the owner, was out of town for the Memorial Day weekend and wouldn't return until next Tuesday. Lauren would go back then.

Until that time, she had four days on her hands. Too many to stay idle and not build upon her nest egg. She really wanted to prove herself in a kitchen before pursuing other methods of income as she had in the past. She'd done many basic jobs but without any satisfaction. She felt the wheels of frustration begin to turn, the tug of putting down roots fade away.

She cupped her hand, looked through the window of the grocery store, and thoughts about leaving fled.

Lauren stepped inside with Billy right behind. The interior was small, cluttered but clean.

The aromas of dill and coffee, yeast and raisins came to her first, followed by the sight of a pallet of foods in every imaginable color. Rich green artichokes, half-sliced red watermelons and carrots with the tops on. Hindquarters of hams and sausages hanging from twine. A scale on the counter, a glass case filled with meats. There was a library ladder behind the counter. The entire wall, from floor to ceiling, was packed with grocery products.

The aisles were more like a maze, pole supports disguised by displays. Six-pound cans of tomatoes made a towering decorative display.

She noticed jars of olives and cans of tuna, both marked with price tags. No bar codes here. This was a market from over two decades ago.

She loved it immediately, felt as if she could stay for hours.

"Help you, ma'am?" The proprietor appeared. A white apron was tied around his middle, and his snowy hair was just as white. His hairline receded, revealing a high brown forehead creased with age lines. He wore a thick mustache sprinkled lightly with gray. The smile on his mouth was genuine, warm and affable. She liked him right away.

"There's so much to look at." At the bins of legumes Lauren sifted dry pinto beans through her fingers. "I think I'll explore for a while."

"I've got a handbasket there in the corner. You can fill it, then get another if you need. I don't have carts, they can't roll through these tight aisles."

She took a basket. "This is fine."

"There's fruit here for the taking, it's samples." Then to Billy, "Or I've got sour Gummi Worms."

"Can I, Mom?" Billy's upturned face was awash with an anxious smile.

Billy rarely ate candy—she didn't buy it, but he was like any normal child. He liked convenient treats when given the chance to have them.

She nodded and followed Billy to the counter.

The scent of fresh strawberries wafted through the air with a sugary sweetness. The red fruits, stems still on, were stacked in a samples bowl.

Lauren tried one, the treat melting in her mouth. She tasted nectar and chocolate. Not just any chocolate, but white and semisweet melded together. Maybe a strawberry torte or a cake soaked with strawberry syrup. Not too sweet. The chocolate would have to be slightly bitter.

While she played with ingredients in her head, Billy took a neon-colored sour worm. She didn't know how he could eat candied rubber, and shivered when he licked his lips with a smile.

The music of the Beach Boys came through unseen speakers as Lauren strolled the aisles. She wished she had a stove to cook on. The Tidewater Motel was working all right for now with a reasonable rate, but when she got a job, she'd move to an efficiency room. Something with a real kitchen and a bigger bathroom. If she was fortunate, an affordable two bedrooms.

A bundle of energy burst through the grocery store while Lauren's small order was being rung up.

Nicky-J, a blur of baseball cap and T-shirt, stopped short of running into the candy display. He made quick work of grabbing two kinds—no thought to it—as if he knew exactly where and what he wanted.

He dropped a dollar on the rubber change mat next to the cash register and snagged a Gummi. "I'm in a hurry. Me and my friends are making a fart machine. You got any rubber bands?"

Only then did Nicky-J pause and notice Billy.

The grocer replied, "I've got a few."

"And some *nen-velopes?*" Nicky-J added in a question.

Folding his arms over the white of his apron, he angled his head at the boy. "So you need envelopes, too? I thought you boys were making them?"

"Yeah, we are, as soon as we get the stuff. Tim and Critter say we need some pages-clips."

"Paper clips, too." The aproned man collected the requested items, but before handing them to Nicky-J, he cautioned, "You boys aren't planning on detonating the noises in your classroom?"

"Huh?"

"Setting them off. The last day of school is next week and I know how it goes—pulling end-of-the-year pranks. I wouldn't feel right giving you the ammo to torture Miss Applegate."

Nicky-J's face brightened as if he'd had a lightbulb idea all of a sudden. "Nope. I wouldn't a' thought to do that. I'm giving her some smelly paper as a thank-you-for-teaching-me-stuff present."

The grocer resumed totaling Lauren's order, punching the keys of the ancient upright register. "That's nice of you."

"My dad's makin' me." Turning to Billy, he stood a little awkwardly. "They're gonna be throwing out candy at the parade."

Billy moved in closer, drawn to his peer's enthusiasm. "What parade?"

Nicky-J shoved the Gummi into his mouth and talked around it. "The parade where we wave flags at the guys who killed people for us."

"That would be Memorial Day," the grocer put in. "We honor the men and women who served this country. It's a national day of remembrance."

"Yeah, that's what it is. My dad told me." Without taking a breath, he sped on in a rush of words running together. "My uncle-grandpa Hal has a rifle and he let me hold it. My dad's going to buy me a BB gun for Christmas. I'm going to shoot at dead fishes' eyes."

Struggling to balance his candy and mechanical-flatulence materials, Nicky-J jarred the door open with his shoulder and left with the same vigor he had used to come in.

"This town has quite a few veterans," the grocer said,

bagging her items. His eyes were like obsidian flints, very observant but very kind. "I saw you and your boy when you arrived yesterday morning. Are you sticking around?"

Surrounded as she was with everything that made her happy, all she could think about were the tastes and smells. Her heart was thudding and her voice level. "Yes, I am."

He held out his hand, the palm a lighter shade than his cocoa-brown skin. "Otis Duncan, but my friends call me Dunk."

"Lauren Jessup," she replied. "And this is my son, Billy."

Dunk took Nicky-J's rumpled dollar bill and added it to the till. "I hand-trim my meat and mark lean ground beef on special every Friday. Dairy goes on sale every other Thursday. Produce prices depend on the seasons. If you want something and I don't have it, I can get it."

The Beach Boys crooned about surfer girls, the smell of garlic drifted through the market, and Otis Duncan had the whitest teeth she'd ever seen.

"If you want to watch the parade—" he lifted a can of cola to his mouth "—I have a couple extra folding chairs. Be glad to let you sit in front of the market with me. We might be a small town, but we do big parades. It doesn't matter what the occasion is, the town rolls out all the fire trucks with lights and sirens."

She was moved almost to tears over the way he welcomed her like an old friend. "That's very nice of you, but I—" She was about to say she couldn't make it, a stock answer when it came to mixing into the crowd. She caught herself, bit down on her lip, then said, "Thank you, Dunk. Billy and I would love to."

* * *

Nick was in a foul mood, an explosive tension in his stride.

He ducked beneath the scaffolding, two stories high, in the main lobby of the Ocean Grove Inn renovation. Dust particles stirred to life beneath each of his steps. The great mantel lay disassembled on the floor, the pieces of oak waiting to be packed and sent out for a luster polish. A miter saw's sharp whine cut through the air. Danny was on the second story working in one of the guest rooms.

The sky was overcast when Nick came to work on Tuesday morning. Almost noon now and the gray haze hadn't cracked a sweat. Still thin and soupy. With daylight in demand, halogen lights illuminated the area, a network of orange power cords winding across the floors.

He checked his watch, thinking he needed to call FedEx. The copper rain gutters he'd ordered hadn't come in yet, as promised. As if he didn't have enough going on. An unforeseen leak in the skylight had caused water damage on the heart pine in the second-floor parlor room. The boards would have to be completely stripped, sanded and resealed. Nick was beginning to wish he had never promised to have the place done and ready for Preservation Week. Every year more and more of the old buildings in Bella Luna were being restored to their former glory, and the first week in September they were all opened to the public so the townsfolk could enjoy a bit of history. It would be an honor to have the place included in Preservation Week this year, but the time constraints were something Nick didn't need at the moment.

The project, an Edwardian hotel originally built in 1908 and later converted to apartments in the 1960s, was always coming up with surprises. Just when he thought nothing else could go wrong, it did. Working under pressure on a historical building and being paid a hefty amount from the investors, he'd hoped, after eighteen months, to be closer to completion. He had a crew of five working for him almost daily.

He unstrapped his tool belt and palmed his cell phone. He didn't call FedEx or Weatherman Gutters.

Punching in the Los Angeles phone number, he connected with his attorney, Bruce Harmon, and spent the next twenty minutes discussing his case.

The interim-custody decision was set for June 10 in L.A., and would determine Nicky-J's placement while he and Debbie prepared for the trial. Bruce assured him that it was very unlikely that Debbie would win this decision. Nicky-J would stay where he was, but visitations over the next three to six months would be legally hammered out in writing.

Nick was pretty much reconciled to the fact that Debbie had legal rights that would alter their current arrangement, but her entering their son's life in this way pissed him off in ways no words could describe. Bruce reiterated that the interim would be pretty straightforward, so not to worry. The custody trial itself would cause the real problems.

Custody trial.

Nick couldn't stand the thought.

He clicked off the connection, fighting the urge to tell Danny about the call—tell his family about what was going down. Every time he wanted to approach them, he talked himself out of it. There was no reason to bring them into this yet. He wanted to watch and wait, to hear what the interim judge would have to say.

And a piece of him was desperately hoping Debbie wouldn't go through with it and leave things the way they were. With the happiness surrounding Danny's wedding, Nick chose not to dampen the mood. If the time came that he had to fight, then he'd take his family into his confidence. He'd need all the support he could get.

He ran a hand through his hair and, in one of those rare moments since quitting smoking eight years ago, he craved a cigarette. Craved one so bad he could taste the nicotine curling around his tongue, and he might have broken down and bought a pack if Danny hadn't appeared at the bottom of the staircase saying something about needing a new blade for the saw.

Safety glasses knocked back on his forehead, Danny brushed the sawdust off his jaw. "Do we have any twelve-inch blades?"

"I've got tens. What's it for, the DeWalt?"

"Yeah. I'm cutting molding."

There was a tension-free atmosphere between them, one Nick welcomed and needed now more than ever. He could always count on Danny to do what had to be done. Rarely did Nick and his younger brother disagree. They shared most of the same ideas for problems and strategies—reasons why they got along so well in business together.

Nick tried to let go of the anxiety fisting tightly around his chest. "I'll have to run up to the hardware store and buy some."

"I can do it."

"I've got it covered."

Boyish pleading filled Danny's eyes. "On your way back, can you get me a patty melt from the Wharf?"

"Sure."

"Get yourself one too." He popped his fist on Nick's upper arm, a playful gesture that had a thirty-year history. "Get two with double cheese. You're turning skinny."

Nick had over two hundred pounds of muscle on his six-foot-three frame. He was far from starving.

After purchasing the saw blades, he entered the Wharf Diner, its shape long and rectangular like a rail car. The exterior had once been shiny tin, but over the years, salty air had corroded the metal to a dull gray. Flower-box geraniums, in bursts of poppy red, brightened the front entrance. The building sat on the front of the pier, a standout landmark for as long as anyone in Bella Luna could remember. The Wharf was located right next door to the Ocean Grove Inn and made a convenient breakfast, lunch, and oftentimes, dinner stop.

Nick could smell today's special before he got to the Formica counter. Verna Mae had put on a pot of navy beans and ham. She must have had a sixth sense to know the damp fog wouldn't blow over by lunch.

"Hey, Verna Mae," he said to her as he took a seat on one of the last vacant blue vinyl stools. The lunch rush had started.

He didn't have to study the menu, he knew it by heart.

"I'll be right with you, Nick," Verna Mae responded without missing a beat in her well-orchestrated diner dance, putting in an order and collecting one at the same time.

Verna Mae had come to town a dozen years ago by way of Santa Barbara where she'd been a cook for one of the mission rectories. It was never confirmed by Verna Mae—and nobody asked—but rumor had it she'd carried on a secret affair with one of the clergymen before it went sour. Verna Mae was a veritable pistol of fire and vinegar for her age, with the charm to stir a so-inclined man to distraction.

She must have been in her midfifties with a fairly supple body. Her movements were fast and concise as she poured coffee with one hand and popped down four slices of white bread in the toaster with the other. Turquoise and orange coral were her favorite gemstones and she wore a lot of the baubles, especially necklaces. While the chunky jewelry caught a person's eye, it was her hair that demanded attention first. The only way to describe its color was lobster red. She wasn't a natural, that much was obvious, but the shade flattered her creamy complexion, so much so, she dyed her eyebrows as well. She kept her hair on the short side, and it crowned her head in shag-style curls.

"I'm in no hurry," Nick said, his usual answer even if he was short on time.

Verna Mae slipped a pencil over her ear, then refilled a water glass for the guest two seats down. Talking in Nick's direction, she said, "Your dad brought me some halibut. I'm having Knox grill them tonight if you're going to be around for dinner."

"I might. Depends on how much I get done the rest of the day."

She stood before Nick, made an efficient wipe of the

counter and stuck a new ketchup bottle in front of him. "What can I get you?"

"Two patty melts, dill pickles and two sides of potato salad. Add one coffee, black, for me. To go."

Verna Mae took his straightforward order and translated it into kitchen slang for Knox Dugan who, sweating over a grill in kitchen whites, wore a paper cook's hat.

Nick folded his arms over his chest and gazed about the diner, pausing when he noticed someone familiar.

Lauren, and her little boy with the cape and dated eyeglasses, sat in a booth. Food plates weren't in front them, just water glasses with puddles of condensation slipping down the outsides. From the looks of things Nick guessed she'd been sitting a while, waiting.

Waiting for what? It seemed odd to be waiting so long for service when Verna Mae had two competent waitresses running the floor.

He took a moment to study Lauren, to read her face for hints or insight into who she was and why she'd come to Bella Luna. Lots of people came and went— this was a given in a harbor town where a third of the jobs were seasonal. But she was different, something he'd noticed the first time he'd seen her in city hall. There was something about her, something he couldn't pin down.

When he'd talked with her, he'd felt heat rush through his body, a purely sexual reaction that hadn't been there in a long while. He worked too many hours, stayed too busy with his son and spending time with family. He couldn't get involved. Especially now with this hearing hanging over his head. Debbie was dragging him into hell and he wouldn't take a new girlfriend down there with him.

When Nick and his wife divorced, he didn't date for

a full year afterward. His first priority was raising his son. Gradually, he let go of his reservations and gave himself permission to see women, to feel like a man instead of a father. When Nick dated someone, he did so without Nicky-J knowing about it in case things didn't work out. He had several short-term relationships that, for various reasons, never went further than a few months.

Two years ago, he'd gotten fairly serious about Kathleen Kirk, an environmentalist who summered in Bella Luna while she gathered information for her dissertation. But she'd wanted more than Bella Luna, more than he could offer, and went back to San Diego to finish her master's degree.

Since then, Nick didn't feel it was fair to Nicky-J to bring complications into their life. His son had grown used to having Kathleen around and her leaving confused him. He thought it was his fault. The day before she left, he spilled his kid's hamburger meal in her car, grease and ketchup staining the upholstery. She hadn't gotten bent out of shape about it, but that was Nicky-J's four-year-old's interpretation as to why she'd gone— no matter how much Nick assured him otherwise.

Now Nick kept himself occupied with the renovation instead of looking for serious female company. Getting remarried was something he'd like to do one day, but for now he wasn't interested. He didn't need a mother for Nicky-J; the one his son had was difficult enough.

It amazed Nick, looking back on those years, how he could have fallen for a woman like Debbie. He'd changed so much since then. His priorities were different, he was a different man. He'd recharted the direction he wanted to go in life and Debbie hadn't. She wasn't willing to compromise and their marriage simply died.

Easing back on the diner stool, Nick observed Lauren. She sat with her spine straight, her hands alternating from being folded in her lap to the tabletop where she'd mop water with a napkin. She was nervous, but doing a reasonable job of keeping it hidden. From their conversation over the parking ticket he didn't take her for the nervous type. She seemed pretty self-assured, a real fighter for a cause.

She corrected her son's posture, nudging him to sit the same erect way she did. The boy's height appeared dwarfed by the table. Estimating him to be close in age to Nicky-J, the kid was a couple inches shorter. He had a thick head of sandy-brown hair and a good-looking face. He took after his mother in many ways.

Speaking to her son, Lauren's lips moved and Nick focused on their shape, full and plump, with a softer red lipstick coloring her mouth. The line of her nose was straight, turned up at the end. The symmetry on her oval face was almost perfect. With a major in housing and urban development, and preparatory work in landscape architecture, Nick's visual mathematics were usually right on target. Not to mention, he took measurements all day with a tape.

Regardless, he didn't have to study her face to figure out he was attracted to more than just her appearance. He liked a woman who had drive and determination and, as far as he'd witnessed, she had both. She was spirited, no nonsense. And gutsy, a word he didn't use often to describe a woman—aside from his mother who'd taught junior high school math for twenty-five years before retiring.

He and Nicky-J had seen Lauren and her son at the Memorial Day parade over the weekend. She'd sat with Dunk, somewhat reserved, as if she weren't familiar, or maybe even comfortable, with the intimacy of a small-town parade.

"Do you know her?" Verna Mae asked, breezing past with an armload of hot plates.

On her return run, Nick shrugged his answer about Lauren. "If you'd call having words over a parking ticket an introduction, yeah—I've met her."

"She's been here for twenty minutes and I haven't had a spare second to sit down. I've gone over twice and apologized, asked her to give me another five minutes. Here it's been ten again. She wants to talk with me and I've got all I can do to keep up. I don't know why we're so busy today."

"The swell was up this morning, rolling the water. A lot of boats didn't go out."

Nick's and Lauren's eyes met in the same moment. She looked away, as if trying to pretend the connection hadn't happened, as if to become invisible to him.

"I'll go tell her you won't be much longer." He got up and went to Lauren's table.

Sliding into the booth, he sat across from them. Lauren opened her mouth to oppose, but he talked first. "Verna Mae told me to tell you, it'll be just another few minutes."

The boy glanced sideways at his mother, an exasperated whimper beneath his breath. Impatience furrowed his eyebrows, but he didn't complain. He took off the glasses and scrubbed his eyes with his fists. His face looked different without the bulky eyeglasses, not so wide-open with wonder. Nick considered why she hadn't gotten him a pair more suited for a kid, not that the ones he had were so bad. But no doubt her son got some teasing at school since the glasses weren't real stylish.

"What's your name?" Nick asked him.

He slouched a little, then remembered to straighten up on his own. "Billy Jessup."

"I'm Nick. You've met my son—Nicky-J."

Billy wiggled his leg. "He told me you were going to buy him a gun to shoot out fish eyes."

Nodding indifferently, Nick said, "He's been after me to get him a BB gun."

"My mom says guns are bad."

"A gun is bad when it's in bad hands."

Lauren knit her fingers together and rested her hands on the tabletop. "Is there something else you wanted, Mr. DiMartino?"

"You can start by calling me Nick. And no, nothing else in particular. I'm waiting for my order to come up. Thought I'd come over here and sit."

She worried her thumbs, rolling them over each other, first forward, then backward. "Um, is the weather always overcast the last week in May?"

"Couldn't say, I haven't ever kept track." He laid his arm over the back of the booth. His long legs grew cramped for space and he shifted his position. The steel toe of his work boots connected with her shoes. She jerked back, shot him a look, then gazed over his shoulder.

She commented, as if to assure herself, "It looks like things are quieting down."

"They eventually do. Are you eating lunch?"

"We had something at the Tidewater."

"You're staying at the motel?"

"For now."

"We're here to get a job." Billy had a toothy grin and dimples. "She's saving money to buy us a house and get me a dog."

Lauren frowned, clearly not liking her private business open for discussion. "I'm thinking about staying in town and I'd need a—"

"Mom, you said I could go to school here."

"Billy, I didn't promise. I said we'd have to see."

His chin touched his chest a moment, before Nick snagged his attention. "Nicky-J and his buddies play baseball in the field on Otter Street by the vacant sardine cannery. I'm sure they'd want you on one of their teams."

"I don't play games like that."

"You've never hit a baseball?"

"I don't believe in competitive sports for boys." Lauren's reply was enunciated clearly and precisely. For a woman with a sexy-as-hell red mouth, she could be a real prude.

Curious, he laid his palms over his knees and leaned forward. "Why is that?"

"It promotes aggression and violence."

Nick snorted, wondering if she was for real. "I played baseball when I was his age and I haven't busted anyone's skull—that I can remember anyway."

Lauren looked at him from beneath thick eyelashes.

"Billy's a good swimmer, he only has something to prove to himself."

"I've got news for you, team sports are a way of nurturing good behavior in boys. He's not going to turn into a man unless he gets clobbered a few times and learns some heroism."

"Then your definition of a hero and mine are completely different, Mr. DiMartino."

"Nick," he growled. His mood, bad to begin with, caused his temper to rise. He pointed a finger. "You're not letting his self-esteem develop."

Her expression, completely reined in as if she practiced not showing her emotions, didn't reveal her thoughts—but her words had bite to them. "I think you should leave now."

"I'm so sorry." Verna Mae came bustling over, her short curls bouncing. "Nick, your order's ready. Shove over so I can talk with her."

Nick slid out of the booth, cursing himself for letting his pisser of a mood get in the way. There was nothing he could do to take his criticism back, so he went after his lunch.

Lauren had scant seconds to arrange her thoughts. Damn that man. Nick DiMartino, a big macho-bruiser-thinks-he-knows-it-all. She'd run across his type before—in fact, Billy's father had some of the same attitude. She wasn't damaging her son, and how dare he suggest otherwise?

She calmed her agitated heartbeat with several quick breaths.

"What can I do for you?" Verna Mae asked. She was pleasing to look at and seemed to be a town favorite.

"I'm Lauren Jessup and this is my son, Billy." She put a hand on his shoulder, lovingly. Her confidence returned in quick order, the strength returned as she reminded herself how much her son needed her, counted on her to be there. "I need a job. I'm a cook, a very good one."

"I don't have any cook positions. Knox, bless his damn heart, keeps up with the orders. Lord knows how he does it. His cousin, Lou, comes in for dinner and mostly takes up all the slack."

"Yes, but I'm a specialty cook. I can make things you've never tasted before, foods that you wouldn't think to put together. I have a way in the kitchen—"

"Sweetpea, we serve hamburgers and the fresh catch of the day in deep-fried batter. I operate a simple joint. I don't go in for all that fancy grass trim on the plate."

Not one to give up, she went with option B. "I can waitress."

"I've got two perfectly good waitresses."

"But they're not keeping up. I watched that table being served their cheeseburgers with fries instead of potato salad. And that table there, they've been plied with so many iced-tea refills, they're too full and they canceled their dessert order. The couple at the counter asked for more croutons on their salads, and they haven't received them yet."

Verna Mae shook her head, a grin stretching from ear to ear. "Well now, you've been just as busy as me on this shift." She looked to Billy, his eyes large and expressive, then back at Lauren. "Down on your luck?"

"Of course not," she sputtered, somewhat stymied by the bold statement. "I can go to the next town and get a job. I take care of my son without any aid. Just because

I'm unemployed doesn't mean I'm having hard luck. You would have hired me before today, but you've been out of town."

Verna Mae cocked her head. "And what makes you so sure I'd hire you?"

"You need me."

"Sweetpea, I need a man and a foot massage."

She didn't relent. None of the other restaurants in town were hiring. This was her last chance. "I can work morning or night shifts. Swing, if that's all you have."

"Lordy, but you're pigheaded." She paused, her lips pursed, a vacant smile for Billy. "Too much iced tea, you say?"

"Five refills."

"I can only use you part-time."

Lauren let out her breath, relief replacing the tightness in her lungs.

"We're open seven to seven, but we never get out of here on time. That's twelve hours of hashin'." Verna Mae rose, favoring her right foot as if she had a corn she couldn't shake off her pinkie toe no matter how much she taped and medicated it. "You'd better have yourself some good nurse's shoes."

"I'll manage."

"Be here tomorrow morning at six and I'll show you around. You'll work with June and me until you can go solo."

"Thank you, Verna Mae." Lauren stood and enthusiastically pumped the woman's arm with a firm handshake. "You won't regret this. And if you're ever short in the kitchen, I'm much better suited as a cook."

"But I'm hiring you as a waitress."

Three

Time to put the moon to bed.

"Can I open the can, Dad?" Nicky-J held on to a can of green beans.

Nick dumped a box of meat helper into a skillet of noodles and ground beef. "Only if you'll eat them."

"You know I don't like this kind of veg-em-table."

"Then you can't play with the electric can opener."

"How 'bout if I just eat the outsides?"

Nicky-J had a food aversion to anything oval. Lima beans, raisins, peanuts.

"What are you going to do?" Nick used a wooden spoon to stir the bubbling mixture. "Pick out all the beans inside?"

"Yeah."

"Go ahead then, dude. At least you'll eat part of a vegetable."

Nick was so hungry that even the smell of processed

food was appetizing. But he knew the dinner wouldn't taste as good as it smelled.

It was Friday and, by the end of a workweek, he was too dead tired to even sit at the Wharf Diner and be served. He just wanted to come home, take off his dirty clothes and get into a hot shower. Then slip into his favorite jeans and T-shirt, go barefoot around the house.

He wasn't much of a cook, knew the basics like opening cans and reading instructions on meat-helper boxes. He discovered that leftover spaghetti and chili mixed together made for a quick night of chilighetti. He did the mac-and-cheese thing, could put together a grilled-cheddar sandwich. In the summer months, he grilled. He had a nice barbecue outside on the deck.

Nick's house was lumberjack rustic, nestled among the cedar and Monterey pines on a hillside overlooking the blue Pacific. A trail to the dunes below carved its way through the pink blooming ice plants. Gray slate stones encircled the property, veering off in various directions: the carport, toolshed, a garden he'd never gotten around to putting in.

He'd purposefully planted all-white flowering shrubs to contrast with the house's cedar-shingle siding and hunter-green trim. Tall windows in every exterior wall gave an open-to-the-woods feel. His bedroom was spacious, with double sliding doors opening onto the deck and a hot tub. He'd put in a shower nozzle outside to wash the sand off his and Nicky-J's feet after walking up from the beach.

Most of the living room furniture was in earth tones, black or dark-painted wicker. The two sofas were made of leather, side tables mahogany. Hung down the hallway were a lot of wood-framed pictures of Nicky-J as a baby, a toddler and his age now.

The motor to the can opener pulled Nick's attention. "Watch the sharp edges when you take the lid off."

Nicky-J used careful fingers to detach the top. He dumped the green beans into a saucepan and handed it off to Nick for the burner. When they cooked dinner together they had a system of moving around each other without the need for directions.

Each man knew his part in the kitchen.

Nicky-J set out a half gallon of milk, moved the step stool below the cupboard and pulled down two plates. He reached higher for the cups.

"Now that school's out for the summer you've got time on your hands." Nick lowered the heat on the main course.

"But, Dad, I washed 'em before I opened the can." He examined his palms.

"I meant, what are you going to do all summer?" Nick needed to keep the conversation as normal as possible, the flow as usual as it always was. He couldn't accept that Debbie might have their son for the summer break, it just wasn't going to happen.

Nicky-J dropped silverware next to the plates, going around the table in a circle. "You got any more wood for me?"

"Some two-by-fours. Nothing big and flat."

"That ought to start us out. Me and Tim and Critter, we're building a fort in the field out back of Tim and Critter's house. There's some dead trees and everything."

The thought of the three boys making a fort brought back memories of him, Danny and John putting up a tree house. It had taken them months, only to have the damn thing blow down in the first windstorm. They hadn't cared all that much, it gave them the chance to work on a bigger and better one, learning from their mistakes. Being with his brothers had been the best part of the summers.

"Remember that lady we saw at city hall?" Nick put the dinner on the table. "She's living here now with her son."

"In our house?" Nicky-J's eyebrows lifted, taking the meaning to be literal.

"No, I meant in town. They're staying at the Tidewater."

Nick wasn't surprised to see Lauren Jessup waitressing for Verna Mae at the Wharf. He'd gone in for coffee this morning and a quick doughnut with Danny. June had taken their order at the cash register, so he didn't exchange words with Lauren.

"I saw that boy a coupla times," Nicky-J said, scooting back his chair.

"You should ask him to play with you and your buddies. He could help you build your fort."

"Do I have to, Dad?"

"I think Billy could use some friends. The kid sits at the diner while his mom works. I've seen him in there. He was drawing with crayons."

Scooping a spoonful of hamburger hash, Nicky-J let it dump in a pile on his plate, the expression on his face showing grotesque pleasure from the *plop* sound. "I don't draw nothin' unless you make me. Are you making me ask him to play with us?"

"No, I'm not making you. I'm just telling you, he hasn't made any friends and you've got some to spare."

"He looks funny in that red cape. I mighta liked him if he thought he was an X-Man or somethin'."

They ate and talked about their day, questioned whether or not the Giants would make the playoffs. After the last green bean was torn apart on Nicky-J's plate, Nick guided the conversation down a different road. "I got a call today from Miss Applegate. She said you and the boys set off fart noises."

The fork in his small hand stilled. "She called you up? I didn't think she had our phone number. I never gave it to her."

"It's in your school records, dude."

"Oh…" His face drew a blank. "Yeah, me and Tim and Critter. We did it. Dunk gave us the idea."

"He told you to do it?"

"No, he told me not to. 'Cept for his sayin' we shouldn't made me think it'd be funny."

"Not a good game plan," Nick said through the ringing of the telephone. "But I'll bet it was funnier than that time you shot wet toilet-paper balls onto the boys' bathroom ceiling."

Nick knew he shouldn't mention a disciplinary incident in a light manner, but when his son did stuff like this, it reminded him of his own normal youth.

Nicky-J broke into a grin as he dashed for the phone. "All the kids were laughing. It sounded like Tim ripped a big one."

Still smiling, Nick began to clean up the dishes.

"Hullo?" Nicky-J put his mouth close to the receiver. "Hi, Mom."

Nick froze midway to the sink, the muscles in his body going hard with knots of tension. Just when he'd been able to put the hearing out of his mind for a while, it came back to him full blown.

Resentment, a feeling he rarely let seize him, held him in its jagged grip.

Debbie had periodically called the house throughout the years, but she'd really increased her efforts lately. Nicky-J didn't suspect why his mother had more than a passing interest in him all of a sudden.

"We just ate dinner. No, I don't gotta no more. I'm building a fort this summer."

The dishes in Nick's hands clattered to the tile countertop as he backed away, running his fingers through his hair. He put the milk away and listened as his son carried on a normal conversation with a woman who had been anything but a normal mother.

"Yeah, I wanna go to Disneyland. Universal Studios, too? I'd have to ask Dad." He talked away from the phone. "Dad, Mom wants to know if I can go to Universal Studios. I wanna, can I when I visit her?"

"We'll talk about it later, dude. Let me talk to Mommy now."

"Mom, Dad's here. Yeah. I will." He shoved the phone at Nick.

To his son, Nick said, "Hey, go get cleaned up in the bath."

Nicky-J stuck his nose in his armpit. "But I don't stink."

"You smell like pine tar."

When Nicky-J disappeared down the hallway, Nick slid the patio door open and stepped outside. Dusk had fallen, the horizon a shade of sherbet orange that faded to midnight blue.

"Debbie." Speaking her name left a bitter taste in his mouth.

"Hello, Nick." Her voice was smooth, like bourbon. She'd always had that appeal to her, a fine southern comfort that a man wanted to slip his hands over.

"You're not having him for the whole summer, and promising him Disneyland and Universal Studios is only going to disappoint him when it doesn't happen." Blood pounded at his temples, creating a pressure that brought an ache to his clenched jaw.

"We'll see about that." There was an edge of threat to her tone.

Nick kept his back to the beach, his gaze through the glass panes of the house to make sure his son wasn't around to overhear him. "Drop the case, Debbie. I swear to God, you're going to fuck up our son if you go through with this. He only knows one house, one family—and it's me."

"Stop sounding so scared, Nick. He's come down here several times now and he likes Steve."

"Yeah, because the guy buys him any toy he asks for and even those he doesn't."

"You're resentful of me because Steve and I make more money than you, and we can offer things you can't."

"That's bull and you know it."

"Listen, Nick, I don't want to fight with you." Her words were cool and clear. "Nicky-J is going to be in first grade this fall and it's time we started shaping his education. The schools are better down here. There's a private school in my neighborhood that's rated one of the best in the country. I can't believe you wouldn't want what's best for Nicky-J."

"I'm what's best for Nicky-J."

"Nick, don't get angry with me." Her voice grew muffled, a short and raspy sound, as if she was being coached, not alone in the room. "I've got every right to my son and you can't keep him from me."

"You should have thought about that when you left him."

"Nick, you're getting nasty. Steve's right here and he said I don't need to take this crap from you."

"Then don't." Nick clicked the connection closed, gripping the dead phone tightly in his hand. He blew off a string of obscenities, a reckless anger engulfing him. Breath burned in his throat. He wanted to hit something with his fist.

Damn her.

He'd never hated his ex-wife, never placed blame or fault for their divorce with her—even when she chose to walk out. But this, what she was doing now, he wasn't going to forgive her. She had no right, no business, to screw up their son's life like this. Nicky-J wasn't up for grabs. Nick would fight her, even if it meant Bruce Harmon had to draw blood, dredge up something—anything, to prevent her from taking Nicky-J.

Nick managed to temper his anger, but an unease held him in its clutches as he returned inside.

What if I can't stop her? What if she wins?

The sand was still warm beneath Lauren as the last slice of sun disappeared and the sky faded to a deep blue. The gulls left the beach at sunset, their gossiping cries gone. The only sounds now were the waves crashing as they reached the shoreline.

She rested her back against a tall rock, Billy's head on her leg, using her as a pillow. He'd fallen asleep after digging for sand crabs then letting them go. He brought her bird feathers and seashell fragments he'd collected; the trinkets lay in a depression of sand by her hand. They'd watched the stars, looked for his, found one and claimed it as the Billy Jessup Star.

In this moment, when daylight drifted to nighttime and the struggle of her life dimmed, Lauren was content. She could spend the rest of her days here like this, with the salty winds and ocean fogs, the twisted and weathered cypress on the sea cliffs above. True peace was her son sleeping beside her, his rib cage softly rising and falling with his deep breaths.

She hated to wake him and head back to the Tidewater Motel, so she stayed, listening to the surf, watching the stream of light circle around from a lighthouse in the distance. The clang of a buoy made intermittent company with her thoughts.

She wasn't making ends meet with the part-time job and tips from the Wharf Diner. Living like this was no way to get ahead, no way to save even pennies. She'd had to make a withdrawal from her savings account to pay her motel bill. The rate was cheaper by the week so she'd converted from daily to weekly. She had a bank account to draw from, a balance of almost nine thousand dollars. She'd been saving for years, slowly adding. Not lately, though, and it was a sore spot for Lauren. She couldn't accept the lack of progress.

She had to get another job.

But where to put Billy? Verna Mae was great about letting him come to work with her and sit on one of the counter stools. June and Knox, Omar the part-time cook and Lou the dinner cook had taken a liking to him and brought him samples of food, French fries and shakes—things she didn't give him, but she looked the other way for now. Billy colored, drew pictures, played with his airplanes, but that only held his attention for so long. It was unreasonable to think he wouldn't grow bored while she worked five-hour shifts.

Guilt sat heavily in Lauren's chest. She'd let him go outside today on the pier and feed the seagulls bread pieces, only if he stayed right where she could see him from the windows. He'd talked to himself, walked the "plank" on the pier and played with imaginary friends.

What could she do? She was only one person and the overload from stress threatened to choke her. Billy counted on her resources, on her to take care of his needs. She wouldn't fail her child, not the way her mother had failed her.

She felt temporarily lost, unsure about where to turn. She had, in the past, been employed by a cleaning service and had worked as a stock clerk at a warehouse. She'd tried telephone answering, but the four walls in a cubicle drove her nuts. She'd graduated from high school with decent grades, and wished she'd been able to achieve more with her education. In the future, she wanted to attend college, but first, Billy would go.

Dampness encroached, the meager warmth of her sweater not staving off its chill. A full moon appeared, looking down at her with a pearly face. She studied it with wonder, not having noticed its unusual luster before. The city lights had been too bright, but now she could see the details clearly. The darkened beach and sky lent the perfect contrasting background.

How ever did the moon turn pink like that? Not a bright pink like a cosmetic, but whipped-cream pink. Birthday-cake pink, and candle pink. The things that wishes were made on. Dreams coming true.

Perhaps if she gazed longingly at the moon, it would hear what was in her heart: the hope and promise she wanted so much for her son.

"It's at its fullest tonight." A man's voice startled Lauren enough that she jerked, but her movement didn't rouse Billy.

Nick DiMartino stood over her, his body tall and cutting off the moon's light. He was a dark silhouette against the darker night. She hadn't heard him approach and chastised herself for not being more alert.

Rather than show him he'd taken her unawares, she asked, "Why is it pink?"

"Don't know. Nobody does. It's been this way for hundreds of years, ever since the Italian fishermen came to town and named it Bella Luna."

"Beautiful moon," she supplied, gently smoothing Billy's hair from his forehead. "Dunk told me."

"Dunk's a good guy. There are a few good guys in town, and I didn't want you to think I wasn't one of them."

Moonbeams shone on his hair, half his face highlighted. His features were strong and masculine, his jaw square. She didn't like that her pulse snagged when she looked at him.

He shifted his stance. "What I said at the Wharf the other day, it's your business how you want to raise your son."

"Yes, it is."

"He seems like a good kid."

"He is."

"I noticed he's artistic, the drawings."

"He likes art."

"Does he take after his dad?"

The surf roared softly, undulating upward, then slipping back down. Lauren let the noise come between them for several seconds.

"I wouldn't know anymore," she said at length, opting—though uncertain as to why—to tell the truth.

"I've got an ex myself." He sat on one of the adjoining rocks, long legs before him. The night reflected on the white of his T-shirt beneath a leather jacket and outlined his dark jeans. He wore hiking boots, the soles sinking into the sand. "She lives in Los Angeles."

"I've never been."

"I lived there for fifteen years. Crowded, smoggy. But the work was good."

"What did you do?" She found a strange comfort settling into their conversation.

"Urban planning and development for a tract of homes on the Los Angeles county border. I went to UCLA—had to put my degree to good use."

A tingling numbness began to creep into her right leg where Billy slept. She felt her foot go to sleep. "But now you're here."

"This is home." He brought his thumb to his lip, dragged the pad cross the lower fullness. The gesture brought forth a churning of awareness, a sharpening of her senses. His masculine scent caught on the air, musky and clean. "Where are you from?"

She swallowed, her throat dry. "Everywhere."

"Originally?"

"Portland."

"Been there a few times. Clean downtown. Good planning."

"I liked living close to the river." She inched her leg to the left, rubbing her thigh where Billy's weight was slightly relieved.

"Folks still there?"

"No." She wouldn't talk about her mother. She couldn't talk about a father she never knew. And the Saunders, speaking of them would mean having to explain why she'd been placed in foster care. Certain things Lauren kept to herself.

Nick scratched the underside of his jaw, running his fingernails up the unshaven skin. She almost heard the rasp of beard, smelled the lingering aftershave from this morning when he'd been in the Wharf for doughnuts. He hadn't sat at her booth for breakfast; his preference was Danish, doughnuts or muffins—foods that could be eaten on the run, and always a coffee to go with it.

She knew from Verna Mae that he was divorced, and that half the women in town were hoping he'd ask them out. The white of his smile was enough to dazzle even June, the middle-aged waitress at the diner.

"I see your father in the morning when I'm on my way to work." She sifted sand through her fist, its texture cool and soft as the grains fell from her hand. "He's on his boat."

Everyone knew the DiMartinos. She'd learned the demographics of the clan already from various sources, and without having asked. They were an old and respected family, reliable and always there to give a help-ing hand. Generations of them had celebrated holidays, special days and the small things in life. Theirs was the kind of family that she had always... It wasn't impor-tant now.

"He's done that for close to fifty years—the old guy won't retire. I think if he did, my mom would go batty having him at the house anyway."

She smiled at the affection warming his voice. The deep undertones raised gooseflesh across her arms. The sun had felt so delicious, she'd only thought to bring a light sweater. Now she was cold. She should leave and return to the motel. Billy was tired, she had an early morning tomorrow.

Lauren gazed at the moon, its pink glow romantic and milky. If this were a different time, if she were a dif-ferent woman, she might have—

What did it matter?

She was who she was and this was now.

Disregarding the moon's whipped-cream allure, she wondered why Nick DiMartino wasn't under its spell sitting in some cove with a willing woman in his arms.

To her chagrin, she caught herself speaking her thoughts aloud. "I wouldn't have guessed you'd be by yourself on a Friday night." She gave a fast shrug, a good save of indifference. "Not that it's any of my business."

The starry light set off his profile. She grew mesmer-ized by the cut of his mouth, shape of his nose and mea-sure of his forehead. Clearly, he was hewn from Italian ancestry. A strong breed, whereas she was a mix of ev-erything and knew little of her family tree.

"I'm not alone right now."

His response, the low-tenored way it was spoken, brought a curl of heat in the pit of her stomach.

He leaned slowly forward, as if in thought, and rested his forearms on his knees. "My mom's at my house watching my son. I had to get out for a couple of hours."

The way he said it arose her curiosity, and her compassion. He must have ghosts of his own to deal with.

"Nothing a drink at the Outrigger couldn't put in perspective," he said, as if knowing she wanted to ask but wouldn't.

She grew a bit nervous acknowledging that she was interested in what had sent him into the night. But she'd never know, she couldn't get involved.

A soupy fog began to roll in and chilled through her clothes.

"I have to leave now." She moved to wake up Billy, but Nick was leaning over her and scooping her son into his arms before she could protest.

"He's out," Nick said, straightening and bringing her baby boy to his chest. "I'll carry him back to the motel for you."

Shock and confusion claimed her wits. She had no idea what to say, what to do. It was a strange moment seeing them together.

Nick walked up the beach, his stride even and steady. She had no fear he'd harm Billy, but in the next endless moment, she stood awkwardly and watched, thinking that they looked as if they belonged together like that.

She shook the thought and defensively willed it away. Her emotions collided with common sense and she quickly found the normal rhythm of her heartbeat and followed alongside.

At the Tidewater, she unlocked the door with her key and Nick lowered Billy onto the double bed—the only bed in the room. It felt painfully inadequate now, her life in this room. All that she owned, everything that was hers and Billy's filled the space. There wasn't a lot, there was more in her heart than what anyone could see.

Even so, she grew embarrassed—a rarity—by her present circumstances.

She stood in the open door not meeting Nick's eyes, questioning and wondering. She wouldn't give him answers. She wouldn't let him read her troubled face.

"Thank you for your help." Her hand lay on the edge of the door, slowly moving it into place as he passed through.

He might have said something further, but she slipped the door closed, inserted the chain in the lock and shut him out. Just as she always did when anyone tried to get too close.

Four

The moon befriends new stars each night.

Wong's Pizzeria was the place to go on a Saturday night. It was located in the now-defunct cannery wharf, a renovated building that was subdivided into smaller rectangles for the variety of businesses it supported. Only the faintest hint of the sardines that used to come through still lingered. The seasoned fisherman could detect the odor, but in Wong's, the average person was likely to smell only the spicy pepperoni and sausage.

The pizza place was small, a twenty-five seater with one high chair, and only Sam in the kitchen unless it was a weekend night. Then he recruited his nephew to handle the overload.

The ping and clang of the pinball machine, the electronic music and the *whop-whop* of Pac-Man, came from the arcade cove. Sam had two classics he'd bought for next to nothing, and even Nick sometimes indulged in a game that brought back memories of his teen years.

Nicky-J bit off a gooey bite of cheese pizza, slugged down a mouthful of orange soda, ripped out a burp, then ran back into the corner to shove another quarter into the pinball machine.

Danny and Heather sat across from Nick, Heather sipping on bottled water and Danny drinking a Bud on tap like Nick. She ate a garden salad while the guys worked on their second slices of sausage and olives.

"Sure you don't want a bite, hon?" Danny asked Heather, tempting her with a slice.

"Get it away. I told you I've got to fit into my wedding dress."

"You look great, Heather," Nick commented, recognizing she'd lost about ten pounds in the past couple of months. Not that she was overweight to begin with, she just looked more toned.

Heather was tall, killer-blond and twenty-seven—ten years younger than Danny. She'd recently completed her graduate work and was a marine biologist at the Monterey Bay aquarium. The way the pair acted, it was sometimes as if Danny were the younger of the two. In spite of that, they were a great complement to each other. They'd been together for three years.

"Thanks, Nick. If I left it up to Danny, I'd put all my weight back on. He thinks I can eat like him—anything I want. I'm like a broken record with him these days."

"You start in on him now, Heather," Nick teased, "you won't have anything left to nag him about once you get married."

"I'm already learning that. I used to critique him in the morning, but I stopped." Heather had an apartment in town, and oftentimes, Danny spent the night. "Now if

I notice his fly's unzipped on his way out, I just say, 'Have a nice day.'"

Danny's bite of pizza stalled in front of his open mouth. "Jesus, that happened one time—and you know why it was unzipped."

Heather was an outgoing person, not quick to blush. She smiled a kittenish smile and shrugged. "You left it down, *hon*."

A trace of envy over their affectionate banter stabbed Nick, but he didn't have a moment to examine why the feeling had suddenly surfaced.

Sam Wong came to the table with another pie.

"Somebody give my driver a bogus address." He presented the large pizza, lid on the box open. "You want this one? Canadian bacon and pineapple."

"Put her on the table, Sam." Danny stifled a belch from his beer, pressing a fist to his chest. "I'll take care of her for you."

"I knew you'd eat it, Danny." To Nick, Sam shook his head with a crooked-tooth grin. "Your brother has a bottomless stomach."

"Yeah, when we were kids he used to eat worms. He's got a leftover one in there. It takes up the slack."

Sam laughed, a deep infectious sound. There wasn't a living soul who would think Sam Wong wasn't on the level. The guy was as honest and hardworking as they came. He'd been born in China, immigrated to San Francisco with his folks, and worked his way through dragon kitchens until deciding he just didn't have a knack for preparing his native food. He preferred putting pizzas together and switched over, much to his mother's horror—so he'd told Nick once.

Pushing fifty-nine, Sam Wong had a salt-and-pepper Fu Manchu mustache, and hair on his chin that drizzled to a long and airy goatee. Eyeglasses made popular in the fifties, a dark gray heavy frame on top with a clear bottom, rested on his flat nose. His skin looked like caramel-colored leather stretched across his angular facial bones. He wore a silver ring on his middle finger and a yellow straw panama hat on his head. A white baker's coat covered his torso, a pair of drawstring pants slipped over his legs.

Sam resumed his kitchen duties, the phone ringing with another order.

Danny and Heather left shortly after Danny did a fair amount of damage to the pizza.

"Nicky-J." Nick called to his son over the noise of the pinball machine. "You about ready to go, dude?"

"I gotta finish this game, Dad. I'm winning." He jabbed the flippers, his body jerking left and right as if his physical movement would take the metal ball in a different direction.

Nick was about to box the leftovers, when he noticed Billy Jessup, with cupped hands, looking through the pizzeria's windows. He shoved his eyeglasses higher on his nose, the tired cape covered his shoulders. When he saw Nick, he gave a tentative wave.

Motioning him inside, Nick pushed out the chair on the opposite side of the table with his foot. "You want to sit down and have a slice of pizza, buddy?"

Billy shook his head. "I can't. I'm waiting for my mom to get off work."

Nick hadn't realized Lauren had taken over the dinner shift. "She's not doing breakfast anymore?"

"Verna Mae needed her to work extra tonight even though she spilled coffee on the floor." Billy eyed the pizza wedges, longingly licking his lips.

"Sure you don't want to sit down?"

He briefly glanced out the window, the corner of the Wharf Diner visible in the early evening. Wong's was located on the pier. The Wharf Diner was the first building across the street where the boardwalk continued and ended on Shoreline Street. "I was supposed to wait out front and not go anywhere."

Once more, Billy's gaze trained on the pizza. Nick suspected it wasn't so much out of hunger, but rather, the kid didn't get pizza a lot and this was a rare opportunity—one he hated to miss.

"You could go ask your mom if it's okay."

"She wouldn't want me to."

"Why's that?"

"We're not charity."

Nick's heart felt a bone-aching sympathy, an almost imperceptible sense of injustice. Last night, this boy had felt weightless in his arms, with an innocence only a sleeping child could surrender. Billy's having to worry about what was a handout and what wasn't concerned Nick. "Buddy, this isn't charity. It's just a piece of cheese pie."

Feet shuffled, Billy's mouth twisted and he scrunched his nose. Clearly a thinker, an analyzer. Nicky-J would've dived into the box by now and had sauce slathered on his face.

Another furtive glimpse out the window, this time Billy was rewarded by the image of his mother bearing down the street, her face awash with panic.

"I have to let her see where I am." He shoved the door open and stood in its gap, but he didn't go onto the street, as if doing so would mean he'd lose all chances of eating the pizza. With one foot literally in the door, he was one hand away from grabbing a mouthful of Chinese, hand-tossed Italian heaven.

"Mom! Over here." The door swished closed and Billy sat his little butt down in the chair and folded hands on the table.

"Yes, please. That one, there. With the cheese."

Nick obliged, was putting the pizza on a paper plate, when Lauren entered the pizzeria looking none too happy.

"Billy, what are you doing in here?"

"Nicky-J's dad invited me to have pizza. It's not charity." He spoke around the latter word, his mouth filled with crust and tomato sauce and mozzarella cheese. Lips closed, eyes round, he chewed, then swallowed with almost an audible sigh.

"Billy." She reined herself in, her chastising voice not so severe as when she'd used it on Nick. "You were supposed to wait right outside for me."

"I was, Mom, until I followed a seagull over here."

Since her son was plowing into another bite, she was momentarily at a loss and just stood there. She had on her uniform, gray and drab like the color of a waterbird, and a white apron, soiled at the skirt, a slight splash of something dark on the bib. Maybe coffee. Her hair was pulled back into a ponytail, a soft sweep of dark brown hair. She appeared tired, maybe not physically, but emotionally. The life in her eyes was empty, as if she was fighting something—both tangible and intangible.

"Have a seat, Lauren." His words weren't a suggestion, they were a command.

"I can't, we can't…. We…" Even she couldn't form an excuse he might buy. She pulled out the chair and sat, purse on her lap, clearly not relaxed.

Nicky-J came over, slowing down when he saw Billy. "Hi."

"Hi," Billy said in return.

"Dad, are we leaving now?"

"In a little bit."

"Cool! Can I have some more quarters?"

Nick snagged a handful from his jeans pocket. "Give some to Billy. Let him play."

"Okay." To Billy, Nicky-J asked, "You know how to play Pac-Man?"

"No."

"Pinball?"

"I did it a couple of times."

"Okay, we'll play doubles on that one."

The boys went into the arcade, leaving slices of uneaten pizza behind. Nick knocked back the last of his beer. "Can I get you a drink? Beer? Pop?"

"No, no thank you." Lauren adjusted her hold on the purse. "But you go ahead if that's what you want."

"I'm good."

Nick eased his weight to the back of his chair, the front legs lifting slightly as he relaxed into the seat. "Billy said you were on the dinner shift tonight."

"Verna Mae was shorthanded. It's been a long day, but God knows I need the—"

She broke off, apparently revealing too much. He'd seen for himself last night that she was living from day to day, moment to moment. He couldn't imagine what that would be like.

Pride chiseled itself in her face and the set of her jaw. Even now when she was dog tired after a long day, she sat as if she didn't need anyone, anything.

He knew the feeling, or at least tried to understand its relevance pertaining to his own life. After Debbie's call last night, he'd asked his mom to come over and watch Nicky-J. He'd gone to the Outrigger for a drink to dull his senses and buffer the anger he felt. Leaving there, he took a walk on the beach and found Lauren and her son. He'd watched her a long moment without her being aware. She gazed at the sky, the moon and stars, and he could almost read her thoughts. Almost feel the sense of permanence she wanted, a kind of fragility that was within her reach, yet too far to grab.

That was how it was for him, with Nicky-J and Debbie. He could still hold his son, watch him sleeping, but for how long? Would she win the right to have him? That thought seized him, so paralyzed his mind at times that he couldn't comprehend how he'd go forward.

"I'm going to have to leave town."

The statement caught Nick's attention, pulling him from his thoughts. He crumpled a straw wrapper between this fingers. "And go where?"

"Anywhere. I've started over dozens of times."

"Why?" This he couldn't relate to. There had been good and bad times in Bella Luna for him, but he'd never pack and leave.

She gave him a wan smile. "I take it you've never lost your job, had your apartment rent go up or chased a lower cost of living."

"Nothing that would make me move," he answered frankly.

"I've moved around so much it's second nature to me."

"What about your son?"

That struck a nerve. "My son is fine."

"Really?"

A deadly silence loomed and Nick knew, in that instant, she was a woman who would never stay and he only wanted a woman who would give herself over to him mind, body and soul. The revelation disturbed him more than he cared to admit.

"Have a piece of pizza," Nick offered, coming back to the present, needing a sense of purpose and direction. Anything to keep his mind from drifting toward Lauren and an unsettled urge to convince her Bella Luna could treat her right.

"I ate at the Wharf."

"I know what's on the Wharf menu and it's not pizza."

A barely visible smile hooked a corner of her mouth. "I had soup."

Lauren eased the purse off her lap, a piece of her defense mode coming down. "We won't be staying long."

"Let it go," he said, knowing he shouldn't give her advice but he did just the same. Nick glanced toward the arcade. "Let him be a kid for a minute. The boys are having a good time."

"Billy hasn't had many friends."

"Nicky-J has a group of friends in our neighborhood he plays with. They all go to the same school."

"That must be nice."

"Yeah, it's good. Keeps them out of my way when I'm trying to clean the house."

Her eyebrows arched. "I can't imagine you over a toilet with a scrub brush."

"Somebody's got to do it."

"I assumed you'd have outside help."

"I do. Mr. Clean."

Lauren laughed, a sound that was so unexpected and light that Nick had to lean forward to absorb as much of it as possible. "She has humor," he remarked, a smile of his own caught on his mouth. "I was worried."

Her smile faded. "I laugh, Mr.—um, Nick. I just don't do a lot of it in public."

"That's a damn shame. You've got a great laugh."

She blushed, the first time he'd noted. A pink flush suffused itself across the high arc of her cheekbones. Following it, a trace of color climbed down the column of her neck to fade at the valley of her breasts. The top two buttons of her work blouse were undone, revealing nothing deep or plunging, but enough to drag his attention.

The timing was all wrong, he didn't need the distraction and she sure as hell had made her intentions clear; when the going got rough, she packed up and left. Yet he found he couldn't put aside his interest in her welfare and that of her boy's. He was, even with everything going on in his life, a man who was born with a deep streak of protection toward women.

"Let's say Verna Mae put you on at the Wharf full-time, what about your son?" Nick folded his arms over his chest, resumed his tilt on the chair and continued to observe her posture, her expression.

"I'm not sure. Sometimes I've had help. A waitress's niece baby-sat Billy the last time I was in food service." She ran her fingertips across her cheek, a thoughtful reaction. "I don't know anyone here yet. I mean, I know Verna Mae and June, but they work, too. Besides, it's only been four days. Not long enough to trust them with my son."

"You don't trust people easily."

Her eyes locked onto his. "Who does?"

"I do."

"Why?"

"Why not?"

"Because it takes time to get to know someone. Why invest your heart and love when they'll only disappoint, leave you and you'll be alone all over again?" A gulp of air was sucked into her lungs and she gave a quick shake of her head, as if to scatter her deepest thoughts and turn them to dust. "Never mind."

"No, don't. I hear what you're saying. I've been fortunate enough to have family to count on during difficult times, so I've always been real lucky."

"Yes, very lucky."

A lapse of time stretched, Nick not sure how Lauren would react. His mind jumped around the possibilities, then he just said what he had to say. "If you decide to stay, my mom watches Nicky-J during the summer months. He plays with two brothers, Tim and Christopher Gilman—the kids call him Critter. Tim's twelve and I'm comfortable enough with that to let Nicky-J go to the store with him or the field. People in town know the boys and they've got to tell my mom where they'll be, and she makes Nicky-J check in with her throughout the day if he's out playing. I'm sure she wouldn't mind keeping an eye on Billy if the boys are together."

She didn't say anything right away. At least she was

being civilized before telling him he was crazy for suggesting such a thing. She began to shrug him off, then stopped herself. Maybe she wasn't sure about his approach or his motives—of which he had none. There was no way he could know what she was thinking, but he could speculate.

"I'm not saying I'm going to stay…but I don't know your mother, and I hardly know you."

His hunch had been right.

"You'll never get to know a person unless you spend some time with them."

"I'd have to think about it."

"I'll have my mom go to the diner and say hello. You can meet her, judge for yourself if you think she's an ax murderer."

"I wouldn't think that."

"I don't know, there was one year when she decided she'd waited long enough for my dad to cut down the dead tree in the backyard. She swung a blade like she meant business. Got a few good chops in before my dad took the ax away from her. She smiled all the way into the house. The surest way to get a man to do something is to attempt to do it yourself first." He grinned. "It's a testosterone thing. We can't help ourselves. Gotta show a woman we can do it better than she can."

"I can do plenty just fine."

"I don't doubt that for a second, Lauren." He liked the way her name sounded, the casual way they conversed. He forgot about Debbie and lawyers, forgot about being stressed by the Ocean Grove renovation.

"So what is it you do for fun?" he asked, stretching his legs out in front of him.

"Fun? I wouldn't know, it's been so long."

Seriousness was fine some of the time, but everyone had to unwind, and some of Nick's best destressing came from Pac-Man chomping his way through the maze. "Ever play arcade games?"

"It's been forever. Some in high school. I doubt they have that kind around anymore."

"Wong has a Pac-Man."

"Pac-Man…" The vagueness in her voice was like a soft remembrance of a fun day, a time past that might have been good.

"I've got a few more quarters."

"Now? We have to leave, it's—"

"It's only eight o'clock. Early for a Saturday."

She looked at her son, noted his big smile and enthusiasm for his and Nicky-J's latest round of pinball. Something inside her must have known that Billy needed this moment, this time to be a boy and play. To not worry about his mom. Nick was glad she saw it, understood it enough to nod.

They joined the boys in the arcade and Nick let Lauren take her turn first. She held on to the knob lever, a smile stretched on her mouth while she maneuvered the Pac-Man through turns, chasing fruit for points. Her body swayed and tipped and tilted. She bit her lower lip in concentration, the visual slamming him in the gut. His heart stood still a moment. He almost gave in to the urge to put his arms around her waist.

He stood back, watching, and thinking that she looked damn fine for a woman whose approach to life was not to lose control. Right now, she looked like an uninhibited kid again. Something that maybe she'd never been before.

* * *

"This is that new kid I was telling you about." An audience of two, Critter and Tim, listened as Nicky-J commanded their attention away from the fort. Wind blew through the tall branches of trees and cloud-dotted sunshine filled the area. "His name is Billy Jessup."

Both Critter and Tim Gilman had been Nicky-J's best buds since Critter and Nicky-J were toddlers and Critter still wore pull-ups. Critter had the best Hot Wheels collection Nicky-J had ever seen.

"How come you're wearing that cape? Is it like your baby blanket?" Critter was the one to ask questions, something Nicky-J could always count on. If a girl in class tried to get away with eating her booger, it was always Critter who hollered, "What are you doing?" real loud. The kid had a hundred eyeballs in his head. Nothing slipped by him.

"It's magic," Billy replied, a smile on his face real eager, as if he wanted to make a good impression in a short amount of time.

Nicky-J had promised his dad he'd take Billy to meet his friends and show him the fort—just for an hour because Billy's mom said that's as long as he could stay out.

"What kind of magic?" Tim asked, standing taller than any of them.

"It protects me."

"From what? The boogey man?" Critter chuckled, his red hair falling into his eyes. He had a lot of freckles, the kind that looked like hunks of cinnamon on his grandma's Christmas cookies. He was nicknamed Critter because Tim hadn't been able to say Christopher when he was a baby.

Tim laughed along with Critter, and Nicky-J had to remember the promise to his dad that he'd make sure Billy wasn't made fun of. But it was hard to keep that promise. Billy was all right playing pinball, but having to bring him to his friends, it was stupid. Billy Jessup was sort of retarded. His glasses were big and the cape was dumb; Nicky-J asked him to take it off on the way over, but he wouldn't. Not for nothing. Not even for his commando-dude action figure.

"It just protects me is all," Billy insisted, his face getting worried, as if he might have to sock Critter or something. Nicky-J's dad would yell at him if he found out Billy and Critter got into a fight.

Nicky-J squirmed. "I told him we were building a fort. He wants to see it."

"What for?"

"I never seen a fort before," Billy said, his cape blowing around his legs. Nicky-J cringed, his mouth tasting sour like he'd sucked on too many Gummi Worms.

"Sure ya seen a fort before," Nicky-J said to Billy, trying to save Billy from looking stupid. "You told me about that big one you built with your friend. You threw water balloons off it and hit girls."

Billy's mouth opened, his eyes scrunched up. "I did that?"

"Yeah, you did." Nicky-J nudged him in the ribs with his elbow.

"Oh...yeah."

Critter and Tim shrugged at each other, sort of like saying without saying that maybe Billy might not be such a weird kid if he threw water balloons at girls.

Tim stuffed his hand into his pocket and pulled out

a bunch of lint and an army guy. "Nicky-J, I'll trade you that horse's tooth you got for this."

"Nope. I already got that one."

Critter reached into his back pocket and showed them all a Hot Wheels car. A police cruiser. "I'll trade you this for it."

"Is this the car that lost the back wheel when your dad ran over it with the lawn mower?"

"Yeah, but my dad glued it back on."

Nicky-J examined the car, flicked his thumb over the wheel and shook his head. "No thanks."

"Why do they want a horse's tooth?" Billy's question took them all by surprise.

"Because it's a horse's tooth," Nicky-J said. He rammed a fist into his pocket and came out with the prize. Holding it up, he let Billy get a good look—root and all. "This horse's tooth come out of a horse at my dad's uncle Hal's ranch. My dad gave it to me, and I can give it to whoever I want—if the price is right."

Billy stared at it in confused awe. He didn't know why he should want such a thing, but these boys made it seem like something he had to have. Something he just couldn't pass up. The trouble was, he had nothing on him to trade.

"I could give you my airplane for it," Billy offered, then suddenly wished he hadn't considered that deal. He liked his airplane a lot more than he'd like a horse's tooth.

"Naw, I don't want your airplane." Nicky-J kicked a rock. "I'm holding out for something better."

"Like what better?" Critter wanted to know.

"I'll know it when I see it, but start putting your money in your piggy banks, you guys, because it's going to cost you."

Tim and Critter mumbled, and Billy could think of only one thing the rest of the hour as the boys hammered out nails from pieces of wood: he wanted that horse's tooth. He wanted to be part of the guys, too. He'd never had friends like these before. Mostly, he hung around grown-ups. He did the things his mom wanted him to do. He had to be a good boy for her, protect her from bad things that might make her cry.

This was a new sensation for him, this feeling of wanting to be away from his mom. It scared him, but it thrilled him at the same time. He felt naughty…and a little guilty for liking it.

The hour passed too quickly for Billy and soon he was back at the Tidewater Motel with his mom. She waited on the bed for him, her face looking concerned. She was so pretty. He loved her best when she was smiling. She didn't do that much. He worried about her, about them.

But not right now. Now he bubbled with excitement, telling her about his day with Critter and Tim and Nicky-J.

"I want to play with them again, Mom."

"Your face is flushed, Billy. Were you cold? I should have made you bring a jacket."

"No." He shrugged out of her hand on his cheek to check if he had a temperature. If he was hot, it was because he was fired up over this afternoon. "Mom, I want to have a piggy bank."

"Whatever for?" She rose from the bed, hands on her waist.

"I need to start saving my money."

"Billy, what is it that you need to buy?"

"A horse's tooth," he declared, knowing by the reaction on her face she didn't understand.

Sometimes he wished he wasn't her little boy. Sometimes he wished he was one of the kids in a school, with a house, a dog in the yard. And a dad who could understand what his mom didn't.

Then he felt so badly for wishing such things, he reached out and circled her waist, squeezing and burying his face into the front of her sweater.

Five

*Visit the moon and you'll find out if
it's made of cheese.*

The grand entrance was filled with scaffolding and cords, the sound of a power tool off to her left, unseen. Lauren held on to the order Verna Mae had given her, a to-go lunch in an insulated box and bagged with a cup of black coffee.

A stairway rose in front of her, stopped at a landing, then split and went left and right. The walls were plastered but unfinished. Lengths of crown molding lay on the floor waiting to be installed. She could imagine what the place would look like with the finished wainscoting and paint, the smell of varnish over new wood.

The Ocean Grove Inn was spectacular, a real grand hotel. It would be incredible when it reopened.

She didn't know which way to turn to find Nick DiMartino. He called in his order, not often Verna Mae said, and Lauren had been sent over to deliver it. Verna

Mae made the assumption that Nick was buried in work and couldn't get out from under it. She joked and told Lauren that Nick could use a pretty face to take his mind off his job for a few minutes.

Lauren hadn't been amused, but as an employee she had to do as the boss instructed.

"Hello?" she called when there was a break in the construction noise.

No answer.

She couldn't be sure if anyone else was in the building, so she proceeded toward the sound of the power tool, taking the steps carefully in case they weren't secure.

Once at the landing, she smiled in remembrance of a movie. She thought of Rose in *Titanic,* at the end, when she's meeting Jack, and for some inexplicable reason, Lauren envisioned Nick DiMartino standing at the second-floor stairway, waiting for her.

She blinked, snapping herself out of the strange musing.

Why she'd thought that, she didn't care to examine. She had been fairly settled on leaving town until talking with Dunk. Now her mind wasn't as made up as it had been. She recalled how a feeling had come over her while Dunk was talking to her, the smells in his store perfuming the air. He'd been telling her about the generations of fishermen, how they held Bella Luna together; they were its heart and soul as much as the tide and moon. Everything he'd said had embraced her as if to make her stay, to not let her go. She couldn't understand that, maybe she didn't want to.

She climbed several more stairs, came to the second

landing and proceeded down a hallway. Both sides were covered with long runners of plastic, except where doors opened onto rooms. Guest rooms, she thought.

Peeking into one, she noted the size and single sash window. Another door and closet took up one wall. Apparently a bathroom and wardrobe.

Lauren had never felt such a curious fascination with the past. Here she was, in modern times, walking where Edwardian ladies had been nearly one hundred years ago. She could almost see them in their long dresses, staring out the window to view the wharf and ocean below.

She left her observation point and continued to track down the blare of what she'd determined was a saw. Having closed in on the noise, she paused in the doorway to a large room, perhaps a parlor.

Nick bent over a table saw and lengths of chair railing. He didn't hear her over the slicing blade and she watched.

His face was set with concentration and focus, his mouth a firm yet full line. Hands, wide and strong, controlled the movement of the lumber as it passed through the sharp teeth that bit into it and sprayed sawdust.

He had on a pair of jeans, hole at the left knee, with a blue plaid shirt open down the front. Beneath, a black T-shirt. The morning had been cold, perhaps in the fifties, and the room was on the cool side. She shivered, thinking she should have put on her sweater before coming next door.

The length of Nick's hair, brushed away from his forehead, was longer than she first thought. A few strands hung over his brow, but they went ignored as he picked up another length of molding.

He made it look so easy, moving pieces of wood like that in a smooth motion, one right after the other. He didn't strike her as a carpenter, perhaps because he had a city edge to him.

Nick said he'd resided in Los Angeles for quite some time. His education and experience showed. He was intelligent, articulate, and right now, very sexy in his element.

She supposed she should say something, maybe even let the floor swallow her, that way she wouldn't have to confront the feelings taking her into a mindless plunge.

Pleasure.

She admitted that much to herself with a frown.

It gave her pleasure to look at him. His body was hard and powerful, and his mouth was something she wondered about...how it would feel pressed against hers.

"Um—" she cleared her throat and raised her voice "—lunch is here."

He didn't cut the switch, turned to acknowledge her, then nodded. He proceeded to slice through another length of molding.

Feeling a bit disappointed, and dismissed, she was going to set the bag on the floor.

Nick must have caught her movement.

"Don't go." His voice was rich, sliding through the room with a husky sound. "I've got two more pieces. Hang on a minute."

She could have left, but her legs didn't move.

When he was done, he brushed the dust from his plaid sleeves and the top of his watch dial. Then he caught the loose strands of hair and raked them away from his forehead.

How was it that a gesture so simple could make her body quiver?

Nick glanced at the time. "My brother's not here today and I'm under the gun on this."

Lauren had been surprised to learn Nick was in the building on a Sunday afternoon. Apparently they had the same work ethic: work when there's a necessity.

"It looks daunting," she remarked.

"Sometimes it is."

"The building is wonderful."

"It will be." He motioned to an open set of large drawings. "I'm fortunate enough to have the original plans to go by."

"You're restoring everything?"

"That's what they're paying me for."

"There's so much detail."

"I've become a bit of a specialist in period architecture. British, Edwardian or American Victorian—it all matters when it comes to columns, ratio of width to height, spacing and design."

"I'm impressed."

He grinned. "I was hoping you would be."

He unbuckled his tool belt and laid the leather pouches on the table-saw bench. His presence wound itself around her and quickened her normal breathing.

Remembering why she'd come, Lauren held out the bag. "The sandwich should still be hot."

He unfolded the top and pulled out the coffee first. Punching a hole in the lid with his thumb, he drank the steaming caffeine. His sigh was a deep, resonant sound.

"I needed that." His face appeared tired, anxious.

"Aren't you sleeping well?" The question was out before she could stop it. His sleeping habits were none of her business.

"I sleep all right—usually I finally nod off around two in the morning, then my alarm goes off at six."

"That's only four hours."

"That's all I can afford right now, my mind's too busy."

"Why don't you go to bed earlier?"

"Maybe because I don't have anyone to go to bed with."

Lauren looked back at him, no words forming a reply.

There was nothing to do but stand and wait for inspiration to hit her. When it did, she uttered, "Then next time you're asked, say yes."

Nick cracked a smile, one that grew broader by the second.

He let his eyes roam over her. Her heart thudded madly, the dusty air felt heavy in her lungs.

He answered, "Maybe I will."

Maybe...*maybe* he was thinking she should ask him.

Lauren felt her pulse jump.

She was strong enough, tough enough to pursue whatever she wanted. In this insane instant, with his blue eyes leveled on her, making her tremble, she wanted to be close to him—but would never dare to allow herself a lapse in judgment.

She hadn't had sex in... God, she didn't want to make a confession, not even to herself. But the answer was there, lingering and strong, so she accepted the truth.

She hadn't had sex with anyone since she got pregnant with Billy.

Needs were there, most definitely, but she pushed them away, putting her mind, soul and body into being a good mother and provider. Of taking each day as it came and working toward a solid future. Doing that made her forget about the touch of a man. The caress of a hand over her cheek, the brush of lips on her mouth. But it was hard sometimes, especially now.

She feared her reaction had erected a barrier, and she made her excuses.

"I have to be getting back to the Wharf." She began to retreat. "Verna Mae's going to wonder what happened to me."

"You're still at the Tidewater?" As Nick's voice carried toward her, she paused.

"I am." She'd asked the front desk if she could do housekeeping to bring in extra. They said they weren't hiring. Her life was upside down, without meaning and purpose. For the first time that she could recall, she wasn't content with upheaval. She didn't want to declare defeat. Something in the way Dunk had spoken to her, and now in the way Nick looked at her, made her want to survive here. But how? The motel was costing her way too much and she wasn't working a forty-hour week.

"How much are you paying there?"

His question threw her, but not so much that she didn't reply.

He nodded. "I know someplace better. A lot cheaper."

Intrigued, yet cautious, she lifted her eyebrows.

"It's on Shoreline, across from the wharf. Three hundred a month."

She gave a huff of laughter, then a pithy observation. "Is it made out of cardboard?"

"It's not the Ritz. Just a row of five summer cottages

with simple furnishings. They were built in 1898. I renovated them about six years ago."

The smirk on her mouth faded, a flicker of renewal coursing through her body. "So you know the owner?"

"I do."

Lauren's mind worked, computing how much her monthly living costs would be. With rent that low, she could afford to build on her savings a lot faster, even with paying minimal car insurance and utilities. Even without having a full forty-hour check in her immediate future—like tomorrow for instance.

"How do I see one?"

"Go to Oceanside Properties, they manage them. Tell Lois you want to see 442 Shoreline."

Somewhat stupefied over what fate had just dropped into her lap, she nearly missed his outstretched hand.

He was offering her a tip.

She started to bypass the bill, then made herself stop. He would have given June a gratuity if she'd brought over the lunch.

"Thanks," she responded.

She slipped the money into her apron pocket, alongside the change and bills she'd collected this morning.

"I almost forgot." Lauren stepped over the remnants of wood on the floor. "Your mother came into the diner this morning."

He teased in a pleasant tone, "Did she bring her ax?"

"No. She was very nice. She offered to have Billy come over this week and spend the afternoon with your son."

Lauren hadn't expected his mother to introduce herself so soon. Things felt too fast, too rushed. She wasn't ready to give up her son to someone new. And yet she couldn't continue to make him spend the day at work with her.

There were few alternatives and Caprice DiMartino displayed a personality that Lauren recognized as genuine. She'd been vivacious and charming. Her eyes were an identical match to Nick's, that blue that really melted a person.

Nick broke into her thoughts. "Are you going to take her up on it?"

Thinking about the agonizingly long hour yesterday when she'd let Billy play with Nicky-J, Lauren wasn't so sure. She'd paced inside the motel room, looking out the window every few minutes. What if Billy had needed her help? What if there'd been an emergency?

When Nick brought her son back, relief flooded her emotions.

He'd been fine. Happy. Excited. He wanted to play with the boys again. He wanted to stay here more than any place they'd ever been, and his happiness was always at the forefront of her mind even if she couldn't always grant his wishes. But with the possibility of a new place to rent...and yet...

Lauren's reply was long in coming, and it was more like talking to herself than anything else. "I might. He was fine. He had a good time. Yes, I think I will."

The commitment, once uttered, was something she would now be forced to study and perhaps keep.

Nick cut the engine to the motorcycle, propped the kickstand and swung a leg over the seat.

He wasn't surprised to see Lauren's Falcon parked

on his parents' gravel driveway. What did throw him off guard was that finding it there felt normal.

A week had passed and Sunday-night dinner might have two new places at the table, he thought, taking the walkway to the side entry door. As if he still lived here, he let himself inside the kitchen and entered into the thick of things.

At the DiMartino house, the kitchen was the central hub. A gathering area where the family talked about report cards, first dates with girls, college applications—or no college such as was the case for John—engagements, deaths and everything else in between.

The room was comforting, always smelling of food. Tomato gravy, sharp cheeses, roasting pork and sweet desserts.

The cabinets were distressed in a forest-green color, giving a timeless quality to the room inspired by Early American color schemes. Recycled bricks from one of the demo jobs he'd done were used as flooring. He and John and Danny had laid and mortared them together. The butcher-block counters were warm and practical, knife-worn in spots from loving hours Caprice spent cooking for her family.

A long day of sweat and breathing in plaster dust took its toll. Nick's body ached, his joints were stiff. He wanted a beer and his mom's spaghetti, and was surprised when the kitchen was empty. There were two tall pots on the back burner though, and the smells of oregano, basil and garlic were nothing short of mouthwatering.

He lifted the lid on the first one and came up with

boiling water. He peeked inside the second, into the depths of softly simmering red sauce, and knew what kind of gravy she'd made by the way it looked. His favorite—sausage.

The refrigerator didn't disappoint him as he snagged a cold bottle of Bud and twisted the cap.

Nick heard voices coming from out back. He followed them through the house, his work boots sounding heavy over the dark-stained pine floors.

The living room was spacious, made bigger and bright by many uncurtained windows. Through them, he saw his mom and dad, John and his wife, Felicia. Danny and Heather. Nicky-J and Billy stalked through the yard holding jelly jars and lids, probably hunting insects with at least six legs.

Lauren Jessup, facing the group, her arms crossed beneath her breasts, looked like a deer caught in headlights. Her skin was pale and he could tell she bit on the inside of her lower lip.

Nick could only guess how she was coming to grips with what she'd stumbled into.

Sunday-night dinners could get loud, noisy, a little crude at times with colorful language during the retelling of old stories, but nobody ever left without feeling as if they'd gotten a little closer to one another.

Observing the scene, Nick watched as his dad said something to Lauren and she had to form an answer. She shifted her stance, retucked her arms and appeared immensely uncomfortable. His brothers, and the women in their lives, stood around adding to the conversation.

Danny and John must have walked over to his mom and dad's house. They lived a few short blocks away, unlike Nick who was higher on the hillside and closer to the main coastal highway.

Before going outside and facing them, Nick held back to get his head on straight. All day he'd felt as if he was drowning, suffocating.

This Tuesday he'd be in L.A. and he was as ready as he'd ever be. He'd told his mom he was going down for the day on business, consulting with an associate on a project.

Several times throughout the day, Nick had fought the urge to walk away from the job site, come here and tightly hold on to his son. Breathe in the smell of his skin, the little-boy scent that defined him as Nicky-J. Dirt, sweat, grass. Nick ached to ruff his hands through his boy's short mess of hair.

He wanted to close his eyes and pretend that none of this was happening.

But he couldn't.

Everyone in that backyard, Lauren included, would understand his pain and support him. He knew that beyond a doubt. But he'd made up his mind that he wasn't going to drag anyone into this yet, in case there wouldn't be a battle to fight.

He'd be okay for now. He'd get through Tuesday on his own, by his own strengths. He was man enough to face what he had to.

Banking on that resolve gave Nick the mind-set he needed to open the patio door and step outside.

Lauren looked half relieved and half cornered to see him.

Arms came down to her sides. She had on her uniform, the apron wilted. Wisps of dark hair framed her face. Her mouth was red from a light application of lipstick. The color suited her, not many women could pull it off without looking overly made-up.

"Nick. You're here." His mother waved him over, a ready smile on her face.

Caprice DiMartino was the anchor of the family, the glue that bound everything together. Anthony might have been the physically stronger of the pair, but his mother was the emotional rock. She'd borne everything from a miscarriage between him and John, to the death of her parents, to sending her three boys out into the world as men with solid footholds on what treating a woman graciously really meant.

Over the past few years she'd added weight to her frame, her face rounding a little. Her ample curves were attractive, somehow suiting her five-foot-seven-inch height. She never looked overweight to Nick, but she complained about it every now and then—only to set out a feast on the table and scoff off the latest diet fad in favor of a traditional family meal.

Her dark hair had begun to thread with silver, nothing real noticeable unless you were standing close. The eyes, they kept their definable blue. The unique color had been in her side of the family for generations of Sicilians. Both Nick and Danny had her blue eyes, John had their dad's rich brown.

"Good Christ, Nick, you look like you haven't slept for a week."

"Anthony," Caprice retorted. She didn't have to spell out the reason she was harping. Taking the Lord's name in vain in her good Catholic house always inflected a disapproving note in the violator's name as she said it.

Nick approached, glancing at his brothers while steeling his resolution to stay closemouthed about what occupied his mind twenty 24/7.

"I'm sleeping." Nick's assurance wasn't bought by everyone, namely Lauren, whose gaze was on him, reading his expression as if there was something more to it than he let his features reveal.

The chance that her intuition was focused on dissecting him, Nick steered the topic in a different direction. "Did you try on your monkey suit, Danny?"

"Decided on the single-breasted black tux." Danny put his arm around Heather and gave her a kiss on the cheek. "Didn't really have a choice, now, did I, hon?"

"You did, too. I said it was either the black tux or me."

Laughter erupted from John, Felicia giving him a warning glare with a full smile attached. "John would have worn his baseball jersey and a pair of jeans if I'd let him."

"What's wrong with that?" he said. "They're comfortable."

Good-naturedly, she nudged him with her shoulder. "Nothing, if you want to stand at the altar by yourself."

Caprice rested her hands on her hips, the glossiness of her hair brushing next to her blouse collar. "It's time to cook the pasta." To Nick, she said, "We were trying to talk Lauren into staying for dinner, but she's stubborn. Maybe you can change her mind."

Lauren's mouth opened to protest, then closed without a word as Caprice headed to the house—and everyone else followed except for the boys.

Nicky-J and Billy were both hunkered down on the grass, jars overturned while they tried to slip the lids beneath them without their quarry taking off.

"Stay for dinner?" Nick's question was straight to the point. He wasn't in the mood for an argument, not even something as simple as this.

He'd spoken to Debbie last night—actually, they hadn't talked, they'd yelled. So he was all out of persuasion and patience today. If Lauren didn't want to stay, she didn't want to stay.

"I've still got some unpacking to do."

Almost a week had passed since Lauren moved into the cottage at 442 Shoreline. Nick was glad that it had worked out for her, but he still sensed an underlying riptide beneath her surface. The first offshore wind, she'd be out of here. He read her instinctively, from a place he couldn't name; it was in his gut, tensing his muscles. She had only relocated from the motel to the cottage. Nothing more.

"You like the place?"

"Yes, very much. Actually...I love it."

Those were probably the first three words out of her that he'd heard that contained unbridled elation. Perhaps the storm wasn't raging all that bad; but in his cluttered mind, he couldn't analyze this further. He was barely able to keep his attention focused on what she was saying.

"Thank you for recommending it."

"Sure." He drank his beer and listened as she told him about her new living quarters.

"It's perfect for Billy and I...for now." She had to expel the last two words, probably more to reason with herself that she hadn't compromised. "The sunporch has the extra bedroom, Billy has his own room and the kitchen is fantastic."

Her eyes filled with life and her voice was light and breezy.

"You sound like my mom. A kitchen's important to her, too."

"It's everything to me. I have a stove and oven now. No more restaurant food."

"What do you like to cook?"

"Anything. I can do anything you'd ever want."

He read another meaning into her response and had a sudden, if not misplaced, thought that maybe she could. Maybe here was a woman who could give him the moon. The trouble was, he needed more than that at the moment. He needed assurances and stability. He certainly didn't need to get involved with someone who both he and his son could get attached to—only to have her end up moving on.

At length, he replied, "I like roast beef."

"Easily done." She slightly closed her eyes, as if envisioning the prepared dish. "Baby onions, fresh sage and bay leaves, shallots and... I'm thinking new potatoes roasting in the juices."

He laid a hand over his growling belly, his disquieted mood lifting a notch. "You're killing me. I'm tempted to pass over my mom's spaghetti tonight."

"Come tomorrow."

As soon as she spoke, a gasp passed through her parted lips—as if she wanted to snag the invitation right back. She must have felt a deep, almost capricious, passion about her cooking or she never would have asked him over for dinner.

Nick could have let her off the hook and said no. But he took a moment to think about it—or maybe talk himself out of it—but in the end it was a no-brainer because all he had to do was look at the pluses.

She was as attractive as all hell, they both had sons the same age and shared that commonality, even if she differed on his parenting views of raising boys. While he wasn't looking for a life partner, he was still a man who appreciated a woman.

And this woman was nothing short of fine, if not mysterious in many ways.

Perhaps going over to her place would be a good idea. He'd be headed out of here early Tuesday. Spending Monday night with her would be a chance to occupy his mind in ways he couldn't at home.

"Yeah, I'll come over. Six o'clock."

"Six o'clock," she repeated, as if she'd grown numb and wasn't sure she heard him correctly.

"Right. Six. I'll bring a bottle of wine."

Six

Baying at the moon.

He arrived at exactly six o'clock, his son standing next to him on the yellow-and-blue porch.

Lauren had tacked on a request that Nick bring Nicky-J over to play with Billy—a tactic to save herself from being alone with Nick in this spontaneous invitation.

The father and son stood side by side, the smell of soap and shaving lather perfuming the sea air. Nicky-J's hair, combed slickly to the side, was the neatest she'd ever seen it; he was without his ball cap and not a single stain scuffed the knees of his pants. His father looked too good for words in a pair of jeans and a laid-back white cotton shirt, untucked. He'd rolled the long sleeves up three-quarters of the way. The collar was open, unbuttoned casually, presenting a very relaxed image.

She wondered if he really felt that way or if it was for show. She had a much harder time with this, every fiber in her body warning her against tonight.

Why she'd made the offer, she couldn't fathom. It had just slipped out. Seeing Nick standing there, she struggled with the uncertainty of what tonight would bring.

A bottle of pinot noir was presented to her from Nick as she stood back to let them inside.

Since the cottage was so small, with only three rooms downstairs, they were able to show themselves to the seating area. It wasn't what she'd call a living room since it ran directly into the tiny kitchen.

"Something smells incredible," Nick said while taking a seat on a wicker chair with its rose-patterned cushion.

"It's almost ready."

Not true—everything was ready. She was not.

She just needed a moment to collect herself before they ate together. She'd never been so compulsively foolish to cook for a man she barely knew. Food was a very intimate thing to share, and she wasn't in the right frame of mind to do that just yet. Not with Nick, not the way her pulse hammered at the base of her throat whenever she flicked her gaze across him.

He was broad and large, filling out the chair and making it appear too tiny for a man of his height and build.

Nicky-J sat beside his dad in the other chair. He must have been coached to be on his best manners. His hands were folded in his lap, clearly a practiced gesture because he refolded them twice before settling on a grip he preferred.

"We would have brought you flowers—" Nicky-J fidgeted "—but this isn't that kind of special dinner. We're only here because we're hungry."

"Nicky-J. Jesus, you don't say something like that— especially when it's not true."

"Grandma would say your name funny because you said 'Jesus' like that without being in church."

Slumping into the chair, Nick ran a finger over his chin and spoke to her, "Sorry. I don't know where he got that idea."

"You said it, Dad. I asked you if you liked her special and you said this wasn't that kind of special dinner."

Lauren saw discomfort flash in Nick's eyes. She felt the same thing and acted quickly. "Is anyone thirsty?"

From one of the kitchen stools, Billy hopped up to man the glasses.

"You got any soda pop?" Nicky-J scissored his feet beneath him.

"Lemonade and milk." Billy waited for Nicky-J to pick from one of the two selections.

"Lemonade."

Billy poured two glasses, mindful not to spill as he walked with them in his hands. He passed one to Nicky-J. "My mom makes her own lemonade with real lemons."

Nicky-J took a sip, then nodded his approval.

"I'll have some of that wine." Nick eased back and crossed his legs.

"I need to do that, Billy," Lauren said when he reached for the bottle. "I have to use a corkscrew."

While she didn't make a habit of drinking, she poured herself a glass of wine, as well. The punch of emotions grabbing hold of her nerves seemed less daunting after several sips.

Since the conversation was stilted, with everyone on formal behavior, there was no more stalling.

She called them to her table, set and displayed with all the mismatched dinnerware she owned. The kitchen was small but quaint. She loved the blue-and-white checked wallpaper and the white cupboards. The stove wasn't full-size, but sufficed nicely with four burners on top. She'd laid a red-and-white flowered tablecloth over the table, arranged candles, and Billy had collected colorful wildflowers from the backyard. They graced the table in a glass vase she'd purchased at the secondhand store. She loved flowers and set them out whenever she could. But suddenly, a bouquet and candles seemed like an extra touch that might be misconstrued as...romantic.

This isn't a special dinner.

Of course it wasn't.

Lauren served the roast with a rich gravy, potatoes and the baby carrots Dunk had just gotten in this morning. She had local fruits, cut in bite-size pieces and sprinkled with spices, and she'd made a tossed green salad with her own blend of dressing.

Waiting for everyone to fill their plates, Lauren observed Nick. The way he moved with tight muscles, the way his vague expression didn't reveal his thoughts. The way his jaw seemed to clench, then he remembered himself and he tried to relax. She didn't think his actions were because of her—because of being here.

There was a great deal more to him under the surface.

But for now, she watched a puzzled smile turn up the corners of his mouth. He'd just had his first taste. She braced herself, waiting, wondering how he'd react. She never knew. Different people felt different things when they ate something she'd made.

Another bite of roast, swirled with gravy, disappeared into his mouth. He studied his plate, as if by doing so he could figure out what had just happened to him.

"What did you say you put in here? This isn't just the onions and bay leaves."

Uneven pleasure warmed Lauren's body, and in this instant, she was happy at her table. Happy that she'd surprised him, even though his response would be difficult for her to deal with. She loved the look that came over someone's face when they tasted her food. "My imagination."

And with that, they shared a conversation with a glance; words unspoken, meanings not quite defined but left there to simmer and meld together.

"What's that mean?" Nicky-J jabbed a carrot.

"I cook with my imagination," she clarified.

His little nose wrinkled. "Like pretend?"

Lauren smiled, truly satisfied and no longer caring that she shouldn't have spent what she had on the dinner. Nor that she had only worked four extra hours at the Wharf this week to make up the difference. She explained, "Not pretend. More like creating fantasies with food."

"I don't get it." Nicky-J ate the carrot.

His son might not have gotten the meaning, but Nick did. He was feeling one hell of a fantasy in his mouth, exploding with flavor on his tongue. He didn't understand why this bite of roast tasted better than anything he'd ever eaten in his entire life.

He'd been raised on old-fashioned Italian cooking, and was partial to it. Give him the choice of fried chicken or *lobster fra diavolo* and he'd pick the lobster every time.

Every one of his senses now seemed heightened, alive. He took another bite, eating slower, savoring. What had she done to the food?

"This is good cooking, Dad. A lot better'n yours." Nicky-J ate another carrot.

His son hated cooked carrots.

"Anything's better than my cooking," Nick responded, trying the salad next, the dressing on the lettuce coming alive across his taste buds.

He hadn't realized how starved he was until he began eating. His cravings weren't solely for food. Forgotten were the problems facing him tomorrow. His thoughts refocused on someone else.

Catching Lauren's gaze on him, he fought against reaching across the table and touching her cheek. He had the urge to skim his work-worn hands down her bare arms, feel the silky texture of her skin, and sift his fingers through her long hair as it fell over her shoulders. He wanted to brush his lips over the corner of her mouth and taste her.

Jesus, he'd never felt like this before.

And she knew it. His reaction was obvious. She was at odds with it, he could tell. He saw the beat of her heart pulsing at the side of her neck, read a sensuality in her hazel eyes that he'd never seen there before. His gaze bore into her in silent expectation, waiting for an explanation he could grab hold of.

She offered nothing. Just a smile, so faint and so tantalizing, it was all he could do not to crush his mouth over hers.

He was damn relieved when the dinner was cleared away and she set out dessert. The strawberries she'd whipped into something indescribably good satisfied his sweet tooth, but he still needed more.

When the boys left to play in Billy's room, Nick drew a breath and made himself stay seated.

"Did you get enough to eat?" she asked, reaching for his empty dessert plate.

His fingers circled her wrist, stopping her from backing toward the sink. "Yeah, but I still have an appetite that wasn't satisfied." His voice was low, sensual.

Lauren's eyes lowered to where Nick held on to her wrist. She shivered, like when she came inside a warm house after being in the cold. Her heart pounded, her stomach quivered. She feared this, wasn't sure what to expect, and when he reacted the way he did, she hadn't stopped him from going this far.

She pretended not to know his meaning. "If you're still hungry, there's more dessert."

"What did you put in the food?"

She chewed on her bottom lip. "N-nothing."

"For nothing, it makes me feel a little reckless."

He rose to his feet, stood over her with his full height and took her into his arms. The weight of him next to her sent a rush of heat through her blood. He slowly dragged his fingertip down her cheek and neck, to her exposed collarbone where he traced even lower to the vee in her blouse.

"Your skin smells good, it feels so soft."

"I don't think—"

"Yeah, that's the problem. I'm not thinking, either."

He lowered his mouth over hers and gave her a lingering kiss, one that maybe she was too willing to return. His lips, warm against the soft part of her own, tasted sweet, like sugar and strawberries. A hint of red wine. The lazy slide of his tongue explored her, his arms tightening around her waist.

She had no control and no desire to gain it.

Everything inside her singled in on this one moment, this one touch of mouths. It was her first kiss in six years, and it felt like the only kiss she'd ever had. So new, so wonderful, it wiped out anyone else she'd ever been with. She wanted to melt into it and never give these feelings up.

Feelings that both thrilled and frightened her, knowing that one man could do something like this to her. Have so much power, so much consuming need for her—and she for him. It erupted, without any thought or precedence, taking her by surprise. She couldn't think, didn't know how to react.

Chaos rebounded inside her.

She should have pushed him away, gained her freedom. But she decided from the instant his mouth covered hers that this was what she'd been after since she'd first seen him in city hall. Admitting her weakness did strange things to her. It was freeing—an inhibition let loose.

Her hands stroked his neck, the warm skin, then upward into his hair. The texture was cool and sleek, thick and soft. She didn't realize that she could feel like this again. She'd never wanted to. It only meant heartache or surrender, losing herself to another person.

With their mouths becoming thoroughly acquainted, they bumped into the kitchen counter and her elbow hit something. A utensil clattered into the sink.

A wake-up call. Loud and clear.

Lauren pushed at his chest, breaking them apart as she gasped for breath. Her skin was alive, burning with unfulfilled desire and a need so strong it scared her. She hated these feelings, hated that she'd let them surface.

She wasn't prepared for romance. Never mind the

flowers on the table or what Nick had said about this not being special.

What just happened was special. There was no denying that. She challenged him with her gaze to deny it. Thankfully he didn't. But it was better to forget that the kiss had happened at all.

She smoothed the hair away from her face, tucked the edges of her blouse down and turned away from him to collect herself. The skin on her face burned, heated from remembering what he tasted like against her tongue.

Bracing herself with both hands on the counter, she took in a series of small breaths. She sensed his presence behind her, close but not so close as to touch.

Knowing he was within an arm's reach, she wanted...never mind. She couldn't.

She didn't like to want things, feelings like that only got in the way. Her life didn't have room for complications. Keep it simple, that was her motto. She lived it as best she could.

And yet, in this combustible moment she'd done something she'd never done with a man: she trusted Nick. Trusted him with the core of her body, her heart, her head and all the thoughts that were mixed up inside.

She quickly denied these things and refused to allow them to take over her sensibilities.

Turning around, she gave him a quick flash of a smile to disguise the fact she was still flustered. "It's quiet upstairs. The boys must be reading."

Nick's hand closed over the back of the chair. She willed herself to forget how warm his touch had been. His jaw grew tight, the wall erected once more.

Good, it was better this way. For both of them.

"When boys are quiet," he said, "it's not because they're reading."

Upstairs, Billy showed Nicky-J his room. He was pretty proud of the large area with the two windows that stuck out over the roof. He was going to make a tent in one of the—what were they called? Oh, that's right—his mom called them dormer windows.

Even though his room was an attic, it had a thick rug on the wood floor and a big bed just for him. Lots of light came through the windows during the day and he was hoping his mom would let him get a goldfish.

His clothes were neatly put away in the drawers of a bureau, a large jar with some coins inside sitting on top. His books were on the floor since there wasn't a shelf. He had a basket of puzzles, comic books and several stuffed animals. Teddy had been with him since he was a baby, but he didn't need it anymore to fall asleep.

The red cape was draped over the doorknob, ready for him in case he needed it.

Nicky-J flopped onto the blue bedspread and glanced around. "You really don't have any baseballs?"

"No." Billy regretted that he didn't. Maybe his mom would let him get one soon.

"What do ya got?"

"Airplanes, books and a piggy bank. It's not really a pig, it's a jar from the diner." He sucked in a breath, then announced, "I'm saving my money to buy your horse's tooth."

Billy shook the jar for emphasis, to make the dollar and twenty-three cents inside sound important.

Nicky-J shrugged. "I might not want money for it. I

might want a trade. Except you don't have nothing good to trade, far as I can tell."

"Puzzles?"

"Naw."

"I have some extra socks I don't need."

"I got one pair that I always wear."

Billy's mind worked fast. "I could tell you a story that might be worth a trade."

"Oh, yeah? Like what kind of story? Something scary?"

Nodding, Billy sat on the floor and crossed his legs. He knew this story pretty good. "It's about a little boy."

Through his missing teeth, Nicky-J slightly whistled. "He kill somebody?"

"No. He almost died."

"What from?"

"I'll tell you." A slight clutch in his belly seized Billy, but he forgot about the discomfort as soon as he envisioned having that horse's tooth. "There was this little boy and he lived by a field of really tall grass. He liked to walk through it."

"What for?"

"Because the field was much bigger than him. He pretended he was in a forest. He could get lost in all the weeds and nobody would know he was in there."

Nicky-J's interest piqued. "Where is this place?"

"I don't remember." Billy wished he could, but he wasn't good at remembering places. "One day, he knew he was going to be in big trouble for not keeping his bike where he could see it."

"So what?"

"It got stolen. He was scared to tell his mom, so he thought if he got lost, she'd be so glad to find him that she wouldn't get mad about the bike."

"That was a good idea."

"He disappeared in the field until he found a barn and sat down next to it. He knocked over a broom by accident and the handle hit a wasps' nest in the roof part."

"I stomp on waspeses," Nicky-J lisped, "and watch their guts squish out."

"I wish this little boy would have stomped on them, too. He got stung."

Nicky-J's eyes grew wider. "He was stupid. He shoulda run."

"He did. You can't run from wasps. They smell you're scared on your skin. It only makes them madder and more come after you. The little boy got stung *fourteen* times." The word caught in Billy's mouth and made his tongue feel too big.

Running his fingers under his nose to scratch an itch, Nicky-J bragged, "I've been stung before by bees and waspeses. Lotsa times."

"Not this little boy. He had an allergic reaction. He couldn't breathe and he swelled up. He had to go to the hospital and spend the night. His mom worried he was going to die—she wasn't mad about the bike anymore. The boy didn't die, but he heard the doctor say if he ever got stung again, for sure he'd probably die. The nurses let him have as many suckers as he wanted. Even if it was two o'clock in the morning."

"I had my tonthulls out in the hospital and I got popstickles and ice cream."

"I wish I could have mine out."

Nicky-J dangled his legs over the bed. "You'd have to get a lot of sore throats."

Holding his breath, Billy asked, "Do you think you'd give me your horse's tooth now?"

"That was a good story, but it's not worth a trade." He bounced off the bed and went to the basket. "What's in here?"

"Toys," Billy mumbled, wishing he'd been able to get that tooth.

Nicky-J gave them a look over, then took out a small matchbox from his back pocket and slid the two pieces apart. Something that moved inside had a thin tail. "You wanna see how fast my lizard can run?"

Lauren arrived at the diner for the breakfast shift on Tuesday morning. She held back a yawn while popping down toast. She'd spent a near-sleepless night, tossing and turning, reliving the kiss every time she dozed off.

By the lunch shift, she was more than ready to clock out, but Verna Mae approached her with an unexpected offer.

"Ruby gave notice today and she quit, effective immediately. How about you coming on full-time?"

Flummoxed, Lauren all but stammered, "Of course. Yes."

"Can you stay on through the dinner and close?"

That would mean a twelve-hour day with tips that could add up to plenty. Ignoring the ache in her shoulders, she replied, "I have to check on my son."

She called Caprice DiMartino to see if Billy could stay that long. There wasn't a problem.

And that was that. She now worked full-time, didn't

have the worry of having to get another job or taking the short way out of town. However, being indebted to Caprice wasn't high on Lauren's list of ideal options. Then again, she rationalized, having her son spend the day at the Wharf Diner with her didn't make the list at all.

She missed Billy. She wouldn't like working so many hours, but she had to get back on her feet without pulling more from her savings. There had been the deposit on the cottage, but thankfully—oddly—there wasn't a first- and last-month requirement. She had not given it a second thought because she just wanted to accept something at face value for a change. The management office had gone out of their way to accommodate her and she was thrilled with her new place.

It was like a dollhouse, yellow and blue on the outside with a pallet of bright colors on the inside. The character and charm was like nothing else she'd ever seen. Carved hearts created accents in the wood trim above the eaves. The Victoriana porch, catching the setting sun, was perfect for potted herbs and flowers.

"I'm done, Lauren," Knox said, yanking on his apron strings. His cousin, Lou, was supposed to have taken over for him at four o'clock, but he'd been a no-show. Knox hadn't been able to track him down to holler at him, but he'd heard Lou had been in the Outrigger for early-bird drinks, and then had left with a blonde. The tops of Knox's ears were still on the red side of agitation.

Lauren had just cleaned the last coffeepot and Knox had scrubbed the grill after putting away the items in his line station—if she could call the row of stainless receptacles that. They weren't what she'd use: infused oils, lemons, fresh herbs and chopped garlic. Knox preferred ketchup, mayonnaise, mustard, relish, oils that looked coagulated and a huge tub of butter.

If she ever got the chance to work the kitchen, she knew just how she'd organize it. The size was fairly large, workable, but it was outdated in equipment, nothing against Verna Mae. Lauren could make do with old pots and pans, but she wouldn't compromise on knives. She had a special one at home she'd bought years ago.

She'd been at the small but wonderfully musty-smelling library yesterday. She looked through cookbooks, and applied for a library card. Then she checked out back issues of *Gourmet, Good Housekeeping* and *Sunset* magazines. Pouring through recipes and picking out what she loved about them was, to her, better than a night at the movies.

Lighting a cigarette, Knox waved out the match. "Flip the Closed sign and I'll get the lights."

She did so and they walked out the door together. He had the key and he locked the door, giving the knob a jiggle for good measure.

Leaving the diner for the lot where he parked his Chevy Vega and she her Falcon, he said, "How're you likin' the new place?"

"I love it, thanks."

He unlocked the car door, the pine-tree-shaped air freshener hanging from the rearview mirror long since fragrance free, killed by curls of cigarette smoke. "I remember when Nick bought those. You wouldn't want a rat to live in them. He did a hell of a job renovating cottage row. He's got the brain for that sort of thing."

She missed that last part. "What do you mean—Nick

bought them? He doesn't own the cottages anymore, they're managed by a rental agency."

"No. He owns them. Has Oceanside Properties rent them out."

Lauren stopped. "Do you know what he gets per month for one?"

The glowing ash of his smoke lit his face in the dusky sky as he sat on the front seat. "Damned if I know. You're the one who's living there."

The car's mufflerless engine ripped through the air as Knox turned it over, then ran through its gears down Shoreline.

Lauren drove to the DiMartino house and waited forever for the door to be answered. In that short moment, her aggravation built to seething. No wonder her rent was so cheap, no wonder things hadn't added up. She'd been given a pity rate.

She had *trusted* him.

She damned her stupidity for allowing two and two to add up to five—and not wanting to confront the miscalculation. She'd been so pleased with the cottage that she'd disregarded a red flag, something out of character for her. Look where it had gotten her—in over her head.

As soon as Caprice opened the door, Lauren blurted, "I need to know your son's address. I've got to talk with him. Now."

"Lauren, it's not a good time," Caprice said, her normal cheery tone flat.

"I won't stay. Send Billy out and tell me how I can find Nick's house."

Anger tainted her sense of judgment, and before she realized what was happening, Nick filled the doorway.

"You're here," she said, her voice strained. "Good. I—"

"My mom's getting your boy." His words were tight, his face a dark mask under the pale yellow porch light. "Take him and go home, Lauren."

"You own the cottage we're living in," she accused bluntly. "I'm not a charity case you have to look out for. I do fine on my own."

He towered over her, broad and wider in the shoulders than she recalled. His masculinity threatened to swallow her whole. She felt the potency of his displeasure...perhaps worse, his thunderous upset. She took a step back, he took one out the door.

In a low and cautionary tone, he growled, "I just found out I'm going to have to fight for full custody of my son in court. Thank God my ex didn't win the interim hearing, so I keep him for now, but I'll have to send him down there on visitations over the summer. I'm so fucking pissed I can't see straight."

He jabbed a finger at her, and she jerked her head back. "So if you think your goddamn pride is more important to me than my son, you don't have a clue."

Seven

La luna porta su la favola di wondrous.
(The moon takes up the wondrous tale.)

When the canneries closed, the heart of Bella Luna died. The corrugated-iron buildings grew silent and the damp streets around them, once active with workers, went empty.

Schoolchildren used to tour the Fruitti di Mare Cannery. Under the factory guide's direction, they observed the fillet lines, hard salting, ice packing and canning into tins. As souvenirs, the students received paper hats with the company logo, and on the cannery's twenty-fifth anniversary, they got a kite with the tuna mascot on the front.

Growing up in a fishing town was exciting. Activity on the boats coming in and leaving port, unloading their catches and working on the gears captured many a boy's imagination. There were engine-repair shops to visit and the boat builders, where hours were spent in fascination watching engines and boats come together.

Only the most resilient and hard-nosed fishermen survived the loss. They were philosophical about the downturn in the industry, drank beers at the Outrigger Pub one night and discussed the outlook. People still ate fish, now more than ever. The canneries might have been gone, but the fish weren't.

The Bella Luna fishermen went out in their meager fleets, continuing to do what they had done for hundreds of years. But rather than barter their catches to the canning outfits, they sold the fresh fish to supermarkets and restaurants as far east as New York.

One such man unwilling to let the economy muck up his life's work was Anthony DiMartino. He'd been fishing on the Pacific for close to fifty years and he wasn't quitting.

The gusty winds that began earlier in the week prevailed as Anthony trolled for salmon, damning the few-and-far-between fish he caught. Those he hauled up from the bottom had belly burns from feeding on shrimp. He brought in sand dabs and halibut, then kissed his St. Christopher medal and gave a silent prayer for an early season of albacore.

He would have liked to rejoice in the day, however windy and poor his haul, but his heart wasn't in it. His little grandson wasn't home, he was visiting his mother—and if she had her way, he'd be living with her by September.

John, his oldest boy, curled 'chovies to freeze for bait. Neither of them had said much over their mugs of hot coffee this morning. It was the kind of week you wanted to forget. The only blessing was that Nick would be bringing Nicky-J back to Bella Luna on Friday.

Nick had refused to let his son go to Los Angeles without him. And rightfully so. Nicky-J needed his father, and good Christ almighty, the DiMartinos were going to fight Debbie with everything in their guts. She wasn't taking their Nicky-J.

Son of a bitch. Goddamn, son-of-bitch-thing to happen.

The cloudy mood wasn't much better at the DiMartino house that night when Anthony returned. Danny and Heather were there creating a wedding registry at the table. When they should have been happy selecting linens and household items, their soft voices sounded as if they were at Sunday Mass.

After Danny and Heather went home, Anthony and Caprice were left alone with their unspoken thoughts. Caprice stood at the oven, not even a double recipe of manicotti pulling her out of her worries.

Caprice wished Anthony would stand behind her, put his arms around her waist and tuck her head beneath his chin. His lack of doing so wasn't out of any unhappiness about their marriage. It was as solid as it ever was, as it would always be.

They had, throughout the years, weathered a great many things together. They'd been high school sweethearts, were completely devoted to one another, but the sizzle had gradually been dying. Anthony was no longer as romantic as he'd once been. She loved him thoroughly, and accepted this, as her own passions had ebbed quite a bit after menopause. But sometimes, quiet comforts were missed, and she reached out to him now.

She held her arms out, walked to him and he embraced her. He was, and always would be, the only man to understand her. And she, with everything inside her, would love him for who he was.

"Tell me this isn't going to happen," she whispered into the front of his shirt. He smelled of the ocean, chum and salt. Many would find that unpleasant. To Caprice, it was comforting.

"I won't let it happen." His rich, deep voice rumbled next to her crushed breasts. The beat of his heart was steady next to hers.

Everything would be all right, she thought, because she believed in Anthony. She had almost all her life.

Over at Moon Cycle, word had spread about Nick having to go to court to keep Nicky-J in Bella Luna. Now, it was a fact the gang knew that nothing definite had happened, and the outcome might not be unfavorable, but in their misguided ways, they took Debbie's court challenge personally and had to let off some steam.

Otto and the gang, their full beards, mustaches and ponytails blowing in the wind, went on a morning motorcycle rally along the coast to clear their heads.

Gathered at the scenic outlook, their legs straddling the bikes and the hot engines still rumbling, Otto revealed he had an uncle in Pomona who could *persuade* people to change their minds about certain things. Nubs took a drag on his cigarette, then gave a brow-raised glance to the others.

The Moon Cycle gang, although biker renegades, talked Otto out of making the call.

"Are you going to hold that tomato in your hand all day?"

Dunk's question worked through Lauren's clouded mind. "Hmm?"

"You're somewhere elsewhere, Lauren."

Yes…she was. Her thoughts were on Nick. Guilt fanned in a hot gust across her cheeks whenever she thought about lashing out at him on the day the ground had been pulled from under his feet.

Regret and shame were two emotions she had a hard time reconciling with. She'd hurt Nick because of her foolish pride and she had to deal with it. Working through it, however, was difficult.

"Mom, can I get some candy?"

Billy was with her today, and had been by her side every day this week. She decided not to leave him with Caprice after learning what the family was going through. Billy would be a reminder that Nicky-J wasn't in town right now. She couldn't do that to them.

"All right. Just for today."

Normally Lauren would have said no, but she couldn't refuse her son's upturned face, the way his big eyes were wide behind his glasses. He was missing Nicky-J and tired of having to stick so close to her.

Inclinations to move along to the next place rose harder than ever before. She felt as if she'd made a mess of things here.

Lauren wished she had a recipe that could turn out the perfect life. Something foolproof.

As Dunk stared at her, his dark face expectant, she had the strangest feeling: she'd miss him.

She never missed anyone when she moved. People's lives intersected with hers without connecting. She wasn't a part of anything, yet suddenly she'd become a part of Bella Luna.

Verna Mae needed her; even Lou and Knox had a friendly smile for her whenever she showed up. Dunk always had sage advice—whether she took it or not. The DiMartinos had been nothing but pleasant, welcoming her into their home.

And Nick…he'd gone out of his way to help her. Such pure kindness was almost unknown to her. She'd never been one to reach out and grasp the benefits of community, but she saw here that she would be looked after for as long as she stayed.

The idea of leaving, of doing what came naturally to her became more frightening than staying put.

These recognitions were a dawning that had never surfaced before. She now saw with reasonable clarity that her constant moving was second nature and there'd been so much she'd been missing as a result.

"Dunk, thank you."

His expression grew curious, his mustache kicked up in the corners. "For what?"

"For being my friend."

He said nothing further and simply smiled.

Nick stood in Debbie's front yard, Steve was inside. The hazy light from a lantern light in the grass gave off enough brightness with which to see her by. His ex-wife folded her arms beneath her breasts, her posture rigid.

She hadn't changed physically since they'd been married. She was still beautiful, still classically dressed and put together.

At one time he had loved her, would have done anything to see her happy, but at this moment he only felt contempt.

Nick reflected on the interim hearing. A judge had heard from both sides and made a ruling, that to suddenly remove Nicholas Anthony Jr. from the only house he'd known would be destructive to the child's well-being. As for Debbie's petition of school-term custody, the court tried mediation to help them reach an agreement, but they couldn't. Now he and Debbie moved into the next phase that would take them to trial: parental analysis, which consisted of evaluation for stability, continuity, community, neighborhood, doctors, church.

The court was going to consider his son's physical, educational, spiritual and emotional needs. For Nick, there was only one answer: Nicky-J needed his father.

Bruce Harmon urged Nick to start keeping a journal of events that affected Nicky-J's life, such as visitations with Debbie, summer activities, family and religious activities and medical appointments.

Everything was almost incomprehensible. Nick never thought he'd be in this position. He damned his lack of hindsight, nobody more hard on him than himself. He should have filed for full legal custody years ago.

Nicky-J sat in the front seat of the rental car, the windows up and the AC on even though the sun had gone down. It was the last day of the required visitation and they were going home. Nick was ready to get out of here.

"Well," Debbie said, inhaling a breath. "I think everything went all right. Considering."

She was referring to the fact he hadn't yanked her head off in the time he'd been here. He'd felt like it, that's for damn sure. But it served no purpose to direct his anger toward her. That was done; she knew how he felt about her petition and yet she'd opted to screw him anyway. Now he'd get his turn in court to vent, and he swore to God, he'd do whatever he had to do to make the judge see that Debbie was only thinking of herself and not their son.

"My being here sucked. You know it, I know," he stated matter-of-factly. "The only reason I'm not raising my voice right now is because my boy is in the car and I'm not going to show him that his mother and father are fighting. And if you told him—"

Debbie must have instantly detected, and heeded, the threat in his tone because she cut him off. "I didn't tell him anything was going on. This visit was like all the others. He doesn't know we're going to court about anything."

"And that's the way it's going to stay. You leave that to me."

She licked her lips, her face half in shadow. Her cheekbones were high, her lips pink and plump. For a flicker of a second, she let uncontrolled emotions shine in her eyes.

He almost didn't read them, almost let the signals go until he realized she was in a slight panic.

Good. He hoped like hell she knew all this was going to be a waste of both their time.

Nicky-J was staying with him.

The next day, down on the beach, an offshore wind hollowed out the waves as a low tide broke before it reached the tide pools.

Dunk rubbed a cake of banana-scented wax on his surfboard, then strapped the board cord to his ankle. The zipper of his wet suit hung open at his navel, his gaze assessing the waves.

The morning was cold, keeping him alert and awake.

"Sets are coming in three to six apart," Sam Wong said. He stood beside Dunk, dressed in a wet suit, as well, his long board nose up in the sand.

The two men had been surfing together longer than they could remember.

Dunk spoke through the dark patches in his mind, absently running a finger over his mustache. "We'll watch the mounds coming in, then paddle out in between."

Sam nodded.

The gulls circled overhead, sandpipers ran on long skinny legs across the wet sand. Blue skies were clear with some bite to them. A lone boat could be seen at the horizon.

"This just no right." Sam interrupted the slush of waves as they came in a foamy spread onto shore. "Nicky-J, he good boy and he belong with father."

"I couldn't agree more, Sam."

"What we do?"

"Nothing as far as I can tell. Looks like it's in the hands of the court judge. But with the whole damn town willing to be character witnesses for Nick, I'm placing my money on him winning."

"Me, too. I hope. We celebrate with free pizza."

"I'll hold you to that, friend." Dunk tucked his board beneath his arm. "Let's paddle out."

As he always did, Sam lit a cheroot and clamped it between his lips. His round face squinted as he inhaled, his eyeglasses on a beach towel, and the brim of his yellow panama hat keeping the sun from his eyes.

The men walked into the crashing surf, waves breaking against their chests. They paddled into position at the point break where waves peeled off.

Waiting for the perfect wave to catch, Dunk did a lot of thinking. Thinking about Nick and Nicky-J. And Billy. But mostly Lauren.

He could see why she felt bad about talking down to Nick, but people made mistakes, and Dunk had known Nick for a long time. Nick wouldn't hold anything so insignificant against her. Lauren didn't see things that way, said he'd probably never talk to her again.

She wore her willful nature like a coat of arms, defensive at the wrong times, something he as a man of color could relate to, having formed preconceived ideas himself that he later redefined. There was a fine balance between tolerance and reason. A person had to be true to themselves—but this wasn't one of those times for Lauren.

Roads got bumpy. Didn't mean you jumped the track and let go of what you had. No telling what else was on the other side.

Dunk might be old, having lived a long life, but doing that gave him the experience to see the bigger picture.

The bigger picture here was that Nick and Lauren were two of the same kind. Both had boys, both were making it on their own and both were dead set against being loved in a way a man and woman ought to be. That just wasn't right.

Sam puffed on his cheroot, his brown eyes scanning the swell coming toward them. "We take this one. It's right."

"Yeah, it is right."

But Dunk's words weren't focused on the wave. They were more about bringing Lauren and Nick face-to-face—however he had to, and quickly.

When two people were fighting for their lives, it was better to do it together.

Dunk caught the wave and stood, knees bent and riding the ocean. The power of water beneath him, the force of waves as they pushed him forward, had him feeling the first surge of vitality he'd felt in days.

Eight

Moon skies are here again.

Hot water from the hot tub blissfully eased tension from Nick's muscles. He stretched his arms out over the decking, leaned his head back and closed his eyes. A week's worth of stress slowly began to ebb as he forgot about L.A. courts, lawyers and long nights spent in a motel.

A starry night enveloped him on the deck, the sunset long since cooled to black, and he half dozed. His mind drifted to a blank space without dreams and he was thankful for the peace.

When he woke, maybe several minutes had passed. Enough time that he felt better.

Looking through the floor-to-ceiling windows, Nick could see Nicky-J in the living room thumb-pressing the controls on PlayStation 2. For his son, this past week had been an exciting whirlwind of Disneyland and Universal Studio visits, toys from FAO Schwartz and indulgences, from new video games to skateboard sneakers and an autographed poster of skateboarder Tony Hawk. Nicky-J was completely unaware that the two adults he loved were at each other's throats.

The timer on the spa bubbles quit and the deck grew quiet. A light breeze moved the dark fringe of tree branches; crickets droned in the woods. Below the hillside, the crash of the surf was like a soothing white noise.

Nick was about to get out, when he heard the doorbell ring. Nicky-J ran to answer it. His son, despite Nick's numerous efforts, had no concept of "Ask who it is before you open the door."

Lauren and Billy stood outside holding a pizza box and a brown paper bag.

Frowning, Nick rose from the hot tub and grabbed a towel to cover himself. He was naked, his trunks inside the bedroom. He hadn't been expecting anyone.

Entering the living room and padding to the door, he ignored the water droplets running down his bare chest and back, and off the ends of his hair.

When Lauren saw Nicky-J, then him, she blinked—as if she hadn't anticipated either of them answering the door.

"What's this?" he asked, glancing at the pizza.

Billy, in his red cape, smiled, also surprised—but unlike his mother, pleasantly. "Dunk gave us some Dr. Fizz root beer—" he shoved the bag at Nicky-J and he took it "—and Wong's Pizzeria said we could bring this order to this address." He displayed a piece of paper showing Nick's address written in Dunk's blocky script. "Sam and Dunk said they'd pay me two whole dollars for making the delivery. I'm saving my money to buy something."

When Nick didn't readily take the box, Lauren clued

in fast. Not only was he sure she hadn't known who lived at the address, a new discomfort took the color from her cheeks when she figured out she'd been set up.

Avoiding the area where his towel wrapped around his hips, she murmured, "I'm assuming you didn't order a pizza."

Seconds ticked by as Lauren controlled her eyes from falling to his naked chest. He could barely remember what he'd told her the night she came by his parents' place, wanting to argue about the cottage. He'd been in a bad place and could have said any number of things.

"Yeah," he said at length. "We ordered a pie from Sam."

"Yippee!" Nicky-J nabbed the box and ran it into the kitchen, Billy close behind. Out of sight, Nicky-J declared, "My favorite kind! Thanks, Dad. Hey, Billy, guess where I've been? Disneyland!"

"What's that like?"

"There's lots of rides, toys, and it's where Mickey Mouse lives."

The boys dug into the food while Nick and Lauren remained at the door.

"Guess this means you're coming in." He stepped aside, and after a long moment passed, she entered his house.

He hadn't been to the job site since returning a couple of days ago, and he hadn't stopped in to the diner, either. He needed to get back to work on the renovation, get back to a routine as normal as he could so he could make Preservation Week on time. Seeing Lauren was, oddly enough, part of his daily life since he saw her at the diner regularly.

She faced him, watched the water trail down his chest before she slanted her gaze across the hardwood floor.

"You didn't have to say you ordered the pizza just to save me the humiliation."

Shrugging, he offered, "I'm hungry anyway."

"We won't stay long."

"I'll be right back." He went into the bedroom and snagged a pair of jeans from the back of a tall chair. Slipping them on, he flicked the metal button closed and reached for a Moon Cycle T-shirt out of his bureau drawer. He neglected shoes, entering the bathroom to rub his hair dry with a towel.

Lauren still stood where he'd left her, her body language uptight. Her eyes drank in his furnishings and possessions with more than a cursory glance. Her gaze ended on the riot of earth-toned pillows thrown across the leather sofa. "This isn't how I imagined you lived."

His eyebrows arched, more over the fact that she'd put thought into where he lived. "What did you see me in?"

"I'm not sure. Maybe something not so contemporary."

She admired the raw-stone hearth, then the art statue he had on the occasional table. "Did you build this house?"

"Yes."

"You're good at building things...restoring things." Their eyes met and locked. "Knox told me about the cottages."

So that's how she'd found out.

With his mind going in so many other directions, he never took the time to consider she'd be this ticked off about his steering her toward Shoreline. He figured she might have a small tirade, then let it go when she cooled down. "Knox talks too much."

"Actually, Knox doesn't say a whole lot at work. I'm lucky to get him to grunt in between his smoke breaks."

Nick smiled. That was Knox.

The boys occupied themselves in the kitchen, enthusiastically chowing down on slices of cheese pizza and pouring overflowing cups of root beer. Nick could swear he heard them laughing as something that splattered hit the floor. He made a mental note to wipe under the table later on.

"So..." Lauren exhaled, walked to the other side of the sofa as if to put a barrier between them. "You sort of tricked me."

"I didn't, not really."

"You omitted the truth."

"There wasn't a truth or a lie to be had in anything I did. I simply gave you the name of a rental agency."

"Yes, but you owned the property and implied you didn't."

"Big deal."

"It's a big deal to me." Her eyes were large and determination flickered in the deep green-gold depths. "I knew the rate was too good to be true, but I ignored my common sense because I fell in love with that place the second I saw it."

"I was hoping you would."

"No fair."

His lips curved. "Fair? I wasn't playing dirty, Lauren. You needed a place to stay. I had something available and you took it."

"That's exactly right—it's like stealing. Three hundred dollars a month is a fraction of what it's worth."

"You're right."

"I don't want to be right."

"Then be wrong and stay there."

"I can't. How much is that rent—*really?*"

"A grand a month."

She groaned. "I can't pay that."

"I'm not suggesting you do."

"I'm not a pity case," she retorted.

He practically threw up his hands. "Jesus, you can't take help from anyone—can you?"

"I help myself."

"But you don't have to." He ran his hands through his damp hair and shifted his stance. There was something about her that put him on edge at times. She was so damn stubborn, so set in her ways and in her mind. In many ways, he liked that quality about her. In many others, he wanted to throttle her independence and make her see that somebody cared about her well-being and wanted to help.

"I'm going to have to—" her voice lowered "—move out."

"And go where?"

He saw her work to come up with a viable plan. "I can get a job in Salinas."

While he thought she might move out after she'd blasted him at his parents' house, he hadn't considered she'd move that far out. "You're talking stupid."

She gave him an affronted frown.

"You heard me. You're being dumb. You've got a job here and your son likes Bella Luna. Think about him."

"I always think about my son first," she fired back.

The boys scooted chairs across the floor and Nicky-J called out from the room, "Dad, we're making root-beer fizzy drinks with the 'nilla ice cream."

"Close the freezer door, buddy, after you take the carton out."

"Uh-huh."

Forcing himself to relax, Nick slipped his fingers into his pockets, stood casually and argued, "If you really wanted to leave, you would have been long gone by now. You want sympathy for a hard life, I can do that. You want me to feel sorry for you, I'm not your man." Now it was Nick's turn to lower his voice. "I think you're scared, Lauren. You're so damn scared to stay, you'll look for excuses to add complications. I've heard enough from Billy when I'm at my mom's. You make the poor dude move all the time. If it wasn't the cottage, it'd be something else. You just can't stay put."

Color fired over her cheeks, crimson anger. Her lips pressed together.

He rounded the edge of the coffee-brown sofa, coming close enough to her that he could smell the faint hint of vanilla on her skin. "Just what is it you're afraid of?"

Chin lifted, she said nothing.

"Did you leave a husband behind? Is he looking for you?"

"No," she snapped quickly. "Absolutely not. I've never been married."

He tilted his head, curious, but added nothing further on the subject.

Going down a possible list, he asked, "Did you do anything illegal in another town? The law's after you?"

Indignant, she retorted, "Of course not."

"If you told me what it was, we wouldn't have to be playing this guessing game."

"I don't have to tell you anything."

He came closer, could see the glitter of dismay in her eyes as he probed. Maybe he was getting close, maybe hitting a nerve. "Do you have a past you want to forget?"

Once more, she didn't reply. Her face was an unreadable mask.

"You can stop this game anytime." He sat on the couch, settled in and cross his leg onto his knee.

"I'm not playing."

"Give me an answer." He pressed, "Is it me? And you?"

A preposterous curve turned up the corners of her mouth. "There is no me and you."

He didn't know why he said what he did. Hell, maybe he'd been thinking too much about needing more in his life right now because he felt so threatened he'd end up with less.

The notion was insane. He had plenty of family to support him, just nobody special at night when the house was quiet.

Family was different than losing himself in a woman's body, kissing her and holding her close after making love.

He sometimes would walk through the darkened rooms, sit out on the deck and watch the moon glide slowly through the sky. Being alone with his thoughts, his fears and uncertainties, left him feeling vulnerable—an emotion he never acknowledged outside of those few hours of solitude. He wasn't weak, wasn't unprepared to handle the stress thrown his way. He never broke down, never. He'd always been tough, strong. Resilient. He wouldn't lose his edge now.

And yet, at the same time he girded his resolve, he felt panic trigger a searing heat into his blood from his nerve endings. A sense of foreboding claimed him, gripping his heart and making him back off from Lauren.

Suddenly the game turned against him. He didn't want to play.

He rose, went to the long row of floor-to-ceiling windows and gazed into the night.

"I can't make you stay in Bella Luna. I can't make people do things they don't want to do. Damned if I'll try, I just can't." He was talking to Lauren but he was thinking about Debbie. He'd tried all methods of reasoning with her and Steve, talking and weighing the pros and cons until he'd been drained and emotionally battered. There was no changing their minds.

He felt Lauren come to stand behind him. "I'm sorry about what you're going through."

He gazed at their reflection in the glass, saw the genuine compassion in her expression as her image was silhouetted next to his.

"I'm also sorry I came after you the way I did that night. I've felt badly since it happened. I wish I could take it back."

"You didn't know."

"Yes...but sometimes I react before I think."

"We all do."

"Well, I'm sorry I did it to you."

"Forget about it."

Her arm lifted, as if she wanted to touch his hand, then she rethought the action and stilled. He'd been bracing himself for the touch, the consolation, and wanting it desperately. When she withdrew, he felt an icy draft run through the room.

While she didn't physically show her sympathies, he

heard them in her voice. "If there's anything I can do. I can't begin to imagine the extent of upset you're feeling. I'm so very sorry."

Nick slid open the doors, letting night air into the house. He breathed in the ocean breeze, the night, the dew-damp shrubs and floral scents—the familiarity was like a balm, soothing and helping to put his thoughts into perspective.

He blocked out the impending trial, blocked out all the things he couldn't change right now.

Instead, he turned and gave Lauren an easy smile, one that he willed to wipe out all the tension charging his body. "You want a piece of pizza?"

"No, I already—"

"—ate at the diner."

She smiled with a soft shrug and he felt undiluted pleasure clinging to him. He wanted to devour her, run his hands over her body and bury his face in her hair. He felt a hot tug deep within his belly. She could give him what he craved in those dark hours.

She was gorgeous when she wasn't frowning. That mouth of hers was made for kissing. Its perfectly shaped lips, red lipstick. He was a sucker for the color she applied. He couldn't think of a better way to spend the rest of his night than looking at them, tasting them.

The consuming depths of needing someone this badly twisted him the wrong way. The thought ran through him like a chill.

The boys' loud laughter from the kitchen drew Nick from a dangerous place where impulses took precedence over reality.

"I'm not a big fan of pizza," Lauren confessed, apparently not reading anything into his sudden tight jaw and clenched teeth. "I prefer my own cooking."

So did he.

Remembering the textures and flavors of her cooking could still heat his skin, evoke the tantalizing smells in his sleep and bring the desire to lift her onto the kitchen counter and give her equal pleasure.

She had some kind of a wickedly sensual touch when it came to food and his senses. He'd had a hard time climbing out of them, of regaining a clear head.

At first, Nick had wondered if she'd spiked the dinner with an aphrodisiac, then quickly discounted the idea. His son had eaten the same thing and his reaction had been entirely different.

His son, who never touched carrots, had been asking for them again. But when Nick opened a can, Nicky-J turned them down flat and said they smelled like sewer water.

To Nick, carrots were carrots, only whatever Lauren did to hers made his son want to eat them. And when they got home that night, Nicky-J wiped the toothpaste off the sink after he brushed his teeth. Nick had asked him about it, and he said he just had to clean up—he couldn't help himself.

Really strange.

There was something about Lauren, something so incredible and amazing, the feelings he had pulled him out of his taut line of control. He couldn't afford to lose his heart. He didn't believe he had enough room in it to share, not with everything that Nicky-J would need from him in the next few months. And yet—

Nick had an instant to pull back his next words, but he uttered them anyway. "Cook for me."

Her lips parted. "Excuse me?"

"Cook for us on your nights off and you can make up the difference on the rent." Wherever the thought had come from, he didn't chase it down. "I can't cook worth a crap and Nicky-J and I eat mostly at the diner or my mom's. When I have to do something in the kitchen, it comes from a box and it tastes like cardboard."

"But I—"

He cut her short, ignoring the deepened lines in her forehead. "If you're so inclined to pay full price on the cottage, you cook for us and we'll call the financial end even."

A stammer caught in her voice. "I—I can't cook for you because I—" she left the rest unspoken, and only after several long seconds, filled in the rest "—because I just can't."

She wet her red lips, his stomach clenched with a slow pull.

There was something mysterious about her, something she wasn't telling, a secret she kept, and he knew it had to do with the way she cooked.

He thought her bewitching, an enigma. Someone who interested him in a way he hadn't prepared for.

"The last time I cooked for you, I made a mistake."

"I didn't notice."

"Not in the recipe…just because I…" Her cheeks grew red, her body head emanated to him. She was feeling the same things as him and neither of them would verbally admit to anything stronger than passing interest. He wanted her; he knew she wanted him.

He could have proved them both liars, could have taken her into his arms right now and proven she had enjoyed that kiss in her kitchen just as much as he had, and wanted it again just as badly.

"Cook for me. Don't think about it, just say yes."

Conflict darkened her face, she worried the inside of her lower lip. He could see she was put off balance by his suggestion, weighing out her options. She clearly considered Nick's solution for a trade.

She lifted her shoulders, then dropped them. She was a great deal more complicated than she seemed. She had a willingness and the strong desire to make things work. From that, her answer must have been formed because she said, "I have Tuesdays, Thursdays and Fridays off from the Wharf."

Nick said, "Get whatever groceries you need at Dunk's and I'll square things with him."

"Is there a particular time you like to eat?"

"Whenever it's ready."

She nodded, looking nervously about the room as if she felt trapped, suffocating. "Billy, we have to go now."

Lauren went toward the door while he slid open a drawer in the dark wood occasional table. "You'll need this."

Puzzled, she took his house key. "So you can let yourself in, I doubt I'll be home when you have to start."

Before closing her fingers around the metal, she studied the key as if there was a symbolism to it she didn't dare examine. "Billy," she called once more, her words crisp. "I'm ready to go."

Billy came flying out of the kitchen, cape flowing behind him. "I'm glad Nicky-J's back. Can I come over again?" he asked Nick.

Nick laid a hand on Billy's narrow shoulder, his clothing warm and his hair smelling like little boy. "I'll see you next week."

After the door closed, Nick stepped back and wondered about the wisdom of such an arrangement with Lauren Jessup.

Nicky-J could tell he was getting a surprise party. Every time he went into the room when his grandma and grandpa were talking, they got quiet. Same with his dad and other people. Then they looked at him real funny, like they knew something he didn't know.

Parties were fun, but he kind of didn't need nothing. His mom and Steve gave him tons of stuff when he visited them. His bedroom was full of new toys and even a Tony Hawk poster, the best skateboarder guy ever.

He liked visiting his mom, but he liked being with his dad better. His friends were here and they did stuff together. Today they were putting up the walls on the fort, and Nicky-J thought that was as good as Disneyland—almost—because he'd puked after he got off Big Thunder. If he hadn't 'a done that, Disneyland would have been better. His mom got sort of mad at him and didn't know what to do, so Steve had to take him to the bathroom and give him a wet paper towel.

Clunk, bump, clunkety-clack.

Thoughts about throwing up were forgotten as Nicky-J pulled an empty red wagon down the street. Nicky-J, Critter, Tim and Billy all were headed for Dad's work to get scraps of wood. His grandma said he could get some more so long as he came right back and didn't forget about telling her they were going to Critter and Tim's backyard again. Tim was the strongest and oldest, so he was going to load the big pieces.

Nicky-J had changed out of his church clothes and

put on his jeans, the ones with the holes in the knees, and his work boots like his dad's. He'd asked Billy why he didn't have to go to Sunday school, then listen to the priest talk about things that he didn't understand. Billy said he didn't have a church and he asked Nicky-J if he could come to his one day. Nicky-J told him he'd have to ask his dad if it was okay.

"Hey, Billy, how much money did you say you had saved up?" Critter asked, chewing on a rope of licorice. His tongue was red and he never remembered to close his mouth when he talked—not that Nicky-J minded. He never did neither.

"My mom counted it for me. Three dollars and seventy-eight cents," Billy replied, his chest puffed out like he was real proud of it. Nicky-J had lots of coins in his piggy bank—more than the paper money. He only liked the coins because they were more. He didn't understand the paper money too good.

"Can I borrow a dollar?" Critter stretched off another bite of candy with his teeth.

Billy shook his head, his silly big glasses slipping down his nose, and he shoved them back up. "No. I'm saving it."

The wagon rattled and rolled across the sidewalk, hitting all the bumps. They reached the wharf, then went past the diner where Billy waved through the window to his mom.

She was nice. She waved back.

Nicky-J thought she was pretty. She'd smiled at him a couple of times, and once, she gave him a free brownie after he ate his lunch—and he didn't even have to ask for it or nothing.

She smelled pretty, too. Just like his grandma when she was baking cookies. Billy's mom smelling good made him want to hug her sometimes. He didn't know why, but he just sort of did.

Billy was lucky he had a mom like her since she knew how to cook carrots. He wondered if she'd make him some more when she came over to cook dinner for him and his dad.

The boys went into the old hotel and hollered for Nicky-J's dad. He came downstairs, his clothes dirty, and showed them where they could take the extra pieces of wood.

"See ya later, Dad." Nicky-J thought his dad looked tired, like he was staying up too late watching television.

"I'll see you at your grandma's."

"Okay, Dad."

Nicky-J brought the wagon back to Tim and Critter's, got the hammers and sized up their supplies. They didn't have a whole lot of nails, only what they'd collected from the floor of the hotel.

"We need some more nails," Nicky-J said after checking out how many they had. "I'd say we need forty-two more."

"I'd say nineteen," Tim offered.

Billy scrunched up his face as if he had a better idea and didn't need to give a count. "How about another box?"

"I know where some are in the garage," Critter offered. "Me and Tim can get some. We know just where our dad keeps them."

"And me and Billy will unload the wagon."

The boys separated. Billy and Nicky-J began making a messy pile of wood, tossing pieces onto the ground. They landed and big puffs of dust came up. Billy kept smiling a lot.

From the way Billy was acting, it seemed like he had never played this much with kids and he was really liking it.

If only he wouldn't wear that dumb cape. It was stupid, all faded from the washing machine, and it got in the way when they were sorting wood.

Nicky-J grabbed a long two-by-four, a really big hunk and chucked it. "Quit pretending like you're a superhero and take off that cape."

The redness in Billy's cheeks went sort of pale. "I can't take it off."

"Why not?"

"Because I don't want to."

"Why not?"

"Just because."

"That's not a reason. My dad says so."

"It's my reason. My mom says that when you feel something, even if other people think it's stupid, you still have the right to feel it."

"I guess. Last year I felt bad I didn't get a red BMX bike for Christmas and I sort of cried about it. My dad told me to take it like a man. I ended up getting one for my birthday anyway."

Billy smiled again, like he was happy Nicky-J didn't make him do something with the cape he didn't want to.

A bee hovered close by and Nicky-J swatted at it, laughing when he knocked it and the bee came back at him.

Billy took lots of steps backward and got as far away as he could. "Don't do that, Nicky-J! Stop it or it'll sting you."

Nicky-J ducked and waited to see if the bee would land. "It's not going to sting me."

"Don't do it." Billy's eyes grew big, like he was real scared.

"I'm not afraid of bees."

Billy looked shaky, as if he just got off Big Thunder and was going to puke, too. His face was funny, his mouth closed tight. He ran behind the tree when the bee flew toward him.

When Billy hid, Nicky-J thought something wasn't right.

He went to Billy and looked him in the eyes. "How come you're so scared of bees?"

"They can sting."

"Yeah, so? I been stung before, it doesn't scare me. Are you scared of waspeses, too?"

Billy's eyes went watery, like he was fighting back whether or not to say anything.

He might have been a little kid, but Nicky-J was also smart enough to figure out that Santa Claus shopped at Toys "R" Us and he knew his dad's credit card number. He was smart enough to figure out something else, too. "You were the kid who got stung in the story you told me. It was you who almost died."

As if he wasn't sure what to say, Billy kept quiet a long while, then finally nodded. "It was me."

Nicky-J felt sorry for him, felt really awful in a way he'd never felt for Tim or Critter. "Did it hurt bad?"

He nodded again. "Real bad."

Nicky-J's forehead wrinkled in thought. For a kid to live through all those stings, he must be pretty brave.

"You won't tell Tim and Critter," Billy whispered. "They'll make fun of me for being scared."

"I won't tell 'em."

"I don't want them to think I'm a baby."

"They wouldn't." Although Tim had just finished the sixth grade, he was pretty mean sometimes and he might say something to make Billy cry.

Nicky-J felt sorry for Billy that he had to run away from bees and waspeses for the rest of his life.

Without giving too much thought about it, Nicky-J dug into his pants pocket and handed over his horse's tooth. "Here, Billy. You told a good story. You can have it."

Billy's face brightened and he took the prize. "For reals?"

"For reals."

"Thanks! You're the best friend I ever had."

Nicky-J had never been anyone's best friend before. Tim and Critter and him always said they were blood brothers because they'd squirted ketchup into each other's hands and shook on it.

Billy Jessup was his first no-ketchup friend.

Nine

Don't ask for the moon when you really want the stars.

She was alone in the house.

Lauren wandered through the rooms, feeling as if she was imposing even though she'd been invited.

Nick's house was spacious, rustic and spectacular. It celebrated a romantic, timeless look with good-size windows and pine paneling. While the furnishings, polished and refined, caught her attention, the details held her interest.

She went down the hallway and studied the row of framed photographs. Nicky-J as a baby, Nick holding him. A woman lying in a hospital bed, Nicky-J swaddled next to her side. Lauren took a closer look at his ex-wife.

She was gorgeous. Beautiful, actually, in that California way that appeared as if it took little or no effort. Blond hair cascaded around her slender shoulders and she wore minimal makeup, a light pink blush and lip gloss.

Lauren recalled the twelve hours of hard labor she'd been in with Billy. By the time he arrived, she'd looked like death warmed over.

The photos were a time line of growing-up years, of first steps, a tricycle with a bow, blowing bubbles from a bathtub, and sitting in the saddle on a pony. Nicky-J smiled, a reflection of his father, and with a happiness that exuded from the film.

He was a content, seemingly well-rounded little boy. He had a vivid imagination, was rough and tumble, and a little too wild and risk taking for Lauren's comfort. He was never without a bandage on his finger, elbow or knee. His shirts were more often dirty, his shoes untied, and he favored baseball caps—backward. He was such a complete opposite of Billy.

She was glad she'd had a son. Little boys bring buddies into their pack and get along. Unlike girls who, from Lauren's memory, could be too emotionally charged, sometimes vicious and downright cruel.

She tried, with no success, to stave off memories of the foster home she'd been in at age nine. The elementary school she'd gone to had been upscale, the girls snotty and distrusting of the "new girl." Lauren had been an outcast, a misfit who didn't have a real mom and dad. She'd been taunted and teased, wasn't invited to be in any of the groups.

Lauren sighed, dusting away the memory. She was so grateful she'd had a son.

Billy was outside on the deck, occupied by the buckets of sand, seashells and beach toys. She gave him a loving smile, a soft wave as he looked through the window at her.

She strode deeper into the home, feeling reluctance pull at her steps, yet she didn't turn back. She knew it wasn't right to give herself a tour, but she couldn't quash her curiosity. How Nick lived intrigued her, filled her with a sense of interest she hadn't had in a long time.

She came to the end of the hall. The bedroom. She peered into a cavernous room that had windows everywhere. It felt as if the room were constructed outside in the lush Pacific woods. Simply breathtaking. If she were ever to be so fortunate, she doubted she'd leave this room for anything. Waking in the peeled-log bed, king-size, and its clean white linen duvet to cuddle into…she could just imagine how soft and inviting it would feel. Warm, cozy, a drowsy smile on her mouth when she looked over at Nick—

Her hold on the doorframe tightened, she started to shift away. Annoyance gripped her.

Lauren didn't enter the bedroom. She retraced her steps, reaffirming her reason for being in Bella Luna. Her life wasn't about Nick DiMartino or his son or a bed that conjured images of a naked man beneath the covers.

She was determined to make it on her own, buy her own house and be the kind of parent her son needed. She couldn't afford to bring anyone into the mix and ruin what she'd been working so hard toward.

What had she been thinking when she agreed to cook for Nick?

His ultramodern kitchen surrounded her with all the very best appliances at her disposal. For that alone, she should have been in heaven. If only her heart wasn't racing and doubts weren't clogging her thoughts.

She liked Nick. Liked him more than she should. Wanted to be here, but didn't like the reason why.

The kiss they'd shared had been in her subconscious ever since. No matter how hard she tried to forget about what had happened, she couldn't. She knew her cooking was special, knew there was something magical about it. People were transformed when they ate what she cooked. She couldn't explain why. But forgotten loves were remembered, friends reconciled, treasures found, pleasures indulged. But never, in all the times she'd cooked for someone, did *she* have a reaction that was completely uncharacteristic and wholly reckless.

Reckless. The word was dangerous, forbidden. Control, that's what she lived her life by. Stay in charge, stay focused. But all she'd had to do was be in the same room with him that night and she'd felt electricity run through her body, her mind and spirit. It was almost an undefinable feeling. Bewitching, maybe.

She hadn't been prepared, hadn't anticipated that she could ever feel something like that so quickly. She'd been consumed by the need to kiss him.

And now what was she doing again? Setting up the same situation.

Insanity. That's what this was.

Damn Otis Duncan and Sam Wong.

When she picked up the groceries today, she'd called Dunk on his little setup and he hadn't denied it. There was no point in going to Sam. The both of them had pushed her toward Nick.

Not one to lie back and do nothing, Lauren asked Dunk flat out why he did what he did. He said that sometimes there didn't need to be a reason when two people shared the same heart. And that's all he'd say about it.

So here she was, caught in this impromptu arrangement.

Lauren, while usually quite ardent about owning up to things, didn't want to take personal responsibility for finding herself in Nick's kitchen slicing garlic to stuff inside a pork loin.

Two hours later, she still felt the same way when Nick came in with an energetic Nicky-J in tow. Nicky-J had been with his grandmother this afternoon.

Lauren had made her peace with Caprice, offered her sincere apology for her disruption that night, and the woman, kind and generous, told Lauren not to give it another thought.

"Smells great," Nick said, tossing his keys and wallet onto the counter.

You smell great. Like new wood, musk and the lingering remnants of shampoo from a morning shower.

The casual way in which he greeted her, stowing his personal items on the countertop and walking through the room with such male presence, wreaked havoc on the tight wind of her resolve.

He went to the sink. His broad back to her as he slipped off his wristwatch and washed his hands.

She stood there, mesmerized. Her blood moved through her like candle wax, liquid hot.

When he stepped back for the towel hanging through the refrigerator handle, she stepped away with a half jump. He gazed quizzically at her and she quickly turned her attention on the oven.

"Everything's ready."

In an effort to make things feel casual, she served caf-eteria-style. Nick took a plate, fixed something for Nicky-J, then himself.

Nick went into the dining room and sat, Nicky-J join-ing him after the sound of a bathroom toilet flushing and the water faucet turning on briefly.

Billy remained in the kitchen with Lauren and he whis-pered, "Am I supposed to stay in here with you, Mom?"

"You can sit on that stool over there."

"Aren't we eating here?"

"No, we're going home."

"But I'm hungry," he complained.

The latter was spoken loud enough that Nick re-sponded, "Join us. Lauren, sit down."

"I can't, we can't..." If she left before he ate any-thing, she'd be fine. Safe. Nothing would happen.

"But, Mom." Billy put his arm around her waist, gazed into her face with large hazel eyes behind glasses. He had a dirt smudge on his cheek and he smelled like the rich minerals of earthworms, an unfamiliar scent she'd never associated with him. "I'm hungry."

Nick overruled further protest. "Go ahead and sit down, Billy."

Billy disregarded Lauren's wishes, something that distressed her. He'd always been a very obedient little boy before. That Nick would overrule her bristled.

Having lost on this one, she took the reins back to have the last word by telling Billy, "Wash your hands first."

Dinner was an array of colors and textures. She'd prepared grilled pork loin stuffed with wild mushrooms and garlic, a demiglaze and fresh sage. She'd had inspiration while shopping in Dunk's that sage would be perfect for the dish, a compliment to the morels. She cooked jasmine rice, then fried patties of it in grape-seed oil for flavoring. For the vegetables, she baked a whole cauliflower—a recipe she'd done many times before with perfect results. There were rolls and fresh fruit— she was very big on fruit with dinner. The sweet juices of seasonal fruits added dimension to a meal.

She'd sampled the food a few times as she cooked and knew everything was perfect. But what little she'd eaten didn't appease her hunger. She had primed herself up for a simple meal at home, but the roasting aroma of sage and meat had ruined her appetite for anything but this. In a way, she was glad to stay.

Nick had wonderful serving bowls and plates, thick white ceramic. When getting them down, she had an instant when she'd pretended they were hers, that the kitchen was hers, as well.

Musings such as those were dangerous. She needed to eat quickly and leave. Staying would be a disaster.

"I have a star named after me," Billy said, breaking the table sounds of spoons against serving bowls.

"Which one?" Nicky-J sliced into his meat.

"One of them in the sky. We're not sure which one, we just pick the one we think it is."

"Do you have the coordinates?" Nick shook salt over his plate. She wanted to tell him he didn't need to do that, the dishes were seasoned just right.

"Do we, Mom?"

"Yes. I have the certificate."

Nick gave the plate a light shake of pepper and Lauren frowned. "You need a telescope."

"We don't have one," Billy said.

"I do," Nick told him.

Billy's face split into a wide grin. "You do?"

"Out on the deck." Nick caught a bite of food on his fork. "After dinner, I'll show it to you."

"Did you hear that, Mom?"

"Uh-huh." The sound was more breathy than weighted.

Nick DiMartino was turning out to be too good to be true. The struggle to stay in neutral territory when her feelings for Nick came into play was becoming increasingly harder.

News about the telescope put a smile on her son's face brighter than the star he had named after him.

"Yeah, we look at stars and the moon." Nicky-J jabbed a piece of cauliflower, gave it a dubious sneer, then knocked it off his fork.

"Eat it, dude," his father said to him.

Nicky-J picked up the vegetable again, sniffed, examined the flower, then tentatively put it into his mouth with an expression that screamed he was anticipating hating the taste. Instead, as he chewed, his lips smacked and he nodded. "What's this stuff?"

"Cauliflower."

"I love it."

Nick gazed at Lauren.

She shrugged, smiled.

"What'd you do to it?" Nick asked.

"Scrambled eggs and parmesan cheese on top, then bake it in the oven. Works every time."

Nicky-J made short order of the cauliflower, then worked on his rice.

Lauren, who could eat like this whenever she had the chance to cook, didn't savor the meal like Nick. Her earlier hunger pangs were gone the moment she reacquainted herself with what eating at the same table with Nick was like: sexy and distracting.

She ate just to eat, but he ate to enjoy every single bite. She looked at him from beneath her eyelashes, observing.

The fork came to his mouth slowly, was removed from between his lips just as slowly. The way his firm lips looked as he chewed, the appreciative expression on his face while he tasted. He drank a glass of wine he'd poured for himself as if he was in no hurry at all, a sip in slow motion. It was almost as if he did everything slowly just to torture her.

She lost all the air in her lungs, felt the blood-pounding need to bring a conversation to light, anything to take her focus away from Nick.

Ignoring the ache in her muscles, she asked, "Nicky-J, what do you want to be when you grow up?"

"A carpenter like my dad."

"I thought you wanted to be a doctor," Billy remarked.

"Naw. Critter wants to be that 'cause he likes to squish bugs with his bike tire. I don't wanna be a doctor 'cause you gotta wash your hands too much."

Lauren swallowed a piece of roll, her mouth feeling dry. She reached for her water glass—only to find it empty.

Nick nudged his wineglass toward her and she gratefully took it, drank, then realized her mouth was exactly where his had been. So much for detached neutrality.

In a half stammer, she asked, "Um, how is the restoration coming?"

"I had the best finishing carpenter working for me a couple of months ago."

"What happened to him?"

"He liked rehab so much he's gone back three times."

"What's rehab?" Nicky-J shoved the last of his rice into his mouth, and chewed for everyone to see until his dad tapped his knuckles beneath his son's chin—a signal to close up.

"A place you go to get help from bad habits."

His face scrunched thoughtfully. "Grandpa needs to go to rehab. He always uses words that has Grandma sayin' his name funny."

Lauren smiled over the little boy's logic. In fact, she almost laughed out loud but caught herself and reined her humor in.

"So, have you replaced him?" Lauren nibbled on blueberries in a sugary lemon sauce.

"I hired somebody yesterday. He's working out so far."

"Having to get things done on time must be a big load on your shoulders."

"No different than anyone else trying to get by."

Whether he meant that as a comparison to their lifestyles, she wouldn't know because Billy tilted his head toward Nick and asked, "How come the moon's pink sometimes when I look at it?"

"'Cause it's made out of Lucky Charms pink marsh-em-hollows," Nicky-J volunteered in a slur.

"No it's not." Nick casually leaned into the back of his chair. "Billy, don't listen to this knucklehead."

Nicky-J simply giggled.

"You'll learn about it in school." Nick emptied the wineglass and set it on the table, his fingers on the stem.

"It's a phenomenon that has to do with the tides. In first grade, you'll go on field trips to the tide pools and study the anemone and starfish. Nicky-J's soon-to-be aunt Heather will take the class around and show you the Monterey Bay aquarium. You can see the octopuses and touch sea urchins."

"I want to so bad." Billy's tiny body all but shook with enthusiasm. "I will, won't I, Mom? *Please.*"

"I…yes, we'll see."

"I never been to school." Billy's confession caused speculation to pool in Nick's blue eyes.

Lauren steeled herself against the inevitable question, and like a clock striking the hour, it came.

Nick didn't ask Billy, he asked her. "Why not?"

"There wasn't a reason. I've taught him since birth. He's done great, very intelligent, as you can judge for yourself." She tried, without much success, to bridle the defensiveness in her tonē. There was no reason for her to feel like this, as if she'd made a bad decision.

"I can say my alphabet, I know how to write my name, all my shapes, and I can sing songs and put on a puppet show."

The questions on Nick's face faded, his eyes gaining a depth and compassion that unraveled Lauren. So utterly dumb that she'd get emotional over his approval of her as a mom and a teacher.

She saw in Nick, in that flicker of a moment, that he cared for Billy, that he thought him as special as she did.

Nick trailed his fingers on the table, tapping them thoughtfully. "That's really very good. You know a lot, Billy. You should be proud of yourself."

The dimples in Billy's cheeks spoke volumes. He

loved the affirmation of validity from an adult male and it almost saddened Lauren as much as it made her happy.

These were the times when she knew that Billy needed a father, was missing that important piece of his life without one. There was only so much she could do for him as a single woman: instill the manners of a gentleman, educate him, support him and let him grow into a maturity that would define him when he entered college. But that was basic parenting dynamics.

She understood that he was missing out by not having a father to go fishing and camping with, to engage in ridiculous horseplay on the carpet, and even do things together in the bathroom mirror like shaving peach fuzz and comparing muscles—when muscles hadn't developed yet.

By vowing to remain free and independent, she was in many ways depriving Billy. But how could she just pick someone to enter her life, to share it, to become her son's father? It wasn't easy. She didn't know anyone, not until—

Lauren gazed at Nick, caught him looking at her, and fussed with her hair, smoothing wisps away from her face.

It wouldn't work, she told herself.

But in the next few seconds, her mind drew a blank on every reason why it wouldn't.

Nicky-J finished off his dessert, then belched.

"Dude, not cool." Nick tossed a napkin to his son. "You have food on your mouth."

Nicky-J scrubbed, tossing the napkin onto his plate.

The next sound in the room was one Lauren wouldn't have guessed could come from her son.

Billy burped, a baritone bear growl that, afterward, sent him and Nicky-J into a fit of giggles.

Lauren wasn't amused. "Billy! That's unacceptable."

"It just came out, Mom."

She knew a burp didn't just come out, especially when Billy's face was still infused with red from the effort.

Nick wasn't any help. He laughed along.

The boys made a fast exit from the table, Billy forgetting to bring his plate to the counter the way she'd taught him.

As if she'd been spun around several times blindfolded, she stood with a light dizziness and a smidgen of shock. "He's never done that before."

"That's too bad."

Her tone went flat. "And you encouraged him."

"I only laughed after the fact."

"Same thing."

A smirk lit on his lips, one she wanted to wipe off and kiss at the same time. Explosive sensations ripped through her, a longing and a need so potent she couldn't thwart the feelings.

She'd promised herself they'd eat and leave, so what was she still doing here?

She felt something…sexual. No doubt about it. Just when she'd convinced herself that she was bigger than the feeling, here it was. Once again, eating her own cooking in the company of Nick DiMartino really messed with her bearings.

For the first time, she noticed he had a scar running through his right eyebrow. The razor-thin line of missing black hair was barely discernible next to his tanned complexion. She had to be standing close to him to tell—and she was standing close. Close enough that she was as transparent as a piece of glass.

"Battle scar," he offered, surmising what had caught her attention. "My brothers made a bridge out of the sofa cushion, ran it from the coffee table to the edge of the couch. I walked across—or that was the plan—and beaned the corner of my head on the coffee table. Six stitches. Danny and John were bawling harder than I was. They didn't mean anything malicious by telling me to walk over it, and when they saw all the blood, they fell apart like a bunch of girls." He brought his hand to his eyebrow, smoothed it, then shrugged. "I forget it's there."

"It doesn't look bad. It looks—" She sliced off the thought. It actually gave his face definition, an appeal that left her brain rattled.

He was too tall, too wide as he went around her to rinse dishes in the sink. When he didn't touch her hair, skim his powerful hands down her arms the way he'd done the last time, she couldn't sort out if she was more relieved or less disappointed.

Lauren picked up the leftovers and brought them to him.

"I don't want you to do that. The deal was cooking, nothing else."

"I can't stand by and watch you clean up and not help."

"Yeah, you can."

He took her by the shoulders, steered her to one of the bar stools and made her sit.

A moment's hesitation, a countless tick of time passed before he released his hold. In that fragment, she lost her breath, lost her equilibrium, and lost her mind.

The sight of his handsome face, the dark hair and piercing blue eyes, and the smell of wood particles that clung to his shirt, had her losing ground she didn't want to stand on anymore.

Nick didn't move for long seconds after lowering his arms to his sides. He wet his lips, something that curled a flame of heat in her belly. He contemplated something, she could tell by the color of his eyes as they darkened.

Maybe he was going to—

In a smooth drawl that evoked shivers up her nape, he asked, "Want some rocky-road ice cream?"

As he backed away, she struggled against falling forward to go after him. Instead, she willed her muscles to stiffen.

Ice cream? She was in crisis here, wanting one thing when she'd demanded another.

"No, I don't want any rocky-road ice cream. Why, do you have some?"

"Brand-new carton in the freezer."

"One bowl."

He grinned, and the impact of perfect white teeth and full lips just about disarmed her.

Sometimes a woman had to revert to chocolate to get her head back on straight. This was one of them.

Ten

There are two sides to every moon.

The Outrigger Pub looked like a dock on the inside. There were pier pilings and ropes, the carpet was a deep blue with a repeating anchor-diamond pattern, and nets were slung from ceiling to wall with glass floats catching the wall-sconce light.

Smoke curled through the air. In the background came the *crack* from a pool table as somebody broke the newly racked balls. Bon Jovi sang from the jukebox as the bartender poured three shots of Jack Daniel's for John, Nick and Danny DiMartino.

The brothers sat together, backs to the Plexiglas windows overlooking the surf. Twilight had passed some thirty minutes ago, the evening sky waking in a wash of navy blue.

"I talked to Bruce Harmon today." Nick slid a bowl of peanuts to Danny.

"What's up with everything?" John hunched his

shoulders after a long day from sunrise to sunset out on the boat.

"He said it's going to be like Debbie and I are going through a divorce today and not years ago. The court's going to investigate me, my house, my lifestyle. They're going to look into my background."

"And find nothing," Danny supplied. "Nick, you're a great father. Nobody can prove otherwise."

"It's not just about me. They're going to do the same for Debbie."

"Good," John said, taking his glass. "I want the truth to come out. She left you and Nicky-J and no judge is going to reward her for that."

The brothers lifted their shot glasses as John made a toast. *"Salute."*

As it slid in a hot trail down his throat, Nick welcomed the instant ease of whiskey to his muscles. "Yeah, they're going to interview Steve, too. Since he's Nicky-J's stepdad."

Danny tapped his fingers on the bar. "What do we really know about this guy aside from the fact he's rolling in cash from movie-studio investments?"

"I'm not worried about Steve, he's on the level. I already had him checked out when Debbie married him. You don't think I'd send Nicky-J to a guy's house and then find out he's an asshole with a record or anything?"

"No." Danny dropped some salted peanuts into his mouth, his hair falling into his eyes. He shoved it out of his face.

John took another drink. "What else is Bruce going to do?"

Nick gazed at his brothers, the rocks on which he'd

clung to all his life. It felt good to talk about everything in the open. They meant the world to him, had been there for him when Debbie left town. He would do the same for his brothers if they ever needed him.

"Bruce asked me if I'd do anything to keep my son."

"And you said yes," John answered.

"Yeah, I did. So he's got an investigator he knows on her—no confidentiality breach since Bruce hired him. Whatever she's done, been up to, no matter how personal or private, he's going to find out. If we can use it in court, we will."

While Nick wanted to win custody of Nicky-J in the worst way, going to such lengths to get something on Debbie didn't sit well with him. A flicker of discomfort clutched his gut. After all, they'd once loved each other, once slept together and created the little boy they now were fighting for. Deep in his heart, no matter how remote, Nick would always care for Debbie as the mother of his child. But that didn't mean he was going to take this lying down without a fight.

Danny inched the peanut bowl to John, who grabbed a handful. "When will you know what they find out?"

Nick shrugged. "Don't know. Takes time."

"When's the next court appearance?" John asked.

"August the twelfth."

"Just about two weeks before my wedding." Danny's boyish expression sobered. "If the judgment doesn't go the way we want, Nick, I can talk with Heather about a postponement."

"The hell you will." Nick knocked back the rest of his Jack. "You're getting married and nothing's going to stop the wedding. Nothing, you got that, *Manny?*"

A wounded smile hooked itself on Danny's mouth. "Aw, for Christ's sake, he goes off with the Manny shit again." Danny shoved Nick in the arm.

John laughed, a low and deliberate sound. "You'll never live it down, Danny."

"I never meant to drop the match."

"But you lit it," John said.

"Only because you dared me to. It was all your fault."

The brothers each, in their own thoughts with distant smiles, remembered the day Danny got the nickname Manny.

Danny, four years younger and always wanting to be like his big brother John, did something incredibly stupid to impress his brothers.

"John," Nick said, "in a way he's right—it is your fault."

"No way. I only found a coffee can of gasoline in the garage."

Danny jumped in, "Yeah, but you decided to pour some down a manhole and light it to see what would happen."

"I never tossed a match down there. You did."

Nick sat on the bar stool, blocking out the world around him, and listened to his brothers' voices.

"Well, you were going to," Danny said, his grin easy on his lips.

"But I didn't. When you dropped the lit match down there, I'll never forget that noise—like a jet engine and then a big boom." John leaned his elbows onto the bar. "The manhole cover flew up and flames shot about fifteen feet in the air. The cover landed on the neighbor's brand-new Plymouth, knocked the windshield out."

Nick was laughing and added, "And all the toilets in the neighborhood blew. God almighty, Dad was pissed at you. Cost him some bucks to repair the Plymouth."

"I know what happened, for fuck sake." Danny turned his glass upside down and frowned. "Manhole Danny."

"We shortened that to Manny," Nick clarified.

John and Nick traded glances, grins.

"Yeah, yeah. Laugh it up. You guys did some pretty stupid stuff, too."

The brothers reflected a moment.

"We tortured Mom and Dad. It's a wonder they still speak to us," John said, his face windburned and red. Creases had begun to line the corners of his eyes and mouth, but he was still a good-looking guy.

"Yeah." Danny nodded thoughtfully. "Nick, you threw rotten eggs out the school-bus window, hit a couple of mailboxes and a cat once, if I remember right. Nicky-J do something like that yet?"

"Naw, but give him time. He's still in his dare phase. If he thinks he can't do something, he does it anyway just to dare himself. Banged up his lip the other day when Critter was riding his bike, pulling Nicky-J along on his skateboard. They hit a rock and Nicky-J went flying. At least he didn't need stitches this time."

Suddenly, childhood reflections turned cloudy and Nick was reminded of the present once more.

His son would be at home waiting for him, along with Lauren and Billy. It was strange to know she was there, but then again it wasn't. He had this sudden urge to see her, to touch her and to embrace her. To bury his head in her hair and hold on. She was something soft in his life, when right now, everything felt so hard.

"I gotta get home," he said, standing and flipping a bill onto the counter.

"So, I heard you've got Lauren cooking for you," Danny remarked, paying his portion of the tab and getting to his feet, as well.

"Yeah, it worked out for the both of us."

John joined his brothers and the trio walked out of the pub and into the brisk, damp night. Collars were turned up, mist formed when they spoke.

"What do you think about her?" John asked, fingering his keys from his jeans pocket.

"I think she's fine."

"Fine, as in okay? Or fine as in, you want more than dinner from her?"

Nick, although normally talkative with his brothers about his feelings for most anything, kept these to himself. They were still forming, still new. He wasn't sure where he wanted them to go, how they'd end up.

"She's got some baggage she's dealing with. I don't know her whole story." Nick went to his motorcycle and swung a leg over the seat.

"But you want to find out." Danny stood next to him, his eyes glittering in the dark.

"Maybe." He turned over the bike's engine. "See you guys for breakfast tomorrow?"

"I'll be there." John began walking toward his truck, Danny to the Suburban.

"Me, too. See you guys."

They all went their separate ways, to separate lives and the people they loved. Only for Nick, he wondered if what he had starting with Lauren was fleeting.

The thought socked Nick's breath from him like a fist

to the chest, and he kicked the bike swiftly through its gears and sped home.

After dinner, Nick and Lauren remained in the kitchen again, having eaten alone. The meal had been quiet and thoughtful without the constant talk of Nicky-J and Billy. The boys hadn't come home for dinner, and instead stayed at his mom's for spaghetti and to help his dad rebuild an inboard motor. Nick saw himself at that age, tagging along in the garage and handing his dad the right tools.

Nick made Lauren sit on the bar stool while he cleaned up the dishes. She'd made another incredible meal. Halibut, one of his favorites. He was going to start putting on weight if he didn't watch it.

"Sorry I ran late." The words were out of his mouth before he could analyze why he felt the need to say them.

He didn't owe her any explanations, could do as he pleased. Yet staying longer at the Outrigger than he'd planned had caused her dinner to sit in the oven, waiting.

"That's all right. You never specified when you wanted to eat." Lauren looked down at her hands. The nails were short, a cut on her index finger. She worked hard. Maybe too hard.

"You look beat," he said.

"I had to work today before I came over." She stifled a yawn, rubbed the backs of her eyes with her fingertips. "Verna Mae had to go to the dentist first thing this morning and she ended up with a root canal. She thought she'd be able to come in, but she's at home on painkillers. I took over her shifts."

He wondered how long Lauren intended to keep

pushing herself. Didn't she ever take a minute to relax? He didn't need her to cook for them, would have been happy to give her the cottage for the current rent, nothing else required. It was her stubborn pride wearing her down, making her look as if she was in need of a full body massage to erase all the strain that constantly held her muscles hostage.

He could go for a hot tub, and caught himself suggesting it. "Let's sit in the spa on the deck. It'll make you feel better."

Instantly alert, her eyes darted to his. "I don't have a bathing suit."

"You can wear one of my T-shirts."

He nudged her off the stool, steered her down the hallway and into his bathroom. She stood in the middle of the room, her bangs falling over her eyebrows and her hands on her hips. She wore a floral skirt and canvas Keds, a sweater that had seen better days but still fit her as if it had been knit next to her body.

He tossed her one of his T-shirts, an old worn-out navy blue one that had been his favorite. The plush cotton was soft and thin, the neck cut into a vee.

She opened her mouth to protest, but he closed the door to give her some privacy.

"I'll be outside waiting for you," he said.

Nick stripped down and put on a pair of bathing trunks. Exiting his bedroom from the sliding doors, he left them open for her. The deck planks were cool beneath his bare feet as he removed the cover from the hot tub.

He turned on the bubble switch, then slipped inside the water with an audible sigh. For a long moment, he sat and closed his eyes, drifting to a place that was simply gray. No tones of black or white, or reasoning.

He sensed he wasn't alone, slowly cracked opened his eyes. Lauren clutched her arms around her waist. The hem of his T-shirt came inches above her knees. The rest of the fabric swam around her, sizes too large.

She'd bound her hair in a ponytail, the severity doing nothing to lessen the delicate features of her face. Her skin was pale, like milk. The shape of her mouth was perfect, the top and bottom lips evenly matched. Eyes that had been tired before now seemed wide-awake, cautious.

He gestured to the inviting water. "Get in."

Without commenting, she carefully sat on the deck, dipped one leg in then the other. She had to hold the ends of the T-shirt to keep them from bubbling around her waist. Even so, the water caught the fabric, brought it up, and he noticed she wore a pair of plain white panties, French cut. Nothing extravagant, very simple. To him, very sexy.

He didn't say anything for some time, letting her adjust to the water, to the night, to him. He could tell she began to relax when her stiff neck loosened up and she rested the back of her head on the deck, her lips parting.

A slight smile, barely discernible, held her mouth. There was no doubt about it, pure pleasure.

His muscles grew taut, not from the end of the day, but in a way that made him want to pull her onto his lap. "Feeling better?"

"I hate to admit it, but you were right," she murmured, not looking at him. "This is really nice."

He was feeling more than nice.

The dark, wet fabric of his T-shirt clung to her skin. She had removed her bra, her breasts pouting without the lift of lingerie.

She wore minimal makeup, something she didn't need anyway. She had a natural beauty, enhanced by the lipstick she favored. There was none on her mouth at the moment, a mouth he felt compelled to kiss, but held back.

If he kissed her now, she'd bolt. He wanted her to stay, to trust him. Even if he wasn't sure he could trust himself.

"Tell me about you," he said into the darkness. "About where you're from."

She slanted her gaze onto him, a low-lidded glance that all but impaled him to the spot. Her eyes were the color of moss, a golden green. "I already have."

"You glossed over the details. I want more."

The meaning had two sides, both the literal and physical.

"I don't like to talk about it." She turned away from him, withdrawing into herself.

"Why not?"

"Because I didn't have the best of childhoods." A frown caught on her arched eyebrows. She lifted her legs in the water, floating, as if needing the buoyancy to not feel anything heavy; she stared at her manicured toes. Red polish had been neatly applied.

Her whisper broke through the motor of the spa. "It's not easy for me to talk about."

He gave her room to organize her thoughts, to evaluate whether or not she wanted to expand on her comment.

"You won't understand what it's like," she began. "You've got memories with your family. It's a movie you watched together or a story that's been retold a hundred times, and you'll always equate that with your mom and dad and brothers, always know that you share that when you get together at holidays, family gatherings."

She met his eyes, in hers he saw a blunt pain. "I don't have what you have. I was placed in foster care when I was three. My mother picked her boyfriend over me, I never knew my father."

He hadn't expected that and her admission packed a punch. He couldn't imagine being raised by total strangers, having no place to call home. No roots, no family. No past to recall with fond memories and smiles.

He thought of all the good times he'd had, the Christmases and birthdays. Fishing trips, picnics, car rides. All that he knew, Lauren hadn't had.

"I lived in a lot of houses, and for various reasons, they didn't work out. When I was thirteen, one foster mother thought I was a threat to her marriage. I thought I was going to be adopted by them..." Nothing in her tone gave away the depth of hurt and rejection she must have felt. "I already thought there was something wrong with me because my mom didn't want me."

His chest constricted. Nick touched her hand in the water, grabbed her fingers and held tightly. She didn't pull away, but she didn't hold on to him in return.

"I was placed with the Saunders when I was seventeen and it was the best thing that ever happened to me. But by then I'd already evolved into who I was. There were some rough moments. I...I wasn't the kind of nice girl who got asked to the prom."

He got the meaning, she didn't have to spell out that she'd looked for affection in ways that she now regretted. Nobody had the perfect past, and what a person did—even if they now realized it was the wrong path to take—shaped them into who they were today.

Her hand slipped free from his. Like a boat breaking from its mooring, she wanted to isolate herself and drift away. He hated for her to think he could be judging.

"Lauren, I'm supposed to think less of you now? Because I don't. Anyone who can come out of what you did has got to be one hell of a strong woman. You have my admiration, all of it."

She sent him a smile filled with remorse. "I don't know why I told you. It's embarrassing. You caught me when I was tired."

"It's not embarrassing."

The timer quit on the bubbles, the water calming to a serene surface. Blue fabric moved like sea grass around her thighs, the sensual shape of her legs murky beneath the water where a yellow bulb didn't do much to illuminate the spa. Her hands caught in her lap, knit together. The strength in her profile seemed to weaken as she lost herself in thought.

The night sounds erupted stronger, less diluted. A foghorn in the bay, the slush of surf below.

The June nights never stayed hot on the coast after sundown. A waxing moon traveled across the sky, its brilliance like a lamp of buttery light.

When he saw a tear slide quietly down Lauren's cheek, Nick reacted by scooping her into his embrace and bringing her down onto his lap.

"It's not embarrassing," he insisted, sliding his arm tightly around her waist and holding fast. "It's not your fault. Look at me. Lauren, look at me."

When she did, he saw it took effort for her to swallow the lump in her throat, blink away the moisture in her eyes.

He wanted to take her hurt away. "What your mom did was wrong. I don't know why she made that choice, but it had nothing to do with you. Sometimes people make bad decisions based on impulses. Sounds like she did that."

Nick caught Lauren's chin between his fingers. "You're doing all right by yourself now, and by your son. I see how you take care of him. You're a great mom. Something inside you knew what to do, how to be there for him. Seems like the Saunders were lucky to have you, too."

"I was the lucky one. I was a mess when I went to them and they made me see I was better than who I thought I was."

Her body quivered on top of his, the softness of her behind a reminder of how feminine and vulnerable she was at this moment.

When her hands reached out to cup his face, his pulse rose and snagged. Her thumbs brushed the fullness of his bottom lip, then she caressed his cheeks. He held still, letting her trace her fingertips over his face, marking out a pattern, a path on which she explored him.

His arms cinched firmer around her waist, the bottom of the T-shirt floating upward. He brought his hands beneath the thin fabric, feeling her smooth, warm skin. The undersides of her breasts were within a fraction of his thumbs; he rested splayed hands on her rib cage, keeping her to him, wanting her closer.

"You're a wonderful man, Nick," she uttered, then brought her mouth over his and kissed him.

He let her lead the kiss, taking him at her own pace.

Her lips against the seam of his mouth was an exquisite tenderness that shot straight through his body. She was in no hurry, the slight pressure of her lips bringing him to a sluggish arousal.

His heart pounded as the slow slide of her tongue parted his lips. Heat fanned through him, his stomach muscles pulsed into a tense grip of control. He saw himself bringing her legs over his, her straddling him while he entered her.

He ran his hands across the curves of her breasts, her skin slick from the water. Breath burned in his lungs. She trembled, gave the kiss over to him, let him take what she offered.

He crushed her fully against him, body to body.

Nick ran his fingers over her ribs, then to the fullness of her breasts where he cupped her bare skin. Nipples were soft, then firmed to tight points under his strokes. She arched her back to him, the shirt billowing about her as he lifted it higher and took her breast to his mouth.

Where he'd felt hollow, he now felt full.

His body strained, he could fall if he let himself. Take her and forget about everything else. He didn't want to think about tomorrows, just today. Right now. This moment.

She moaned, her legs falling over each side of his. It would be so easy to slip aside her panties, take what he wanted. Give her what she wanted.

Part of him was on the brink of doing just that, part of him was sober enough to acknowledge the consequences.

He couldn't use her for sex, couldn't lose himself in her for only his pleasure. Whatever she gave, he would have to return equally—mind, body and soul. She was fragile, whether she knew it or not.

Their seduction was mutual, her low throaty moan proof of that, but he denied himself the pleasure of her scented skin, and instead, brought his hand lower to her panties.

She took in a long gulp, let him slip his fingers inside. While he sucked her nipple, he stroked the delicate folds of her body. She reached for him, was on the brink of release. With her hands around his neck, she kept him close. Moving against his palm, she sought crossing that line of control and let herself tremble against him.

Pants, in quick and choppy gasps, filled his head as she hunched forward, her forehead pressed to his. He was hard for her, but ignored his needs, sucking in the crisp night to cool his lungs.

"I…oh, my God," she breathed against him. "I didn't expect that. I might have, we could have…and I wouldn't have cared. Oh, my God."

Arms draped around him, her cheek pressed next to his as if she couldn't move, didn't have the inclination or desire and was completely content as is.

He held her, kissing her hair where it smoothed above her ear.

"I don't do this kind of thing with just…anyone."

"I didn't think you did."

"I haven't…not since—" her breath was warm and moist against his neck "—Billy's father."

Quick math added up for Nick. Six years was a long time to deny, ignore, sexual needs.

Lauren lifted her head. "You really are wonderful...great. I didn't realize how badly I needed you until just now. But you've got so much going in your life right now and I—I'm just floating. I have no ties to anyone, any place."

He now made the connection as to why she had difficulty settling down.

Kissing him quickly, fiery with a firm press of her mouth as if it were the last time she'd allow herself, she said, "We're too different, I think. I can't make promises."

"I'm not asking you to promise anything."

"I know...maybe that was presumptuous of me. But I don't know how to be settled. It's not my nature."

"Because you've never tried to make one place your home."

"I have. Honestly." She touched his jaw briefly, and the touch warmed him. "It's a struggle for me. I don't need the extra pressure of you right now. And how can you even consider anything with me? You're in the fight of your life for your son."

"I'm aware of that. But right this second, that's not something I'm dealing with. I'm with you. What do you need?"

His words put a margin of panic in her eyes, as if no one had ever wanted her for herself. As if no man had ever asked her what she wanted.

"I don't need anyone. I'm okay by myself." She shifted her position, the emotional walls rebuilding. "This isn't going to work out. I can't do this. There isn't going to be anything between us."

Not believing she meant everything she said, Nick questioned, "Is that how it is or how you see it?"

"It's how it has to be." She got off his lap, water

sloshing, and sat down on the other side of the hot tub to collect herself.

Lauren was more shaken than she first realized. The climax that Nick had brought her to was earth-shattering. Yes, it had been a long time, but there was something intensely special about Nick, about how he'd touched her, that left her aching and burning for more. Wanting more, wanting him right now and knowing it would be a mistake.

She couldn't believe she'd fallen under the spell of lust again. She'd always been so controlled about it and made sure she didn't repeat the past. Just moments ago, she would have made love with Nick and not thought about anything else. No consequences.

Trembling at her lack of resolve, Lauren willed her thoughts to get back on track, reminding herself that she'd done this once before and look where she'd ended up.

She'd fallen for Trevor, thought he was the one for her and would give her what she'd been missing all her life. She'd taken precautions not to get pregnant, and had been surprised to find out they'd failed. Nothing was foolproof. Bitterly she added, not even her so-called love for Trevor. He'd never been truly happy about it, never taken responsibility the way she'd hoped.

He left her with a one-week-old baby, signing a termination-of-parental-rights agreement. She hadn't seen him in six years, knew she never would again.

Stupid. Lauren hadn't known her father, now Billy wouldn't know his. She hated how history was repeating itself. She never would have chosen this path in life, but she had to deal with it.

She'd thought Trevor would be different. The one

time she let herself trust a man, he let her down. So why was her heart trying to take her places now she wasn't prepared to go?

Nick was an incredible man. He was everything she'd ever dared to hope and wish for in flesh and blood. A real person. Why then couldn't she embrace him? Why was she afraid?

The answer was slow in coming, but ultimately, she realized she didn't want to hurt him. She couldn't bear it. She cared too much for this man.

Gazing at Nick, she forced the longing for him out of her tone. This was so difficult for her. He was entitled to an explanation, she felt she owed him. No matter what happened between them, she did care about him, had feelings for him that she couldn't deny.

"I learned early on not to have too many expectations about life, about people and about myself. But I do want my son to grow up feeling confident about himself, I want him to be whatever he wants to be. It's up to me to help him reach his potential."

"And I can see you're doing that just fine. But have you ever taken a moment to put your needs first?"

"I do all the time," she said in a frustrated tone. "That's why I move. That's why I'm angry with myself for not thinking about what Billy wants. In that regard, I'm not the best parent. But everything else, everything that matters about me being his mom—that's where what I want doesn't matter."

"I think it does, only you won't accept that."

Almost snappishly, she replied, "You know as well as I do, when you have a child, you don't think about your needs over his."

Nick challenged, "My son doesn't need what you just felt a minute ago. Admit it."

"A person doesn't need what they don't think about."

"I think," he said, drifting toward her, "that you think about it a lot."

Lauren licked her lips, was on the verge of arguing against his assumption, then resigned herself to the verity of his statement. Sometimes if she said a truth aloud, she could handle it better, face it head-on and move forward. "You're right. I think about it, I miss it. I want it. Right now, I want to have sex with you."

His eyes darkened. "You're wrong. I don't want to have sex with you. I want to make love to you. There's a difference."

Lauren sucked in a breath, his words clutching her heart and making her want to believe there could be more...

She knew he'd held back for her sake, wanted to embrace him for his consideration, but was afraid she'd send the wrong message.

Flustered, she couldn't confront the feelings running rampant throughout her head. Better to take the sensible approach, the more analytical side of things.

"But I also have to look at the reality of my life," she added. "At twenty-nine, I realized that there was only one person I could count on. Me. I might have gone to the Saunders when I found out I was pregnant, but Bob suffered a stroke that year and Betty had all she could do to take care of him. I couldn't have imposed in their home, and I didn't tell them about Billy until he was six months old. By then, I'd gotten the rhythm of parenting on my own. No help."

So many regrets. She should have told them. They would have made room for her, taken her in. Her life might be different. But she couldn't turn back the clock and play what-if. There was only one place to go—forward.

She learned from trials, learned from errors. She had no right to, but when Nick didn't readily comment, she dared add something further. "Your ex-wife."

Nick's chin shot up, giving her his full attention.

"At least she wants to see your son. Billy's father wrote him off when he was a baby." Lauren could see the lines of tension coming to play across Nick's face.

She elaborated, "Billy hasn't grown in certain ways because he doesn't have a father's influence in his life. A strong male for him to look up to. Dunk's been pretty patient with him in the store, but it's not the same thing. I understand you don't want your ex-wife to win custody of Nicky-J—and I agree—but maybe she deserves a chance to get to know her son better. Spend more time with him."

"You don't know anything about it," he returned, his voice a low growl. She flinched, an abrupt blink of her eyes. "Let me see how you'd react if Billy's father wanted to take him from you."

"I'd be upset."

"Damn straight."

"I'm just saying that at least she wants to be in his life."

"That's not how she wanted it five and a half years ago."

With muscles corded and tight, Nick pulled himself out of the spa, walked through the open glass doors and disappeared.

Lauren stood for extended minutes, her hands trembling and her heartbeat sounding in her ears. She'd said too much, she knew that. She'd imposed her opinion—uninvited. Conclusions had been formed based on her own experiences and she'd upset Nick. That hadn't been her intention and she wished she'd said nothing at all.

Why did this happen? Why did she push away the people she cared about? All her life she didn't get close, and on those few times she had, she'd learned that heartache wasn't invincible. She'd been hurt, crushed, on more than one occasion.

She'd promised herself she wouldn't do it to others, and yet, she'd just done it with Nick. The one person who seemed to have true feelings about her, about Billy.

Going inside, Lauren dressed and found Nick pacing in the kitchen, drinking a beer.

"Nick, I'm sorry," she said, breaking through the silence in the room and wanting to reach out to him; but she knew enough to keep her distance. "You're right—I don't know what you're feeling. I wish I did—"

She turned, saw Billy and Nicky-J entering the house with Caprice not far behind.

Anything she would have said to Nick was cut short.

After Caprice said hello, she followed Nicky-J, who wanted to show his grandma a baseball he'd gotten in California. Billy was left with Lauren and Nick.

Billy gazed at them through his heavily framed glasses, then broke into a nose-wrinkling smile. "You were talking about Nicky-J's surprise party, weren't you?"

Nick's eyebrows came together. "Surprise party?"

"He told me you're planning a party for him."

"What gave him that idea?"

"He said you're always whispering to his grandma and grandpa and then you get quiet when he comes into the room. Like right now, you and Mom stopped talking when I came into the room."

Nick's jaw clenched, a muscle ticked at the corner of his mouth.

Lauren ached for him. She knew he was experiencing a rush of emotions, the first of which was that time had run out.

He had to tell his son what was going on.

"Brush your teeth, dude." Nick leaned into the bathroom doorway, folded his arms across his chest as his son spread paste over a colorful toothbrush.

"I got a splinter today, Dad," he said while scrubbing his teeth.

"You get it out?"

"With my toothes."

Nick worked hard to remain steady, his heartbeat slamming him in the ribs. "Break the skin?"

"Yeah, but I don't need a Band-Aid." He rinsed then wiped his face on the towel, leaving a smear of green mint paste. A glob of toothpaste remained in the sink, something Nick would have normally commented on. He let it slide tonight.

Nicky-J went into his bedroom, cleared the toys off his bed with a shake of his bedspread and lay down in the racing car. Nick had built the bed for him, painted it yellow and red like a Hot Wheels. A twin mattress fit perfectly inside and the covers had a competition stripe down the middle. His mom had sewn the bedspread.

His son's room was a mix of everything colorful. Posters on the walls, inline skates on the floor, a hockey stick in the corner. He liked all sports, had a baseball collection and a basket of elbow pads that he never remembered to wear. Nick liked to come in here at night when his son was sleeping and watch him.

A tightness closed Nick's throat as he clicked off the light. The faint yellow glow from a night-light illuminated the wall at the baseboard.

When Nick's eyes adjusted to the meager light, he moved forward.

"Nicky-J, shove over a little." Nick sat down, his long legs awkward over the twin bed's side.

Nicky-J's face blanched, his eyes darting swiftly away from his father's. "I didn't break nothin', Dad."

Nick put his hand on his son's shoulder, little-boy muscles hard beneath his palm. "I know you didn't."

"What's the matter then?"

The breath Nick let out was a shudder. His pulse lurched, a knot in his stomach tightening. "Buddy, I have to tell you something."

Nicky-J fell quiet and listened as Nick went on.

"Billy said you think you're having a surprise party."

With a pout, his son murmured, "I'm not having a surpriseth party, I can tell from the way you're lookin' at me. All the whisperin' is 'cause I *am* in trouble."

Nick leaned down and pressed his mouth against his son's forehead for reassurance. Soap and shampoo lingered on his soft skin, the spikes of his hair from his fresh summer buzz cut. It wrenched Nick's spirit, disquiet in his tone. "You aren't in any trouble."

"Yeah…I am." He grew quiet, then confessed, "I broked one of Grandma's ladies." Nick's mom decorated her flower beds with fairies. Nicky-J frowned remorsefully. "I didn't want to get in trouble so I buried the arm. I'm sorry, Dad. Are you gonna yell at me?"

"No."

"Why not?" His voice sounded worried.

"I love you very much," Nick began, plumping the bed's pillows and making sure Nicky-J was tucked in.

"I love you, too."

There had never been a macho wall preventing either of them from getting "mushy"—as Nicky-J called it. Nick had taught his son to speak his feelings. He'd always have a right to the way he felt and it would never hurt him if he was open about them.

"Your mom loves you, too."

"I know, Dad."

"We both love you."

"I know, Dad." His lower lip trembled slightly.

"Your mom and I both love you so much, we both want you to live with us."

"I do, Dad. I live with you and I live with her sometimes, too."

"But your mom wishes you'd live with her more." Nick blew out a hot breath, steeling himself. "She wants you to spend more time in California."

He blinked, sniffed. "Do I gotta?"

Nick swallowed, collected himself. "Do you know what a judge is?"

"Yeah. That lady on the TV who's always yellin' at people and callin' them stoopid."

"Well, she's one kind of judge. There are other kinds, too. There's a family-court judge. He decides where kids live."

"How come the kids can't decide? I wanna stay here."

"Sometimes it's complicated when the daddy and the mommy both want the little boy to live with them. The judge has to help them decide."

"I already decided. I wanna stay with you."

"I want that, too. And I'm hoping that's how the judge will see it. But he might not. So I wanted you to know that maybe it might turn out that you start living with your mom more." Nick ran his hand beneath his nose, sniffled. He closed out the heat in his eyes. "I don't want you to worry about it. Everything is going to work out."

Nicky-J sat up and threw his arms around Nick's neck. "I want it to work it out with you, Daddy."

"Me, too, buddy."

"Can you p-promise?" His voice cracked.

Nick's jaw ached. "I can promise that your mom loves you just as much as I do."

Nicky-J's body shook as he sobbed into Nick's collarbone. His small hands made hard fists, clinging to his dad's T-shirt. "I don't wanna live with my mom. I wanna stay with you and Grandma and Grandpa. I don't wanna go to California. I don't care about Mickey Mouse. I don't wanna leave. Tell the judge I'm not going."

Nick let his son cry it out until he grew exhausted.

"I want my sipper cup," he mumbled.

Going into the kitchen, Nick poured milk into the plastic-lidded cup Nicky-J had graduated to when he got off his bottle. The blue sippy cup was a nighttime comfort for his son, much like a blanket or a stuffed animal.

Nicky-J had stopped sucking his thumb at age two, but hadn't been able to give up the milk. Every morning, the cup was empty. He drank it in the middle of the night, not aware he'd even woken to take a drink.

Nick handed the cup to Nicky-J, who took a sip, then set it on the nightstand. Shifting his pillow, he showed Nick what he'd put beneath it while he was in the kitchen.

"I got my tommy-hawk under my pillow and if the judge comes to get me, I'm going to chop 'im up." He settled his cheek on his pillow, stared at the wall with the night-light, then took another drink of milk.

Nick stroked his son's back, his hair, rubbed him and soothed him until some time later, after Nicky-J's eyes drifted closed, Nick laid down in the narrow bed beside his little boy. He stretched out, Nicky-J's warmth burning into his chest.

Nick had held on to a weighted grief with the last grasp of resolve he could maintain. Everything that he had locked so tightly inside him came seeping out.

Like a dam with a slow crack that eventually gave way, Nick released all the pain inside his heart.

The broken sound of his raw sob startled him.

In the darkened room, with the smell of Nicky-J cloaked around him, Nick DiMartino quietly cried.

Eleven

Even the moon has dog days.

Salty white foam rolled over Billy's bare feet. The surf rushed next to his ankles, through his legs, and washed sand from under his heels. He held out his arms to balance himself, liking the rushing-fast feeling of icy-cold water and warm summer air, the smells of the ocean and its sounds. If he could swim far out into the ocean, he'd bet he could find a whale.

Dunk and Sam were in the water surfing. Billy waved to them. It was okay for Billy to be by the water as long as Dunk was watching.

Him, Nicky-J, Tim and Critter came to the beach to hunt for things people forgot when they went home at the end of the day. So far, they'd found some coins, three beer-bottle caps, a baseball hat and a radio battery.

Critter poked a stick at some fish guts, flies swarming up from the stinky bone pile. "Sick," he hollered,

AN IMPORTANT MESSAGE FROM THE EDITORS

Dear Reader,

Because you've chosen to read one of our fine books, we'd like to say "thank you"! And, as a **special** way to thank you, we're offering you a choice of <u>two more</u> of the books you love so well, **and** a surprise gift to send you— absolutely **FREE!**

Please enjoy them with our compliments...

Pam Powers

Peel off seal and Place inside...

What's Your Reading Pleasure...
ROMANCE? _OR_ SUSPENSE?

Do you prefer spine-tingling page turners OR heart-stirring stories about love and relationships? Tell us which books you enjoy – and you'll get **2 FREE "ROMANCE" BOOKS or 2 FREE "SUSPENSE" BOOKS with no obligation to purchase anything.**

Choose **"ROMANCE"** and get **2 FREE BOOKS** that will fuel your imagination with intensely moving stories about life, love and relationships.

FREE!

Choose **"SUSPENSE"** and you'll get **2 FREE BOOKS** that will thrill you with a spine-tingling blend of suspense and mystery.

FREE!

Whichever category you select, your 2 free books have a combined cover price of $11.98 or more in the U.S. and $13.98 or more in Canada.

And remember... just for accepting the Editor's Free Gift Offer, we'll send you 2 books and a gift, ABSOLUTELY FREE!

YOURS FREE!
We'll send you a fabulous surprise gift absolutely FREE, just for trying "Romance" or "Suspense"!

® and TM are registered trademarks of Harlequin Enterprises Limited.

Visit us online at
www.FreeBooksandGift.com

THE EDITOR'S "THANK YOU" FREE GIFTS INCLUDE:

▶ 2 Romance OR 2 Suspense books

▶ An exciting surprise gift

YES! I have placed my Editor's "thank you" Free Gifts seal in the space provided above. Please send me the 2 FREE books which I have selected, and my FREE Mystery Gift. I understand that I am under no obligation to purchase anything further, as explained on the back and opposite page.

Check one:

ROMANCE	
193 MDL DVFN	393 MDL DVFQ

SUSPENSE	
192 MDL DVFM	392 MDL DVFP

FIRST NAME   LAST NAME

ADDRESS

APT.#   CITY

STATE/PROV.   ZIP/POSTAL CODE

▶ DETACH AND MAIL CARD TODAY! ▶

(BB2-04) © 1998 MIRA BOOKS

The Reader Service — Here's How It Works:

Accepting your 2 free books and gift places you under no obligation to buy anything. You may keep the books and gift and return the shipping statement marked "cancel." If you do not cancel, about a month later we'll send you 3 additional books and bill you just $4.74 each in the U.S., or $5.24 each in Canada, plus 25¢ shipping & handling per book and applicable taxes if any.* That's the complete price and — compared to cover prices starting from $5.99 each in the U.S. and $6.99 each in Canada — it's quite a bargain! You may cancel at any time, but if you choose to continue, every month we'll send you 3 more books, which you may either purchase at the discount price or return to us and cancel your subscription.

*Terms and prices subject to change without notice. Sales tax applicable in N.Y. Canadian residents will be charged applicable provincial taxes and GST.

If offer card is missing write to: The Reader Service, 3010 Walden Ave., P.O. Box 1867, Buffalo, NY 14240-1867 stirring the smelly mess as insects winged skyward. "You guys, look. There's a fish head with eyeballs."

Nicky-J, who was usually the first to be on the scene of something that smelled really bad or looked really bad, didn't rush over.

Something had been bothering Nicky-J for three days.

He sat on one of the rocks, his bare feet tucked under him and his chin on his knees, a pair of board shorts hiked up on his thighs. He had a scab on one knee and his left finger was bandaged. He had to get stitches yesterday on his finger because he accidentally cut himself with a piece of sheet metal they'd dragged off his dad's job—without his dad knowing they'd taken it. Only now, his dad found out because of the hospital.

The bandage was made of blue tape and he'd written his name on it. Nicky-J said his dad hadn't gotten mad at him for hurting his finger. His dad hugged him after they were done in the E.R. that smelled like medicine, then he let him have a cheeseburger, fries and a chocolate shake, with a king-size bag of any candy he wanted.

Sometimes Billy wondered if he hurt himself again, like with the wasps, if he'd get special attention. Not counting how scared he was at first, he liked when he was in the hospital because he got to watch TV whenever he wanted, ring a button for the nurse to bring him a book or soda pop—any flavor, mostly 7-Up. But even with special attention, and maybe a cheeseburger on the way home, he was afraid to go back to the hospital. He knew his mom didn't have extra money to pay big bills, so Billy tried his hardest not to play with dangerous stuff. Sometimes he forgot.

"I already seen fish eyeballs before." Nicky-J jumped down and wandered over to the water's edge beside Billy.

"We can collect floats," Billy suggested, then pointed to the wharf where the captain of the *Morning Star* waved at them. "Cap'n Mike said any glass fishing-net floats we find under the pier we can have. So we wouldn't get in trouble."

"I don't feel like it," Nicky-J replied.

Tim and Critter came over, a dog suddenly appearing with them.

"Hey, whose dog is that?" Billy bent down on one knee and petted the scruffy reddish tan dog that wagged its stump of a tail. He smelled like dead seaweed, his fur all tight and twisted in spots. The dog had the brownest, biggest eyes, and a black nose that was cold and wet against Billy's cheek when he hugged him.

"I dunno," Critter said. "He just showed up this morning at our house and we can't shake him off. I thought we ditched him when we came here. Guess not."

"You don't think he has a home?" Billy felt the dog's neck for a collar. He wasn't wearing one.

"Maybe he does." Tim patted the dog's head. "I saw him over at Moon Cycle sniffing in their garbage. Could be he belongs to Otto or Nubs."

Just when Billy wanted to reach around the dog's neck and hug him again, stink and all, the dog ran up the beach to chase birds. He barked at the squawking gulls, then at the skinny-legged sandpipers, before taking a pee on a rock and bolting over the dunes and disappearing.

Billy felt an empty pit digging in his stomach, like when he drank too much soda and needed to burp but couldn't get one up his throat. He liked that dog, even though it was dirty and might have belonged to Nubs, the guy who painted the motorcycles.

Critter sank onto his knees in the sand, his face sunburned with a peppering of freckles. "I'm hungry. Anybody got anything to eat?"

Tim checked his pockets, came up with a rubber ant, one hunk of bubble gum—unwrapped—and bluejeans lint. He popped the linty gum into his mouth. "Nope," he replied, working around the wad of bubble gum.

Nicky-J didn't respond, Billy shrugged. Critter got up and held on to his stomach. "If I don't eat, I'm gonna be sick from not eating. Mom's got a whole box of Ding Dongs."

"She does? Let's go home." Tim's eyes got real big.

"Sure. You guys want to come over, too?"

"Nah." Nicky-J pitched a seashell fragment into the churning water. A gray-and-white seagull with beady eyes went after it, must have thought it was a potato chip.

Billy could tell something was bugging Nicky-J. Even though he would like to have a Ding Dong, he declined. "Me neither."

Critter called, already halfway up the dunes, "Then see you guys later."

Nicky-J sat down, his board shorts wet at the knees from where the ocean hit him high on the legs. He didn't mind, he never even rolled his pants up like Billy. Nothing bothered Nicky-J, he was never scared of anything. Not like Billy who worried lots about doing something that would upset his mom, like losing his glasses.

At that moment Billy took his glasses off, rubbed the lenses clean with his cape, then squinted out to sea. Everything was blurry. The water, the sky, the sunshine and the sand. There were times when seeing things all fuzzy was better than clear. It meant he didn't have to figure stuff out so hard because there was nothing for him to try to figure out. His head got tired of thinking, so he'd take a rest. By being in Bella Luna, he was having more resting than thinking. He liked it here, he didn't ever want to leave. So he had to make sure that his mom would be happy here.

Billy slipped his glasses back on. The world around him came into focus again. Abalone shells glittered in the sand, their insides more colorful than a rainbow of Skittles candy.

The cape around Billy's shoulders felt annoying, bothersome. With a jerk, he swept the edges behind him so he wouldn't be reminded he wore it. Sometimes it was hard to hold on to magic powers. Sometimes he didn't want them anymore. He wished he could be a regular kid, like Nicky-J.

"You okay, Nicky-J?" Billy only asked when Nicky-J's eyes got watery, like he'd just sneezed or coughed. Only Billy knew that wasn't what happened because he'd been sitting next to Nicky-J all this time.

His friend was quiet a long time. Billy let him be quiet, because there were times when he liked to be quiet himself.

After a few waves crashed onto the shore, wetting Nicky-J's legs and shorts even worse, he finally said something in a really soft voice. "There's no surprise party for me."

"There isn't?"

"My dad told me that my mom wants me to live with her."

Billy had to take a minute to figure this one out. His

dad had never asked him to live with him. He didn't know his dad, never met him before. Nicky-J was lucky to know who his mom was. He'd seen her picture at Nicky-J's house before. She was real pretty. She had a new husband now, so Nicky-J had two dads and that just didn't seem fair when other kids didn't even have one.

Puzzled, Billy asked, "How come you don't want to do that?"

Nicky-J's face turned sour. "I want to live with my dad."

"How come you can't live with both of them?"

"Because they don't live together. My mom lives in Losangels and my dad lives here. I don't want to move to Calif-thornia."

Billy didn't understand the problem. "Then don't move."

"But I gotta do what the judge says. If she says I gotta live with my mom, I gotta. But I'll run away if she says I have to. I won't go to my mom's house. I don't wanna…" His lower lip went rubbery like a jellyfish.

"You can't just say you want to be with your dad?"

"No. My dad said the judge decides. I hate her."

"The judge?"

"My mom."

Billy's heartbeat slowed, skipped. "Don't ever say you hate your mom."

"What do you know, your mom is nice and you don't have a dad to take you away."

It was Billy's turn to feel like crying. "I want a dad."

"How come you don't have one?"

"He never wanted to be my dad, even when I was a baby. I must have been a bad baby for him not to want to be with me." Billy had no idea what his dad looked like, his mom had never showed him a picture. She said she didn't have any.

Nicky-J checked to make sure he had his red Ferrari Spider in his pocket, then wiped his nose. "It's that bitch of a moon."

"Huh?" Billy had never heard a kid swear before, and it wasn't like Nicky-J to cuss.

"It's the moon. That's what my grandpa says when things are bad."

Billy felt awful for him.

Nicky-J went on, "I don't wanna visit my mom this summer, 'cause she might keep me there and I'll never come back here."

Billy chewed on his lip, thought about what he could do to cheer up his friend. Without reluctance, he reached inside his pocket and handed over his best treasure. "Nicky-J, you can have your horse's tooth back. Maybe it's good luck for you. Nothing like this happened when you had it."

Nicky-J didn't take the offering. "I don't want it. I want my dad." Tears rolled down his dirt-smudged cheeks and Billy was thrown into a situation he'd never been in before—another kid was crying and it was up to him to help him out.

Billy had never had a friend like this, he'd never been so close to a boy his age. And for good reason. That reason stayed inside him, tight and closed off in a dark space because it hurt him too much to think about all the mean names he'd been called.

But he sensed that Nicky-J wouldn't call him anything mean or make fun of him. And even if he did, Billy supposed it was worth it since it would make Nicky-J feel better.

"You want to know why I wear this superhero cape?" Billy's question wasn't answered at first, Nicky-J was too busy wiping his nose on the sleeve of his shirt. Then, finally, he looked at Billy, his eyes sparkling and the underpart of his nose red.

"Because it's magic," Nicky-J supplied, his tone flat like the bottom of a drinking glass.

"That's what I told you, but there's another reason. The *real* reason."

"What is it?"

Billy, keeping his lips together and knowing there was no going back now, reached behind him for the cape's edge and he brought it forward. Inside the narrow seam, running down the front part, was a secret pouch, a pocket. There was a long, hard tube inside. It was as long as a pencil and round as a penny.

He took the tube out and showed Nicky-J—who had no idea what it was.

"It's my epinephrine pen."

"An ep-frun? What's that for?"

"It saves my life."

Nicky-J's blue eyes narrowed and he leaned in. "What's it do?"

"If I get stung by a bee or wasp, I take it out of the tube, then see that gray part on the end? I take it off, then hold it like this—" he demonstrated with his right hand, holding firmly "—and then I give myself a shot in the thigh through my pants. My mom makes me practice."

"There's a needle in it?"

"Yes, with medicine inside."

Examining the epinephrine pen, Nicky-J held on to the tube as if he was afraid he'd accidentally give himself a shot—even though that was impossible. "Why don't you keep it in your pocket instead of wearing that cape?"

"It's too big to fit in my pocket." Billy demonstrated, about four inches of the pen protruding. "See. I can't keep it there because I might lose it." He slipped the pen back inside his cape. "I'd rather have kids making fun of me for my cape than knowing I'm scared of wasps and bees. Boys aren't supposed to be afraid of anything."

"I'm sometimes afraid of the dark." Nicky-J swatted a tear off his cheek; Billy pretended he didn't notice. "Now I'm afraid of havin' to live with my mom and not my dad."

Both boys stared into the ocean, the sun a globe of orange that sizzled over the blue-green horizon.

Wasps and Calif-thornia—they were both bad things that could make a kid cry.

On Friday Lauren had thrown together a simple spaghetti and a salad, left both dishes on the counter and hadn't been there when Nick came home.

After the way they'd left things on Thursday, she feared she wouldn't be good company for him so she'd made herself scarce.

Come Monday, she confronted her inane thinking. She had to stop doing this—running from people and places that felt too good to be true.

She realized this when she talked with the Saunderses over the weekend. Hearing their voices always brought her a sense of being grounded. Strange how she'd spent a year of her life with them, and she'd never been able to call them Mom and Dad. It was easier thinking of them as the Saunderses, or Betty and Bob.

Lauren didn't talk about anything between her and Nick, but she'd given them an update on Bella Luna, having sent them her new address over a month ago. Their encouraging words fell on her heart like warm water, giving her the reassurance she needed, not knowing how badly she needed it until after hanging up the phone.

Now, as she closed the diner, her heartbeat thumped steadily in her ears. Billy was at the movies tonight with Verna Mae. Verna Mae said she wanted to see that new full-length Disney movie and she thought Billy would enjoy coming with her.

Lauren had written Nick a note on his lunch ticket this afternoon, asking him to meet her on the pier at eight-thirty when she left work. She had no idea if he'd come or not, since she'd been surprised that he ate in the diner for lunch rather than take his meal to go. He'd sat at her station with his brother Danny but there hadn't been a moment to talk in a meaningful way during the rush.

Lou cleaned the grill, scrubbed down the floor, then stubbed out his cigarette on the bottom of his boot before lighting a fresh one for the road.

"You done yet?" he asked, whipping off his soiled apron and tossing it into the laundry bin Verna Mae kept by the back door. All the dirty kitchen towels, cook aprons and floor cloths went in there. She said that nobody did laundry the way she did, with bleach booster. Claimed that the Wharf would never get a bad health inspection so long as she owned it, and true to her word, that's how it had been for years.

"I'm ready." Lauren snagged her purse, removed her

apron, as well. The waitresses were in charge of their own uniforms. She wished she wasn't wearing the gray dress and stained tennis shoes to meet Nick. She slid her arms into her sweater, left the front unbuttoned, and walked through the door.

They locked the diner, Lou taking off into the night, no doubt to have a drink at the Outrigger. Actually, more than one drink. The man wasn't reliable and would probably have a hangover tomorrow and not show up for work.

The sound of waves rolling onto the shore was a soothing tempo to slow her racing heart. A mugginess claimed the evening air. Pink neon lights spelled out Ice Cream in the diner window; the coils buzzed as she walked past.

She arrived at the pier and headed toward the end, relieved to see a man's silhouette at its far end—the place where fishermen dropped their lines. The backdrop behind Nick was a hazy, full-circled pink moon making its once-monthly appearance.

The moon did its best to illuminate him, but the closer she got, she realized she could only marginally make out his features. All she could see was his rugged profile, the kind portrayed in one of those cigarette commercials. She half expected to see a curl of smoke coming from his lips, a Marlboro clamped between them.

There was something about him... Every time she was near him, heat tracked across her skin and baby-fine hairs tingled pleasantly at her nape. She drew closer, trying to smile nonchalantly as if this weren't any big deal for her when, in fact, her pulse skipped at her wrist like the pinball game they'd played at Wong's Pizzeria.

"Hi," she said, stopping beside him, her words floating into the crescendo of the breaking waves beneath them.

"Hey." His cheekbones set off his face in an angular, masculine way that made her throat go dry.

A puddle of moonlight surrounded them, and the strangest thing, she could swear she heard an Italian ballad coming from Wong's—even though the kitchen lights were dim and the dining room closed.

"I got your note. I wanted to talk to you, too," Nick said, his words penetrating her heart.

Her mind went soft, she felt like a cream puff—all sticky and gooey with not much substance.

"Thanks for coming."

"Sure." Both his hands were jammed into the pockets of his black leather jacket.

So much for small talk. She breathed in his scent, loving the smell of his skin—a natural hint of sawdust, shampoo and a kind of musky soap. She recalled how strong and hard he'd felt next to her in the hot tub. What he'd given her had been a gift, something so special…she'd thought about him, about that night almost constantly ever since.

No matter how much potential she thought she had, she never fully believed herself. Nick gave her resolute confidence she hardly recognized and a piece of something she was missing—a truth about herself.

She was lonely.

And so was he. She could see it across his face and in the way he stood.

Even with Billy, she had a woman's longing, an emptiness in her body that ached to be filled. Like a shipwrecked soul, she'd been thirsty for what he offered, taking and sating herself until she could fill herself no more. She hadn't asked what he needed, sex aside, if maybe he just wanted to be held. Instead, she'd spoken across lines and boundaries. She hated upsetting him about his son, about his ex-wife. She had no business doing that. She was here to offer her apologies.

"Nick, I wanted to say I'm sorry about what I said the other night. I truly don't know how you're feeling, I can only guess." When he didn't add anything, she rambled on. "When I said that you should be grateful your ex-wife wants to see Nicky-J, I didn't mean that she should take him from you. I'm sorry, I wish I hadn't said anything at all."

The pounding surf crashed, thundered against the rocks below, before sliding, like a whisper, back into the sea. Bells on a buoy clanged, the lighthouse light circled softly in a muted sky filled with a blue so deep, it was nearly pitch black.

Nick didn't respond.

Lauren feared she might be losing something before she even had it.

There was no hostility, no sarcasm in his voice when he finally spoke. "You don't know how it is with me and Debbie. I can't blame you for what you said, Lauren."

"Tell me." The gentle coaching in her tone wafted through the night air. "I'd like to understand."

Nick turned toward the ocean, resting his arms on the railing made smooth by years of wind and rain. Clasping his fingers together he brooded, his face lit by the moon.

She grew mesmerized, drinking in his features and memorizing every detail. The set of his full mouth, the corner of his jaw where it clenched.

"I met Debbie in Los Angeles. I was thirty-one, she was twenty-four and in beauty school."

No wonder the woman came across so put-together in her photos. She was a beauty specialist. Lauren tamped down the sudden, and unreasonable, feeling of inadequacy.

"We dated for two years, busy schedules and both of us going in our own directions. I was doing a Housing and Urban Development project that took a lot of my time, while she tried to get started in the movie industry. She wanted to be a hair and makeup artist, and was starting to make some headway, small assignments, then she found out she was pregnant with Nick. It was a surprise to both of us, but one I was happy about."

Lauren realized his son's conception had been an exact parallel to her own son's.

"We got married. Debbie kept working, was getting some jobs, but after Nicky-J, she was tied to the house. She said she needed help, she was exhausted. I was sick of the city, ready to be with my family again and make a quieter life. I suggested we move to Bella Luna.

"I thought she was fine with it, she seemed okay to make the sacrifice, put her career on hold. My parents welcomed her, we bought a house on Seaside Road, a fixer-upper that I worked on when I could. Danny and I started the restoration company and my first project was the cottages."

He continued in a low and direct voice. "My life was really great. I loved having a baby boy." A smile caught the corners of his mouth, curving and widening. His teeth were white in the murky dark, his expression distant yet happy.

"I thought she could be content here, she said as much when she came. She had ambitions of opening a salon in town, doing hair and makeup, but Bella Luna never held her attention and she soon realized her grander dreams would die here." A gentle wind picked up Nick's hair. He ran his fingers through it, smoothing it, his profile hardening. "She left him when he wasn't even six months old. How a mother could just do that— I don't get it. I never will. She carried him for nine months, she had to feel something for him. I know she loves him, but I'm talking about something deeper."

Lauren kept her silence, staring mutely at him.

"We never filed for joint custody, she didn't want him that way. After our divorce, I told her she could see him anytime she wanted. She came a few times before his first birthday, then her visits tapered off. She got into a job in L.A., started her own business and it took off. I don't begrudge her her success, but I damn well take it personally when she comes back into Nicky-J's life and wants to pull him out of my house, the one I created just for me and Nicky-J. I sold the other place, couldn't stand to live in it." A rage lit into Nick's eyes, a fire that grew hotter as he turned toward her. "So when you said I should let my son get to know her, I honestly don't think she deserves the chance. I've let Nicky-J go visit her, I put up with some shit she gave me, because I do think a boy ought to know his mom—but what she's trying to do to me, to us, I won't forgive her for it. I'm going to fight her with everything I have. I'll make her life so hard, she's going to wish she never started this. And if that makes me a son of a bitch, then fine."

Lauren gulped back potent emotions. Something

more than compassion drew Nick inside her heart. She felt a deeper sense of connection to him, beyond anything physical.

Neither of them spoke for a few moments, Lauren thinking that she'd never felt closer to another person, had never felt their emotions in the way she felt Nick's.

She leaned closer to him, dared to touch his shoulder. The finely tooled leather was cool and smooth beneath her fingertips. "If there's anything I can do. If you need a character witness…I've seen you with Nicky-J and there isn't a better father. Nick, I want you to know, I'm on your side."

His eyes turned the color of the moonlit ocean, a velvety blue. "I know. That's why I wanted you to understand exactly where I was coming from the other night. Why I got so pissed off at you."

She nodded.

The boardwalk beneath her felt solid, firm. She stood tall, was glad he'd come and glad they'd cleared the air.

But her resolve went spineless, as if she were a jellyfish, as soon as he said, "So you made me spaghetti—from a jar, and a salad out of a cellophane bag. Bottled dressing." A teasing note lifted his tone. "Hell, I could have done that myself."

She had indeed done a "quick" job of dinner. She'd wanted to be in and out of his house before he got home. "I was hoping you wouldn't notice."

He smiled easily, the leather jacket and white shirt beneath taking her breath. "I noticed."

"I'll make up for it tomorrow." She had to crack a dumb, ineffectual joke. "My creativity was on the blink."

"Right." His face sobered, their interplay turning serious once more. "You're not off the hook all the way, you know."

"I'm not?"

"No. I want to know your story. You and Billy's father."

Excuses gathered in her head, a wall began to build around her trust genes. "It's late and I—"

He put a finger over her lips. "Not tonight. I need to get home. You've got to pick up Billy from my mom's."

Relief surged, but with it, confusion. He gave up too easily.

"Fourth of July's this Friday. Spend it with me and my family. We'll do the beach thing, we do it every year. I'm bringing my telescope, you bring the coordinates and we'll find Billy's star."

Without her answer, he brought her closer, held her in his arms and stroked her hair. He smelled incredible, while she had the lingering scents of grease and gravy on her dress, on her shoes.

She looked up at him, at the night sky, and saw so many things she wanted to have. It seemed he was offering the most simple of them all—his company, and all she had to do was take it.

"I'd like that."

"Good. You need a break from the Wharf," he noted. "Your serving technique is off. You gave me decaf today for lunch."

"The pots look the same to me. You should have asked for another cup."

"The first one tasted bad enough."

"I'm sorry. I feel awful I didn't please the customer."

"Don't worry about it, you please me plenty."

Gooseflesh rose across her skin, her body felt overly warm. "I might be insightful about what's supposed to be done or not done, but I'm not a very good waitress. I've been trying to convince Verna Mae I'm a much better cook."

"I know." He caught her dismayed expression and added, "Come on, let's get out of here."

They walked back toward the diner, side by side, shoulders touching with every other step. She felt in sync with someone for the first time, a normal rhythm with another body.

Tonight was the start of something wonderful and promising, something Lauren welcomed without an ounce of resistance.

Twelve

It was a good night for moon gazing.

Swag banners in red, white and blue draped over the railings of the Tidewater Motel and every other downtown business in Bella Luna. Flags waved everywhere, from Victorian homes to Otto's Moon Cycles. Everyone was bit by the patriotic bug.

The day started with a pancake breakfast sponsored by the Allegiance Fishermen's Association. Anthony DiMartino flipped his traditional creation, started some ten years ago as a joke but it caught on: the sardine pancake. Nubs put away a tall stack with syrup.

At one o'clock, the annual dinghy boat and balloon-capture race commenced. The boats were manned with oars, and whoever's team collected the most red, white and blue balloons with a fishing net was proclaimed the winner of a dinner at Wong's Pizzeria—a family feed with three pies, unlimited toppings and all the soft drinks and salad they could eat.

Children ran along the wet sand with their faces painted in Fourth of July themes; the adults conversed around a fire pit and roasted hot dogs in the wind shelters of grass-covered dunes. The Lions Club gave away sparklers and safety lighter sticks.

By secret ballot, Otis Duncan was declared Mayor for the Day and was presented with a stars-and-stripes baseball cap. With a ripple in his mustache, he angled the brim on his head just right and thanked the commissioners. His duties consisted of being the grand marshal in the parade and judging the boat-decorating contest.

The Seal Avenue parade started at three, the Bella Luna Convalescent Hospital winning the Drill Team division with the best wheelchair formations. Knox Dugan, the cook at the Wharf Diner, won for best costume; he dressed himself as a psychedelic Abraham Lincoln with a red, white and blue stovepipe hat. The entire Bella Luna Engine Company 11 emptied the firehouse and participated, sirens wailing and lights flashing as the firefighters tossed candy to the spectators.

In the marina, salmon trawlers and tuna boats clustered and rocked on swells; masts and decks were festooned with strings of lights and streamers. Pelicans flapped their wings, watching the fishing fleet with curiosity, bills flapping in readiness in case a net appeared with something they could plunder.

Lauren and Billy were on Anthony DiMartino's fishing boat, *Lady Caprice,* decorating the stern with paper lanterns. Nick had climbed the mast and was putting miniflags on the deer antlers. He heard Billy ask why there were deer horns up there, and his dad said that in ancient Sicilian times the fishermen thought the horns brought luck, and since it worked for a thousand years, Anthony had always had them on his masthead.

After the boat was decorated, Nick threw some baseballs for the boys. He waited to see if Lauren would object, but she folded her arms across her chest and shrugged her okay. Billy didn't have a natural sports bone in his body, the poor kid was left traipsing down the shoreline after missed balls. But he loved playing, loved the feel of that glove in his hand, and would have run after sliders for hours if Nick's arm hadn't given out.

The colors were presented at sundown, the crowd growing somber and reflective as they sang the national anthem. A molten sunset intensified, eating up the blue sky, and a liveliness came to light in the dusk.

When nightfall curtained the sky, the waning moon gazed down upon a shoreline that looked as if shooting stars were erupting from the sand—fiery bursts of multicolors, flying and circling into the darkness.

Nick had Lauren sit on a folding chair he'd brought down to the beach, Nicky-J and Billy were on the blanket. They watched as the boats came from the harbor, around the wharf to the point where everyone was sitting. The festive lights lit the ocean, twinkling and shining. High-pitched horns blew, sails whipped and the low hum of engines churned the ocean.

Dunk had a hard time choosing a winner, settling on Captain Mike's tuna boat made out to be a mermaid.

After the boats came in, the fireworks on the beach started. John and Danny went overboard and bought several boxes' worth. His brothers might be closet pyros with all the Screaming Toads and Big Dragons they spent money on. Danny was like a kid setting off skyrockets into the air, him and John fighting over who'd light the next one. Nicky-J and Billy got into the thick of things, picking out which fireworks they wanted Nicky-J's uncles to set off.

The bright bursts of color illuminated Lauren's face as she gazed skyward. Nick held out his hand, lifting her to her feet.

"Let's take a walk."

Her fingers felt slight in his grasp, his grip tightening as they left the crowds and noise behind.

The cool, soft sand soothed Nick's feet. He'd slipped out of his flip-flops hours ago. A lightweight pair of shorts covered his legs and a Tommy Bahama camp shirt floated around his middle.

The night was still, a marginal breeze barely moving the tall grasses.

Nick was completely focused on the woman beside him, the brief message from Bruce Harmon on his cell phone forgotten. It hadn't been urgent; Bruce said he needed to run some preliminary testimony past him. Nick had meant to call his lawyer back, but got busy on the job site. He'd catch Bruce first thing Monday.

"So," Nick said through the sound of water sluicing onto the shore. "It's your turn."

He glanced at Lauren. She bit the inside of her lower lip as was her habit, and contemplated turning back.

He could read her profile as clearly as if it were a newspaper.

Headline: I'm not ready for this.

News in Brief: I don't want to talk about it.

Nick wasn't buying the late edition. He'd told her his history, now it was time to flip the pages.

"How did you meet him?" Nick threw a question at her to get her started.

She let it digest a moment, then said, "In my apartment building. He lived on the first floor, I was on the second."

"What'd he do?"

"Electrician."

"Handy."

"When he was working."

Nick shook his head. "And you fell in love with him?"

"I thought so," she answered without looking up from her bare feet. He appreciated the dark polish on her toenails, her slender ankles tan from a day in the sun. She had on a skirt and tank top that fit her body perfectly. Her hair was loose, framing her face in the moonlight. "I didn't plan on getting pregnant."

The words fell like a flat line.

She hastily continued, "I wasn't irresponsible. You know what I mean. Sometimes things just don't work. Nothing is one hundred percent."

"I hear you."

"And when I found out I was pregnant with Billy, I just sort of went into shock. At first I was scared, then I was excited about it. Until I told Trevor."

"Trevor—the electrician."

"Yes." She flipped a length of hair over her shoulder. "He wasn't thrilled. We stayed together while I was pregnant and I thought we would work things out. We had differences from the start, but I overlooked them because I was so—"

The rest hinged in the night.

He waited, wondering if she'd be completely honest.

"—so," she continued in frustration, likely with herself, "desperate for someone to be *in love* with me, I ignored all the bad and only wanted to see the good. But there wasn't much good.

"After I had Billy, I was home two days and he still refused to move in with me and help me with our baby. I begged him to work things out. I was sure we could make a go of things, but he refused. The next morning, I went to his apartment. He'd moved out in the middle of the night."

Nick slanted his gaze across her. "Talk about a deadbeat."

Lauren's face paled.

"That was all it took for me to sober up and realize I was in this alone. I tracked Trevor down at his friend's apartment. I told him I'd take him to court for child support if he didn't sign over all his rights to Billy. Trevor signed the termination of rights. While I was sad it ended like that, I was glad our relationship was over. I didn't want Trevor showing back up in my life claiming something he had no right to claim."

A sting sort of zapped Nick, not that he thought Lauren said what she did with him in mind. But if he'd had Debbie sign over her rights to Nicky-J, he wouldn't be headed to court now. But hindsight was twenty-twenty and there was nothing Nick could do. No telling if Debbie would have signed such a paper anyway. In all likelihood, she wouldn't have, and all this time, Nicky-J might have ended up twenty, thirty or forty percent of the time in Los Angeles with her. But no going back and wondering.

"So it's just been me and Billy from the start, and I

plan on keeping it that way. Uncomplicated. He won't ever be subjected to the pain of a bitter childhood like me. He won't know what it's like not to have his own things, a sense of place and belonging—and I don't mean that in reference to a street address. I mean he'll always belong to me. Nobody will move him, take him to another home. He won't have to wonder if he's loved or not. He won't have to feel like he doesn't matter. I won't do that do him. *Never.*"

The foster care.

Nick held her by the arms and gently steered her to a large rock. Her back pressed into the hard surface as she tried to lean as far away from him as possible, to put as much distance between them as she could. She'd done this too many times with him. No more. He wanted to be close to her, to get inside her head and know what she was thinking.

He saw her fear, at first wasn't sure where it came from, then slowly a dawning came.

"Don't be afraid, Lauren. You aren't your mother."

Her chin shot up. "I won't be my mother. Ever."

"Then why do I see fear in your eyes?" He touched her cheek, cupped it with his palm and tilted her face to his. Their eyes met, held. She was so beautiful, so vulnerable and fragile, at times he couldn't believe this was the same woman who went after him at city hall because of a parking violation. "Don't let your laundry pile up, Lauren. You ever hear that expression? My mom says it all the time. You let it pile up, and you'll feel like you can't get close to anyone because you haven't aired all your feelings out. So dump on me, tell me what's got you so scared."

Her voice broke in a whisper. "I'm not scared."

"I think you are. That's why you move so much. You're afraid. It's your way of deciding, when you leave nobody can leave you. You're the one choosing your fate, nobody else."

She tried to look away, he brought his other hand to her cheek and held her still, making her stay connected with his gaze.

At length, she licked her lips. "I didn't have what you have when we were our sons' ages. I only learned what true devotion to a child was when I was placed with Betty and Bob Saunders, but by then, it was almost too late for me. I'd done things I wasn't proud of."

"But at least they made you see that you didn't have to be like that. It was up to you."

"Yes. I'm so grateful for them. There is good in the foster-care system, I know this. I just wish it hadn't been so long in coming for me. I wish that I'd never had to enter it. I wish my mom…"

"Wishing doesn't make it happen, Lauren."

She nodded, and he sensed she knew deep down that every day lived was a day that shaped their lives and made them who they were this moment.

In a hushed tone, she asked, "But what if I've messed Billy up with all this moving and what if—"

"You don't need to go there. Your son is a normal boy. I've seen him with Nicky-J and they're two of a kind even though you can't see it." Nick's insistence punctuated his words.

"But Billy's different—special in the way he's different. He's so smart and insightful. He's mature. He's lived through a lot. I just want him to—" emotion filled Lauren's voice "—to be happy."

Nick's gut twisted for her, he felt the pain in her body transport itself to his. He tried to take as much of it as he could from her, cupping her face, stroking her hair, soothing the knots in her shoulders. But she resisted his comfort. She stood stiff, tall and proud. Unbroken.

He couldn't begin to imagine what it would be like to have his parents abandon him, to live with a feeling of hopelessness for so long. Family was such an integral part of his life, he'd be lost without it.

Lauren's perseverance in the face of adversity garnered his awe, his complete respect. For a woman who'd all but grown up on her own, she was stable, smart and self-sufficient. Surely she knew that.

"Lauren, you're doing a good job as a parent," Nick reiterated. "He's a good kid. He washes his hands after he uses the bathroom, he looks before crossing the street, and he helps my mom bring in groceries."

"Those are fundamentals. Manners and common sense." She pulled out of his arms, walked to the water's edge and let the dark ripple of ocean wash over her toes. "I'm talking about preparing him to be a man. How can I know? I'm a woman. I don't think like a man. I try, but it's just not in my head."

Nick's mouth broadened into a smile. "I'm glad you don't think like a man."

"I wish I did."

"No you don't. Then you'd have a whole set of worries you didn't realize you had." He cracked a grin. "You'd start straining pond water through your socks."

"Why?"

"To see what bugs were in it."

Lauren frowned, not taking his quip the way he had intended—to lighten the tension gripping her shoulders.

Her sigh filled the night. "You dream through your kids, you want better for them than what you had. I think about doing things wrong with Billy. You said yourself that I should have let him play team sports. And I saw tonight how badly he wanted to catch that baseball, but he was horrible at it. See—" she raised her hands as if in surrender "—I have messed him up. His self-esteem could be ruined. You said yourself because I don't let him play—"

"Lauren, quit it." He inhaled. "Jesus, you're so hard on yourself."

"I have to be. He's all I have."

The ocean rode in and out, breaking softly. The sky was deep and endless, stars blanketing the edges as far as a person could see. Smoke curls rose to the right where the picnic was still in full swing on the beach. The pungent odors of spent fireworks drifted in the air. Spurs of fireworks darted through the sky, blowing up in bright colors.

"You're right about me," she said, time defining the moment as a cherry bomb exploded in the sky, a brilliant fan of red, white and blue popping to life. "I move frequently because I'm afraid to get close to people." She gazed up at the stars. "It's stupid, I know that. I recognize I need to get over my past, but I try and try and I just can't seem to break the pattern of my childhood." She hugged herself. "Hell, maybe I should call in to a radio talk show and get free therapy."

Nick laughed but not at her. "I think this is the first time I've ever heard you swear."

"Did I?"

"Yeah, and I liked how it made you look so... naughty." His grin broadened.

Lauren turned away, collected herself, then looked at him as if he were a dessert she'd made and she wanted a heaping helping of him. "I'm better off when I keep things simple, keep my life simple and don't get involved."

"Look, Lauren. You're doing okay. Coming to Bella Luna was the right move. Your *last* move. You're involved here. With me, my family. Dunk. Verna Mae. Sam Wong always gets a smile when he says your name. A lot of people are glad you're in their lives."

Lauren shook her head in a gesture of sardonic defeat. "I know...I know. How did this happen?"

"Maybe because you wanted to be a part of something so bad, you didn't realize how much until you were deep into it."

She vented a half laugh, half snort. "Am I really in that deep?"

"I'd say about knee-deep for now. Enough that you'd need a pair of waders to walk out."

"Great," she moaned, her liquid eyes cast heavenward as if to plead for help.

Nick chuckled, the picture of her burning in his brain. He hadn't felt this way about a woman in a long, long time. He wasn't sure if he should embrace it or run. He suspected the latter. He had so much going on in his life, he kept telling himself he couldn't get involved. And yet, that was the very thing he told Lauren she needed to do.

Giving advice was easier than taking his own.

He thought about these past few days of hell. For Nick, waiting was the hardest part. On one hand, he wanted life to hurry up so he could get the trial over with. On the other, he was looking for all the extra hours he could get to spend with Nicky-J, to keep creating new memories with his son.

He couldn't have it both ways.

Right now he didn't want either. He just wanted this moment. There were no courts, no lawyers and petitions. No appointments for home visits, personality and psychological testing evaluations. No phone call to return to Bruce. It was as if that part of his life didn't exist right now.

The thunder of fireworks shot into the sky, flowering bursts of colors. Reds and greens. Then an explosion of near-blinding white.

"They're setting off the fireworks," Lauren said, holding her arms about herself to ward off the slow-creeping chill. "We're missing it."

"I can see just fine right here."

"But the boys—"

He took her into his arms, drawing her close. "The boys are fine. Are you, Lauren?"

Her eyelids drew slowly closed, then opened. The shape of her mouth was lush and full, the corners lifted in a vague smile. A floral scent warmed her skin. She felt soft and feminine in his hold, felt really good. Too good.

"Yes," she whispered. "I'm fine. Thank you, Nick. Thanks for making me see that I'm not so bad."

He brushed her hair away from her cheek, tucked it behind her ear. He stroked her neck, held her close and lowered his face over hers, his mouth catching over her mouth.

The kiss was leisurely, long. A dusting of lips together, lightly, softly. Her arms reached up around him, held him close to her and she surrendered.

His heart constricted, came alive in strong beats. Satisfying warmth filled him where he'd been cold. The silk of her hair slid between his exploring fingers as he cradled her head, keeping her mouth next to his.

Surprise flicked through him, instantly arousing, as she slanted her lips, parting his with the tip of her tongue. Blood shot through his body and straight to his groin. He trailed his fingertip across her bare collarbone, then lower to her breast, cupping. He felt a rush, a desire for this woman that was so powerful, he almost couldn't restrain its potency.

She affected him like no other, he wanted her like no other. It would be so easy to bring her down onto the sand, to take her here and forget that the world around them existed.

But to do that would mean giving up, giving in and bringing her into his life when it wasn't his to give right now. His fate was in a court, a thought he struggled to accept. He wasn't ready for any commitments.

So Nick contented himself with holding her, touching her, stroking her pliant body. Kissing. He loved kissing her, the moist heat of her mouth fusing with his. She, with a simple touch of her body next to his, controlled his thoughts, his breathing.

He slowed the beats of his heart, needing to savor the feel of her, savor this moment between them. There was a quiet pleasure in the kiss that he held on to, that he took and wrapped into his mind like a present to be opened and remembered later.

Her lips were so warm, so willing, it was easy to forget. Easy to want this to go further. Her hands lifted, dug into his hair and stroked. She toyed with the shorter hair at the nape of his neck, touched his warm skin. She splayed her fingers over his back, drawing him as close to her as she could.

The fly at the front of her skirt crushed into his, a soft moan escaping her. He could have her, be inside her. There were so few layers separating them. She was as hungry for this as he was.

It had been a long time since he'd wanted to lose himself in such a way, lose himself in making love.

Not sex.

Making love.

She was sexy, her body swaying against his, the lazy slide of her tongue sweeping through his mouth. He gathered her hair, its length like skeins of satin in his fist. Her palm raised, flattened between them to lay on his chest, a low growl rose from his throat.

He kissed the corner of her mouth, her cheek, lower to her exposed throat.

The night filled with the songs of the Fourth, and anyone who ever spoke the cliché about hearing fireworks while kissing someone wouldn't think he was crazy for imagining he could hear them louder, stronger.

Nick encircled her waist, so slender, fitting perfectly in his wide hands. She was slight, but tall. Breakable, but resilient. There were so many things about her that he admired. She was one of a kind, a woman who was independent and fierce, yet self-conscious and questioning at the same time.

In Lauren, he saw the worst and best parts of himself. A woman who lived her life with her heart, who gave everything to her son. He understood that, recognized her devotion in his own eyes. Maybe there was something about opposites attracting, but this woman—she was him in so many ways that it felt as if he'd known her all his life, felt as if he'd lose a part of himself if he ever lost her.

Nick's brain switched gears, a startling clarity coming to life.

He wondered, in that split instant, if he was falling in love with her.

He kissed her fully on the lips, one last time, then pulled back.

Moonlight reflected in her eyes, her face pale and beautiful. She caught his cheek in her palm, pressed her lips to his once more, as if to take back possession of something he'd started.

She didn't step out from his arms, she stayed. He could feel her pulse pounding at her wrists where her hands lay gently over his shoulders. Her heartbeat thumped next to his, her lips wet from their kiss.

A part of him didn't want to move, the irrational side that told him something more would be there for them tomorrow. That they'd have endless tomorrows together. Another part of him projected his cynical side. He wasn't so all-consumed that he forgot the promise he'd made to himself.

He wasn't going to get sidetracked, not now, not when his son needed him to be there one hundred percent.

Nick drew in a hard-fought breath. He hated to let go of the perfect rhythm he felt, the harmony flowing through his body making him feel, oddly enough, calm.

He leaned forward, murmured into Lauren's ear, "We should head back."

As he drew away, her eyes were still closed, a dreamy smile on her mouth. "Hmm."

"I promised Billy I'd find his star for him," Nick said, his voice hoarse.

She gazed longingly into his face, her fingers laced through his. "He'll like that."

They retraced their steps, not touching one another, and yet he felt a charge surrounding them, like the current generated in the sky with the fireworks.

When they returned, hot chocolate and coffee had come out to warm the evening crowds that had begun to thin. They found Billy and Nicky-J with his mom and dad, the boys waving the last of their sparklers in their hands.

Nick had set up his telescope earlier. "Billy, you want to find your star?"

"Sure!" He ran up to Nick, eyeglasses steamed from the heat coming off his head. Like Nicky-J, Billy was fired up, a turbo charge of little boy and sweat, damp hair and smelling of salty air and gooey-sweet marshmallows that they'd roasted rather than dunked in cups of hot chocolate.

"Your mom gave me the coordinates. I looked them up." He dialed them in to the refracting telescope, and gazed through the eyepiece to find a bed of constellations. He charted the degrees of the Billy Jessup Star using the equatorial system, bringing the star into focus. "It's that one. The one brightest to the right. You can count over six and you'll see it."

Billy anxiously nuzzled himself in between Nick's chest and the telescope. The boy wasn't unlike Nicky-J in his curiosity and interest as he winked and squinted, removed his glasses and wiped them off, then peered into the eyepiece to see his most prized possession.

"One, two, five, six…I see it!" He jerked his head away, to shout at Lauren. "Mom! I see it. It's my star! Come look."

Lauren sidled next to them, peeking into the scope and taking a look. "I think I see it, too. I'm sure I do. There it is, Billy." She straightened, mouthing a silent *thank-you* to Nick. Her gratitude was better than a sky filled with a million stars.

To her son, she said, "This is great. I'm so glad you finally got to see your star."

"I love it, Mom." His little body turned toward his mother and he hugged her, pressing his cheek into her waist. Then he turned to Nick and hugged him, the gesture catching Nick by surprise.

Billy squeezed Nick's middle, the temple of his glasses pressed into the flat of Nick's stomach as he held on, squeezing. "You're the nicest guy ever. Thanks, Nick."

Nick swallowed, his throat tight, uncertain how to organize the flood of emotions swelling at the same time. He patted Billy's slim back, probably a little more gruffly than he should have, given he was so touched, so taken by the boy, that he guessed his next move and didn't respond in the way he would have with his own son. "Sure, Billy. No problem."

Then as quickly as Billy had embraced him, he dashed off. Nick felt the cool emptiness, the place where warmth had been and disappeared. He feared that he might feel this forever if Debbie got her way with Nicky-J. It was impossible to imagine living with this kind of longing and hollowness gripping him in its clutches.

Nick refused to be felled by the unknown. Being

afraid had never been one of his shortcomings. He'd always been competent and assured.

Only this time, he was up against something he couldn't control.

Nick jerked a hand through his hair, tried to get his bearings in more ways than one.

Nicky-J poked the stem of his last sparkler between his bare toes and swung his foot around—just the thing to take Nick's mind off his worries. "Dude, get that out of there. You're going to set fire to your jeans."

"Grandma said that they're flame retarded."

"I said no such thing," Caprice interjected, still sitting in one of the reclining beach chairs with a mug of coffee. "And it's retard*ant,* not retarded. I told you that your Halloween costume wouldn't catch fire—your jeans are a different matter, so take that sparkler out of there."

Nicky-J moped and pulled it from between his toes, then he danced along the shoreline, waving the sparkler with its sprinkler of light looking like a cluster of fireflies.

Billy was about to follow him, when he paused, then ran toward a small object not far up on the beach. He dropped onto his knees and petted an animal.

It was a dog, and mangy as far as Nick could tell.

Hugging the dog, Billy fed it something from his pocket and led it to the group.

A reddish tan dog with short fur sat on its haunches and looked at Billy, waiting for food. Marshmallows, Nick realized.

"Billy, you shouldn't feed that dog," Lauren said, standing clear of it as if she knew what was to follow.

"Mom, can I keep him? Oh, please, *please.*" Another toss of a marshmallow was quickly snapped up with a lick of canine chops.

Lauren stood her ground, uncomfortable as if this scenario had played out before. "No, Billy. We don't know whose dog this is. He could belong to someone."

"He could be a stray. We already saw him before, didn't we, Nicky-J? If we find out he's nobody's, can he be mine?"

"I don't think so. The landlord won't let us have pets in our cottage." Lauren shot Nick a stare that spoke volumes. She wanted him to back her up, but he wasn't biting. This wasn't his business.

"Why not?"

"Dogs...um, chew the furniture in the house and we'd have to pay for the damages since we don't own the property."

"Why don't we own it?"

"Because we rent."

"I don't want to rent anymore."

"Well, I'd have to find a house to buy and that's just not happening tonight."

"Tomorrow can you buy one?"

"Of course not. That takes money." Lauren folded her arms over her chest, taking on a defiant stand.

"But you have money. You said we have nine thousand dollars in the bank."

That revelation was news to Nick, not that he'd lost sleep over considering her financial status. It was just that she lived so frugally, he'd assumed she didn't have much of a monetary backup system.

Lauren's posture became erect, stiff. Clearly she

didn't like her financial business discussed in public. "No, Billy. No dog."

The dog apparently understood the verdict and pranced off in a well-timed jog, as if beneath the grime there was something regal about him.

The mutt's departure had Billy chasing it, only to stop on the dunes and slump his shoulders in dejection.

For Billy Jessup, that dog meant hope.

He'd be one step closer to having what he'd wanted his whole life.

A dog, a dad and a house.

Starting tomorrow, he was going to find out if that dog had an owner. He'd color Lost Dog signs and put them up all over town.

Then he would figure out how his mom could buy a house for them.

And for his last wish…he was positive he could find himself a dad.

He already had one in mind that he liked—very, very much.

Thirteen

Chasing moon dreams.

An offshore wind made fishing unstable and half the Bella Luna fleet stayed in the harbor. The Wharf Diner had been busier than usual midmorning, the fishermen milling around over coffee and plates of bacon and eggs, hoping for a shift in the wind only to be disappointed. Booths and the stools along the counter began to empty around two and the dinner-hour crowd started to trickle in about five.

Lauren waited for an order of burgers to come up. She was working the last shift until closing. She'd spent the past ten minutes busy with customer requests: more iced tea here, ketchup over there, a high chair needed at table six. No matter how long she waitressed, she still ran a little behind.

She should have the foresight to bring the ketchup to the table as soon as an order was placed—people being strange about ketchup. The condiment wasn't just used for fries and meat loaf; it got poured on chicken wings and fish sticks, and once—on a slice of toast.

When she wasn't occupied with serving, she had to sweep, scrub, slice, refill and restock. June managed with a real fast beat from years of practice; Lauren moved slower, but Verna Mae was somewhat patient. She puckered a red eyebrow, and coral earrings would dangle as she shook her head. That was about the extent of things.

Billy had come to work with Lauren this afternoon. The last time she checked, he was still outside at the diner's rear entrance calling for that lost dog.

Lauren picked up her dishes, juggling them on her forearms as she walked into the dining room. She'd already returned midmeal to table four to inquire how everything was—the answer had been great; now they—the two of them—were waving her over as if there were a three-alarm fire underneath their booth.

She served the burgers and removed an empty glass to give it a lemon-lime soda refill. On her way to the fountain machine, she stopped at the hand wavers' table to ask, "Can I get you anything else?"

The older woman wore an I've Traveled Route 66 T-shirt. False eyelashes swept clear up to her penciled eyebrows when she blinked her eyes. "We were wondering if you've ever seen Clint Eastwood 'round these parts."

Lauren switched the empty soft-drink glass to her other hand. "The movie actor?"

"He used to be the mayor of Carmel," her husband said by way of clarification—Lauren not needing any.

"I'm sorry, I've never seen him in here."

"Well, shoot, Ethel," he remarked, lifting his ball cap with the RV logo on it to scratch his head.

"We'll just have to go up farther," the woman said, dabbing her mouth on a napkin stained with crimson lipstick. "We were hoping he might come down this way."

Her husband laid his hands over his ample belly. "In that case, we'll take two apple pies, à la mode."

Lauren gave them her cheeriest smile. "I'll get those right away."

As she went into the kitchen, the DiMartino group came in. Anthony and Caprice, Danny and John, Nick and Nicky-J, and Heather was with them this time.

Lauren waved to the younger woman, liking her immensely. During the brief times they'd spoken, Heather had been nothing short of refreshingly outgoing. She spoke her mind yet remained thoughtful and caring. Lauren thought Danny and Heather were perfect together.

The DiMartinos occupied their usual booth, sliding across the vinyl seat and not bothering with menus. They were at June's station, and the waitress passed their table with a quick hello on her way to take plates of the battered fish special to customers at table ten.

Caprice gave her a wave, then sat down. She nudged herself quite closely to Anthony; he draped his arm around her shoulder and kissed her temple. Lauren couldn't recall ever seeing the two of them so affectionate—and certainly not in public.

Nick sent her a glance, one she returned and was rewarded with his smile. Just looking at him could bring out the best in her, even on a bad day.

She had to stop herself from reaching out and grabbing him by the shoulders and bringing him to her lips, slipping her tongue inside his mouth.

He was every woman's best dream, the best waking thought as they started their day. Lauren was no exception.

With everything on her agenda, dating men just wasn't a priority, it never even made the list of "things to do." Maybe she'd just set her expectations so high, they were up there with the moon.

At the pie dome, she asked, "Verna Mae, what do you look for in a man?"

"A pulse."

Affectionately smiling, Lauren said, "Seriously."

Verna Mae's creamy complexion offset her turquoise earrings. Russet hair curled around her rouged cheeks. "Kindness. You can never go wrong with a man who's kind. He'll treat you right."

Kindness.

Nick had done so many acts of kindness for her, she'd lost track.

Lauren cut two pieces of pie, thinking the crust looked like soggy crepe paper with lumpy canned apples and a spice that was supposed to smell like cinnamon. Verna Mae had a pastry vendor she bought from, and nothing against a company trying to turn a buck, but the pies were awful.

As Lauren plated the desserts, she plunged headlong into a subject that had been on her mind all day. "Verna Mae, can I bring in some of my homemade raspberry muffins and we'll sell them in the pastry dome?"

Lauren came up with the idea after Caprice DiMartino had raved on and on about the muffins. They were a thank-you gift to Nick's mom for watching Billy so often and not taking a penny for her time. Caprice called the muffins a "decadent whisper" in her mouth.

Verna Mae poured dressing on two salads, then shot a swirl of whipping cream over a bowl of cherry Jell-O. She didn't say anything right off and Lauren assumed she'd been shot down, until Verna Mae asked, "You want a percentage of the profits?"

"Yes. Eighty." Hope bloomed inside her chest. She'd already figured everything out.

"Eighty? Are you crazy? It's my dome."

"It's my baked goods. You'll see, it'll be worth it." She pressed on. "I happen to have a muffin with me, there on the counter. Lift that overturned coffee cup, and on the plate beneath is something that will make you want to sing."

"Sweetpea, I only sing in the shower." She turned the cup over and took a peek. "I was about to accuse June of not cleaning up from the breakfast rush. I wondered about this cup, just never got a chance to investigate. Raspberry muffin, you say? Lordy, it looks good." Her eyes appraised the plump muffin with its golden streusel topping and red berries baked through to add color. She took a nibble, then a hearty bite. A curious light came into her blue eyes. "Did you put brandy in this?"

"Not a drop."

"Then why am I feeling so warm and generous all of a sudden?"

Lauren knew when she'd won someone over, and this was a case of a unanimous-approval rating. "Do they taste like a decadent whisper in your mouth?"

"They taste like how I felt when I had my first kiss— tingling and yummy."

Lauren laughed. "Well, I didn't put anything like that in there."

Verna Mae ate some more, then swallowed with a shake of her head. "I'm feeling a song coming on." She hummed a few notes of a popular tune. "This is delicious. Sumptuous. You can bring in a dozen to start, sweetpea—so long as you put a warning label on my pastry dome." She took her order to the end of the counter.

Smiling, Lauren was quite pleased with herself. She could use the extra money, and even though this meant she had to buy more groceries from Dunk, she'd already calculated she'd be ahead if she sold each muffin at a certain amount.

Lauren brought the refill of lemon-lime to her table, then made a short stop at the DiMartinos'.

"Hello," she greeted. "Sorry about the weather today."

She'd seen Anthony DiMartino go out on his boat, but come back early this afternoon without a very big haul. Interestingly, he hadn't seemed all that bothered by it. Caprice had been waiting for him on the dock.

"That's July for you. Always have that damn offshore to wreck your day," Anthony replied.

Caprice gazed at him and Lauren felt the sparks flying between the two. Clearly something had transpired to make them seem as if they were newlyweds.

Heather smiled. "I like your earrings. Where did you get them?"

Lauren absently raised her hands to her ears. She'd had the little dangling gold earrings forever. They were dated to the sixties, she was sure, but she loved how they moved when she swung her head. "I bought them at a thrift store."

"Goes to show how much good stuff they have," Heather said, making Lauren feel comfortable. "Next time I'm in Santa Cruz, I'm going to check out that place on the beach. I've seen wonderful old pieces of furniture in the front."

"How're things coming with the wedding?" Lauren asked.

Danny replied, "She's making me take dancing lessons."

Nick chuckled, his eyes trained on his brother. "I didn't know that."

"Heather says I suck as a dancer, so she's got me going two nights a week." He playfully glared at his fiancée. "Told me that she didn't want me to embarrass her for our first dance."

"No, hon, I said I didn't want *you* to embarrass *yourself.*"

Everyone grew amused, Nick's sexy smile sending a cascade of shivers through Lauren. She loved seeing him like this, not so pent up with tension. Unguarded, relaxed and with his family. She was sure the trial was on his mind constantly, but when he let the hard features on his face soften, there was no one who could melt her heart faster.

"How are you doing, Lauren?" Nick murmured, his voice sounding like silk in her ears.

"Good. Fine, actually. Verna Mae said I could sell raspberry muffins in the pastry dome. I'll bring some in tomorrow."

"They'll go fast," Anthony remarked, his sun-weathered hands clasped in front of him on the tabletop. "I wolfed down five of them at the house."

Caprice added with a soft laugh, "They're addictive."

"I'm glad you liked them." Lauren felt a sense of well-being, of satisfaction she couldn't define. It was unlike anything else, it was closer to a feeling of protection—as if no possible harm could ever come to her so long as she was here, in Bella Luna.

It felt as if she'd known the DiMartinos all her life. It would be so easy to fall in love with everyone at this table. Day by day, the tug to move on wasn't as strong, the lure leading her away seemed to be illusive.

Maybe she was falling in love with Nick and she didn't know it, didn't dare embrace it. Letting her guard down would be so easy, if only it didn't require unrequited vulnerability. She didn't want to think like that, but retraining her brain to channel differently didn't come overnight.

Lauren didn't know if she was capable of giving herself to a man in such a way. She had no experience with marriage or the kind of compromise it took to live with a husband.

Husband.

That word came out of nowhere, almost startling Lauren to the point where she backed into June who'd come to the table and had her order pad poised and ready.

"Hi, folks," she said, her voice breathless. "What'll it be?"

Lauren bid her goodbye and went to total two tickets at the adding machine, an unnamed feeling making her move with thoughtfulness.

June called in the order. As she was within hearing distance of the DiMartino table, Lauren could hear their conversation. She glanced at them several times.

Nicky-J sat, fidgeting with his legs as he scissored

them to and fro, his tennis shoes clunking into the booth until Nick told him to cut it out with a hand on his knee. Nicky-J usually had a hello for her, but she sensed he had other things on his mind today.

On her way to drop off the checks, she overheard Nicky-J say, "I ain't going to my mom's never again."

"You *aren't* going," Heather said.

His pout remained in place. "I'm glad you thunk so, too."

Heather put her hand on his shoulder. "I was correcting your grammar."

"I don't got no bad grandma, just a bad mother."

Nick's deep voice sounded bottomless and powerful when he spoke, and he kept his words tight and concise. "You don't have a bad mother."

She paused at their table, daring to think she might be able to do something to help. "Nicky-J, Billy's outside on the wharf looking for that lost dog. If your dad says it's okay, maybe you'd like to help him while you're waiting for your dinner."

"I wanna."

Nicky-J didn't ask his dad, he simply slipped out of his chair, under the booth, and came out from the underside of the table.

Lauren hoped Nick didn't think it presumptuous of her to have made the suggestion, and when she looked at him, his muscles were taut and hard.

"I'm sorry, maybe I shouldn't have—"

"No," Nick cut her short. "It was a good idea to get his mind off everything. Thanks."

Caprice gave Lauren a shrug and an understanding smile.

Lauren left them, suddenly feeling like an intruder, a person who didn't belong.

When she reached the kitchen, she brought a hand to the base of her throat as if it would help bring more air into her lungs.

She felt a terrible tenseness in her body, almost as if she and Nick were one and the same, sharing a beating heart and breathing in the same jagged tempo.

Perhaps they both wanted to protect and keep their sons with them so badly, they were becoming one and the same person. They were close to thinking each other's thoughts.

It frightened her that she could feel something so emotionally shattering.

Maybe she truly was falling in love with Nick DiMartino.

Maybe she already had….

"Grandma," Nicky-J hollered from the patio. "Can we dig in the dirt?"

Nicky-J's grandma came to the sliding doors at the back of the house and opened them. Looking into the green backyard with all of its colorful flowers and big trees, she settled a hand on her hip. She had soft-looking hair with eyes the same blue color as Nicky-J's. Billy thought she was a nice grandmother. She gave him cookies and lots of milk.

"You can dig in that flower garden." She pointed to a bare piece of dirt alongside the fence way out to the left.

Nicky-J squinted, his nose wrinkling funny. "But there's no flowers in it."

"That's why it's perfect." Nicky-J's grandma smiled, then she went back inside and closed the door.

"I don't get it." Nicky-J shrugged and brought the buckets with shovels and tiny plastic army men. Billy had his airplanes in his pockets. Square bathroom tiles filled Billy's beach bucket to the top. They'd picked them up from Nicky-J's dad's job. The tiles were the size of Hot Wheels cars and army guys. Him and Nicky-J were going to tunnel out the dirt and make secret caves with the tiles.

They'd left the diner together after Nicky-J ate his dinner, but he told Billy he hadn't been hungry and he hadn't felt like shooting at the ketchup bottle with his fries. Billy listened to him, feeling sorry for Nicky-J who was normally talkative as he ate his dinner. For the past few days Billy hadn't played with him because he was looking for his dog so he could adopt it.

As they began raking the dirt away, creating a damp mound that would be good for packing down, Billy couldn't keep his mind all that focused on tunnels. "I just have to find that dog."

"That dog stinks. Why not get a fresh one from the pet store?"

"I don't want a fresh one. I want this smelly one. Where do you think it is?"

"I dunno. Did you ask Nubs?"

"He said he hasn't seen that dog since last week." Billy pushed his eyeglasses up his nose. "It's got to be around here somewhere. It wouldn't just leave, I know it. I even put up signs."

"Maybe nobody lost it. Maybe he doesn't got a home."

Remorse settled like a rattling cough in Billy's chest. "I don't want to think about that. I'd be sad if I imagined that dog never having a home, a bowl of water and a box of treats."

They worked in the dirt, piling it higher, then they started laying tiles in the dirt for the flooring.

"How are we going to put the roof on?" Billy sat back, his cape tossed behind his shoulders.

"You put the floor, then the side walls, then the roof. I done this before."

"I haven't."

"You haven't done very much ever, Billy."

"I've been doing more stuff with you." And that was true. In the short time he'd been in Bella Luna, Billy had gotten the dirtiest he'd ever been, chased more birds, eaten more candy, got to see the best parades, and even roast marshmallows.

This town was like a magic place. A place where little boys got to live when they wanted all their dreams to come true. This was better than a fairy tale, better than *Hansel and Gretel,* one of his favorite bedtime stories.

Billy commented, his thoughts drifting to the way he used to see things. "I used to think little people lived in rainspouts."

"What're those?"

"The pipes where the rain comes down."

"Oh." Understanding lit Nicky-J's face, then he scrunched it up. "What kind of little people?"

"Little fairy people."

"How come you thought that?"

"I don't know, I just did. Maybe because when the rain came down, it brought little twigs and leaves with it that looked like fairy people used it for their houses."

"You're a funny kid sometimes, Billy."

Billy didn't take that the wrong way, he knew Nicky-J was just talking.

Nicky-J arranged the white tiles, his mind not fully on what he was doing. Normally he'd be making army men holler and noises from crashing helicopters blowing up. He was moving his hands and scooping dirt, but not really thinking about that as much as he was thinking about having to go to Calif-thornia in a week to visit his mom.

He'd been trying to hate Disneyland lately. Same with Universal Studios. He talked himself out of ever wanting to go there again, only sometimes he slipped up when he thought about how much fun he had on Tom Sawyer Island and how good those mouse-ear pancakes tasted with blueberry syrup.

Nicky-J had always loved his mom. He might not have seen her very much, but a kid always loves their mom. Especially when she bought him so many good toys and rubbed his forehead when he was trying to go to sleep. But all the toys in his bedroom wouldn't make him trade his dad's house for his mom's house.

He didn't love his mom right now. He tried to hate her like Disneyland, but no matter how hard he tried, he still loved her, only not so much as he used to. He just wished she wouldn't have told a judge that she wanted him to live with her.

Every time he was in Calif-thornia, she hugged him and said he was such a good son, that she was happy to have him as her little boy.

Scowling, Nicky-J spoke his thoughts aloud. "She thinks I'm such a goody-goody. She's always kissin' my cheek and tellin' me I'm such a great little boy. But if she wins me, I'm gonna show her what a bad boy I can be." Nicky-J stopped talking suddenly, his eyes growing real wide. "I got an idea!"

Billy started.

Nicky-J felt his cheeks grow hot as if he'd eaten too many cinnamon sticks. "My mom wants me because I'm a good boy. If I'm a bad boy, she won't want me."

Taking a second to figure that one out, Billy eventually nodded his agreement. "What are you going to do that's bad?"

"I dunno."

Nicky-J looked around the backyard and zeroed in on his grandma's best flowers, the ones she spent all her time on with the watering hose and a box of blue powdery stuff. Some of them were taller than him. She'd been growing the plants since they were seeds. He stood and marched over to brightly colored rows and contemplated.

His grandma sure loved these flowers.

For a minute, he was too scared to do it.

I gotta do it. I gotta make it for real.

He took his shovel and began digging, crushing stalks and leaves and the pretty flower heads, petals floating onto the dirt.

"Not your grandma's flowers!" Billy stood over him.

"Yes-huh," Nicky-J said, swiping at the pom-pom flower with the yellow centers.

Billy backed away, staring in amazement that Nicky-J really had the guts to go through with it. His grandma was going to be awfully mad.

"Be careful for bees" was all Billy added, sitting on his heels and watching his best friend be bad.

Really bad.

Lou squeezed out of the diner fifteen minutes before closing, leaving Lauren alone. Thankfully it was a slow

Monday night and nobody to speak of had come in for an hour after the DiMartinos left.

One of these days Verna Mae was going to have to replace Lou, and Lauren wanted to be around to get the afternoon-cook job. Lou never complied with the rules, he came and went as he pleased—if he showed up at all—and tonight he just walked out after muttering something about needing to buy some smokes.

When Lauren had asked his retreating back if he'd return, he shrugged and had given her a one-syllable "Nah. I cleaned the grill, it's quittin' time."

More like Miller time, Lauren had thought.

In his absence, she worked on her tasks, dumping leftover coffee down the drain, washing the pots and turning off the warming burners. She used the big sprayer to wash utensils, then she swept the floors and was just scooting in the last chair, when a customer came into the diner at three minutes till closing.

He took a seat at the counter, laid his hands out in front of him and sighed as if he carried the weight of the world on his shoulders. The collar of his white shirt was heavily starched, his firmly creased pants a deep utility blue. She'd seen him in here before. He worked at the cemetery on the wind-gnarled cliffs—the night watchman who patrolled the grounds and made sure nobody disturbed anything.

Lauren was flustered, the big kitchen warm and empty behind her, the fishy-smelling grease from the deep-fat fryer perfuming the air in a bad way.

"I'm sorry," she said, approaching him, "we're closed."

With his chin down, he gazed upward at her through

eyelids that could have used a nip and tuck. His dark hairline receded, his cheeks were round and he had a cleft in his double chin.

"Can you give me a break, miss?" His plea was quite heartfelt, although she had no idea why he was in such misery.

She bit the inside of her lip, pondering what to do. "Are you okay?"

"Bad day. My wife and me, we got into a beef."

"I'm sorry to hear that." Lauren wasn't a very good counselor on the job, but she did lend a sympathetic ear. "I'm sure you'll work everything out."

"Don't think so. She's dead set in her ways."

Without really thinking about it, Lauren placed a glass of iced water in front of him.

He took a sip, wiped his mouth with his hand, then told her his story in detail as she patiently listened. "I say the kid's teeth ain't so bad, she says he needs braces tomorrow, them fancy clear kind so he won't be ashamed. I tell her, braces cost money. I got insurance, but it only goes so far, you know, and they don't cover the clear ones, you know. We got into it and I left—she didn't give me my lunch box or nothing. So here I am, thinking I gotta come up with the extra for the clear braces or she won't speak to me no more."

Lauren shifted her weight, the balls of her feet hot and tired in the Keds she wore, and her shoulder blades aching. As tired as she was, there was no dispute over which one of them was having the more taxing day.

"What can I make for you?"

"Thanks, miss. I'm awfully hungry."

She smiled wanly at him while he perused the menu.

"I'll take the batter-dipped special with onion rings."

Cringing, Lauren nodded and went into the kitchen. Why was it that everyone wanted their food saturated with oils that were going to kill them?

Determined to fix the poor man a dinner that could take him to work for the night, she looked for the pieces of fish in the freezer. The chrome-fronted, industrial refrigerator wasn't stocked well, the afternoon delivery had been held up, so they were short on items. Battered shrimp were in the freezer, and who knew what else with the disorganization. She was aware of the shrimp because Lou had dumped a handful down into the fryer basket for his dinner just before he left.

For all her looking, she came up short on the seafood special. They must be all out. In the refrigerator, there was a plastic bag of fresh-caught Pacific red snapper that one of the fishermen brought in. Verna Mae had a deal with most of them—they bring her fish and she feeds them meals at a discount. This ensured she had fresh fish and the fishermen got hot meals for their part of the deal.

"I'm sorry," Lauren said through the cook's window, "but we're all out of the special. But I can fix you something, don't worry. It'll just take me a minute."

It might take her more than a minute to calm the racing pulse at her throat. Adrenaline began to pump hard through her body, the spark of an idea in full flame.

She'd been in this kitchen too many times to count, watched Lou and Knox at the grill and stove, observed how they operated the equipment, and she'd logged the procedures in her memory just in case.

Well, this was an "in case" if she ever had one.

Lauren worked quickly, taking out the snapper.

Thankfully the fisherman had removed the gills, guts and scales. The red-skinned fish smelled fresh and felt firm. She knew just how she wanted to prepare it.

Rummaging through the refrigerator, she grabbed the grocery bag she'd stuck in there on her break. She'd walked to Dunk's and picked up a few ingredients for her muffins. While she was at the store, she bought a few herbs. Her herb garden hadn't fully come in yet, not enough to harvest anything.

She had a shallot, the finest olive oil and some garden greens. Not the kind you got in a cellophane bag, but the spring mix with all the tenderest pieces.

Heating a skillet, Lauren poured olive oil into the bottom and waited for it to heat super high while she rinsed the fish in cold water. She wished she had kosher salt, but made do with table, generously rubbing the cavity with it. She added black pepper, again wishing for better—crushed would have been preferable. From her grocery bag, she added fresh sprigs of thyme and rosemary where the guts used to be. She chopped the shallot, sprinkled it inside as well. The last thing to go in, sliced lemon.

She laid the fish, head first, into the pan and let it sear while she piled greens on a plate and improvised a salad. She wasn't fond of the side salads the Wharf served—tomatoes, cucumbers and shredded carrots. Too common. So she used the greens, tossed them with olive oil, vinegar, salt and pepper, and a pinch of sugar. To her surprise, she found fresh blue cheese in the refrigerator and she sprinkled several crumbles on top.

The fish was ready and she prepped the plate, arranging the fish beside the salad. The dish was simple, yet smelled like heaven.

She walked it over to the night watchman and presented it.

He took one look and said, "You didn't have nothing that was deep fried?"

The strong thrust of Lauren's proud shoulders caved in a little. "No."

"What's this? Cod?"

"Snapper."

"This thing's looking at me. You left the eyes in." He turned a pleading gaze to her. "I like fish sticks."

"We didn't have any." Trying to keep her smile from falling, she urged, "Come on, try it."

"You gave me a wilted salad."

"It's not wilted. You're thinking of iceberg lettuce that's white and pale—marginally good for you. This is better."

He scratched his throat, then one beefy hand picked up his fork and he took a bite of salad. After several chews, he nodded. "It's pretty good. Yeah, not bad. I like it."

She smiled. "Try that snapper."

"Where's the tartar sauce?"

"I guarantee you won't need any."

The fish flaked on his fork, done to perfection. He broke the skin, steam rose in an aromatic curl, wafting through the diner and giving it its first genuine breath of culinary cuisine meant for gods and kings.

And a night watchman who was in a beef with his wife.

He ate, then he ate some more, his face heating. And another bite, and another. He didn't say anything further, just devoured the dinner and scraped his plate, then almost looked confused as he saw the skeleton of bones, a tail and head.

His napkin was swiped across his mouth, his big hand grasped the water glass and drained it. He appeared as if he couldn't figure out what had just happened to him.

On a stifled belch, he stared at his plate then at her. "I'm glad you were out of the special."

Her breath let out, a curve to her mouth. "I'm glad Lou was all out of smokes."

"Lou?"

"Never mind." Lauren cleared his plate, and he asked her what he owed her and she conjured a reasonable figure in her head.

"Can I use the phone for a minute?" he asked.

"Sure. It's by the register."

She took his plate into the kitchen, lowering it into the sink. As she held on to the sprayer, she heard him talking.

"Baby doll, it's me—Hank. Listen, I'm sorry about everything, it was my fault. If you think the kid needs the clear kind for his self-esteem, then I'll make sure he gets them. I love you, love you lots."

Water ran through Lauren's fingers, soap pooling in the bottom of the sink. Her thoughts swirled around the drain, her smile still in place as she heard Hank making kisses into the phone.

She liked to think Hank would have come around on his own...

...but Lauren knew differently.

Anthony settled into the bed, tucked his arm around his wife and brought her close. Funny...he always thought she smelled like carnations. Now he realized she smelled like roses. Her skin was still soft, her body still fit neatly next to his.

She'd finally calmed down after discovering Nicky-J had dug up her flowers.

"I don't understand why he did it," she murmured into the dark room. "And when I asked him, he refused to tell me."

"I think he's acting out. He doesn't want to go live with his mother."

"I know..." Caprice drew in a breath, a little shaky, a little unsettled.

"Do you think Billy dared him to do it?" her husband asked.

"No...not Billy. He wouldn't."

Caprice thought momentarily about Billy Jessup. He had the kindest and biggest eyes, the brightest smile. So inquisitive, but not mischievous. Besides, he wouldn't have gone near where the bees were. Not after what happened to him.

Lauren had told her about her son's accident and said he wore a Medic Alert necklace in case of an emergency. Dunk knew about it, too. Caprice had never had experience with a child—or anyone—who needed to carry an epinephrine pen.

Caprice laid her hand on Anthony's chest, felt his heartbeat beneath her fingertips. His skin warmed the knit of the thin T-shirt he slept in. She loved lying here like this. It seemed they hadn't done so in forever, but lately...

...lately the sizzle had returned to their marriage. It seemed as if they couldn't stop touching each other. Hand-holding, caresses on cheeks, kissing. And other things.

Caprice, who was rarely coy, felt herself blush.

She couldn't trace the change in their marriage, and didn't want to question what was happening.

She did know one thing, however, and that was this morning after they'd eaten Lauren Jessup's muffins—they couldn't keep their hands off each other.

They'd barely made it to the bedroom...

Caprice felt heat across her cheeks once more.

"Anthony," she said into the murkiness.

"Yes, honey?"

"I love you."

"I love you, too."

Fourteen

The moon had the wind and the sun on its face.

Lauren had the day off and she took the opportunity to clean every corner of the cottage. She never minded cleaning, preferring organization over clutter.

She dragged a mop over the floorboards, rinsing the dirt in the sink. These days, Billy brought in more dirt than she could keep up with. He'd always been pretty neat before, but now he came home with mud on his shoes, sand in his socks, seashells in his pockets and buckets of treasure he'd collected on the beach.

She knew he was loving it here, growing in ways he never had before. School started in less than two months. She had little time to make a decision. She either registered him soon or he'd miss out.

After the kitchen was clean, she worked her way through the lower level, dusting and sweeping. Her bedroom was at the side of the house, a converted sunroom. She loved how the sunshine slanted through the windows to brighten the already bright whitewashed walls. The floor was painted sea-green-and-white plaid, with a compass pattern directly in the center, flowers all around. Whoever had painted it had talent. The bed was plain and simple, a silver iron headboard and footboard, looking like something from the turn of the century. A large painting hung over the bed, a colorful burst of all the local wildflowers packed in vases and pots.

Since the room was so narrow, her bed could fit only one way, leaving barely a foot of space on either side. She'd moved a wicker pedestal table to the right, set a lamp on it and a fern. On the windowsill that looked through to the kitchen, she had tin pots of herbs. It was strange how living in a little side porch could bring her such comfort. Perhaps because the space itself was so confining—like a cocoon that kept her wrapped up snug and safe.

She made the bed, its patchwork quilt colorful greens and roses, then she plumped the white eyelet pillows. When she could buy her own house, her own bed, she'd want something just like this. She was going to ask Nick who picked out all the furniture.

Moving through the house, she set her cleaning items on the kitchen sink and then gazed inside the refrigerator thinking about what she'd prepare for lunch.

The homey-sweet smell of raspberry muffins wafted through the cottage. She'd baked several dozen and had taken them to the diner early this morning. Fingers crossed that they sold.

Absently staring at fresh vegetables and cream, cheeses and yogurt on the refrigerator's shelves, Lauren wondered if Verna Mae had found out yet what she'd done last night. There was no telling if she would or not. Hank would have to speak up, come back in…

Lauren debated telling Verna Mae herself. Her reaction would be one of three things. Verna Mae might fire Lou on the spot for leaving early. No matter how badly Lauren wanted to be the cook, she wouldn't intentionally sabotage Lou and get him fired. Verna Mae could easily not care that Lou left—he had a habit of doing so that was no secret—and she might be happy that Hank had been so pleased with the improvised dinner that she'd have Lauren cook it again. Or…Verna Mae could tell Lauren she'd overstepped her duties and she was fired.

Somebody knocked on the front door and Lauren went to answer it. Billy didn't charge for the door like he normally did. He wasn't home. He was at Dunk's helping him in the grocery. Billy had formed a close friendship with the man, and Dunk, in turn, enjoyed having Billy around to arrange canned goods in decorative columns and listen to the Beach Boys while Dunk told him about his surfing days.

Funny how, barely two months ago, Lauren wouldn't have let Billy out of her sight to do something like that with a stranger. But Dunk was no more a stranger than most everyone else in town.

Lauren opened the door, pleasantly surprised to find Nick. A white T-shirt stretched taut over his broad shoulders and chest. His hair, freshly washed, was still damp and combed away from his forehead. He had on his black leather boots beneath a pair of bleach-faded jeans.

"Hi," she said, unable to stop smiling. "I was just going to make myself something for lunch, then I was headed to Dunk's to pick out your dinner. Now that you're here, you can tell me what you want tonight and—"

"Take a ride with me."

"Ride?"

"On the bike. I gotta get out of here for a while and I was hoping you'd come with me." Sunshine had deepened his tan, his eyes bluer than she'd noticed before.

She gazed at her khaki shorts, her knees scuffed from cleaning. Water spots created a pattern down the front of her V-neck shirt, her hands were chapped from scrub water and hours at the diner where she constantly had them in and out of water. She'd thrown her hair into a ponytail, wasn't wearing a speck of makeup, and she was barefoot.

"Well…it might take me a minute to get ready."

"You look great."

"Liar." She hastily added, "And I'm not looking for compliments, it's just that I'm not prepared, I need to change and to—"

His expression was dark and troubled. "I only have an hour and then I have to be back home."

It dawned on her that it was a Tuesday and he wasn't at work. Something was going on. "Are you all right?"

"I don't know."

"I'll be right back."

Lauren left him in the doorway, grabbed her clean tennis shoes, slipped them on without socks, and made a quick telephone call to Dunk to tell him she'd be gone for about an hour and asked if he could keep Billy there a little longer. He said not a problem.

She snagged her house key and met Nick. "I'm all set."

He lowered his head, brought his mouth to hers and

gave her a kiss she hadn't anticipated. His lips were warm and tasted so good, like a fine mellow wine that melted on her tongue as he parted her lips seeking more.

The unexpected kiss left her reeling.

She didn't question why he did it. She just raised her arms around his and held him close as the kiss made her delirious. So dangerous...so crazy to want him so badly.

The kiss ended as abruptly as it began, Nick's face over hers, his hair falling over his forehead. It felt right, comfortable, to brush the hair away from his brow, to stroke her thumb over his forehead.

"What's the matter?" Her voice broke, ached for him, as she could sense he was conflicted.

"I need to get my head on straight."

She nodded, needing nothing more. She'd been there before, knew what he meant. She let him lead her into the warm afternoon and to his gleaming chrome-and-black motorcycle. Two helmets sat on the leather seat and he handed her one.

She wasn't sure how to put it on. He helped strap her chin, then he swung a leg over and she did likewise.

His powerful legs straddled the machine, her body sliding into his back, his buttocks, as she positioned herself so she wouldn't fall off.

"Arms around me," he said simply.

She complied, slipping them around his waist, resisting the urge to press her cheek to his heavily corded back muscles. The helmet was too bulky to allow her the intimacy. She sat tall, ready and waiting.

She'd never ridden a motorcycle before.

The bike's energy, its strength, felt hard and caged beneath her. Nick kicked over the engine, charging to life in a deep rumble that sounded like the growling rage of a hundred pent-up lions.

Her thighs pressed Nick's, gripping as he ran the bike through its first gear and nearly jerking her backward. She held on tighter, her fingers gripping his T-shirt.

They crossed Shoreline and went up Seal, then higher to the coastal highway where Nick turned right and headed south toward Santa Barbara.

As the ocean-scented wind blew against her cheeks, and the bike purred beneath her, Lauren began to feel more relaxed and less afraid of the steel-and-mechanical beast she rode.

She hadn't ever been this far south. The long sandy beach seemed endless, the tide driving the sea up against the cliffs. She'd never really thought about the ocean being the edge of a continent, but here it hit home in a way that had her gaze searching the vast expanse of water.

Bush lupines lined the road, and sparrows flushed from them as the bike rumbled past. Down below, a long line of pelicans flew across the water toward the marshes. Mudflats stretched ahead, birds she couldn't name winging over the ground.

Trees rose on her left, climbing the hillside. The road was interspersed with shade and light, the afternoon sun not reaching its highest point. In the distance, barely visible and oh, so vague, the ghost of the moon—waiting its turn to rise in the sky as soon as the sun and wind were finished with the day.

Nick turned off onto a narrow dirt lane, followed it down and then up until he came to a wide clearing. Once there, he held on to the handlebars and simply admired the sea for a long moment, then he cut the engine.

She felt the iron strength in his legs as he held the bike between them before punching down the kickstand.

Lauren slid off the seat, her legs still tingling from the thunderous vibration of the motorcycle as it had cut up the miles of highway to this place. Nick took her helmet, then her hand, and led her to the edge of nowhere.

The earth was soft beneath her shoes. "Where are we?"

"Lovers' Point."

"Oh." She thought his choice of location was interesting, but said nothing.

Yucca and aloe and other exotic plants grew in a profusion of colors and textures. Ice plant, something that Billy nicknamed green French fries, grew wild in thickets of stunning pink. The landward slopes were thick with carpets of orange poppies and millions of tiny lavender blooms.

"I used to come here when I was in high school." Nick stood at the cliff, larger than life, the wind in his hair and his gaze hard and focused. "We'd drink beer, listen to music, smoke."

She filled in the blank. "Not cigarettes."

"Whatever we could roll into a ZigZag."

She'd tried marijuana herself, reflecting on days long since past. She was so different now. So glad she wasn't that misguided teenager looking for a way out, looking for love that felt so elusive all the time.

"It's beautiful here." Lauren walked around, investigating the perimeter. For a place that obviously drew people, it wasn't trashed by partygoers. No beer cans, cigarette butts. It was pristine, really. Simply heavenly.

Nick came to stand behind her. His strong arms slipped around her waist, he held her tightly, his chin resting on her head. Stubble from a day's growth of beard caught in her hair, snagging, yet comforting. Such a simple masculine thing, but it brought out sensations in her of deep longing, of cherishing this one little piece in her life and wrapping it up in her memory storage box.

The restless sound of the sea drowned out the constant beat of Nick's heart against her back.

The rock cliffs disappeared into the sea, passing the breakwaters to form islands where the water exploded in a crash of spray as the tide pushed and pulled. The rocky bluffs were wind-formed, shaped by years of sea-salt mist.

"This afternoon I'm being evaluated. The court is sending somebody to my house to interview me, interview Nicky-J."

Lauren's hands rose to cover his forearms, to hold him close to her as she leaned her body deeper into his, wanting to melt into him and give him the confidence to know that everything would be fine.

"I'm not worried for you, Nick," she said, easing her arms around him. "You'll say what you have to and they'll know that you're truthful and sincere."

"I've gone over everything a hundred times, been coached by Bruce about it." His voice, deep within his chest, rumbled through her. "But I still keep having this bad feeling. What if they think Nicky-J isn't well adjusted? I mean, the kid has a vivid imagination and he swears sometimes. I heard him slip out a few words, but I never made a big deal about it. What if they tell me I'm not the best father?"

Lauren turned to face Nick, cupping his face with her hands. "You are a wonderful father. I've seen you with Nicky-J. You will get through this. I have faith in you."

Nick's eyes held hers, deep and incredibly blue, so filled with anguish, with love for his son. She wished she could slip inside him, be with him this afternoon and hold him in her heart.

She laid her hand over his chest, on the place where his life pumped. "Trust yourself, Nick. You can never go wrong with that."

His forehead touched hers and she felt his breath on her nose, her cheeks. "Nicky-J's not doing well with this. Yesterday, he tore up my mom's flowers. He won't say why he did it, only that he felt like it."

"He's confused, he doesn't understand what's happening."

"He understands."

Lauren swallowed, feeling lost from the world in the emotional space they'd created for themselves in this place. It felt surreal, like nobody else existed or was around.

She drew from within herself something that she hadn't thought about, hadn't dared to examine or to confront again in her lifetime.

Just the thought of the memory created chills over her skin. Her breath came in a tight release of air. Then she broke a self-imposed silence and spoke words that she vowed she never would. "When I found out I was pregnant with Billy, and Trevor didn't want the baby...I—" She licked her lips, forcing herself to go on. "I almost did something."

Nick held her tightly. She clung to him, as if without his support, she'd falter.

"I went to the clinic, I had the appointment to...to..." She couldn't form the word. "But I couldn't go through with it. I swore I would never, *ever,* do anything to hurt my child. I was his mother and I would do whatever it took to fight for his life, to give him the best that I could." She raised her chin, forcing Nick to meet her gaze. "You fight for Nicky-J. You fight for him with everything you have."

Her throat closed as Nick brought his roughened cheek to hers. "You're amazing. Thank you for telling me."

They were reminded of the time, of the seconds passing by, bringing him closer to his fate, by the intermittent sounds of the surf below. And on the hillside, they heard the cry of a lone cormorant who sang into the wind.

Nick sat in his living room, every bone in his body feeling like ice—cold, unyielding. A wrong move and he'd snap.

He'd prepared for this as best he could. He'd finally hooked up with Bruce, and the lawyer told him what to say, what not to say. Some of it involved Lauren. Nick hadn't told her about that this afternoon, didn't see a reason to. The questions would be basic and the answers simple—no, he wasn't seeing anyone seriously.

But even as he thought it, Nick felt disquiet.

He hadn't told Bruce his true feelings about Lauren, hadn't felt a need since he wasn't pursuing anything beyond a trusted friendship with her at the moment. But he had told Bruce he had brought someone new into his son's life to cook for them. To phrase it like that sounded distant and didn't sit well with Nick. But from outward appearances, nobody in town could link them—romantically anyway.

There was only one problem, and that was Nicky-J.

Bruce had questioned if Nicky-J would make something more out of Lauren than she was. Nick debated that issue. If he had talked to his son about not discussing Lauren, chances were, he would because he wasn't supposed to and it would be on his mind.

So Nick opted out of talking to Nicky-J about the evaluator and allow his son to answer the questions naturally. Nick decided to let the conversation come at him in whatever way it did. He could handle it.

The court evaluator had taken the chair across from him, a notepad in her hand.

She wasn't what he expected. He'd figured it would be somebody with a severe hairstyle, a real bruiser of a woman who enjoyed this sort of thing. On the contrary, she was midsixties, pleasant-featured and she had a friendly smile.

Her name was Susan Bright.

Susan had an even tone when she spoke. "Mr. DiMartino, what's of paramount importance in determining custody is the child's welfare and best interests." When he didn't say anything, she added, "I'm not on anyone's side. I'm here to compare the location of the parents' homes, their proximity to schools, churches, day care, medical facilities and other services—baby-sitters." Sitting taller, her shoe touched the battle-worn briefcase at her feet. "Your lawyer told you to have photos of your house, interior and exterior, for me."

Nick leaned forward, grabbed an envelope. "I have them right here."

They disappeared into her caramel-colored briefcase. "I have to ask you a few things."

Nick readied himself, dragged in a few breaths, then forced himself to be relaxed.

Susan began her interrogation, asking him many questions relating to his home; how long they'd lived here, where the school was, if they went to church. At one point, she asked to see Billy's room. She brought her notepad with her, making scratches on the legal yellow paper.

They returned to the living room, her smile never faltering, so it sideswiped Nick when she inquired, "Are you romantically involved with anyone in a serious relationship?"

Nick absently moved his leg, his mind working. He knew he'd be asked this question. He guessed he just wasn't prepared to deny his feelings even though his answer was truthful. "No."

"Have you ever had a woman spend the night in your home?"

"Yes. But it was years ago."

She made a notation.

"What hours do you generally work during the week?"

He had a much stronger guard up now.

His voice sounded defensive in his ears. "Forty-plus."

"Plus how many?"

"Depends. Ten maybe."

"And your son is where when you're working?"

"My mom watches him, or he's in school."

Susan nodded. She asked him if he participated in Nicky-J's school activities.

The time moved as slow as a growing barnacle, and it felt as if he had been under Susan Bright's microscope for days.

Finally, she set her pen down. "And your son will be home soon?"

"You said to have him here at four, so my mom's bringing him over."

"Great." Susan sipped her water, set the glass back onto the coaster, then gazed about the living room. "You have a very nice home."

"Thanks." Guard still up, higher than ever, Nick sat as if he were on a bed of nails.

The clock's second hand barely moved.

Nick ground his back teeth, fingers knit loosely together on his knees. "Have you interviewed my ex-wife yet?"

The question was out before he could stop it.

Susan simply smiled politely. "I'm not at liberty to say."

The front door opened and Nicky-J came inside, not with his usual bluster and knock-over-anything-in-his-way walk. His chin was down, his shoulders sloped and uneasy. He peered over the sofa at Susan. Nick's mom had her hand on Nicky-J's back, protective, watchful.

Nick introduced the women.

Caprice said a tight hello, then left, but not before giving Nicky-J a firm hug, a kiss on the cheek and telling him she loved him.

Nicky-J sat beside his father, feet dangling over the edge of the sofa, kicking back and forth until Nick put a hand on his son's knee to make him sit still.

Susan didn't go straight for the questions but, rather, she asked Nicky-J what he liked to do, what were his favorite foods, his favorite subjects in school and television shows he liked.

The more she talked, the more relaxed Nicky-J appeared, then finally, with her smile in place, Susan asked, "Do you know why you're here?"

Nicky-J mumbled, "My mom's tryin' to take me away."

She made a note in her log. Nick hated the legal pad and all the words written on it.

"Nicky-J, do you like your school?"

"I'm gonna be in first grade and so are my friends. I don't got no friends in Calif-thornia."

Nicky-J went on to answer the woman's questions, talking about how much he loved his grandma and grandpa, his house, his dad. Said he'd never been spanked, never been yelled at and, except for yesterday when he dug up his grandma's flowers, he'd never been bad on purpose.

And he was sorry he was bad, since it made his grandma upset.

On that, he gave Nick a woeful stare. Nick hadn't punished him last night, but he was going to make Nicky-J plant all new flowers for his mom, and he'd have to use his own money to help pay for them.

Susan sat taller. "Does your father give you restrictions?"

"I don't think so—'cept for the time I had an earache."

She questioned him, her features puzzled. "Oh, you thought I meant prescriptions, like medicine."

Nicky-J picked at a scab on his knee. "That's what you said."

She smiled.

If the woman smiled one more time, Nick was likely to tell her to knock it off.

"I was talking about restrictions," Susan clarified. "Does he punish you?"

"Only when I do somethin' bad."

The smile broadened, amused.

Notations, more notations, then: "What are you doing this summer?"

"Building a fort with my friends."

"How long have you known these friends?"

"How long, Dad?" He shot his gaze to Nick.

"Since you were born."

"Since I was born," Nicky-J repeated. "I got a new friend now. His name is Billy." Nicky-J scowled, his hands folded together as if he were in church waiting for the priest to bless him. "His mom is nice. She's a nicer mom than my mom and I like her. She smells nice when she comes over."

Susan's eyebrows lifted, she gazed at Nick.

Nick's face gave nothing away. "She cooks for us."

"How often?"

"Three nights a week."

"She cooks good," Nicky-J said. "I like her. My dad likes her and we done special dinners."

Nick closed his eyes a moment, inhaled and felt his nostrils flare. He quickly composed himself.

"Are you seeing this woman romantically?" Susan asked, the skepticism in her tone evident.

"No." The sound rode heavily on his tongue.

Lowering her pen, Susan looked relaxed when every sinew, every fiber of muscle in Nick's body felt stretched to the limit.

"Nicky-J, do you understand why I'm here?"

"You want me to live with my mom."

"I want what's best for you."

"My dad's my best friend."

Nick's throat tightened, his arms flexing and wanting to drag his son onto his lap and squeeze him.

"My dad, he's the best dad ever. He don't yell at me, he brings me my sippy cup with milk. He lets me use the opener can even though it's sharp and I can't never watch TV out here with food 'cause I might spill it. We look at stars and we go fishin' and he never yells at me or nothin'." Nicky-J's little face was filled with so much worry, Nick fought back the burn in his chest. "He's the best daddy ever and I want to live with my dad. 'Cause he's my best friend."

Nick's breath was caged in his chest, love for his son filling him.

Susan folded her notepad, arranged it inside her briefcase and stood. "I have everything I need. Thank you so much, Mr. DiMartino."

At the Wharf Diner, Verna Mae was pondering the benefits of support hose and nurse's shoes over dollar-store stockings and sneakers when Hank came in.

Hank wasn't a regular. He favored a lunch pail—his wife made him a cheese sandwich most nights. But once in a while, he popped a squat on her vinyl stool and ordered from the menu—usually something with kick to it.

"Evenin', Verna Mae," he said, taking a spot at the counter.

"Hi, Hank."

Verna Mae was bone-ass tired from a long night, made longer because Lou didn't show. Knox was in the kitchen, having put in almost twelve hours and he was fit to be tied. At least he'd stopped swearing and threatening to string up his cousin on a fishing line and drop him overboard Cap'n Mike's trawler as shark chum.

The odor of unfiltered cigarettes permeated the kitchen, Knox smoking one right after the other from outside the alley door. The rickety screen door did little to mask the odor pouring through the mesh every time Knox stepped out to take another drag. Verna Mae hadn't said anything about the kitchen being a non-smoking environment—she valued her neck, as skinny as it was.

"I'd like the fish special," Hank ordered, a smile on his mug so broad, she didn't think she'd ever seen anything like it on his face before.

He'd either come in to some money or gotten laid.

"One battered special," she said, noting it on her order pad. She was about it clip it to the revolving ticket ring, when Hank stopped her short.

"No, ma'am. I don't want it battered. I want it just the way it was last night."

"It was battered last night."

"No, ma'am. This was served whole, no tartar sauce."

"All our fish is served with a cup of tartar sauce, Hank."

"Not this fish. Snapper. With lemon and some green stuff inside."

Green stuff...?

Lauren Jessup was on shift last night with Lou. They'd closed and Lauren wasn't working today; however, she'd brought in some of those raspberry muffins this morning before Verna Mae came in, and by noon, every last one had been gobbled up.

As for green stuff on the menu... Verna Mae hadn't noticed anything different in the kitchen from last night.

She didn't keep a tally on her snapper or fresh fish, nor did she weigh the freezer goods. She knew Knox and Lou fixed themselves something to eat on the time clock.

"What do you mean by 'green stuff'?"

"Herbs. Like little pieces of grass. They smelled like, I don't know—herbs. Just great, if you want the truth. Eating that snapper last night, something washed over me, you know. I felt like a new man, all vigor and damn-me-I-can-do-anything." His face reddened. "My wife noticed the difference when I came home. I was still feeling it, you know, even after eight hours on the hill, you know?"

No, she didn't know and she didn't want to imagine Hank's bedroom and picture things that she would rather not picture. But she did have a sneaking feeling about who had cooked that snapper.

"Was it Lauren who served you, Hank? She's that cute little gal I have working for me. Looks like she belongs on one of them fashion magazine covers instead of in a waitress uniform? She's tall, dark hair, red lips."

"That's her!"

"Hmm. Well, whatever she cooked for you, we don't have that on the menu, and I wouldn't know what it was."

"Darn shame, Verna Mae. I was really primed. You think you could have her fix it for me sometime?"

"Oh…" Verna Mae poured herself another cup of decaf, the joe keeping her going through the long day and even later night. In a voice that was low and smooth, she said, "I'll fix her, all right."

Fifteen

The old devil moon made him do it.

Lauren had barely stamped her time card when Verna Mae appeared in her office doorway and waved her inside.

Dread worked its way up Lauren's spine.

Verna Mae wasn't smiling.

Easing out of her sweater and setting her purse in one of the employee lockers—no lock but safe just the same—Lauren straightened her shoulders and marched forward.

Myriad thoughts swirled through her mind. She needed this job and she shouldn't have done something to jeopardize it. In hindsight, she recognized she'd been waiting for the chance to prove herself to Verna Mae, so she'd jumped on it when the opportunity arose. From the expression on Verna Mae's face, Lauren thought she would have been better off if she'd sent Hank on his way that night.

While her own troubles were at the forefront of her mind, Nick's weren't far behind.

He'd telephoned her last night, telling her not to come by. He and Nicky-J were going to spend the evening by themselves. Lauren understood perfectly, gave them their space. She asked him how the interview went and his only response was, "It's over."

Pushing the door open, Lauren stepped into the windowless office. Verna Mae had a penchant for red and the room swam in it. Like a velvet-lined box of Valentine chocolates, the walls were painted love-struck red. Her desk was so piled with receipts—no CODs as she was often proud of saying—the actual wood grain was indiscernible. She collected troll dolls, their fuzzy colorful hair sticking straight up, their big glass eyes staring off into space from their shelf. Saltwater taffy filled a glass candy jar that was within reach should Verna Mae be so inclined to have one.

"Have a seat," Verna Mae said from behind her mound of paperwork. She sipped on a cup of coffee, its surface steaming and oily black.

Lauren took a chair, one of the legs shorter than the other so it wobbled when she tucked her ankles together.

Without preamble, Verna Mae got down to business. "Last night, Lou got himself into a barroom fight at the Outdigger. He didn't show for his shift because the cops put him in the slammer to cool off. That man drinks like a fish, don't know why I put up with him. Knox said he was going to knock his block off, but I saw Lou this morning so I know for myself he's still alive—but the hangover he's carrying around is as big as a jumbo jet and I'm sure just as turbulent."

Wondering why Lou got called in so early, Lauren remained silent. She hadn't seen him in the kitchen.

"I canned his sorry butt." Verna Mae's declaration made its way through Lauren's brain. "Effective immediately."

Lauren's silence held, uncertain where, if any place, she fit in here.

Verna Mae helped herself to a taffy, offering Lauren one. She declined, unable to sit comfortably in the chair until she knew what was going on.

"Hank came in last night," Verna Mae said.

A flinch threatened Lauren's steady composure. This could be bad...

With an arch of her red eyebrow, Verna Mae went on, "He talked about some snapper you cooked for him."

Now or never, Lauren thought. This was it. She had a feeling she wasn't leaving this office with the same status she had when she'd entered it.

Making no excuses, Lauren said, "We were all out of the deep-sea batter special."

"So you decided to serve him something else, something not on my menu."

"He was hungry."

"He was sniffing for a second helping last night."

Optimism rose, a tiny bud blooming to life. "Verna Mae, I didn't intentionally go against any rules of the diner, but I didn't know what else to do. We didn't get our order in and the kitchen stock was short. I made do with what we had."

"You could have turned him away."

So much for optimism, it buckled and crumpled like a house of cards stacked one too many high. "I suppose."

"But you didn't." Verna Mae leaned forward, her curly titian hair framing her face. "Instead, you fired up the grill and you fed him. You kept the customer happy."

Trying to discern whether or not that was a trick question, Lauren remarked, "Yes, I did."

Verna Mae busted into abrupt laughter, startling Lauren into sitting taller. She wasn't sure what to make of her boss's sudden humor.

"I can tell when a man has that look of love and he was happy in love." Her tone lowered into that serious businesswoman voice of hers. "Your raspberry muffins sold out before noon."

Lauren barely had a moment to be joyful.

"Don't look so pleased about it." Verna Mae's statement sliced Lauren's elation short. "I don't think you'll have time on your hands to be baking them anymore." Popping another taffy into her mouth and talking around it, Verna Mae flattened the wrapper on her desk, a habit more than anything else. "Here's what I'm going to do. I'm moving Omar from part-time cook's helper—to full-time cook on weekday mornings. You can work the kitchen on the nights Knox isn't in there. This means you'll be doing the Saturday-night dinner shift, and four nights weekly."

Speechless, Lauren couldn't breathe. She was trying to make sure she heard Verna Mae correctly. "You're making me a cook?"

"Not full-time, only part-time. You can waitress the other hours if you want."

Lauren nodded, a thought surfacing in her mind. Hank had loved her red snapper dish—would she be making that again, or nothing more creative than dropping a prebreaded item into a vat of grease? "But what about the menu? I don't really think—"

"I'm not paying you to think, sweetpea, but I'd like

you to fix me that snapper for lunch so I can see for my-self what all the fuss is about. If I like it, we'll add it on for tonight's dinner."

Verna Mae stood, the conversation was over.

"Thank you, Verna Mae." Beside herself, Lauren rose to her feet. "You won't regret your decision, I promise you. I'll be the best cook this place ever had."

"That's good to hear." Verna Mae gave her a pat on the back and a smile that warmed Lauren to the core. "Now—are you up to date on your tetanus shot? I've never had a cook yet who didn't cut the tip of their fin-ger off with a sharp knife the first week in my kitchen."

Blinding sunlight slashed through the six-on-six win-dow in guest room 208 as Nick took a measurement for the ceiling cornice. He stood on a sawhorse, squinting against the sun as he drew his yellow tape across the wall. Tools hung from his hips, his movement creating sounds from the leather pouch of nails and the hammer that dangled next to his thigh. His hands were stiff from fin-gering nails. It had been a back-breaking six hours so far today, but he needed to immerse himself in something.

Anything to take his thoughts away from the phone call he'd had with Bruce Harmon.

Last night after Nick put Nicky-J to bed, he had called Bruce to talk about the interview.

"Define romantically involved," he'd asked Bruce.

"Do you have a stepmother in mind?" the lawyer had countered.

Nick's body had tightened, he didn't say anything.

Bruce noticed his unresponsiveness. "I asked you when this thing started if you had a serious girlfriend.

You said no, just the woman who cooked for you. What's changed?"

"You asked me if I've done anything lately I wouldn't want a courtroom to hear. I told you I haven't. That still stands, only there was a little misunderstanding with Nicky-J's interpretation of my relationship."

"How so?"

"My son said Lauren Jessup would be a nicer mom to him than his real mom."

"Not good. If Debbie's lawyers get wind of it, they'll put your girlfriend's life—"

"She's not my girlfriend." Not in the way he would have liked.

"—under crossfire. Call her what you want at this point. Your son has implied she's something more than a cook in your house. Her past could be dug up and she could be brought into court."

"How certain are you this could happen?"

"The judge is going to factor in every piece of your life and figure it into the equation." The lawyer tone in Bruce's voice dimmed and eased. "Nick, we've known each other a long time, so be up front with me. Is this a woman you want in your life?"

Nick had swallowed, contemplated. "I'd like her to be, but the timing sucks."

"Judges aren't going to rule a dinner and a movie as anything detrimental to your son's well-being. They know you have a life—but it's a life that's under a microscope right now. Anything you do can be held accountable in court. That's the key word here—*accountability*." His deep voice cleared. "Keep things simple. I don't know if your ex has a P.I. on your tail. It's a possibility."

"Christ, I don't know. Maybe Steve would think of it." Nick had taken another drink of his beer, his body fatigued. "I just don't know. Haven't felt the fine hairs on the back of my neck on edge, if that's any indication."

"Nick, I'm not telling you to stop having a life—just be careful what kind of life you're living right now."

And that had been that.

Nick had hung up feeling beaten. All the emotions that had been evolving, growing, deepening for Lauren sort of evaporated. He had to make them go away, had to forget he felt things he did.

He had to cool things down.

Stepping off the sawhorse, Nick strode through the room and into the hallway where lengths of golden oak lumber filled the floor. Plaster dust circulated in dust motes, the cacophony of construction filled the air around him. While Danny worked in room 209 with a nail compressor, three carpenters plastered ceilings on the ground level. The plumber completed the lobby rest room and an electrician was rewiring a kitchen wall up to code.

The Preservation Week committee had walked through last week and had been impressed. All in all, Nick was on track with the project, but he just wished there were more hours in the day to get things done.

He turned toward the main stairwell and caught sight of Lauren as she walked in his direction. Pausing, Nick girded himself, a tightness holding him still.

She looked great.

He'd never seen her smiling so freely, so beautiful. Her hair was tucked behind her ears, her cheeks blushed from excitement. Nick had skipped lunch today, so he hadn't seen her, which was an excuse anyway. He chose not to go into the diner with the others at noon, staying here, immersing himself in work and trying to forget he had ever kissed her, held her or ever wanted more for himself than he had before she came to Bella Luna.

Nick held himself in check. "Hey," he said before she could speak. "I'm sort of busy right now."

"I won't stay long." She stepped over a network of orange electrical cords, a box of plaster and a mud tray with a trowel. "I wanted to tell you something—something really great."

The cords of his neck muscles stretched taut. He willed himself to ignore the feelings that had surfaced and were attacking his resoluteness.

Pride broadened her smile. "Verna Mae promoted me to cook."

He hadn't really guessed that that had been her news but he should have expected as much. Lauren was persistent and she was an incredible cook. "That's good, really great, Lauren. I'm glad for you."

She went on, not noticing he was conflicted, not noticing his hands had balled into fists to keep himself from smoothing her hair and holding her close.

"I start tonight," she said in a rush. "I'll work alongside Knox, get a feel for the kitchen and the equipment I'm unfamiliar with. It's going to be amazing. Verna Mae loved what I made her for lunch. She's adding it to the menu tonight." Her enthusiasm bubbled, her features stunning with confidence and a happiness he'd rarely seen in her eyes.

He wished he could let go, forget about obligations, just be with her the way he wanted to. Bring her into his arms, congratulate her properly. Kiss her mouth.

"I knew you could do it." He picked up a length of wood. He had to put something in his hands to keep them off of her, to keep from doing something stupid.

Lauren's smile faded, her elation cooling. "Nick, what's the matter? Did you hear from the court?"

"I'm good. Nothing's happened yet." He brought the lumber into the guest room. Lauren followed.

"What aren't you telling me?" The cynicism in her tone, something he'd heard before, rose full-blown. He hated knowing that he had put it there.

He owed her an explanation. He wasn't such a hard-ass that he'd let her walk out without knowing why what had started to grow between them had to die.

He lifted his arm to the window and leaned into the sill, staring through the glass. The ocean was serene, the wind had died down and the sky was a vivid blue.

Turning to Lauren, he drank in her appearance, the way her shoes were double tied and her apron pocket stuffed with her order pad. The way her lips were red and full, her skin the color of a pearl. "I talked with my lawyer last night. He cautioned me about getting seriously involved right now. You can't cook for me anymore. It gives Nicky-J the wrong impression and it...Christ."

Lauren's expression remained stoic. Whatever she was thinking, she hid it well.

"I care about you, Lauren. Too much. That's the problem." He snagged a raspy breath. "But I can't do anything that could be interpreted unfavorably by the court."

She nodded slowly, a sight that pained him. Her eyebrows lifted slightly, she let out a shaky sigh, her lips pursed briefly. "Yes, I understand." Then she smiled, a forced smile that cut him to the quick. "Too well."

She'd come here with happiness and cheer, and he'd snuffed it out with words he hated to say. "Lauren, I don't want to give up our friendship."

The statement sounded lame even to his ears. He despised himself right now.

"I agree. We shouldn't have to pretend we aren't friends. That would be ridiculous. I still consider you someone I trust, that hasn't changed." *Trust.* That was so hard for her to do, and yet, she gave it over. Torment wrenched through him, a knifelike pain that stabbed. "I appreciate your honesty." She turned to leave, he couldn't let her go.

"Lauren, wait." He caught her by the arm, and her gaze slid to where his hand touched her—as if it burned. She removed herself from him, stepped away.

"It's okay, really. Anything you have to say won't make a difference to me. I'm a big girl," she half joked. "If you think I'm going to cry about it, don't worry. I'll be fine. I always am."

"I don't want to do this." He grappled for the right words, the right thing to say to make things okay. "We can still see each other, just not in a way that would make us want to take things further, not until after the trial. I just can't."

She kept smiling, that defeated smile he wanted to erase from her mouth with a fiery imprint of his own. He wanted to hold her and make all the hurts he put upon her disappear.

"I know you can't. It's okay." She pulled in a breath. "Listen, if you're hungry when you get off work, you should come by the Wharf. I'm making snapper tonight. It's really good." With that, she gave him a little shrug, showed just the tiniest hint of buckling under to emotions, then erected the strong facade once more.

She turned and left, his gut feeling as if it were made of lead.

He went through the cavernous building, found the electrician and bummed a cigarette.

Pushing through the side door of the hotel, Nick rested his forearms on the edge of the wharf's railing. The water was a deep ultramarine blue with little whitecaps of foam flicking the swells. Silent boats bobbed on the sun-glistened surface. The air smelled like rust, motor oil, the daily lunch special at the Wharf Diner.

On an exhaled puff of smoke, he promised himself he was going to get through this and make things up to Lauren.

Sixteen

Porta la luna per questo.
(It takes the moon for this.)

Curious things began to happen in Bella Luna.

The metal walls on the canneries gleamed in the sunshine, as if winking in conspiracy. Marine animals appeared more colorful in their tide-pool beds; vivid bursts of purple urchins, orange sea stars and green anemone.

Seabirds that walked on empty beaches to watch the final passing of the day, their spindly legs scissoring swiftly along the wet sand, seemed confused by the changes.

Like shifting sandbars, the daily patterns were different, life courses were changed.

The pink moon was nowhere to be seen, and there was nothing to account for the occurrences of fortune and well-being and in this case, thanksgiving.

One morning when the sun rose over a river of fog filling the streets, Doug Carlyle, one of Bella Luna's finest, sat behind his desk eating a raspberry muffin he'd purchased along with a cuppa joe in an insulated cup. Paperwork was the bane of his existence, and he had a mountain of it. But what would normally give him indigestion didn't bother him in the slightest. He couldn't figure out why, but he felt better with each bite of that muffin until he eventually had a clean desk and the urge to take his wife to the new chick flick playing at the Rialto.

At the diner, Miss Applegate was enjoying a respite from the classroom this summer, wishing she could take a vacation getaway to Hawaii. She'd gone as far as stopping by the travel agency and taking several brochures. She dreamed over the glossy pictures of white sandy beaches over dinner, sampling the Wharf Diner's latest offering when a two-week Kona-Kauai-Big Island package caught her attention. It was doubtful she'd be able to afford such an extravagance, but she opted to inquire anyway by making a call on her cell phone. To her amazement, the package was within her budget and she booked the trip, giddy with anticipation. She even passed on dessert, determined to fit into her bikini.

During Sunday Mass, the priest lost his train of thought, suddenly feeling the Holy Ghost descend upon his spirit like a page out of the Bible. He'd never given a more profound and reverent message. The congregation wept, touched by his words of wisdom and strength. Prior to the service, the coffee hour in the rectory had been supplied by the choir—who didn't lift a finger baking—but rather bought a box of raspberry muffins from the Wharf Diner.

Verna Mae didn't have one single regret about her decision to promote Lauren to cook, and she gave thanks to the angel above who'd decided to send that pretty little gal her way. In fact, Lauren wasn't out on the floor much this last week, having done such a bang-up job in the kitchen the week prior. Verna Mae's business had kicked into high gear, the place was full most every night Lauren was on shift. The two of them went over the menu and, depending on what fish were running that week, what produce was freshest, Verna Mae was writing something new onto the chalkboard special a couple of times a week.

Life couldn't get much better for Verna Mae, unless she won the lottery or something grand. Not since she'd been with the rectory over Santa Barbara way had she seen such a flock of hungry diners sitting down at a table.

Bella Luna was literally aglow, people were friendly and lives moved in new directions. Overdue book fines were paid at the library, parking meters always had leftover minutes on them for the next car, and spam ceased to clutter people's e-mail. It was as if the heavens had sprinkled them with pixie dust.

But in a dark corner on a Saturday night, a little dog shivered against the damp sea spray that thickened over the pavement, his short breaths coming out in little mists.

Seventeen

Under a smiling moon, she let down her hair.

When Lauren should have been the happiest she'd ever been in her life, she was easily distracted, longing for something that she didn't have but had tried hard to reach for. She missed the way things had been between her and Nick. Friendships were fine, but she felt more than friendship for him, so she threw herself into working at the diner. Nicky-J was still a constant in Billy's life, since the boys still played together under Caprice's care.

In the last couple of weeks, Verna Mae had turned out to be a gem. The woman, while opinionated and stubborn, relinquished her old-school thinking and let Lauren offer input to the new menu. The diner was fast becoming a popular place to go in the evenings and Lauren, while loving the energy and newness, was so tired she dragged at the end of the week.

Maybe it was losing Nick, maybe it was something else, but a restless discontentment smoldered to life in her heart. Why did this feeling have to come now? She wanted it to go away, to disappear. She had finally found a good place and a job that she wanted, so why did she feel the tide pulling again?

Nick.

Always back to Nick.

She hadn't cooked for him in weeks, and not one to disregard a deal, Lauren had begun to increase her rent money by increments. Her pay as cook was more than what she'd earned as a waitress. Eventually, she would find another place to stay but, for now, paying Nick extra was the best she could do.

As Lauren sat in the diner's kitchen, a notepad before her while she sorted through what to get done first on Monday night's shift, she grew distracted by the pouring rain on the rooftop. The sound was like needles, sharp and tinny, hitting the shingles. She glanced through the window, watching as the drops fell from the sky in white jets under the lamplight on the empty pier. The rain had started to come down hard about an hour after closing. The two busboys had cleaned up, and Verna Mae had left after they'd discussed which supply orders would be coming in next week.

Lauren had a key, something that symbolized trust on Verna Mae's part because as she'd said she didn't give it out lightly—not after changing the locks after firing Lou.

Alone in the quiet restaurant, Lauren was occupied with her thoughts, letting them drift and ebb like the tide.

There was no rush to return home. Billy was at his first-ever sleepover. Critter Gilman had just turned six and Billy, Nicky-J, Tim and several other boys were attending a pizza party at Wong's Pizzeria, then a camp-

out in the Gilmans' backyard, which—because of nature—had probably been changed to the living room.

Lauren's attention turned to what she wanted to cook
for the special on Monday. Beefsteak, she thought, with
a demi-glaze. Baby vegetables. Dunk had said he'd be
getting in summer squash, and some zucchini blos-
soms. Closing her eyes, she envisioned the flavors, tasting and adjusting them in her mind, then she wrote on
the notepad.

She was certain a trained chef would never go about
kitchen duties in the manner in which she did. Strange
how knowing what to do came to her without effort.
She'd never been able to pinpoint why, but she dared
once, and only once, to perhaps attribute it to her
mother. As a small child, she recalled many aromas in
the house, the scents of roasting meats, cookies and
spices. Comforts which were taken from her when her
mother decided her boyfriend—Lauren couldn't recall
his name—came first.

Satisfied she'd come up with a crowd pleaser, she
made sure the diner was secure, all the faucets turned
off in the rest room. Verna Mae said she'd once come
in to work to a flood—someone had put chewing gum
in the men's-room drain, then turned on the faucet.

The grill was cool after a long hot night of searing
fish, and sizzling chicken breasts and crabmeat. The
low hum of the big refrigerator sounded louder when
Lauren switched off the lights. Her sweater did little to
ward off the rain. She didn't own an umbrella and had
to step outside with only the side-street overhang to
temporarily keep her dry while she locked the door.

She refused to look at the Ocean Grove Inn, directly

behind the diner, so she failed to see the lone construction light coming from the upstairs window. It was turned off as she checked the door lock.

To her left, and barely five feet down the alley, the large rubbish bins stood guard like sentinels. If the lids hadn't been closed, leftover food made late-night meals for cats.

Against her will, she gazed briefly at the Edwardian hotel, damning her lack of fortitude. The building was dark, of course. Nick had long since gone home.

He'd been seldom seen in the diner, having Danny come in to grab their to-go meals. DiMartino dinners were, more likely than not, missing his presence. Once she overhead Anthony say that Nick was going to work himself into an early grave the way he'd thrust himself into the renovation, barely sleeping, barely eating.

Lauren wished, for Nick's sake, he wouldn't be so hard on himself. Feelings for him still remained, as much as she hated to admit it. She wanted him to be happy, wanted him well. Wanted him to continue to be a good father and finally have the trial behind him, a dim memory.

But what he was thinking, how he was feeling, Lauren wouldn't know. So she looked away from the Grove and pushed forward.

Rain pelted Lauren as soon as she stepped onto the sidewalk, but her steps were short-lived when she heard the whimpering cry of an animal coming from behind her. She paused, turned to look, and gazed down the alleyway. Two glowing eyes blinked, a small body quivered.

Lauren bit her lip, inhaled and really didn't want to deal with whatever it was, but something in her wouldn't let her go home.

She trudged around, walked into the alley and stopped.

A grimy lightbulb from the building's back entry lent enough muted light with which to see.

The lost dog Billy had been searching for was huddled on a wadded pile of wet, greasy newspapers Knox had tossed out after cleaning the deep fryer.

Rain soaked her through, her jeans and blouse sticking to her skin, the sweater sodden and heavy over her shoulders.

Crouching, Lauren extended her hand, unsure how the dog would react to her. If it was hurt, it might be aggressive.

She spoke in gentle tones, reaching her body farther and farther toward it. The little dog shook, the tail unmoving.

"It's okay," she crooned.

The dog let her touch its head, and give it a few strokes. It smelled like motor oil, wet pavement and dirt. Poor thing. As she smoothed her hand over its coat, it lay down, beaten and forlorn.

She wondered where it had been all this time. More importantly: What was she going to do with it?

Feeling down the flanks and legs, she didn't think the dog was hurt or had broken bones. Just cold and hungry.

How could she turn her back on it, but how could she take it in? She didn't have money for a vet, couldn't care for a pet when she wasn't home, and certainly didn't need the burden.

Whimpering, the dog rose on its haunches and came to her, leaning its matted body next to her thigh. The physical effort was too much and it collapsed onto the flooded alley pavement. The rain pelted down, bouncing off the concrete.

She could barely see as she attempted to pick the dog up, cradling it in her arms. It felt like a dead weight. Her heart thumped, adrenaline surging through her veins. She didn't know where she could find a vet and hoped that a warm home, water and food would do for tonight.

In this rain-soaked night, as she took steps down the alleyway, she felt as alone as the dog.

Old wounds resurfaced, as she remembered nights gone by when she'd lain in a bedroom that wasn't hers, unable to fall asleep and feeling like an outcast. An outsider never let in.

At the corner, she stopped cold.

Standing there was Nick DiMartino. Water ran down his T-shirt, his hair and face. His silhouette was one of a kind; imposing, yet comforting.

"I found the dog," she muttered, thinking of nothing else to say. Feeling incredibly sad from missing him, from longing for too much, seeing him there made her want to melt.

"Where are you taking it?" he called over the roar of the rain.

"Home."

"Give him over. I'll carry him."

She shook her head. "I want to do it. He trusts me."

Without argument, neither his nor hers, Nick stayed beside her as they half ran in the pelting rain to just past the pier and Cottage Row. She never drove to work, and she wondered briefly where Nick had come from—where his motorcycle was parked.

On her porch, she couldn't reach inside her purse for

the house keys so Nick rummaged inside and found it. He opened the door, and stepped aside so she could enter ahead of him.

There was no time to ask him what he was doing, why he'd followed her home. No time for her to analyze why she'd let him come inside. The dog took precedence and, for the next hour, she bathed and fed it some leftover chicken, dried it off in a towel, tried her best to run a brush through its fur. She dumped out the toys in Billy's basket, laid a blanket in it and gently set the dog into the warm depths.

It stared at her with grateful brown eyes, a little flick of pink tongue on her hand before circling once, twice, then curling into a tight ball. Within a few minutes, it slept soundly, snoring softly.

Lauren had a moment now to realize she was cold and still wet through, and that Nick was sitting on a kitchen chair with his shirt and shoes off.

She gazed at him, dumbfounded, and blurted out, "You aren't staying."

"Take your clothes off."

Her mouth dropped open.

She went around him, his arm caught her hand. "Lauren, you're wet. It's cold. You're tired. Get something warm on, I'll make you dinner."

"Why were you out in the rain tonight?"

"I was working next door and saw you on my way home." He rose to his feet, standing in front of her, imposing and broad. Her breath hitched in her throat.

"And that's where you should be. Go home, Nick."

"No." His hands slid up her arms, held on to her shoulders to steady her. She hadn't realized she was close to faltering. She was exhausted, emotionally spent. "Right now, I need to be here. With you."

The day had been long, the weeks even longer. Withdrawing from Nick was worse than moving from place to place. In Bella Luna she had to catch glimpses of him, had to see his mom and his family, had reminders of him at every turn.

On shaky knees, she resisted him. Couldn't fight, couldn't even muster the energy to form words that would make him leave. A part of her didn't want him to go.

He smelled like damp wood, rich oak and the storm outside; rainwater and night sky.

The outline of his lips was sensual, his jaw chiseled and hard. He'd combed his dark hair from his face with his fingers, his forehead smooth and tan. Blue, depthless eyes stared at her, reading her mind.

He knows.

He knows I want him, that I missed him. That I caught myself falling in love with him. He knows my heart, my hopes. He knows who I am, where I've been, and he still looks at me as if I matter.

A moan of surrender rose from her throat. She could no more fight him, fight this, than she could keep on denying she'd forgotten about him.

She expected herself to willingly fall into his arms, but something kept her still, frozen and unyielding. Waiting, wondering.

"I can't just be your friend," he whispered huskily. "I don't have promises to give. But I'm here, it's now…and I want to be with you."

She found herself saying, "But nothing's changed. You still have your reasons."

"They aren't my reasons. And nobody is outside that door to question my judgment right now. It's just you and me."

That was as honest as she could expect. Whatever happened tonight was only for tonight. Whatever happened tomorrow, he couldn't say.

She'd had too many tomorrows of uncertainty. This was real, this was right now. She felt it in her mind and soul, a connection to Nick like she'd never felt for another man in her whole life. To turn her back on it because there was no guarantee would be like buying a lottery ticket and never scratching the surface to see if she'd won.

"Then stay," she said, her voice so slight it was like a fragile piece of lace. "Stay with me…but no regrets."

"No regrets."

She wrapped her arms around his shoulders, her wet clothes pressed into his body. Thigh against thigh, breasts crushed next to his chest. An explosion of heat erupted where he touched her. She floated, let herself fall into the kiss as his mouth covered hers and he took her away from the present.

The only thing that mattered was Nick, and this moment.

She wanted to explore everything about him, every nuance, all that he had to give. She'd drink from him, thirsty for his body, hungry for his touch.

She arched her back, wanting the sensation of his exposed flesh covering hers. She had to be rid of this sweater, the blouse. Shrugging out of the heavy knit, she didn't break the kiss. Nick helped her, pulling on sleeves, his tongue sliding into her mouth.

The buttons of her blouse were tiny, awkward to unfasten when her hands were trembling. Nick caught them within his own, examining the battle scars of the kitchen.

Her hands ached from the blisters on her palms. At the base of her forefinger, a cut had healed into a scar. The cuticles were in bad shape and both her hands were raw from being in water all day. Her knuckles were callused and the fingernail on her pinkie finger was filed down so low, there was no white left.

The scrapes and wounds made her who she was, and Nick touched each one as if to mend the ravages. She shivered from his touch.

She went to unbutton her blouse once more, but Nick brushed her hands aside. She ran her hands over his chest, languid with desire for him. He felt so warm, so sleek. Like liquid heat, taut with muscle, burning-hot skin.

She hooked her right hand around his neck, head back, and exposed her throat to his mouth. The blouse fell in a soggy pile onto the kitchen floor, and she backed into the table, her butt pressing against the edge.

Nick's lips traveled over the delicate skin on the column of her neck, moving higher to her ear and the sensitive skin of its shell. He traced her ear with his tongue, a slow and sensual pattern that left her breathless.

His heartbeat was steady, hard and fierce beneath her left palm. In the chilled room, her nipples tightened, her plain white bra feeling tight. She skimmed her short fingernails down his biceps, falling in lust with the strength he exuded.

To Lauren, there was nothing better than a man who stood a head taller than a woman—it was a dominance thing—but in a good way that made her feel completely feminine. Nick towered over her, in command, his sexuality reined tightly, drawing each second out with a sweet agony that caused her toes to curl.

Her stomach muscles quivered as he flicked his tongue over her lips, parted the seam of her mouth and took his entrance in a deep and bone-searing kiss.

She took both his hands, held them in her own, his arms raised over his head. She had to control something, had to be master over him in some way, even if it was small. She walked him through the house, guiding them backward toward her bedroom.

Once there, the patter of rain filtered through the room's many windows. In a ritual, ages old, they danced their dance of undressing.

Nick worked the metal button of his jeans, shrugged out of the cumbersome denim and kicked his feet out of the legs. He wore briefs that fit him like a glove, leaving little to her imagination. He was thick and full, the definition of ridge making her throat go dry.

Breath burned inside her body, closing in her lungs. This was so different than how she'd imagined it. She'd seen them on her bed, naked, slowly making love. There was an urgency to her beating heart that she couldn't quell even if she wanted to.

He stroked his hands down her bare arms, then reached behind her and unhooked her bra. It fell from his hands and she stood before him, meeting the fire in his eyes.

"You're beautiful."

The valley of her breasts rose and fell with her breath, her skin sensitive to the air as gooseflesh appeared. The tightness in her nipples increased, and she ached for his hands, his mouth, to discover her.

She rid herself of her shoes and jeans, the frenzied pulse of excitement racing through her body. It was so strong, she felt dizzy from it, aroused to the point where she was unsteady on her feet.

Nick removed his briefs, stood before her, and she fell into his arms. His chest was warm, so warm and felt so right next to hers. They kissed, mouths fused, their minds relieved of the outside world. All that existed was this, the here and now.

His hands slid over her waist and hips. He caught the elastic band of her panties in his thumbs and pulled downward, their kiss accommodating the motion.

She felt as if she were falling. He touched her very center, gently stroking, softly touching. He'd gone there before, and had brought her to gratification. She wanted that again, wanted him to feel it, too.

She turned her face to his. "I want to make you feel good."

"You make me feel good just by looking at you."

Her fingers rose to his hair, she loved its texture, could never get enough of the rich thickness and how it felt. "That's not the same thing. I want your body to belong to me the way mine belonged to you that night at your house."

In a guttural tone, he said, "You have it."

She kissed him the way she liked it, the way she knew he liked it. Full mouth, open lips and tongue. She explored and nibbled, bit and grew daring. She liked the way he moaned, and the hum of pleasure that rose from his throat.

It felt good to be in control, to take charge of him.

His skin was scented by rain and she traced her tongue along the ridge of his shoulder. "I've thought about doing this since forever."

She stopped at his collarbone, pressing light kisses.

"Coming in to the diner and seeing you but not touching you, it was driving me crazy—" He sucked in his breath as she slid her hand down his chest, moving lower and cupping him in her fingers.

"You're touching me now."

He pulled in a hard gulp as she stroked the length of him, favoring the smooth head. The wide stretch of his hand flattened against her belly, then higher to her breast. He teased her nipple, pulled and coaxed a purr of sinful pleasure from her throat.

Blood rushed through her, making everything she did more sensitive by tenfold. The room seemed lighter, the air warmer, her body in heightened awareness.

She clung to him, reaching her arms around him and holding him as close as she possibly could. He brought her back and they fell across the bed, the worn springs giving way to their weight.

The storm raged outside as a different storm raged within the cottage. Sighs fell from her lips, sensations she hadn't felt in aeons curled through her belly.

His mouth was on her. Her hair, her neck, her breasts. He felt her control unraveling and she gave up, knowing she would have him but not in the way she'd assumed. This was no give-and-take. It would be take-and-take. Demand and devour. Hard and fast.

She clung to the edge of reason, almost forgetting, almost giving way—

"It's a little late to ask," she gasped, her fingers fisting into the coverlet, her body damp with perspiration and need. If he hadn't brought protection, she'd go crazy. But they'd do other things, she wasn't going to let him go. Not yet.

He was gone from the bed only briefly, came back to her and covered her body with his. "No worries."

She kept her eyes locked on his, knowing she had no worries in this moment. Everything she had, everything she could offer was his.

His smile melted her. She had no idea until now that she'd been waiting for this from the second she'd first laid eyes on him.

Lauren's lips met his, a lingering brush of a whisper kiss. "I don't want to feel empty anymore, Nick."

"You aren't." And as he said it, he slipped himself inside of her, and filled her up with his body.

She tightened around him, slightly shocked, giving a little gasp. He was big and it had been so long.

Nick let her get used to him, slowly moving, just barely giving her a silky friction of movement. Her legs hugged his, calves intertwined.

"Look at me," he commanded.

She hadn't realized she'd closed her eyes. The world moved at a rapid pace around her, but she didn't feel it. All she saw was Nick. All she felt was Nick.

All that she was she gave to him.

He moved and thrust into her, bringing her to the brink of something exquisite. She wanted to let go, but she held on, wanting even more to savor every second of pure bliss.

Clutching onto his shoulders, her legs fast around his,

she moved and rocked with him, took him as deeply inside as she could. When she could hold off no longer, she found her release in a shattering flex of her pelvis, arching it high into his powerful thrust.

A moan passed through her lips, caught by Nick's mouth as he pushed himself into her several hard times and groaned his climax.

His body tensed, she held him and he fell onto her with a shudder. He buried his face in the crook of her neck, breathed into her hair.

"Lauren." He rasped her name, his voice jagged.

She would have spoken, but the only words that she could form were three:

I love you.

She didn't dare say them aloud for fear it would make all this splendor disappear.

Just being with him had to be enough.

Eighteen

Things look different when the moon disappears.

He spent the night.

Waking in the sunroom with the bright morning light slashing over his face, Nick was momentarily disorientated.

His eyes opened, blinked, then he took in his surroundings.

The room was colorful and homey, just as he remembered, only better. His mom had decorated the cottages; he had no knack for colors, preferring earthy, masculine tones.

Rolling onto his side, he discovered the bed was empty.

Nick sat up, pushed off the bed and noted his clothes were gone. No sooner did he wonder when he looked at the footboard and found them hanging over the railing—dried and neatly folded.

He fumbled for his wristwatch on the wicker side table.

Quarter past seven.

He never slept this late. He'd drifted off with Lauren in his arms and had slept soundly. He should have gone home last night. It was pointless to think about a choice he hadn't made. What he'd done was something he couldn't, didn't, want to take back.

Sliding his legs into his briefs, he slipped on his jeans and went searching through the house on bare feet.

He found Lauren kneeling by the dog.

"How is he?" he asked, coming up behind her, Nick's leg touching the small of her back.

"He seems to be okay. He slept through the night—" she lifted her face to his "—like somebody else I know."

"I was beat. Sorry. I haven't slept like that since, hell, I don't know."

"I told you that you weren't sleeping enough."

"And I think I said I wasn't sleeping with the right person."

A smile found its way to her mouth.

In one glance, he felt her pleasure, trust and maybe love. *Love.*

There were so many things he wanted to say, had to say.

She stood, hands on her hips. She must have taken a shower. Her hair was a little damp, pulled into a sleek ponytail. She didn't wear any makeup, but didn't need it. She had luminous eyes, her lips were full and seductive even without the red lipstick.

"Wait until Billy sees what I've done. I can't believe we have a dog," she said, moving toward the kitchen as if she was nervous about being so close to him.

He watched her go, stayed where he was, given the cottage was so small. He had a view of anyplace she went—except the bedroom.

"I fed the dog some more chicken, but now I'll have to see Dunk about dog food. And then I'll have to take it to the vet and figure out about shots." She braced her hands on the countertop, her slim back to his view. "I don't know why I have this dog. I can't afford a dog, I don't want to take care of it, but it seems like it was meant to be."

She faced him, kept her arms at her sides. She had on a pair of blue shorts and a knit shirt that fit loosely around her shoulders. "Are you hungry? What time is it? The boys will be done with the sleepover at ten and I've got the morning off. I guess we could eat, or maybe you should leave."

On that last part, she sucked in a sigh.

He knew what she was getting at, but anyone who knew him, knew he was always up early. He could have come by this morning. Could have, but he hadn't.

His being seen here in the light of day was a lot different than slipping in during a dark rainstorm.

But he'd needed her last night, more than he'd needed anything he could recall in the past couple of years. Being with Lauren had made him feel whole, like a man.

He'd been with a few women since his last girlfriend and he had parted ways, but it wasn't the same as wanting to see them on a long-term basis. A night of sex was easy, it was the wanting-more part that was hard.

And he wanted more.

He grew troubled, his stomach tight with unease.

"Lauren, you don't have to pretend that what happened last night didn't happen."

Her cheeks paled, composure hard fought. She wrung out a dishcloth in her poor beat-up hands, as if needing something to do. She wiped the cloth across the already clean counter.

"Lauren, don't."

"I'm not doing anything, Nick. I'm just getting on with my Sunday. Don't you have to be at Mass or anything?"

"Trying to get rid of me?"

She all but snapped, "I'm trying to make this easy on you, you idiot. Go ahead and leave. I put your clothes on the back of the bed, I guess you saw them." Her gaze leveled on his bare chest, lower to his jean-clad hips. "You forgot your shirt and shoes."

He couldn't let her dilute last night into nothing, a little capsule of sex that meant nothing. He went to her, trapped her in his arms, his hands holding the counter's edge. Terror lit in her eyes, a fear of falling. Not literally, but falling into his arms. He sensed it. She moved left, then right. But she had no place to go.

Nick framed her face in his hands, wanting desperately to give her something to pin hope on. She felt like silk beneath his fingers, her cheeks so smooth and sweet. She smelled good, like floral soap and herbal shampoo.

He wouldn't speak until she looked him in the eyes, and when she did, he murmured, "Next to my son, you're the best thing to ever happen to me, Lauren."

Discomfort stretched across her features, her mouth a thin line of displeasure. She attempted to duck away from him, but he held her still. Resigned to his hold, she half choked, "You said you couldn't get involved. Nothing's changed, Nick. If you keep talking, you'll regret it."

"I don't regret last night."

"Me neither, so let's just leave it at that. You need to leave now. I've got things to do. Billy will be home soon—"

"In three hours."

"Well…I need to go over the menu once more. There's a hundred things you're keeping me from, Nick."

"But there's only one thing that you want."

He didn't say it to be arrogant, he only spoke what he was feeling, too. Then he showed her, lowering his lips to her mouth and kissing, nipping and gently sucking her mouth into a long and passionate kiss.

She melted next to him, her body crushing into his chest. The feel of her weight next to him heightened his desire. In a short moment, he scooped her into his arms and carried her to the bedroom, the bed still rumpled and tangled from last night.

He laid her down, took off her clothes, skimming his hands over the flat of her belly, lower to the apex of her legs. She opened for him and heat flashed through his body. He brought her to a swift arousal, gave her what she sought, then he kicked off his jeans and let the rage in his blood burn hot.

After sheathing himself, he took her, made love to her slowly. He gave and she returned. She guided the tempo, her body writhing beneath his, her hands locked onto his shoulders. And when they were both at the same pinnacle, they abandoned themselves to each other.

Afterward, he caressed her cheek, kissed her mouth. A tendril of hair escaped her ponytail and he touched its silkiness, running it between his thumb and forefinger.

She was so beautiful, he felt so much love for her, his heart ached.

They dressed, Lauren almost immediately closing herself off from him again. So it was to be like that. Only letting feelings surface when they were in bed.

Time had drifted away and Nick should have left an hour ago, a startling reminder when Billy flung the front door open and found he and Lauren in the living room—dressed, thank God.

Billy and Nicky-J came inside, Nick pulling himself together as his mom appeared right behind the boys.

"Hi, Nick." His mom wasn't particularly surprised to see him here this morning. She had an uncanny sense for reading between the lines, not to mention school-teacher eyes in the back of her head.

Buzzing into the living room, she said, "I picked up the boys this morning. Critter got sick right after breakfast. Too much junk food so the party ended earlier than expected. Mrs. Gilman called your cell phone and said you didn't answer, so I told her I'd pick up both boys."

"My dog!" Billy squealed. "You found my dog!"

Billy stood over the basket, his mouth open wide enough to fit a semi.

"I heard him last night." Lauren's gaze went briefly to Caprice, then to her son. "He was at the diner so I brought him home."

"Oh, Mommy! This means I get to keep him." Billy fell to his knees, hugged the dog and smoothed his hand repeatedly over its furry back. "Hi, boy."

Nicky-J dropped down and petted the dog's head. "Hey, buddy."

The dog licked Billy's fingers, then Billy's eyes grew

wide and he stuffed a hand into his pocket, came out with a few smashed marshmallows. "You smell these, boy?"

Holding out his hand for the dog to eat the treats, they quickly disappeared.

"You can't keep feeding it marshmallows, Billy," Lauren advised, taking Billy's backpack from Caprice. She gave his mom a wan smile, as if to say she knew they'd been found out. "We'll have to go to the grocery and buy some dog food."

"Okay," Billy said, his face alight with happiness. "Hi, boy. Did you miss me? You won't ever be hungry anymore."

"Hey, Billy," Nicky-J asked. "What are you going to name him?"

"I don't know." Billy's expression grew thoughtful and a short moment later, he said, "Marshmallow—because he likes them."

"Mash-em-allow." Nicky-J shrugged his approval. "He likes it. He wagged his tail when you said it."

"Hi, Marshmallow. Hi, buddy." Billy petted the dog, touched his nose to the dog's wet nose.

Nicky-J looked around, finally dialed in to the fact that his dad was in the living room. "Oh, hi, Dad. What are you doin' here?"

Without missing a beat, Nick replied, "I came to see how Billy's dog was. I helped his mom bring the dog home last night."

Caprice gave him a look that said she knew he'd never gone home. She wasn't a judgmental woman, never had been.

Nick drew on his sunglasses, taking them from his belt loop. "Come on, Nicky-J. Let's go home."

"I'll come over later and see your dog." His son bounded through the room, let himself outside to do a two-foot hop off the three-stepped porch.

"Thanks for your help," Lauren said awkwardly to Nick, then to Caprice, "And thanks for bringing Billy home."

"You're welcome, Lauren." His mom gave her a hug, a Sicilian hug that packed a dose of compassion.

Nick knew then that his mother was saying it would be okay.

Lauren, confused and unsure as to what to make of the gesture, stood in the doorway and waved goodbye.

On a last look over his shoulder, Nick felt let down when the door closed and he lost sight of Lauren.

Nicky-J walked ahead of him and his mom, giving her the chance to say, "Danny went to the job site early this morning. He said your motorcycle was in the same spot as it was last night. I wondered, sort of figured out where you'd be."

"You're not surprised."

"No." She reached for his hand. "Just be careful, Nick. This whole business in Los Angeles, I just want it to be done and over so we can all move on. You've got so much to give to a woman. I'm happy for you. She's a wonderful person and she deserves you. Billy's terrific. He's an old soul in a young body and he needs a father in his life. I think you'd be great for him. Nicky-J and him get along so well." His mom shook her head. "I just want everything to be the way it was, only better."

"Me, too." He slid his arm around her waist and brought her close to him as they walked in sync.

Caprice DiMartino, the rock in the family, was be-

ginning to crumble. The frailty in her eyes was like a
fist in his heart.

He was sick of feeling desperate, sick of not knowing what was going to happen.

Worst yet, he was tired of living a lie.

He was in love with Lauren Jessup and wanted her
to know it.

Buckets of flowers bracketed the entry door to
Dunk's grocery store. Colorful zinnias, coneflowers and
stargazer lilies exploded with summer-warm petals that
lent a sweet fragrance to the air.

Inside, it smelled of turnips and eggplant, basil,
thyme, rosemary and oregano. Dunk had brought in ed-
ible pansies, their petite faces blue and yellow, purple
and orange.

Lauren hooked a basket through her arm and shopped
for cake flour and chocolate, heavy cream and vanilla.
Heather and Danny had asked if she'd bake a cake for
their rehearsal dinner. Lauren had never been more honored. She told them she'd love to and, since then, she'd
been playing around with several recipes, finally deciding which one would bring smiles and love to those who
ate it.

Several items caught Lauren's interest and she studied them; smelling the citrus and checking out the pale-
ness of the veal.

"Lauren, hello." A woman's voice broke into her
thoughts.

"Hi, Maxine."

It seemed aeons ago since she'd first met Maxine at
city hall to file a complaint about her parking ticket.

"I'm coming by the Wharf tonight for dinner. Love what you do with all that fancy food." Maxine's smile stretched wide as she nosed around the cookie aisle.

Lauren, as odd as it felt to her, had become a celebrity of sorts in Bella Luna. When she first came to town, she walked in almost nondescript anonymity. Now she was stopped on the street and praised for her culinary skills.

It felt good, great, in fact, to be recognized. Never would Lauren have thought this would happen for her. If only…

No, she wasn't going to do that today.

Nick wasn't going to land in her thoughts and muck them up. She had tried—somewhat in vain—to move on. Yet whenever she caught a glimpse of him, she could feel her lips pull into a smile, and her body turn traitor and want to wrap itself around his.

Stupid, stupid, she berated herself.

Billy was just outside the grocery, training Marshmallow to sit and stay. It had taken a pocketful of dog treats to get the dog to mind. Getting Marshmallow, what at first seemed like a horrible idea, had been nothing short of wonderful.

Nicky-J and Billy had come up with a shorter nickname for the dog—Mel. After a clean bill of health and a grooming, Mel was the cutest thing she'd ever seen. His personality shone.

Mel took her mind off Nick in ways she hadn't anticipated. The dog could just look at her with those brown eyes, little white crescents beneath, chin on forepaws, and she'd have to bend down and give him a pat on the head. He had a cute way of begging for treats, front legs up and on his haunches like a prairie dog. Mel brought Billy around from a serious little boy to a carefree kid who took his dog with him wherever he went.

Setting her order next to the cash register, Lauren waited for Dunk to ring up her purchases. He simply stared at her with that smile of his, so white and so all-knowing, his mustache a full bristle above his lip.

She had a feeling about what was to come and she held her hand up to stop it before it started. "Don't go there with me today, Dunk, or I swear I'll stop shopping here," she threatened without much threat.

"No place else to shop, so you don't have to get snippy with me."

She frowned. "I'm not in the mood."

Dunk didn't care, he plunged right in. "I've seen how you and Nick have been dancing around each other lately. You do any more sidestepping, you'll end up off the pier. He's a good man."

"Hmm, hmm, hmm," she returned, planting her hands on her hips. "He's also in the middle of something he doesn't want to mess up, so anything you have to say, Dunk, isn't worth saying."

"Too bad, I'm going to say it anyway." He put on bifocals to read the price on the bottle of vanilla. "There's no law against two people talking to one another, two people sitting down to share a meal in a public restaurant. Her lawyer can't bring that kind of thing into court."

Lauren didn't respond. Dunk's weathered brown fingers punched numbers into the upright cash register. "If you ask me—"

"I didn't."

"—you're both missing out on a friendship in the meantime. I can't say that's real smart."

"I like to be stupid, Dunk. I think it makes me look much better."

Dunk looked at her over the rims of his glasses. "Lauren, you've got a smarty mouth on you today."

She grinned, feeling a smidgen more at ease. "Just trying to dog-paddle my way through life."

"I think you're doing more than that." He put her groceries into a brown paper bag. "How'd it go at the school?"

The trepidation that would normally follow an answer to a question like that was nil. She announced, "I registered him."

"Glad to hear it, glad to hear it," he repeated with a happy nod of his head.

She took heart in Dunk's praise—it meant the world to her. Yesterday, she'd gone to Sea Cliff Elementary School and registered William Robert Jessup for the first grade. Billy had never been more elated. He'd stood by her side, his shoulders thrust back and a smile on his face. They'd been given a tour of the school and Billy was shown the first-grade classrooms. Last night they'd celebrated with ice-cream sundaes.

She paid Dunk, and as he handed over the grocery bag with its handles, he commented—in what she knew was more than an offhand manner, "Nick's back in town. Came in early last night."

Lauren thought she was on her way to a smooth exit, but Dunk's words held her to the spot. She knew Nick had gone to Los Angeles during the week, one last visitation for Nicky-J before the trial next week.

Damning her curiosity, she wondered why he'd returned early.

She had to put on her face of indifference.

"Don't know the details," Dunk said. "Something about his ex-wife getting called out to a movie and having to cut the visit short."

Lauren refused to ask questions and instead said, "I'll see you around."

"I'm sure you will."

She'd barely turned when Dunk called out for her, "Do me a favor, Lauren?"

"Depends. The last time, you had me taking a six-pack of soda pop to Nick's house and I didn't even know it *was* Nick's house."

"You know where he lives now, so I can't fool you."

Still half-skeptical, she asked, "What do you want?"

"I borrowed Sam's flippers for my boogie board. I told him I'd give them back today, but I can't leave the store. Can you take them to the pizzeria for me?"

He dangled a pair of blue rubber fins within her reach.

She said, "I suppose I can."

"Thanks."

Lauren went outside, lifting her face to the sunshine. It was a wonderful day, but deep in her heart she felt sad. She pushed the feeling aside, not letting it remain.

Yet as she walked, the smack of her flip-flops seemed to keep singing:

Nick is back in town.

With Billy and Mel trotting alongside her, Lauren covered the short length of pier to Wong's.

"When I go to school, can Mel come with me?" Billy asked.

"Mel will have to stay home."

"But we don't have a home." His red cape floated in a faded river over his shoulders.

Dismayed by his line of thought, she countered, "Of course we have a home."

"But we can't plant a tree in the yard without getting in trouble."

"Yes...well..." He had her stumped. "We were able to have a dog and it worked out."

"I want a house of our own. We've got a dog and I know who I want to be my d—" He clipped his sentence short.

"To be your what?"

"Nothing."

She gave him a hard stare. "Are you planning on any kind of mischief?"

"What's that?"

"Are you thinking about surprising me with anything?"

"No, Mom. I just wanted a house and a dog. And something else good if I can have it, only I don't want to tell you what it is in case you get mad."

"Billy, I never get mad at you."

"If I lost my glasses, you'd get mad."

Lauren stopped, gazed at her son and knelt down to his level. Since he was wearing his eyeglasses she knew he hadn't done anything to them. "Billy, if you lost your glasses, it wouldn't be the end of the world."

"But I always thought you'd be mad."

Setting down the groceries and flippers, Lauren brought him into her embrace, breathing in the smell of his little-boy hair, while Mel jumped up to try to give kisses. "Billy, I'm sorry I made you feel that way. I know it hasn't always been easy for you. But this time we're going to be all right. You're going to school and I have a great job. It's different now. I don't want you to worry."

He looked up at her, his face tanned from a summer on the beach. "You mean, this is for real? I can always be friends with Dunk and I get to keep Mel and Nicky-J, Tim and Critter and me we can build forts and go to school? I'll be able to fly kites on the beach, roast marshmallows over the fire? I can see Verna Mae and color at the diner? And I can collect the glass floats when Cap'n Mike says it's okay?"

His enthusiasm proved she *could* do this, *could* make a life for them here—because Billy already had one he loved. "Yes."

"So we're really staying?"

"Of course. I registered you in school."

"I know—" his eyes rapidly blinked "—but I couldn't believe it was for real."

"Oh, Billy." She kissed his cheek, held him close, her heart breaking for all the times she'd made him feel so unsettled and displaced. "We're staying for good. I promise."

Nineteen

When the moon rages, the skies weep.

Nick rested his feet on the chair in Wong's, watching Nicky-J play pinball. His son's body was fatigued from the trip and the flight, but he wouldn't give in to it, not yet.

The days in Los Angeles had been a bust, emotionally tiring for Nicky-J, but Nick told him they could have pizza the night they got home since that's what he wanted. But neither of them were in the mood for cheese pie and arcade games. It seemed as if they were only going through the motions of being here.

Taking a long swallow of beer, Nick closed his eyes and relived the trip. They'd gotten there and everything was all right, or as close to, given the situation. Debbie spent two days with their son, then she called Nick on the third to say she had to cut the visit short. The studio had called her out for a retake and she had to do the makeup.

Nick had been relieved that they were out of there a day early.

Steve apologized about it, but Nicky-J was glad to go. It had been strained between him and his mom ever since he found out about the custody trial. Nick had a talk with Nicky-J, told him he couldn't blame his mom for wanting him, too. He had to be a man about it and show her the same respect he always did, that meant no screwing anything up in her house. No jamming toilets or digging up flowers. Nicky-J agreed, but with a rubber lip that had a lot of stretch to it.

Nick took another drink of beer, casually glancing up to see Lauren coming into Wong's Pizzeria holding a pair of flippers. He could see Billy through the window with his dog.

Her steps slowed as soon as she made eye contact with him.

"Hey," he said, his voice worn-out.

"Hi," she responded, then gazed at the flippers. "I don't suppose these are yours?"

"No."

She made a face. "Sam, are these your flippers?"

Sam called from the kitchen, "What flippers you talk about?"

She held them up to dangle from her fingers.

Sam studied them, read the droll expression on her face, then said, "Yeah, they mine."

"I'm sure." The sarcasm in her tone was so thick, it could be cut with a knife. "You tell Dunk I'm never talking to him again."

On a big smile, Sam simply nodded, then went back to tossing pizza dough.

"Set up again?" Nick asked, having a hunch he knew the answer.

"Seems like it."

He loved how the light played across her sun-hued skin, her rich hair. The deeper shadows of her body, the vee at her breasts was inviting. She'd become too much a part of his life for him to let a minute go by without thinking about her.

"Sit down." The sight of her made him want to ease her onto a bed.

Hesitation held her, then she said, "Billy's outside waiting for me." But she didn't leave right away. "I heard you had to leave Los Angeles early. I hope everything's all right."

"It's the same." He instantly wished he hadn't said that. Because it wasn't the same, not with the way he felt about her.

He damned himself for not giving promises and assurances. This was a situation where he couldn't trust his own instincts, he had to trust the advice of his lawyer. But it was so damn hard. He was ready to disregard everything.

Then he heard his son at the pinball machine, saw his strong profile with the baseball cap on his head. Nicky-J interpreted things in his own way. As it was now, his son wasn't supposed to testify; but what if he was called? Nicky-J would say things that might hurt the case. It just wasn't worth—

Nick's cell phone rang, pulling him out of his thoughts. He was slow on the draw, not ready to let Lauren go, but she'd already headed toward the door.

Longing for just a fragment of quiet satisfaction, Nick punched the phone. "Wait."

She shook her head, then waved, a slow sweep of her hand in the air.

"I'll see you around, Lauren," he called after her, then she was gone.

Nick spoke into the receiver, "Hello."

"Nick, Bruce Harmon."

Nick's muscles grew taut. Hearing from Bruce was the last thing he needed right now. "What's up?"

"The investigator found something," Bruce said in a voice that managed to be both brisk and cautious. "She can't have another kid."

Momentarily lost, Nick took in a breath. "Excuse me?"

"Your ex-wife was seeing a fertility doctor for a year. Nothing worked. She can't have another kid so she filed for joint custody."

Nick's pulse rebounded after momentarily stopping. Hands on the table, he asked, "How do you know this?"

"I've got the medical records and a statement from one of her friends confirming it."

Inasmuch as he wanted to feel differently, Nick only felt destroyed by the sad fate of Debbie's decision. She'd had a son, but she'd walked away from him. And now that she was ready to be a mother, she couldn't have a child.

Jesus...

So she wanted their child back.

"How do we use this?" Nick asked, his mind racing with the news.

"It changes things—no arguing that. But this doesn't give us an open-and-shut case. It could come back and work against us."

"How? This means she wants Nicky-J more as a consolation for not being able to have a child with Steve."

"Whatever her reasons, she has a valid leg to stand

on. She's the child's mother. This case could go either way, Nick."

"I'd say more our way now."

"And I'd be inclined to agree if I were a betting man, but I'm not. This is something we have to really think over—be prepared for the backlash in case things go the other way." Optimistically, Bruce said, "One good thing—we got assigned a judge who's a real ballbuster. I'd drop a C-note on the table that he'll side with us, but you know there are no guarantees."

"Fighting for my son is worth the risk."

"I see your point. But just so you understand, the judge could end up being sympathetic to Debbie's cause. If so, then using this information won't be in our best interests."

"Who'd be sympathetic to her? This makes her look selfish in my opinion. God, this is so unbelievable." Nick drank the rest of his beer with a long swallow. "So what do you think?"

"I think we're ready for court next week."

Nick felt too sober, and he needed another beer. "I want to call her."

"That would be a mistake. Leave it alone and let me handle things." Bruce's other phone rang. "I'll see you soon. If anything else develops, I'll call you."

Nick and his son moved around each other in the kitchen, each man handling his share of the dinner preparations, but being sloppy and unorganized.

Nicky-J got out the milk and was reaching for the glasses when Nick went for them at the same time. Gone was their usual in-sync choreography. Nick manned the stove, burning his finger while stirring noodles into a skillet of meat helper. The spoon dropped to the floor; he swore.

Nicky-J looked at him wordlessly.

While Nick cleaned up the mess, the whir of the can opener sounded. A can of corn got dumped into a pot, half of it missing its target, and was handed off from son to father.

Neither said anything.

The loaf of bread and butter were brought out. Nicky-J went for the plates, almost dropped one and cast his gaze down and sniffed softly before rubbing the underside of his nose. Silverware showed up on the table, then chairs were scraped back and seats taken.

It wasn't the usual Monday-night dinner routine and they both knew it.

Tomorrow at six-thirty in the morning, Nick was on a flight to Los Angeles to attend Family Law Court.

Nicky-J wasn't hungry, but he ate a bite of food. It tasted bad, not that his dad was a bad cook. He just wasn't in the mood to chew anything, not even bubble gum. He didn't want to hurt his dad's feelings so he smashed his noodles in his fork, stirred them around, and made it seem as if he was doing something when he was really doing nothing.

"You think the Yankees will win the World Series?" his dad asked, his plate not looking too empty, either.

"I dunno, Dad."

"San Francisco's doing all right."

"Yeah."

They ate some more, Nicky-J's stomach sort of hurting. Not a hurt like he was going to puke, just an aching hurt as if Tim had kicked him in the privates. He did that one time when they were rolling around on his floor. Tim didn't mean to. It was an accident.

Nicky-J wished his mom wanting him was an accident. He hadn't had much fun at her house the last time. She talked on the phone a lot, and Steve, he was always using his computer. Steve didn't know nothing about baseball. He liked to golf.

"When's Grandma coming over to stay with me?" Nicky-J asked, taking a drink of milk and trying his hardest not to spill it. He'd poured the glass too full and it ran over his fingers as he tilted the cup. A dribble fell down his shirtfront.

"You'll still be sleeping, buddy."

"I want you to wake me up and k-kiss me goodbye." Nicky-J almost slipped up, almost started crying.

His dad gave him a smile, one of his "big man" smiles that said he was doing a good job of taking it like a big guy. But that's not how Nicky-J felt. He felt like a little guy, small and scared. He didn't want none of this to be happening. He just wanted...

...his dad.

Tears swam in his eyes and he had to drop his fork. He dropped his chin to his chest, little pants of air working hard in his lungs to keep him from letting go.

"Daddy..." he murmured. "I can't take it like a man. I don't wanna. *Daddddddyyyyy.*"

He flung himself onto his dad's lap, held on tightly and sobbed.

His dad hugged him so hard, Nicky-J thought he might just puke. But he didn't care.

He just wanted his dad to hold him forever.

* * *

Nick was flanked by his brothers, Danny and John, and his father, Anthony, whose face was somber. They stood outside the courtroom, waiting.

Through open double doors they viewed the court-room. It was paneled in heavy mahogany, and they could see tall gray chairs sitting behind two sets of desks that faced the judge. Raised on a higher plat-form was the judge's large black leather chair, the American flag on the left, the State of California flag on the right.

A podium was angled directly in front of the judge's desk, a microphone in place.

The room's smell came at them in a faint wave—an odor like cleaning products, ink and sweaty leather.

Anthony asked in a strained voice, "When do we go in?"

The tie around Nick's neck felt as if it was cutting off his airway. "Bruce said he'd meet us here."

They spoke in soft voices, waiting.

A woman appeared at the end of the hallway, a tall and sexy blonde, with endless legs and a California tan perfectly dressed in a suit and made up to perfection. His ex-wife, Debbie McConnolly.

He felt the DiMartino muscles bulk around him, two brothers and a father, all tensed, all wanting to verbally lash out. But Nick had already warned them to stay quiet.

She was with Steve. He had on an expensive suit. They looked like a really put-together couple. Nick studied them, wondering what the judge would think.

He made eye contact with Debbie, not breathing when he looked at her. She gave him a fleeting glance, hooked her arm through Steve's, and they went inside the courtroom.

He gave her retreating back a cold glance, his heartbeat an erratic tattoo. Fending off his emotions, Nick ran a hand through his hair.

Bruce arrived, marching down the hallway wearing a black suit and carrying a compact briefcase. "We need to go in, but Nick, there's been a change in the judges." His gaze looked turbulent, maybe even nervous. "Judge Palmer is out sick. They've replaced him with Judge Lewis."

Nick wasn't really listening and asked, "What's that mean to us?"

"Lewis is a woman. No children."

The implication couldn't have been any clearer. An uneasy feeling rose in Nick—he was in for trouble. But there was nothing he could do. He'd prepared for this day for months, now all he could hope for was justice.

They took their seats in the courtroom and the judge entered.

She was in her late fifties and had silver hair. The robe she wore made her seem bulkier than she probably was.

The proceedings began with lots of background testimony. Nick would glance at Debbie every so often, but she kept her eyes straight ahead. He felt his father's gaze on his back, strong and supportive. During one exchange, he heard Danny mutter an expletive under his breath.

It was Nick's turn to take the stand and he was sworn in, his pulse jumping through his body. The judge gave him a smile. She could be on his side…he wasn't sure.

Jesus, he didn't know anything right now.

Debbie's lawyer questioned Nick, asking basic questions, and Nick felt he answered them honestly, and in a nonbiased way.

"Has your son ever had to go to the emergency room?" the lawyer asked.

"Yes."

"Has he ever had stitches?"

"Yes."

"Is your son accident prone or does he lack supervision?"

"Objection," Bruce cut in.

The judge countered, "Sustained."

Nick followed along, thinking that Debbie's lawyer couldn't ask a question like that.

The lawyer adjusted his collar, glanced at a notepad and continued. "Mr. DiMartino, would you say Nicholas Junior is properly supervised?"

"Yes." The word sounded flat, ugly. He tried to keep his temper from boiling.

"Who watches him?"

"He's at school or with my mom during the summer."

"Why don't you watch him?"

"I work full-time." Jesus, they'd been over this during the family evaluation.

"I have records from the hospital emergency room that show Nicholas Anthony DiMartino has been in their care three times in the past year. This doesn't make you feel as if you're neglecting your son, Mr. DiMartino?"

"Objection!" Bruce rose to his feet.

The judge's voice was a soft but effective threat. "Counsel, I'm giving you a warning. Sustained."

By the time Nick was off the stand, he felt washed out, as if his blood had been drained from his body, and he could barely stand on his legs. He wasn't sure what to make of what was going on. It felt surreal, as if it were happening to someone else, not him.

Debbie took the stand and Nick sat back, anxious to hear how Bruce was going to present their side.

The same monotonous questions were asked of her, then Bruce changed gears.

"Mrs. McConnolly, before you petitioned the court for custody of your son, you were seeing a fertility doctor."

She paused, checked with her lawyer before answering. If she had any reaction to the question, she didn't show it. Her lipstick was perfectly in place, her hair a sunny blond upsweep. "Yes."

"It must be difficult to go through all that without the end result—a baby."

"Yes," she said through clamped teeth.

"You tried for a year to get pregnant."

"Yes."

"It must have been upsetting for you when you thought about your son with his father."

"Yes...no." She looked at her lap, then up. "I don't think Nick is a bad father, I just think—"

"If Nick isn't a bad father, why are we here in court?"

"Objection!" came the call from Debbie's lawyer.

The judge tsked. "Sustained. Mr. Harmon, refrain from the hypothetical."

Bruce lowered his hands, clasped them behind his back to regroup. "Isn't it true that the only reason you want Nicholas Anthony Junior is because you can't get pregnant with another child so you want the one you abandoned?"

"Objection!" The lawyer's complexion turned ruddy. "It hasn't been proven that she abandoned her child and we aren't arguing that point, Your Honor. Debbie McConnolly has a good relationship with her son and has seen him since he was born."

"Sustained. Mr. Harmon, continue—without the assumptions."

Bruce inhaled. "Mrs. McConnolly, isn't it true you waited until after all methods of conception had failed before you petitioned this court for school-calendar custody?"

"No, that's not true. I want my son because I'm his mother." A tear rolled down Debbie's cheek. Her hands were clasped on her lap, trembling. She gazed at Nick, wet her lips. "I love my son. I made a mistake leaving him. Something I wish I could go back and change every day of my life. But I can't go back. I only want to go forward and be a good mother for him—"

"How can taking him away from his father make you a good mother?" Bruce interjected.

Debbie ignored the question, crying as she faced the judge. "I'm in a much better place now. My son loves me. He tells me all the time. I'm not trying to hurt him, I just want to give him the best that I can. We can afford a private school, give him a wonderful life. I'm not taking him away from Nick—" she turned to him "—I'm not. He is and always will be your son. I just want my turn now. I'm sorry for everything. I just want my child back."

She broke down, her shoulders shaking.

Nick felt a niggling stir of sympathy toward her, but quickly snuffed it out. Whether or not she felt this way, or whether her show of emotion was for the judge's benefit, he didn't care to speculate.

The next half hour dragged on, Nick listening but not hearing the testimony of the court evaluator and other parties with a vested interest in the case.

When the judge retired to her chambers to make a decision, Nick rose and went into the hallway.

He walked through the heavy double doors, outside into the smoggy afternoon before anyone could follow him. Sucking air into his lungs, he braced his arms on the railing and closed his eyes.

He had no idea what to think, couldn't guess what the outcome would be.

His mind was on one thing, and one thing only: the feel of Nicky-J trembling in his lap, hot tears making the front of his T-shirt wet.

Twenty

The moon comes and goes with the tide.

Lauren moved with organization and skill as she seasoned tuna steaks, then pressed the flat of her knife on the cutting board to crack peppercorns. After dicing Italian parsley, she wiped down her station with a damp towel. She was always cleaning, keeping things neat and operating smoothly.

June bustled past the order window, tagging a new ticket onto the rounder. "Order in! Got a deuce."

"What's hanging?" Lauren asked, removing the tuna and making a quick reduction of cream for the sauce.

"Steaks, burn 'em. Spuds with all the decorations, salads on the sly with bleu—all in a day."

Lauren got started on the sirloins.

Using the back of her hand, she wiped the moisture from her hairline. The kitchen was overbearingly warm, the back door open to let in a cross breeze that lost its effect by the time it neared the commercial stove and oven.

Yellow-orange flames licked the bottom of pans, tongs flew from her hands and she never stayed in one place long. The pace was frantic, the orders kept pouring in. She was hot, she was thirsty, the balls of her feet ached.

But she loved this.

Loved it like nothing else she'd ever done.

She had more energy than a pot of coffee could manufacture. Adrenaline charged her system along with the steady noise of conversation from the customers in the dining room.

For the next couple of hours Lauren kept up, creating one dish after another that pleased the customers eating at the Wharf Diner.

It was a Tuesday night and she hadn't been able to take a break since coming on at noon to get her menu in order. Knox arrived, as he sometimes did on his nights off, to see if he could help with prep work. He'd been a lot less grumpy lately since Lou had moved out of their shared apartment and gone to Alaska to stake his fortune in the pollock-fishing industry—"As if," Knox always added.

By the seven o'clock closing, Lauren was worn-out. She took off her apron, soaked her battered hands in a sink of warm water and hunched forward over the sink to release the kink of pressure on her spine.

"I'll finish up for you," Knox said, giving her a pat on the arm. "Anyways, Verna Mae wants to see you in her office."

Lauren straightened, taking the cotton towel Knox handed her. "Thanks." She wiped her hands, threw the towel over her shoulder and proceeded to the office.

Wearing a pair of half-rim glasses on a chain of little gold beads, Verna Mae gazed at her over the rhinestone tops. She sat at her desk, papers piled in a haphazard way. "Come on in, sweetpea. Take a load off."

Lauren gratefully took a seat, leaning into the chair with a soft moan. The day had been long physically, but a piece of her was mentally taxed. She'd been wondering about Nick, wishing she knew how the trial had gone. Nobody was talking in the diner, so no news was good news—as June was fond of pointing out.

Sitting taller, Lauren asked, "Have you heard anything about Nick's custody hearing?"

"Not a peep." The even coat of lipstick on her mouth fell in a grim line. "I got feelers out, though. Maxine lives almost across the street from the DiMartinos. She said she'd give me a jingle soon as she saw any activity over that way."

Lauren eased into the chair's back once more.

"We did a bang-up business tonight." Verna Mae held up the cash receipts. "More food flew out of here than airplanes flew out of San Francisco. I'm thinking I might have to start taking reservations by the look of that line out the door. It's been one wild ride, Lauren, and I don't know what I was thinking by not hiring you as my cook in the first place. You said you knew what you were doing, and you damn well do. Every time I eat something you make, I'm whistling Dixie."

A smile caught on Lauren's mouth. "I'm glad you think the arrangement is working out."

"It's more than working out—and that's what I wanted to talk to you about." Verna Mae pulled open the lid on her taffy jar, offered one to Lauren, then unwrapped her candy. "I ran this past Knox already and he's good to go, said it works out fine for him. So here's what I want to do. I propose to hire you full-time to be the head cook. Knox'll do the breakfast runs, help out some in the evening. I can bring on a prep for you, or you can have Omar and I'll replace him, but the deal is—you cook for me six nights a week. And I'll—" the taffy disappeared into her mouth "—put you on salary and give you benefits."

She was too physically tired to jump up and down, but her heartbeat did a big dance.

To have medical benefits meant a huge increase in financial status. She wouldn't have to pay out of pocket for dental cleanings or trips to the doctor.

"Verna Mae, that's really generous."

"You deserve it. You brought life into this place. And I don't mean just the diner. You brought something special into Bella Luna. Your boy, he's a fine kid, and you…I wish you all the best in the world, sweetpea."

Appreciation, and fond affection for Verna Mae, made Lauren smile. "Thanks."

"No thanks necessary. Just tell me you'll take the promotion."

"Of course I will."

"Have another taffy." Verna Mae offered the jar and Lauren selected a pink candy.

Verna Mae declared, "I'm going to hire Nick to remodel the whole damn place. We'll put in new carpet and booths, really give the joint some class. I might even leave off the 'diner' part in the name and go for the Wharf Bistro or something elegant-like."

At the mention of Nick's name, Lauren's train of thought was altered.

The job, the friends she'd made, and even bringing home Mel as an addition to her and Billy's family—all that had happened was everything she wanted. While she was happy about accomplishing so much, she would have liked to share her joys with Nick.

The office phone rang and Verna Mae jumped on it as if it were a winning scratch ticket.

"Hullo?" Her eyebrows furrowed. "They did? When? Just now, huh. Okay. You know anything for certain? No…all right then. If you hear, you call me again."

Verna Mae hung up the phone.

"Was it Nick?"

"He's back." Her eyes grew worried. "Maxine said they weren't smiling. I don't have a good feeling about it."

Already on her feet, Lauren said, "I'm going to find out. Can you watch Billy for me? He's still in the dining room with June."

"Sure, sweetpea." Taking another taffy, Verna Mae tried to manage a smile, but she just couldn't work her lips into a curve. "I hope it's not what I think. Oh, God. That poor man, he's not going to be the same if his little boy gets taken away."

Nick wasn't at his parents' house.

His mom told her he'd gone down to the beach. Lauren found him in the sunset's striking glow, walking along the sand wearing dark dress slacks and a white shirt. He'd rolled the sleeves up his forearms and pulled the tails from the waistband. Barefoot, he bordered the water's foamy edge, glittering sand and a splash of water marring the bottoms of his pants.

Caprice gave her the unthinkable news.

Nick DiMartino had lost custody of Nicky-J during the school-calendar year, the complete transition to take place before the first week of September.

Lauren walked toward him, her heart breaking. His head was down, his thoughts clearly occupying his entire body. His every breath, his every move, must have been knowing and understanding the terrifying reality that he must relinquish his child.

Unable to even remotely imagine what that must feel like, Lauren could only guess. Every ounce of her compassion and sympathy grew tenfold.

Nick looked up, his eyes hidden behind a pair of Ray•Bans. His hands were in his pockets, his shoulders hugging the air as if he needed its very help for support. She'd never seen him like this before. So…defeated.

"Nick," she whispered. "I heard. I'm so sorry."

He swallowed, his throat working to form words. She could tell he was barely holding things together, his lips pressed firmly together. "Yeah, it didn't go how I wanted."

She laid her palm on his arm, trying to ease his pain and give him comfort. "Is there anything I can do?"

"Not unless you can get me out of this," he replied, giving the first hint of a glib expression on his face. He slid his sunglasses off, slipped the temple into his pocket.

They walked together toward the sun, its glowing sphere washing them in a fusion of marmalade sky.

"How did this happen?" Her simple question lingered in the wind.

"Been asking myself that a hundred times on the plane ride home." His voice sounded low, gravelly, as if he'd smoked a few cigarettes. "The judge was a single lady who'd never had kids. She saw Debbie's side of things, said Nicky-J deserved a chance to know his mom the way he knows me. She didn't say I was a bad father, didn't say Debbie was a good mother, which struck me as a screwed-up thing. Why put a kid someplace where he's not going to be better off? Why take him from the only place he knows and make him—hell. I can't believe this is happening."

Lauren stared at her feet, the water running up to her tennis shoes, then slipping back into the ocean. "What are you going to do?"

"The judge ordered me to have him there by August 25."

"That's two days after Danny and Heather's wedding," Lauren blurted out without thinking. She wasn't trying to point out the bad timing, it was just that a wedding meant joy and happiness. But on its heels, taking Nicky-J to Los Angeles was going to tear the family to pieces.

"School starts the first week in September. She's got him enrolled at a private academy, some snobby place that'll probably make him wear a uniform. He'll hate it."

The way Nick was talking sounded as if he was disconnected, not talking about his own son but someone else's.

Dread worked through her, she feared he might not be fully accepting of the circumstances. She knew she wouldn't be, she'd take Billy and run away with him, leaving and never looking back. She couldn't stand to have a judge tell her where her son would live, with whom and for how long.

"Nick, are you thinking about doing something?" she asked, speaking her thoughts aloud.

He looked at her if she'd spoken some taboo. "You mean like taking him and hiding in Mexico?"

"Well, not exactly...but sort of."

Gazing into the sunset, his profile was hard-set. "Yeah, I thought about it. But after a couple of gin and tonics on the plane I knew I couldn't. I don't want to run, I don't want to put Nicky-J through that. He's got grandparents and uncles and aunts who love him, I'm not taking that away from him, too."

She felt her throat burn, wanted to help.

The misery on his face made her chest ache, her heart was torn with grief. She loved Nicky-J, had gotten to know him. He was precocious, a bundle of energy and fire with a ready smile for trouble and comedy. And he'd done so much for Billy.

She slipped her arm around his waist, the expensive fabric of his dress shirt cool against her fingers. "Nick, I wish there was something I could do."

He stopped walking, turned to her and put his hands on her shoulders. "There is."

"Anything." She was a part of his life now. She wanted to be there for him in any way she could.

"I had some time to think about what I want to do, how I'm going to handle this. There's no way in hell I'm leaving my son in Los Angeles without me." Nick's adamancy shone in his blue eyes, the set of his mouth. "I've decided to leave Danny in charge of the business and I'm moving back to L.A."

Lauren checked the beat of her heart, waiting for him to elaborate.

"I've still got contacts there, I'll get back onto my old job, spend ten months out of the year doing that, then come up here for the summers. I've figured it out in my head and I think it'll be all right. I have to make it do-able, I know I need to fix this for my son and, yeah, I've worked it out."

From his rambling tone, he hadn't really sold himself on anything, and Nick knew it. He was dying inside, trying desperately to hold on to any thread of optimism from an unraveling rope that was failing him by the second.

Son of a bitch, how had this happened?

When the judge read her ruling, Nick couldn't have been more shell-shocked. Who in God's name takes a boy away from his father?

The shock was dying, the resentment had turned to rage and now he was just plain scrambling to come up with solutions. He hadn't been able to face his son yet, talk to him about it. For the first time that Nick could recall, he was avoiding the truth. It was going to kill him to tell Nicky-J he had to live with his mom. How could he do it? How could he fail his son like this?

Jesus Christ, why?

Grief rolled up tightly in his gut, made him feel sick. He was trying to come up with answers, trying to make this acceptable.

"So I figured I'd move down there," he went on, "and make it seem like no big deal. That it would be all right for Nicky-J to live with his mom and Steve. But I'll be around so I can watch him in a school play or something—"

God, was that his voice that cracked?

"—you know, stuff like that. And I'll be there for Halloween because me and him always carve pumpkins together and I take him out trick-or-treating. I have always done that for him, and I…"

His chin lowered. He couldn't go on.

He felt Lauren's arms come around him, gathering him close to hold and comfort. He took what she offered, sucked it dry, wanting so badly to feel normal again. Feel the way he used to, not this man who was beaten and coming up with lame plans to make things seem all right when they weren't.

Nick lowered his face into the crook of Lauren's shoulder, closing his eyes and breathing in the skin at her neck. She smelled like the perfume of a kitchen: herbs and butter, sweet wine and rich cream.

They stood that way for a long while, the surf crashing behind them and the sun making its last descent into the horizon. All that was left was the hazy aftermath of an orange sky, the deepening blue of the ocean as it settled to bed.

He dragged himself taller, pulled his mind together and got his head on straight. Pulling in a few breaths, he collected the edges of his torn life and pulled them together. What he'd proposed wasn't so bad, not if he entered into it with the right attitude.

"Seriously, I am moving to Los Angeles," he said, more shaken about his decision than he let on. "It's the only thing I can do. I don't want to get into an argument with Debbie about this. Two people have to be civil to one another in a case like this where I'm legally bound to bring him to her." Speaking that aloud, a knife couldn't have twisted in his heart and caused a deeper wound. "As much as I resent the hell out of her, I've got to put on a front to keep things calm for Nicky-J. He's a smart kid, I want what's best for him. He doesn't need to take me on and think I'm upset with anyone. For everyone's sake, the transition has to go smoothly or else Nicky-J suffers."

He hunched his shoulders. He had to slow his mind down, had to focus on what he wanted to say next. Escaping all the baggage piling up, he centered his thoughts on Lauren.

She was amazing. Strong, determined and a wonderful mother. Nicky-J favored her, talked about her over dinner. She had a quality about her that not many women had, something that shone brightly. He wanted to hold on to that, to her. He wondered how he could live his life without her.

Nick gazed into her eyes. "They say don't change anything more than necessary in his life right now, but you're something familiar and good. You'd be great with him, with me. The four of us as a family." When her lips parted in surprise, he shook his head as if to confirm what she was thinking. "I know, the timing stinks. I wouldn't ask this way, but I don't have a lot of time to think about it. I need to make decisions now and I want you to be a part of them." He held her hands, squeezing gently. "I love you, Lauren. I'm asking if you'd be my wife and come to Los Angeles with me."

He could see her surprise, the sense of upset and indecision. He hadn't wanted her to feel that way when he asked her to marry him. And he'd thought about asking her dozens of times, had been waiting until the right moment. He'd screwed it up now, and he just hoped she could overlook that part and accept him.

Lauren cupped his cheek, kissed his mouth.

She tasted like summer, warm and sweet. Her fists crushed into his chest, hard knots as if she was afraid to open them and embrace him. She pulled back, and the heat pumping through him spread as he waited for her answer.

She found her voice. "I wanted you to ask me one day. I imagined it. Ever since I came here, you've been on my mind, in my heart. Your son has brought out the best in mine, and I can't think of a better man as a father." She wet her lips. "It's just that I promised Billy we were staying, that he'd go to school here. I enrolled him and he's so excited. I've made us a home…and my life is in Bella Luna. I wish, oh, I wish I could, I want to say yes." She held his face in her hands once more. "Nick, I love you. I love you with everything I hold dear inside, but I can't marry you."

Twenty-One

Be careful when the moon is asleep.

The bride and groom moved into the reception room, smiles on their faces as their name was announced:

"Ladies and gentlemen, it's my honor to present to you, Mr. and Mrs. Danny DiMartino!"

Cheers and applause rose from the crowd. Music struck up from the disk jockey's speakers and the couple headed toward the main table, stopping to accept well-wishes and hugs.

Lauren and Billy sat with Dunk and Verna Mae; Sam Wong admired the centerpiece and kept adjusting his tie. Maxine and Lois from the rental agency were drinking cocktails with miniumbrellas.

By all accounts, it looked like a joyous day.

The wedding had gone off as planned, Nicky-J the ring bearer and Nick was Danny's best man. John stood up for him as well as Anthony. Heather's father walked her down the aisle, heartfelt emotions showing on his face. Sitting in the front row, Heather's mom kept dabbing her eyes. With grace and dignity, Caprice DiMartino put on a brave front and didn't shed a tear. She sent a reminding gaze to Nicky-J when he was fiddling with the ribbons on the pillow.

So like the DiMartinos to band together, to make the best out of a worst-case situation. Lauren knew Nick had insisted on it. Danny was ready to postpone, but Nick told him if he did, he'd have to kick his butt.

Things were calming down a little, perhaps because their attention had been diverted by the wedding—a bright light of hope in a dark swirling sea. Neither Anthony nor Caprice wanted their son to leave Bella Luna again for Los Angeles, but they were both resolved to accept Nick's decision. After all, it was for Nicky-J's sake that Nick was making the sacrifice. They'd sat around the family table, talked over the pros and cons, and sided with Nick on this one—deciding everything had to be upbeat, and it was all for the best.

Even Nicky-J, who hadn't wanted to go, was beginning to see that maybe living by Disneyland *and* his dad could be okay. He was still sorry to leave his friends, didn't want to. Days passed and he forgot about having to pack and move out of his bedroom—until he saw the boxes and missed a toy that had been taped up inside.

Lauren remained strong, unfaltering. After all, she was good at that. She, better than anyone, could put on a front that didn't hint that she was breaking inside. Her heart was completely torn in two.

For the first time, she was on course with her life and she liked the direction she'd taken. She would have loved to have said yes to Nick, would have gone to Los

Angeles with him if she'd been in the same frame of mind she'd been in when she arrived in Bella Luna. But she'd changed.

For Lauren, probably one of the hardest decisions in her life was to turn Nick down. She wouldn't jump ship, bail…leave.

She was staying. For good.

Inasmuch as that conflicted her at times, she had to be true to herself and, more importantly, to her son. This was their home now. She wouldn't leave it, wouldn't ruin what she had here for a man. She was not her mother. She'd made a promise to Billy, and she intended to keep it.

Billy was confused by the turn of events, not sure why his best friend had to leave, why the judge didn't let Nicky-J stay with his dad and friends. Bright and intuitive, Billy knew enough that whatever was going on with Nicky-J, he had to accept the outcome.

Nicky-J sat at the long table, fidgeting with his water glass and catching ice with his spoon. He'd fished a cube out, and transferred it to his glass of soda pop. He glanced Billy's way and smiled. His tooth was missing, giving him an endearing smile and expression that Lauren wanted to wrap up in a bundle of love and squeeze.

She'd miss him, no question. She'd miss his father even more.

Lauren caught sight of Nick as he shook hands with a few people, and made his way through the room. He filled out his tuxedo in a way that stole her breath. Broad shoulders, narrow waist and tapered hips. He had the body of a football player, and she caught herself wondering if he'd ever played. She knew him, but there were so many details she didn't know, wanted to know. But now there would be no time.

He stood tall and athletic. His hair was combed neatly, a dark contrast to the white of his collar; his tie fell into place at this throat, a clean knot. The tan of his skin made him look healthy and happy—an outward show when inside she knew he was holding things together by a will and a prayer. A white rose boutonniere was pinned to his coat.

Catching her eyes on him, he gave her a vague smile, an indication he saw her, perhaps was thinking about her. Lauren smiled back, wishing for more, wanting more. But this was all it was to be.

Nick hadn't liked her answer, but he'd understood where her heart was. He accepted she had a life here, and didn't try to change her mind.

She'd probably hurt him, maybe not hurt…disappointed. She hated that word, what it stood for. She didn't want to disappoint anyone, but it seemed as if for most of her life she'd disappointed herself. Now when she wasn't, now when she'd gotten herself together with a great beginning and fulfillment of her potential, she'd disappointed the one person she'd ever been in love with.

She still loved Nick.

He still loved her.

Funny how loving each other wasn't enough. Maybe not funny, it was sad.

The bride and groom took their seats at the main table, a toast was made by Nick. The families both spoke, sang the other's praises, then the first dance took place.

Lauren watched Danny and Heather, so in love…it was a bittersweet moment. A feeling of loneliness swept over her, held on and wouldn't let go.

When the newlyweds' first dance ended, the music

changed tempo and others joined the floor. When the next slow song came along, she felt a hand on her shoulder.

Nick.

"Dance with me," he said, his voice low and soft.

Lauren rose, feeling momentarily unsteady in her heeled shoes.

She took his hand, let him lead her to the dance floor. He put his arms around her waist, held her close, and she laid her hand on his arm. He smelled of cologne, something wholly intoxicating. She wanted to drown in it, in him.

His cheek touched the top of her head, her fingers in his were held tightly.

The music flowed over them like a current of water, the ebb and flow of notes and a perfect harmony. She didn't want the song to end.

Not now. Not ever.

The BMW's engine was noiseless as the odometer rolled off miles of coastal highway.

Debbie McConnelly opted not to fly up to Bella Luna. She needed to drive. Driving, even in heavy traffic, always helped sort things out in her head.

She'd been a wreck since the trial. Things between her and Steve were strained, worse now than before. She truly had a good marriage, a solid marriage. She loved her husband dearly and he loved her, no doubts. It was just that trying to get pregnant for a year would tax anyone's relationship—the numerous doctor appointments, the procedures, hopes lifted then crushed.

Bringing her hand to her forehead to ward off the sunshine, she gazed through her sunglasses and kept telling herself she'd done what any mother would have done in her situation.

She wanted her baby back.

Who would have thought that after Nicky-J, she couldn't have another child? She never would have assumed, not when she got pregnant once. But she'd developed a condition that prevented her from conceiving. Tests upon tests confirmed there was nothing wrong with Steve, it was her. To Steve's credit, he never made her feel badly. Not being able to have a child of their own had been something Steve had had to work through, and then they were left to consider their options.

Adoption or a surrogate mother. Neither choices thrilled them because each method wasn't a one-hundred-percent guarantee that the child would be theirs. Too many factors played into a mother changing her mind.

During her year of trying, Nicky-J came to visit her and she had had a great time with him. Nick was doing a wonderful job with their son—she never questioned that. He was smart, wild and a handful. Sometimes she felt he was too much for her. She worked long hours at the studio, but in between projects when Nicky-J came, she was able to devote herself completely to him.

She thought about all the years she had rarely come to Bella Luna to see him. She'd been wrong. She'd relied on the convenience of her son coming to her.

How she wished she could turn back time and make things right.

But by putting him in the best school, by giving him her full love and attention now, she hoped to make up for past choices that hadn't been in his best interest.

Even the judge had seen her side, had known she would be a wonderful influence on him.

Why, then, had Debbie not slept a decent night since the ruling?

She began to think about having a six-year-old son every day. Steve was excited, said he'd take him to Dodger stadium and Laker games. All well and good—except for the fact that Steve was very wrapped up in his job, and wasn't used to rearranging his schedule. Neither was Debbie.

She'd been trying to get everything in order this week. She had Nicky-J's room repainted, bought him a new bed and even got a saltwater aquarium with fish. She was looking forward to parent-teacher conferences, luncheons with the other moms, helping out at school.

She just had to be careful about her schedule. She'd turned down a movie that was going to be shot on location in New Mexico. There was no way she could commute to and from home. While she knew she'd done the right thing in not taking the project, she wished she were working on it. The picture was already getting early Oscar buzz.

Debbie shoved thoughts like that aside. She had made a decision to be a mother to her son, she had to be there for him. She'd take other projects. Lots of movies were filmed in Los Angeles.

She was wrapping up a movie now. She'd felt badly for leaving early on Nicky-J during his last visit, but it couldn't be helped. She was surprised Nick didn't use it against her. But Nick, being Nick, was fair. He'd always been, if anything else, fair.

He'd never put boundaries on her as to when she

could see Nicky-J. Never told her she couldn't take him for a weekend if she wanted to. The trouble was, she hadn't asked for him as much as she should have.

In hindsight, she saw that she was young and unworldly when she married. She was just starting out with her career, just figuring out who she wanted to be. Having Nicky-J turned her in a new direction, one she hadn't been prepared to handle. Leaving him had seemed right at the time—Nick was a wonderful father—but looking back, she never should have.

Now it might be too late.

Nicky-J would never love her in the same way he loved his father. She could feel his attitude changing the last time he'd come down. She wished he would embrace her the way he used to. She missed how he called for her to tuck him into bed, read him a story. This last visit, he hadn't said much. Hadn't wanted to do anything with Steve.

And could she blame him? She'd taken his life and turned it upside down to suit herself.

This is what she had to talk to Nick about. She didn't want to destroy the love from her son, she couldn't bear it. But she couldn't give him back, not when she had won the right to have him.

Reflecting on her own thoughts, it sounded as if she'd gone after Nicky-J as a prize. Maybe she had…maybe she'd done it because she felt so sad she couldn't have a baby.

She didn't want to examine her reasons, because what if she had to confront something horrible about herself? She considered herself a good person, a strong person. Smart. A good businesswoman. She had many friends, had a wonderful husband, a great life. She was fulfilled in every way except one.

A child.

Maybe she'd missed the whole point. She had a child, a son who wanted to spend time with her. Now she had a little boy who didn't give her hugs, didn't want a mommy.

Nervousness worked up her spine, dread filling her heart. In her mind she knew this was right, knew that Nicky-J needed her just as much as he needed his dad. Nick had had his turn, now it was her turn. There was nothing unfair in that. But deep down, deep inside her heart, she knew she'd been slightly pressured. She wanted to make Steve happy.

In that quest, she forgot to be completely true to herself. She'd been doing okay with their arrangement all this time. Yes, she got caught up in the baby stuff, yes she wanted to hold a little baby in her arms and buy cute clothes and decorate a nursery...

But it wasn't about just any baby. She wanted to do that for Nicky-J. She wanted to turn the days and months and years back and be the kind of mother for him that she should have been.

But there were no second chances, no going back. She was taking their son to her home, but she would never be able to fill in the gap of those missing years. What she longed for, what she really wanted, wasn't meant to be.

Nicky-J was six. He needed a mother, yes. But he didn't need to be babied...and she wanted a baby.

Debbie turned off the highway and drove into the scenic town of Bella Luna. It had been ages since she'd been here. Its streets looked the same, the canneries gleaming in the distance. The water sparkled, the boats bobbed on the ocean. So picturesque, so serene. She sometimes imagined living here again, then changed her mind. It was a wonderful place to come and regroup, but her heart beat in the frantic L.A. pace where traffic conditions were broadcast on a radio station twenty-four hours a day. Where the horizon was steepled with highrises, the air quality usually hazy. It was the people, the diversity, the way everything moved quickly, that drew her. That kept her there.

Driving down Seal Avenue, she was fortunate to catch Nick walking across the street at the end of the block.

She drove down, parked her car and got out. She found him as he entered a large building. Some sort of renovation project as far as she could tell.

"Nick," she said, catching his attention before he went inside.

He turned, looked puzzled a moment, then slipped his sunglasses off his head. "What are you doing here?"

"I wanted to talk to you."

"You could have called."

"No. Face-to-face."

His expression grew cynical, his mouth thinned with distrust. At one time, they used to be friends. She wished that were the case now.

"Can we go someplace?" she asked, her heartbeat thumping in her chest, her pulse surging as if it were the tide in a storm.

"Come on inside." He entered the building, an Edwardian hotel, and she followed him into a sunny room with a block of windows. The air smelled of paint, of wood.

Leaning into the windowsill, he folded his arms over

his chest. He wore jeans and a T-shirt, work boots. He hadn't aged a bit in the five years since their divorce; but she'd found a few lines at the corners of her eyes she wasn't thrilled about.

Looking at Nick made her feel petty, cheap in some way. As if she weren't content with her own life so she'd had to go and screw his up. That wasn't how it was, not by a long shot. She'd had no chance to explain this to him. Everything leading to the trial had been spoken in anger and upset, through legal go-betweens.

"Nick, I wanted to apologize," she began. "I know this is really difficult for you. I just wanted you to know that I didn't mean to hurt you or our son."

"Too late for that." He words practically ripped out of his chest.

"I know what it must look like...I'm not trying to be selfish or mean." She walked toward him, her shoes sounding on the hardwood floor.

"Why didn't you tell me you couldn't have another kid?"

"It wasn't your business."

"When you file for custody of our son based on that single truth, I'd say it's my business."

"I didn't mean it like that, I meant that talking about my not being able to get pregnant was something between me and Steve. We had to work through it on our own."

"So you worked up a plan to take our kid. Well, it worked, so I don't know why you aren't looking a little more happy about it."

Debbie licked her lips, trying to form her thoughts. "I want to really try with him, Nick. I want to be a mother for him the way you've been a father. I think it's only fair that I be given the same chances."

Nick ran his hand through his hair, his shoulders bathed in sunshine. "As far as I'm concerned, you forfeited those chances the day you walked out on us."

"I'm not proud of my actions." She stood closer to him now, saw that his eyes were still the most incredible blue. She'd loved this man once, wouldn't have dreamed of ever leaving him. So why had she? What had possessed her to put ambition and her own personal needs above his, above their son's?

That's what was bothering Debbie. There was a part of her that still loved this man. They'd have to be friends, or at least civil to each other for the rest of their lives. Through Nicky-J's wedding and if he had children of his own. She and Nick would always be connected.

"I don't know how to say this without making you think I'm not sure. I am…but—"

"But what? You won. Frankly, I think it's fucking ballsy of you to come into my town and gloat about it."

"That's not why I'm here," she denied, her anger rising a little. She didn't want to get into an argument with him. "I came so I could see where Nicky-J lives with you, I wanted to talk myself into thinking I could do better for him. That's why I came. I wanted to prove to myself that I did all this for the right reasons." Tearful upset made her vision blur. "I just don't want to make another mistake with our son."

Nick rubbed his chin, sighed heavily. The sound of his breathing was ragged, his jaw clenched tightly. He was strength and resoluteness while she was willowy and bending. She wasn't sure which way to go, wasn't sure what she should do. She only knew that she had to come here, had to confront the pressures that were making it increasingly hard for her to breathe.

When Nick finally spoke, some of the hostility had left his voice. "Where are you staying?"

"I don't know. I just got here."

"I'll get you a room at the Tidewater, then you can come up to the house. Nicky-J and his friend Billy are out on the beach. You can see him if that's what you want. Prove whatever you have to. I don't give a damn. Just don't go giving him any false hope that you've changed your mind unless that's why you're here."

Billy watched Dunk and Sam as they sat on their surfboards in the ocean. Him and Nicky-J weren't allowed to go in the water any deeper than their knees, even with Dunk watching them. It was okay, though. Billy didn't feel like it anyway.

Billy was going to miss Nicky-J. He was the only person in Bella Luna he'd ever told about his epinephrine pen. That was a big thing for him to confess; he couldn't imagine telling the secret to Tim and Critter, and he really liked those guys.

Nicky-J was different. He didn't laugh at kids, he didn't make a guy feel like he was stupid.

The two of them were on the beach hunting for the best seashells that Nicky-J could take to Los Angeles. His mom didn't live by the beach, she lived in a city where people got paid to walk dogs.

Nicky-J said, "When I get old enough, I'm going to walk dogs for people and make enough money to move me and my dad back here."

"How many dogs you think you'll have to walk?"

"Hundreds probably."

Billy looked around for Mel. He was on the dunes, digging a hole in the sand. Sprays of it flew from his back legs and Billy giggled. "Guess he found that marshmallow I buried for him."

"I'd like to have a dog. I could ask Steve. He'd get me one. He buys me anything I ask for."

"Sounds like he's nice."

"He's okay. I liked him better when I knew I didn't have to live with him every day."

Billy went to the water's edge, got his feet wet and poked around the compacted sand with his toes. Sand crabs made little airholes on the surface, and if he used his foot as a shovel he could overturn several of them. When he'd first moved here, he'd dug up lots, now he still liked to look at them—only he didn't take them home in a bucket anymore because his mom said they stinked.

Gazing at the ocean, he waved to Dunk and Sam. They waved back. He liked watching them, thought that surfing was neat. Dunk said he'd teach him how to surf and he'd even had him on his board a couple of times and let him lie on his tummy on it.

"Let's go down there," Nicky-J said, but he stopped short as he looked up. "Mom."

Billy turned toward the direction Nicky-J was staring. He saw a really pretty lady coming toward them. She walked on the sand like a flower blowing in the breeze. Really nice and not stumbling on her bare feet. Her hair was the color of sugar cookies and her face was soft. He'd seen her picture before, but he'd never seen her in person.

"Hi, honey." She went to Nicky-J, reached down and hugged him, but Nicky-J didn't hug her back. He stood still, as if he was practicing to be a statue or something.

"How come you're here?" Nicky-J asked.

"I came to see you."

"How come?"

"Because I love you."

"Oh."

A salty breeze lifted Billy's superhero cape off his shoulders. Nicky-J's mom gazed at his costume funny, like she was wondering why he was wearing it.

"You're Billy."

"Yes," he responded, thinking she talked in a sweet voice, too.

"What are you two doing?"

"We ain't in no trouble," Nicky-J quickly replied. "Dad said we could come down here if Dunk watches us, and since you don't have any beach at your house I gotta say goodbye to this one."

"We have Malibu Beach."

Nicky-J's eyebrows knit together. "I'm not going to no beach for Barbie dolls."

His mom smiled, and when she did, Billy thought she looked like an angel.

"It's just the name of the beach, lots of people go there. Grown-ups and children. All kinds. Movie stars, too. Sometimes I see a few. Let's see, I saw Barbara Streisand once."

Billy didn't know who that was.

Stepping back from his mom, Nicky-J looked into her face, his eyes small and his lips sort of shaky. "Do we gotta move today? Did you come to get me?"

She didn't answer real fast. "No. Not today."

"Oh."

Billy could see the relief relax Nicky-J's body.

"Why don't you keep playing." She lowered herself onto the sand, sitting nice even in a dress. "I'm going to sit here for a while."

"What for?"

"To watch you."

"What for?"

"Because I love you." Her voice got quivery, like Jell-O.

Shrugging, Nicky-J said, "We're getting shells. I saw some over that way. Come on, Billy."

Billy followed, looking over his shoulder once. He couldn't help thinking Nicky-J's mom was pretty, but she looked sad. Like she was trying not to cry. She had that way about her that his mom sometimes got.

"Where are we looking?" Billy asked.

"Over there."

Once they reached a pile of driftwood, Nicky-J climbed over the gray tree trunks and rough granite rocks. He sat down, felt in his pocket and pulled out two lollipops.

"Want one?"

"Sure." Billy selected the purple one.

They sat together, looking at his mom sometimes. Neither of them said anything, but Billy suspected they were both thinking the same thing.

This was the last time they'd be able to have suckers together on the beach.

"I guess I gotta go talk with her," Nicky-J said, reaching into his pocket but coming up empty-handed. "My car's missing."

"Your Ferrari Spider?"

"Yeah." Nicky-J stood up, turned his pocket liner inside out and gazed around. "It must have fell out of my pocket when we climbed up here."

Billy searched the area, saw something small fly by in the breeze.

A bee.

He was scared to death of bees.

"There it is." Nicky-J jumped off the granite rock and crouched down by an old hollowed-out stump wedged between the rocks. He was reaching inside when Billy saw the angry bees.

"Nicky-J! There's bees in there! Don't do it!"

"But I can get it quick," Nicky-J said, reaching farther. The car slipped and disappeared, but Nicky-J's arm stretched in farther until Billy couldn't see his hand.

Nicky-J let out a yelp and a scream, stood, and his eyes grew wide while his face went white. "I got stung. *Ow-eeeeee,*" he cried, looking at his pulsing finger. He held on to his hand, his lips trembling, the stinger pumping venom into his body.

Billy staggered back, fright burning through his blood. Terror twisted around his heart. Just like the drill he'd practiced so many times, he pulled out his Medic Alert necklace from under his shirt, holding on to the tag and wishing on it that the bees would go away.

But more bees were coming out of the log now and they buzzed in an angry group, rising into the air current.

Petrified, Billy brought his hand over his epinephrine in the seam of his cape. He fished it out, the cylinder slick and slippery in his sweating palm. He didn't want to stay here. "Let's go tell your mom."

Nicky-J's mouth opened, but he couldn't speak.

Billy wanted to run away, and yet his feet wouldn't move. Not without Nicky-J.

Nicky-J barely made it onto the sand when he dropped to his knees, hunching his body over. His breathing came hard and he put a hand on his chest like he was trying to rip his shirt off.

He gazed at Billy with helpless eyes, as if he didn't know what was happening to him.

Billy blurted, "You never been stung before, have you, Nicky-J? You lied to me! You've never been stung!"

His friend couldn't answer, he only gasped for air, then his eyes started to flutter closed.

Not thinking, just moving, Billy popped the cap and held the pen correctly in his fist. He bent down and stabbed the medicine into Nicky-J's leg at the same moment he felt a prick on his neck, then another on his arm.

He didn't move, kept giving Nicky-J the epinephrine and holding on to the pen the way he was supposed to. This was the first time he'd done it for real.

Nausea rolled in his stomach, he didn't feel good. His head got dizzy, but he kept that pen feeding Nicky-J the medicine. Until Billy couldn't keep it in Nicky-J's leg no more. He had to lie down and he just sort of flopped onto the sand.

His eyes were half-open, he saw a seagull in the sky.

He heard a noise. Wheezing. It was him.

The venom worked quickly through his blood, carrying with it the darkness that had come last time.

His tongue felt too big for his mouth.

His muscles felt hard, like knots of fishing rope.

The last thoughts in his conscious mind were that he'd dropped his lollipop in the sand…

…and he'd never see his mom or Mel again.

Dunk heard a woman's frantic screaming from the beach as he rode in on a wave. He was on this feet and pulling off his leash before he even took a breath.

"Over here!" she cried, waving him over.

Running in the uneven sand, his heartbeat pounding, Dunk found Nicky-J and Billy lying still. Nicky-J was partially conscious. Billy was not.

"I don't know what happened," she said, her face white, her arms cradling Nicky-J's head.

Debbie, Nick's ex-wife. Dunk thought he knew her.

In a split second, Dunk knew what had happened. Lauren had told him about Billy's previous anaphylactic shock.

Dunk noticed a fat pen in Billy's hand and quickly concluded that Billy hadn't injected himself. Fighting off a momentary panic, Dunk was aware that second-time victims were always worse off and every half second counted.

Lord help me, Dunk thought as he scooped Billy into his arms.

"Sam!" he hollered while breaking into a run up the dunes.

Sam was already at Nicky-J's side while Debbie fished a cell phone out of her purse.

Dunk, although sixty-eight years old, sprinted the eight blocks to the community hospital with Billy tightly held in his arms.

A short moment later, the E.R. doctors accepted a patient from a winded black man wearing a wet suit, his bare feet raw from the hot summer pavement. He refused water and a chair, all he wanted to know was if Billy would be all right.

But nobody could assure him Billy Jessup would even live.

Twenty-Two

It's a honey of a moon.

Debbie stood in the doorway of the emergency-room cubicle and caught a glimpse of her ashen face in the mirror above a scrub sink.

Nicky-J lay on the gurney, his body looking small and frail beneath the white sheets. Nick sat on a stool with wheels, his broad shoulders to her as he leaned forward and tucked a blanket tighter around Nicky-J's shoulders.

Everything had happened so fast.

One minute the boys were playing, and the next both were on the sand…Billy Jessup in respiratory distress.

If Dunk hadn't been there.

Debbie shuddered. She could have handled it, and she would have, but she'd panicked. Panicked in a way she hadn't thought she would. She thought she could mentally focus, be there and act quickly. If only she'd been more astute. Hindsight left her quite shaken.

Nicky-J gazed through heavily lidded eyes, focusing on Nick first, then on her. Debbie pushed off from the doorway, took a step forward, but stopped.

Their son cried, quietly asking for his father...not her.

"I'm here, buddy." Nick's voice was soothing.

"Daddy..."

"It's okay, son. You'll be all right."

"B-Billy...?"

"Billy will be all right."

Tears streaked down Nicky-J's cheeks. "I lied."

Nick lifted himself a little taller, taking Nicky-J's small hand in his. "Lied about what?"

"I told Billy I'd been stung before."

Nick grew quiet, thoughtful. Then in a calm and reassuring tone, he said, "I'm sure he's not mad at you. He'll still be your friend."

That Nick could be so intuitive about what his son was trying to reach out for left her confused, and feelings that she'd kept tamped down began to surface. Debbie experienced a gamut of emotions as she watched Nick...saw him for who he was at this moment. He was a very selfless father who instinctively knew exactly what to do for their child.

It was Nick who comforted him. It was Nick who put Nicky-J at ease. She realized what an extraordinary parent Nick was and how much Nicky-J depended on him.

Her mind was reeling. After a troubled night of soul-searching and a long day's drive, now this. She felt the effects wearing on her, felt as if she had difficulty breathing.

She knew the answer in her heart. Perhaps it had been there before she'd ever left Los Angeles this morning.

Where the rationale came from wasn't important. Her decision was, ultimately, a truth she couldn't suppress.

And she would tell Nick how she felt....

For now, she stepped noiselessly out of the room. She dug through her purse for a tissue to blot the tears on her eyelashes.

The activity around her reminded her where she was and how lucky her son was to be alive.

But down the hallway, another recovery was not so easy.

Billy remained in critical condition, suffering from acute anaphylactic shock. Thanks to Dunk's quick thinking, Billy was brought to the hospital faster than if he'd come by ambulance.

In the emergency room, doctors administered diphenhydramine, methylprednisolone, aerosolized albuterol and intravenous epinephrine. Billy's anaphylactic episode was complicated by frequent runs of premature ventricular beats.

He was a very sick little boy.

Lauren rushed to his side, holding his hand, uttering soothing words to him and telling him he needed to get better. She didn't understand how something like this could have happened. Billy knew to give himself the injection, they'd been over it many times.

Then she found out Nicky-J had also been stung, and had had a reaction. And Billy had given his friend his epinephrine, only too late to realize he had none for himself.

Lauren's heart swelled with pride over his selflessness, but at the cost of losing her son...

She wouldn't accept it. She could not.

Nicky-J had recovered within a couple of hours, the irony of two little boys having the same reactions still cause for conversation by the nurses.

Lauren vaguely remembered the room filling with people; she saw various faces coming in and out. Dunk's the most prominent. He practically tripped over her, and stayed in the room if she had to leave for a short moment. Verna Mae came by, and Caprice DiMartino. Danny and Heather showed up. They'd changed their honeymoon plans after their wedding, not wanting to leave without being there for Nick and Nicky-J's final days in town before moving.

She recalled Nick's hand on her shoulder, his voice in her ear as he whispered reassurances. He was taking care of his own son when he made time to take care of her. She didn't expect him to stay, she knew firsthand that the first time something like this happened, it hit you without warning. Emotions weren't all there, coherent thoughts fled. All you thought about was how close you came to losing your child.

Nick must have been going crazy with worry. Thankfully Nicky-J would be all right.

The sound of hospital machines, the muted noises from the nurses' station kept Lauren half-awake all night. She sat by Billy's side, her head finally lowering onto her forearm.

She drifted into a state of semiconsciousness, her mind like a pillow; feathery, light, supporting her dreams.

In them, she saw herself coming to Bella Luna, holding Billy's hand and standing on the wharf. They were looking at a new life, a new start. The fog folded through the streets, a gray blanket that cloaked everything. But the flowers. So vibrant, so alive.

When she stopped to smell them, she saw Billy's face in the center, his smile, his eyeglasses. He was happy, truly. In his eyes she saw youth and hope, purpose and mischief. Things she'd never seen in them before. She knew Bella Luna had given her son those things, but now the town and the damn moon wanted to take it all away.

She tried to pick the flower, to save Billy, but when she did the stem withered in her hand. She gazed at it, the flower gone. Her son was gone.

Sitting up in a startled gasp, Lauren leaned forward and felt for breath under Billy's nose. He remained in respiratory distress, his tiny chest rising and falling in a choppy motion. But he was still alive, still with her.

The beats of her pulse tore a jagged path through her body and she was losing the battle to stay strong for him. The clock hands were blurry, it was perhaps two in the morning.

Down the hallway, she could hear the soft hum of a floor polisher as the janitor ran a buffer over the linoleum.

Hands came down on her shoulders, warm and solid. She took immediate comfort in them, turned her head and looked into Nick's tired face.

"Nicky-J?" she asked, barely getting the word out.

"He's at home now. He'll be fine. Danny and Heather are with him, my mom and dad, too. I thought you might need me."

She rose to her feet, brought her arms around his neck and held on.

"I need you, Nick. I need to be strong, but I'm afraid. Help me." She buried her face in his chest and cried, her hands bunching the fabric of his shirt. The strength of his embrace held her up, his arms like bands of steel supporting her. He smelled so good, so familiar. The even beats of his heart echoed in her ears, a cadence that she'd grown so accustomed to.

What was she going to do without him?

The despair in her heart emptied, lessened the longer she leaned on him. When she could cry no more, she closed her eyes and pulled in slow breaths, unable to move or to think.

She just wanted to be assured. Assured that everything was going to be fine, that Billy would be with Mel and they'd run on the beach and dig in the sand. That Billy would start first grade and he'd grow up to be a wonderful young man and she'd see him go to college and become somebody important.

Pulling herself together, she wiped her eyes only to have a hospital tissue handed to her. She thanked Nick, blew her nose and took in a deep and calming breath.

"Thank you." The simple words seemed inadequate.

"I love you, Lauren." He took her chin in his hand. "That hasn't changed."

She reached up and brought her fingers around his wrist, taking his hand and putting it against her cheek. "I love you, too."

The night ebbed into morning, light trying to work its way through the seams in the blinds. Where the day began and ended, Lauren wasn't able to tell.

Dunk was here, then he was bringing her a coffee and a cellophane-wrapped pastry. He wouldn't leave her

alone until she ate it. The flaky dough tasted like note-
book paper, the fruit inside not any kind of cherries
she'd ever eaten. The coffee roused her sluggish head
with the fringes of a headache surfacing in its wake. She
knew she needed to lie down, to sleep, but she was fear-
ful if she left Billy's side, something would happen and
she wouldn't be here.

Throughout the day and into the night, Nick remained
a constant and she never questioned his presence, only
knowing she took comfort in it; never thought to ask
why he hadn't talked about going to Los Angeles.

Nicky-J came with him today, but she wasn't sure
when—a cartoon was on television.

The little boy came to her with a bouquet of flowers
and he held on to her neck and sobbed. "I'm sorry. I
didn't mean to lie."

Confused, Lauren held tightly to Nicky-J. "Lie?
What are you talking about?"

"I lied about being stung before. If I hadn't tried to
get my Hot Wheels car, I wouldn't have gotten the bees
mad. Billy told me there were bees. He was scared of
'em and I...I'm sorry. I'm sorry!"

"Oh, Nicky-J." She held his face in her hands, looked
at the heartache in his startling blue eyes. She kissed his
cheek, gave him a reassuring hug. "It's okay. You didn't
do anything wrong."

"I'm sorry," he said once more, the color on his face
a healthy pink while Billy lay drowsy and pale.

"Why don't you talk to Billy, tell him you're here?"

Nicky-J went to Billy's bedside. He gazed at Billy's
hand where the IV tube went in, then swallowed hard.

Nick stood behind his son, there for him.

"Billy, it's me, Nicky-J. You gotta open your eyes now 'cause your mom is here and she wants you to get better. Me, too. And Dunk, too."

"Right here, Billy," came Dunk's deep voice. "Got some things around the grocery I need your help with so you better wake up now."

They stood by Billy's bedside, watching and waiting. Hoping.

Later in the day when it was just Lauren sitting beside her son, she read to him. *Hansel and Gretel.* Nick had gone to the cottage and picked the book up for her. He was in the hospital somewhere, but her mind was not clued into the details. Coffee? Had he said he was going for coffee?

As she read, she glanced at Billy's face, checking the opening in his lips as air passed between them. When she read the page about the wolf, she paused, "Mel misses you, Billy. Nick said he was sleeping on your bed when he went into your room to get this book. Mel wants you to wake up so you can take him for a walk and give him marshmallows."

Lowering her head to the pages of the illustrated book, Lauren tried to remember where she'd left off.

"Mel…" came the weak sound of Billy's voice.

Lauren's heart skipped a beat. The book fell out of her hands onto the floor. She moved to Billy's side, laid a hand on his chest.

"Billy, it's Mommy."

Through the drugs, he willed his eyes to open and he stared at her. "Mom?"

"Yes, Billy. It's Mom." She squeezed his hand, her words coming in a gasp of joy. "I'm right here."

"Mel?"

"He's at the house waiting for you."

"Nicky-J?"

"He's fine. You saved his life, Billy. You were so brave." She kissed his forehead, his cheek, his dry lips. She brushed the sandy hair from his forehead. "So strong and I love you so much."

"I'm hungry."

She sat up, put a hand over her heart as laughter lifted from her throat. "Oh! All right. Yes, they have food here."

"Ice cream."

"I'm sure they have that."

She was reaching for the nurse's call button when Nick came into the room with some food.

"He's awake now," Lauren said, a smile spread on her mouth. "He's going to be all right."

The doctors came into the room, examined Billy and agreed he would come out of this without problems. Dunk appeared, and as soon as Lauren saw him, she gave him a hug.

"Thank you, thank you," she murmured.

"No thanks necessary, Lauren. I'm just glad I was there."

The moment overwhelmed Lauren and she staggered, fatigue overtaking her muscles and senses. Nick caught her, supported her with an arm around her waist. "Come on. Outside for some fresh air and you can eat something, too."

"But I want to stay with Billy," she protested.

Dunk's face was resolute. "I'll be here. I'm not going anywhere."

Lauren was led onto a patio, made to sit in a chair

and eat a bagel with jam. Nick had brought an orange juice. Pampering her, he peeled back the foil top from the cup. "Drink."

The bagel and juice revived her enough that she actually felt a bit more human, her thoughts much more clear.

"It's going to be a change for you and Nicky-J." Lauren dusted crumbs from her lap, not realizing she'd been so hungry. "He'll have to carry an epinephrine pen on him at all times. You'll show him how to use it, but you'll pray he never has to."

"The doctor gave him a pen. We watched a video on how to use it, and we used a sample pen to practice with."

"He can't lose that pen, they're so big, too. They don't fit in a pair of jeans."

Nick stared at her quizzically. "Sure they do."

"No, they don't." She shook her head adamantly. "They don't stay in a pocket—not with any reliability, that's why we came up with the superhero cape idea."

"You mean that's why he wears that cape?"

"Uh-huh."

Nick laid a hand on the back of her neck, massaged and gave her a funny look. "I don't know how you'll take this, given the last time I told you how to raise your son when it came to team sports—" he threw in a grin for her sake and she grinned right back "—but the answer's real simple. It's called—carpenter's pants."

"What's that?"

"The pants with the hammer tabs and slots for tool handles. They've got plenty of deep slashes and pockets for an epinephrine pen. A boy can play all he wants in them and not worry he'll lose a lifesaving device."

"Carpenter's pants? That's so…simple."

"Men are simple when it counts."

His suggestion about the jeans was wonderful, one she wished she'd had the insight to figure out on her own. "You're not simple, Nick. You're complicated." Rubbing her temple, she asked, "What day is it?"

"Tuesday."

"You're set to leave tomorrow?" she uttered, the hazy sunlight suddenly seeming too bright. The reality of their separation hit her full thrust and she tried to be relaxed.

"Not exactly," Nick replied.

Her eyes passed over him. "Then when?"

"Never."

She couldn't have heard him correctly. "What do you mean?"

"Debbie was here the day the boys were on the beach."

Angling her head toward him, she responded, "I had no idea."

"She came up to see me, we talked. Before she went to the beach, I showed her the house. She wanted to see Nicky-J's room. We got some things cleared up. I guess we should have done that before the trial, but neither of us were willing to see the other's perspective."

If something was wrong, he wasn't saying so. "And what happened?"

"When Nicky-J was in the E.R. she admitted she'd made a mistake. She told me our son should stay with me."

"So you're saying...?"

"Debbie changed her mind. We're going to work things out, keep the custody arrangement close to the way it was, only this time it'll be in writing. She agreed."

The heavy lashes that had shadowed Lauren's vision flew up, and her eyes opened wide. Astonishment gave way to a cry of relief that broke from her lips.

Nick's voice wrapped around her, warm and strong. "There is no more dispute. Nicky-J is staying with me, and I'm staying here."

He told her to be ready at eight o'clock.

Nick spent the day making last-minute preparations, making sure everything would go off perfectly tonight for Lauren.

The last few days had passed quickly. Danny and Heather had taken off for Jamaica—after a family dinner at the house where the wedding was toasted without any sadness on the horizon, and Nicky-J's staying with them was celebrated with a cake.

Nick was going to reveal the newly restored Ocean Grove Inn for Preservation Week; his work was on schedule, just as his life was back on track. And it would be even better in an hour.

John and Felicia had taken the boys to a movie, leaving him and Lauren free for the night. He stood at her door, holding a bouquet of red roses. The suit he wore felt right, comfortable. He'd told her to dress up.

When she opened the door, she took his breath away.

She had on a black cocktail dress, very low cut and showing a hint of breasts. Just the top swells where her skin was pale and looked like satin. The sleeves were short, barely-there ruffles of lace. The cut fit her body like a glove, molding to curves and making her look stunning. A very understated dress, but it aroused him as much as if she were standing there naked.

"Hi, Nick," she said, somewhat out of breath as if she'd hurried over the last few minutes to get ready.

Her hair was swept up on her head in a high pile of curls and tendrils that were sexy and wispy. Makeup had been applied to her eyes, making the irises seem darker, more sultry. Blush colored her cheeks, her mouth the same deep red color of the roses in his hands.

He extended the flowers. "For you."

Her smile warmed him to the core. "Thank you. I'll just have—"

Verna Mae came from behind Lauren. "I'll put them in water for you, sweetpea." To Nick, "Doesn't our girl dress up nice, Nick?"

"She looks amazing."

"I worked on her all afternoon. We even did her nails."

Lauren blushed, bringing her hands together. The nails were short, painted red. She smelled like floral lotion, her knuckles still sporting some scars from the kitchen.

"You don't think it's too much?" Lauren questioned, her self-conscious state evident.

"Not a chance."

This was probably the first time Lauren had ever dressed like this. She should do it more often.

"What's that you've got on there?" he couldn't help saying, his gaze falling to her feet.

"High heels."

"Three-inchers."

"Verna Mae took me shopping."

"You done good, Verna Mae," Nick teased appreciatively. Then he held out his arm for Lauren. She took it and they stepped into the late-August night.

The air was unseasonably warm, the ocean scenting the street with a spray of salt. The sidewalk was uneven in spots and Nick made sure he held fast to Lauren. Her shoes were a slip on kind, a black strappy style that showed off her ankles and red toenails.

"Where are we going?" she asked, her voice light and happy.

If she was happy now, just wait.

"You'll see when we get there."

He took her across Shoreline, his thoughts hammering inside his head as he ran past every detail one more time. He'd never done anything like this, never had wanted to be so elaborate and so planned out.

They reached the boardwalk and Nick guided her past the shimmering canneries.

A full pink moon, its fringes faded like the color of new garden petunias, hovered high in the midnight-blue sky.

At the end of the wharf, a table had been set up with a white cloth and two seats, a bottle of champagne and tall-stemmed glasses. Candles winked from hundreds of glass holders along the boardwalk railing and rose petals littered the weathered board planks.

Pausing, her eyes bright, Lauren asked, "What's this?"

"I said I was taking you out to dinner."

"I didn't think...I assumed a restaurant."

"This is a restaurant and the moon is our maître d'." He held out her chair.

She sat, tall and perfectly poised. Her face was lit by the moon, vividly beautiful.

His throat ached, his heart swelled.

How had he gotten so lucky?

"And where is the menu for this fine establishment?"

she queried playfully, her lips so red and plump, it took everything not to take her from her chair, bring her onto his lap and kiss her senseless.

"There isn't one."

On cue, Knox Dugan appeared carrying two salad plates. He looked like a penguin in his suit and tie, his freshly shaven chin held high.

"For you," he said in the tone reserved only for butlers and dignitaries, as he set the salad in front of Lauren.

She smiled. "Knox, you look so handsome."

"Thank you." He stayed in character, serving Nick his salad.

"This looks familiar," she said, assessing the greens.

"I watched you," Knox stated in a reserved tone. "Your recipe."

Laughter, the sweetest sound, floated from her mouth. "Well, then I'm certain I'll love it."

They ate, speaking in low voices as the surf broke softly against the pier pilings below. The lighthouse beam made its revolutions from the jagged point in the distance. A weathervane from the boathouse creaked, while ropes mooring the boats rubbed softly against the iron cleats.

The main course was filet of beef with everything done in subtle colors: saffron potatoes, pale sauces and new asparagus. Lauren gave Knox her praise; he didn't crack a smile, but Nick suspected the man was walking on air. He'd been working hard to get everything just right for tonight, using the diner's kitchen to prepare the food.

Throughout the meal, and over sips of champagne, he and Lauren talked as if they'd known each other all their lives. He reached across the table, touched her hair, the curling tendril that had captured his interest all through dinner.

She held his hand, they sat and reminisced about their pasts and how they came to be who they were today.

Nick thought that Lauren was more than fate could have ever brought him. He was in love with her, wanted to spend the rest of his life making her and Billy happy. He wanted to give them a home and sense of belonging. He wanted to share his family with her, his brothers and their wives. He could see Christmases together, Lauren's and Billy's names on gifts under the tree.

Dessert was served, nibbled and shared, the chocolate cake melting in their mouths. Afterward, Nick popped the cork on another bottle of champagne and poured two glasses.

He lifted his glass and made a toast, "To the best cook in all of Bella Luna—the most beautiful and talented— a woman I'm honored to be with tonight. To us."

"To us," she said, touching the rim of her glass to his.

Their eyes held, loving and tender.

The right moment had come, the time when he knew that he would give himself over to her completely and fully.

Like a teenage boy, he felt his male ego tested and tried. He'd asked once before, and the end result had not been what he'd expected. But things were different now.

Slipping off his chair, he bent down on one knee in front of Lauren and took her hands.

His own were unsteady, his breath just as uneven in his chest.

She gazed at him with love in her eyes, a smile on

her lips and a quiver to her pulse. He took a second to collect what he wanted to say, how he wanted to say it.

"Lauren, I didn't do this right before."

She pressed her lips together, maybe to keep emotions in check.

Nick gathered his mind, sorted the expressions of love and gratitude for her being in his heart. "You came to town and the first time I saw you, I think I fell in love with your stubborn pride. The way you didn't back down, you held your head high. I've watched you grow as a person, you're someone I respect and admire. You've raised a fine son, a boy any man would be proud to call his own. I imagine my future with you and me, Billy and Nicky-J. I see us looking at stars, roasting marshmallows on the beach, watching sunsets and running in the rain. Everything that I have I'm offering to you. My heart, my love, my undying loyalty." The heavy thump of his heart urged him to reach into his coat pocket and produce a jeweler's box. He lifted the velvet lid and presented a diamond engagement ring to her. He'd chosen a three-carat solitaire set in platinum. "This ring is you. It has heart and grace, yet it's simple and classic. The metal is precious, but strong and resilient. All that it is, is all that you are." Gazing into her eyes, he said, "Lauren, I love you. Will you marry me?"

She leaned forward, kissing him on his mouth, his cheeks, his forehead. His lips caught hers, kissing deeply, thoroughly. He felt her love so strongly inside him, it was as though it was alive, breathing new meaning into his life.

"Yes," she said between kisses. "Yes…a thousand times yes."

As he slipped the ring on her finger, he knew this was the beginning of forever.

Epilogue

Bella luna!
(Beautiful moon!)

Ten pink moons later...

They had the wedding at the Ocean Grove Inn, the Saunderses in attendance with Lauren introducing them to the guests. Later on at the reception, Verna Mae would comment that the whole thing reminded her of a scene from *Titanic* the way Lauren had walked down the grand oak stairway in a flowing white dress, on Otis Duncan's arm, to Nick in his tuxedo at the base of the stairs.

The couple had danced on the wharf, champagne glasses in hand, smiles on their faces until the velvety moon drifted behind a curtain of clouds, the finale on a grand night.

Life in the small coastal town of Bella Luna marched forward, as it had done for hundreds of years.

The creamy pink sphere of a moon rose each month, its arc in the sky a beautiful phenomenon.

Verna Mae and Lauren went into partnership together serving the best food between San Francisco and Los Angeles. Tim, Critter, Billy and Nicky-J were primed to spend the summer together with Mel tagging along. Otto and the boys at Moon Cycle had a collision with infamy. Clint Eastwood came down from Carmel and was impressed with how Nubs painted bikes. Mr. Eastwood ordered a custom-built soft-tail motorcycle, and before Otto knew it, he was deep in orders and PBS wanted to film a documentary on the shop.

Nick's next project was figuring out how to expand the house since he and Lauren were talking about expanding their family, thinking of trying for a girl to even things out. Until they were ready, he was busy renovating one of the canneries for retail space.

Sam Wong delighted in the news that his daughter was going to add another grandson or granddaughter to the family. Verna Mae won five hundred bucks in the lottery. Billy's mom let him add a horny toad to his pet collection.

Sergeant Doug Carlyle wasn't so lucky, however. While on the night shift, he noticed a stalled car with its hood up in the gift-shop parking lot. Like any good officer, he helped the guy out and gave him a jump with a set of battery cables he carried in the trunk. It turned out the man he'd assisted had robbed the store and Sergeant Carlyle had helped him with his getaway!

That sly moon could bring out the best and the worst in people, but that's what made life in town so interesting.

Out on the pier, as the night settled in, Sam Wong turned the Closed sign on his door and locked up. As he disappeared from sight, music drifted from the eaves of the pizzeria.

The notes were romantic, infused with accordions and strings, a Dean Martin-type of voice singing lyrics to a song that played to the sounds of the ocean.

> *Itsa moon, thatsa big,*
> *and so high in the sky, that we know!*
> *This is home, this is heart, this is love.*
> *Where we gaze at the night and we sing:*
> *Itsa our beautiful moon,*
> *Itsa our—Bella Luna!*

Literary Times calls *New York Times* bestselling author Brenda Joyce's writing "…like silk! Powerful, evocative and emotionally charged!"

BRENDA JOYCE

VENGEANCE RULED HIS DAYS…AND NIGHTS

An infamous sea captain of the British Royal Navy, Devin O'Neill is both feared and respected—and consumed with the need to destroy the man who murdered his father. And his ingenuity has paid off. He has nearly ruined the Earl of Eastleigh financially and is waiting for his moment to strike the final blow. And it comes in the form of the earl's spirited young American niece, Victoria Hughes, who is about to set his cold, calculating world on fire. As his hostage, she will soon find her best-laid plans thwarted by a passion that could seal their fates forever.

The PRIZE

"For scorching sensuality and raw passion, Brenda Joyce is unrivaled."—*Romantic Times*

Available the first week of October 2004, wherever paperbacks are sold!

MBJ208

From the **USA TODAY** *bestselling author of*
Mesmerized *and* **Beyond Compare**...

CANDACE CAMP

Despite its graceful beauty, Winterset remains
shrouded in the mystery of its dark past...

For years Reed Moreland has been unable to set foot in
the house that was the backdrop of his ill-fated romance with
Anna Holcombe—Winterset. The eerie Gloucestershire mansion
remains a painful reminder of a love that was never meant to be.

But when Reed begins dreaming that Anna is in danger, he puts
his heartbreak and bitterness aside, determined to protect the
woman he cannot stop loving. Once again passion flares between
them, but the murder of a servant girl draws them deep into the
foreboding, deadly legends of Winterset...and a destiny neither
Anna nor Reed can escape.

WINTERSET

Available the first week of October 2004,
wherever paperbacks are sold!

STEF ANN HOLM

66949 GIRLS NIGHT   ___ $6.50 U.S. ___ $7.99 CAN.
66730 UNDRESSED   ___ $6.50 U.S. ___ $7.99 CAN.

(limited quantities available)

TOTAL AMOUNT $_____
POSTAGE & HANDLING $_____
($1.00 for one book; 50¢ for each additional)
APPLICABLE TAXES* $_____
<u>TOTAL PAYABLE</u> $_____
(check or money order—please do not send cash)

To order, complete this form and send it, along with a check
or money order for the total above, payable to MIRA Books,
to: **In the U.S.:** 3010 Walden Avenue, P.O. Box 9077, Buffalo,
NY 14269-9077; **In Canada:** P.O. Box 636, Fort Erie, Ontario
L2A 5X3.

Name:_____
Address:_____ City:_____
State/Prov.:_____ Zip/Postal Code:_____
Account Number (if applicable):_____
075 CSAS

  *New York residents remit applicable sales taxes.
   Canadian residents remit applicable GST and provincial taxes.

MIRA®
www.MIRABooks.com   MSAH1004BL